Praise for P. T. Deutermann's

# THE MOONPOOL

"Exciting…Chilling.…Thriller fans will look forward to further entries in this fine series." —*Publishers Weekly*

"Richter is an easygoing, likable series hero, and Deutermann has a strong, fluid writing style.… The series is still relatively young, but it's already proven to be a winner." —*Booklist*

## SPIDER MOUNTAIN

"Fast-paced… imaginative plotting." —*Publishers Weekly*

"Another pulse-pounding thrill ride…An unnerving, tightly woven thriller." —*Cincinnati Library*

"The stuff of series heroes...a battle royal."

—*Kirkus Reviews*

"Non-stop action." —Mysterylovers.com

"One of the crime genre's more original and memorable creations…a welcome change from the usual sort of thriller villain." —*Booklist*

## THE CAT DANCERS

"Gripping...original and intense." —*BookPage*

"Full of surprises...keeps you reading past your bedtime." —*Charlotte Observer*

MORE…

"A spellbinding novel of suspense...quite possibly his best."
—Nelson DeMille

## THE FIREFLY

"Complex...fascinating." —*Washington Post*

"A first-class page-turner." —*Atlanta Journal Constitution*

"A deft thriller...impeccably authentic!"
—*Library Journal*

"A top-notch thriller from a top-notch writer."
—Nelson DeMille

"Addictively enthralling...(wait till you get to the jaw-dropping ending!)." —*Entertainment Weekly*

## HUNTING SEASON

"Explosive tour de force....The author exceeds his near-perfect *Train Man* with this ripped-from-the-headlines plot pitting a middle-aged Rambo with a small but deadly arsenal of spy gadgets against spine-chilling villains, corrupt agency brass, and powerful political forces. Deutermann never sounds a wrong note in this nonstop page-turner."
—*Publishers Weekly* (starred review)

"You think you have read this before. Trust me. You haven't. And you should...a great read."
—*Tribune* (Greensburg, PA)

"One of the lasting conventions in thriller writing involves putting the hero in a situation where the reader is

forced to ask, 'How can he possibly get out of that?'…
Deutermann…exploits that convention to the hilt in
*Hunting Season*."                              —*Houston Chronicle*

"Enough techno and black ops to satisfy Clancy fans,
enough double-dealing, back-pedaling internecine treach-
ery to keep le Carré fans reading, and enough plot turns
and suspense to keep Crichton and Higgins Clark devo-
tees guessing."                          —*Florida Times-Union*

"Deutermann's previous novel, *Train Man*, was a marvelous, bang-up action novel…in *Hunting Season* he equals
the thrills…Deutermann writes with authority and inven-
tiveness. Add in top-secret gizmos, heroes meaner than
villains…and you've got one of the best by one of the best
at what he does."                       —*Telegraph* [Macon, GA]

"The tale is loaded with political and bureaucratic skulldug-
gery, and there are plenty of well-banked curves and clever
twists. A solid read from an author whose own tradecraft is
every bit as good as that of his characters."        —*Booklist*

"Deutermann has sold three novels to Hollywood already.
They're blind if they pass on this one."      —*Kirkus Reviews*

## DARKSIDE

"Gripping…thoroughly absorbing."        —*Publishers Weekly*

"Deutermann…writes page-turners. And this one has a surprise ending—one that comes as a bombshell."
                                            —*Houston Chronicle*

"A dead-on sense of place and appealing characters in tight
corners…satisfying."                           —*Kirkus Reviews*

# NIGHTWALKERS

### P. T. DEUTERMANN

St. Martin's Paperbacks

NIGHTWALKERS

Copyright © 2009 by P. T. Deutermann.

All rights reserved.

For information address St. Martin's Press, 175 Fifth Avenue, New York, NY 10010.

Library of Congress Catalog Card Number: 2009007280

ISBN: 978-0-312-36537-0

Printed in the United States of America

St. Martin's Press hardcover edition / June 2009
St. Martin's Paperbacks edition / May 2010

St. Martin's Paperbacks are published by St. Martin's Press, 175 Fifth Avenue, New York, NY 10010.

10   9   8   7   6   5   4   3   2   1

# APRIL 1865

They came out of the darkness, riding lean, hungry horses. The engineer put down his unlit pipe and reached for the shotgun in the cab, but then relaxed. The riders were Reb cavalry, not goddamned bluecoats. He could tell by their slouch hats, the mishmash of uniforms and weapons, and those big CS belt buckles gleaming in the engine's headlight. The officer who appeared to be in charge rode right up to the locomotive. The others slowed to a walk and spread out in a fan around the train's guard detail, who were lounging in the grass beside the tracks while the engine took on water. The riders were greeting the men with soft drawls and questions about what was going on up there in Richmond city.

The officer wore the insignia of a major, and he tipped his hat to the engineer with his left hand while holding the reins close down to the saddle with his right. He was wearing a dirty white duster that concealed the lower half of his body.

"Major Prentice Lambert, at your service, suh," he declared. He had a hard, hatchet-shaped face with black eyes and fierce eyebrows. "This the documents train?"

The engineer said yes, a little surprised that the major knew. There were only four cars behind the engine and its tender, three of them passenger cars stuffed to the windows with boxes of official records from the various government departments up in Richmond. The twenty-man guard detail rode in the fourth car, but they were all disembarked for a smoke break and calls of nature. The guards, who were an odd mixture of old men, teenagers, and even some walking wounded from the trenches at Petersburg, seemed relieved to see Confederate cavalry.

The major nodded, as if the engineer's answer were hugely significant. The engine puffed a shot of steam from the driver cylinder, spooking the major's horse sideways, but his rider held him firmly.

"Any more trains behind you?" the major asked, shifting his reins to his left hand as the horse danced around.

The engineer shook his head. "We heard ol' Jeff Davis took one south two nights ago, but ain't nothin' comin' down thisaway that I know of. Jig's 'bout up in Richmond."

"All right, then," the major said. He raised the big Colt Dragoon he'd been holding down beside his saddle horn, pointed it at the engineer's belly, and fired.

The engineer sat down hard on the steel grate of the engine cab, the wind knocked clean out of him and this awful, ripping feeling in his guts. He grasped his midsection with both hands and felt the blood streaming. He was dimly aware of more shooting now, as that arc of cavalrymen also opened fire, shooting down the stunned soldiers where they sat in the grass or leaned against trees, all their weapons still back on the train. He bent over to look down at his middle, lost his balance, tumbled off the engine steps onto the cinder bed, and then rolled into the grass. His knees stung where he'd hit the track bed, but then that pain faded and he relaxed into the sweet feel of that long, cool grass against his cheek. His middle was going cold now, and his legs were buzzing with pins and needles.

He looked back up at the train, his vision shrinking into a red-hazed tunnel. He saw a single white face at the nearest window in the front car, a young face, no more than a kid, maybe fifteen, sixteen. One of the guards? He tasted salt in the back of his throat, and it was becoming really hard to get a breath of air.

Why hadn't that kid gotten off the train? What was he doing in there among all those boxes, while his comrades outside were being slaughtered like beeves?

One of the horsemen saw the kid's face and surged his horse forward, his black cap-and-ball pistol pointing at the window. The engineer heard the major's voice call out, "No. Not him. Leave that one be."

The horseman reined up. "That's your spy? That boy?"

"Train was right here when it was supposed to be, weren't it?"

"Yeah, but you said, now. No goddamned witnesses."

"There won't be," the major said, getting down off his horse, "but I need to know one more thing."

Then the engineer heard the other horseman swear. He realized he'd been spotted, eavesdropping on their conversation. He tried to crawl up the bank, trying to get under the locomotive, but his limbs had turned to rubber. He thought he heard the major say, "Oh, goddammit," and then a bolt of lightning exploded in his head and he was gone to see the Baby Jesus.

# THE PRESENT

Right here's where it happened," the Realtor said, puffing a little as we climbed the embankment to the abandoned railroad line. "April 4th, 1865. Right up here. About an hour after sundown."

It was an early spring day, and the faded right-of-way pointed down to the Dan River on my right. The rails and ties were long gone. All that remained of the nineteenth-century trestle was the stone abutments on both sides of the river and the stumps of pylons out in the current. The abutment on the Carolina side was fortified, complete with a tower for sharpshooters and two pads for cannons. On the Virginia side the abutment was a plain stone wall. Beyond it stood a dense grove of what the Carolina locals called Virginia pines, supervised by a few ancient, lightning-bit oaks.

"They waited over there, in those woods," he said, pointing to our left, where the rail line bent around the base of a small hill and then disappeared into a notch in the woods. "This was a waterin' stop—see that iron tower?"

A four-legged, rusting steel structure crouched to our left. At its base were the remains of a barrel-shaped water tank, perhaps ten feet in diameter. The wooden staves were gone, but the hoops and bands were still there.

"The locomotives would stop under that tower and lower a water hose into the tender. That's what they were doin' when them bastards rode out of those woods yonder and started shootin'. They caught the guards with their pants down, some of them literally so."

"They were after gold?"

He frowned. "That gets a little fuzzy, history-wise," he said. "Supposedly the train was carryin' important documents, government records and such. It could have been carryin' part of the Confederate treasury, but ol' Jeff Davis had already come through with the bulk of it, on his way to gettin' caught wearin' a dress down in Georgia. Even so, yeah, most folks think there was gold behind what happened here."

I'd heard the story when I first started looking at the property, two months back. The plantation was called Glory's End, a seven-hundred-acre cotton and tobacco farm in Rockwell County, northeast of Triboro. One of the disclosure elements was that there were two graveyards on the property, one dating back to the end of the Civil War, the other lost on the property somewhere.

"They kill all the guards?"

"They killed everybody, guards, train crew, the lot. Just shot 'em down. Local folks heard all the shootin', but they was afraid to come out in the dark. Next mornin' they found the train sittin' right here, the firebox gone out, and all those boys stiffened up on the ground. Musta been a helluva sight, you know?"

"Most battlefields are," I said.

"Wasn't no battle here," he said with a sniff. "This here was murder, plain and simple. Buncha cavalry deserters from Georgia who knew somethin' they shouldn'ta. Wasn't leavin' any witnesses, neither. The railroad company carried off the train crew that day. Rest of 'em are all buried yonder, on that hill."

"I want to see that," I said.

"Ain't much to see," he said, eyeing the hill warily. Mr. David Oatley was a portly individual and apparently wary of hills. "Ticks'll be comin' out, you know."

"Still," I said.

"Right," he said. We crossed the overgrown right-of-way, stumbled down the gravel embankment on the other side, and walked up into the knee-high grass.

The graveyard was a collection of rectangular stone markers and stumpy white tombstones. A few were formally inscribed; others were just plain rocks with one smooth face bearing a name and life dates. Many of the markers were flat on the ground, and there was no fence or other enclosure. I counted twenty-nine graves that I could see. Wild cedars had sprung up everywhere over the years, now standing sentry duty over the remains of the slain guards. Mr. Oatley wiped his face with a handkerchief and pulled up a pant leg to see if he'd acquired any passengers.

"These are Confederate war dead," I said. "How come this place isn't state maintained?"

"They was ashamed, I reckon. This was gray killin' on gray, you know? The government up in Richmond had pretty much gone down, Grant had Lee's army by the throat over near Appomattox, lotta folks was runnin' for their lives. That's how the property got its new name, by the by. Used to be called Oak Grove. After this mess, right here, that's when they called it Glory's End."

"Highly appropriate, too," I said. I'd been moving closer to a decision about buying this property for some time now, ever since learning that it might be available. Surveying this poignant piece of history, I made up my mind.

"Okay. I'll buy it."

Mr. Oatley's perspiring face broke into a big smile. "Wonderful, sir. That's wonderful. You won't regret it, I can promise you that."

* * *

We drove back to town in his SUV. I'd already done quite a bit of research on the property before actually approaching a Realtor, including a flyover in a small plane for an aerial look. The plantation had just over a mile of river frontage on the Dan, five miles of road frontage on a two-lane highway, and about four hundred acres of rolling land laid out in abandoned crop fields and woods. The remaining three hundred acres was in forest. It was commonly stated that none of the prominent families in Rockwell County "ever" sold big parcels, but apparently their heirs did. The elderly lady who'd owned Glory's End had died the previous fall, and the two surviving "children," both in their sixties, had let the local Realtors know that they might be persuaded, reluctantly, of course, most reluctantly, to let it go for two point five mil to the right kind of people.

Besides the tragic history, the most interesting feature for me was the original plantation house, a redbrick, white-columned pile overlooking a long sweep of cleared ground down to the river bottoms. It dated from the 1830s or so, when Rockwell County was the single most prosperous county in North Carolina, supported, of course, by a slave-based labor force. It wasn't a huge building, as the real ones often weren't, but it was pretty much in its original configuration. There were none of the blighting additions I'd seen tacked on to other nineteenth-century houses in the area. I intended to restore it and then live in it.

My crew of retired cops at Hide and Seek Investigations, all city boys at heart, thought I'd gone senile. One of them even bought me a video of that movie *The Money Pit* just to make sure I knew what I was getting into. For me, however, it was time to make a change. I was tired of living in the ever-expanding suburban densepacks of the Triboro area. The peaceful old farm behind my house had been acquired by a developer, so now I got to watch them rape the hillside with giant yellow machinery in preparation for yet another mansion graveyard of million-dollar homes, shoddily built by heavily leveraged builders, a whopping twenty-five feet between them. I had known that all this was inevitable, so I'd been looking for some country property for a year or so before the big Caterpillars showed up.

I was also getting bored with herding court papers and the general tedium of missing persons cases that were the bread-and-butter jobs for our little company. There were some really interesting cases, but for the most part we chased down people who didn't want to be found and served them with paper they didn't want to see. When I sensed that I was getting on my guys' nerves, I decided that I needed a change of scene and a project. Glory's End looked like it would do.

We did the necessary preliminary paperwork, and I gave Mr. Oatley my banker's name and number to begin the money dance. His eyes really lit up when I said there would not be a mortgage. I did want a title search, a survey bring-up, and all the other usual due diligence normally required by a bank. He thought we could probably close in thirty to sixty days, barring complications. I asked what kind of complications.

"This is an old, rural county, Lieutenant," he said solemnly. "Titles can be complicated, depending on how far back they go and how long a family has owned it."

"Shouldn't that actually simplify it?"

"In the early days," he said, "the big cotton and tobacco planters would work the ground until it was exhausted. Then they'd abandon it and move on to new ground. Technically they still owned it, but if some small farmers moved in behind them, things could get murky."

"Well, time I've got," I said, "and, of course, the money to buy it."

"That should help considerably," he said, rubbing his hands together.

"One more thing," I said. "I would like permission to

stay at the house from time to time. I'll rent it if that's what it takes."

"I'm sure that can be arranged," he said.

I drove back to my office downtown, where Pardee Bell told me there was an urgent message from a Mr. Ray Garrett.

"Dude says he's the TPC at Alexander state prison."

"What's a TPC?" I asked. Pardee had no idea.

I went down to my office and called Mr. Garrett. "Okay," I said, when he answered. "What's a TPC?"

"Transition placement coordinator," he said with a chuckle. "The new and improved name for the prisoner release paperwork guy. I started as a main pop screw, but now I've moved up to upper middle corrections management. Ain't that something?"

I agreed that it was most impressive and asked what was up.

"Back when you were on the job there with the Manceford County Sheriff's Office, do you remember sending up a bad boy named Breen? Billie Ray Breen?"

I searched my memory. "Yeah," I said. "Nasty little bastard. Got drunk, got mad, beat his common-law wife and her sister almost to death with a baseball bat one night. Gorped the sister, as I remember. The wife had to testify by blinking her one good eye yes or no. We took him down in some no-tell motel that same night with the MCAT. Crack-thin kid, rat faced, weird eyes."

"Well," he said, "that still describes him. He's done twelve on a twenty-to-life jolt in the red level here. That's the good news."

"Okay, and?"

"The bad news is he's getting early-released."

"How in the hell did that happen?"

"Don't ask, Lieutenant. Here's the thing: I think you're getting a ghost."

*Oh, great,* I thought. In cop parlance, a ghost was someone who got out of prison and then went after the cop who
put him in. When I said we took him down, I should have
said that I had personally taken him down when he shot one
of my guys and tried really hard to shoot me. I'd put one
through his right lung and two more into his plumbing, but,
unfortunately, we were issued nines in those days, and,
thin as he'd been, he'd survived, after soaking up a great
deal of the taxpayers' money.

"He been talking trash?"

"Not so's we could bust him for it," he said, "but we have
ears out there. Word is that he's gonna make you, by name,
his new life's work."

"When exactly does he get out?"

He named the date.

"Parole supervision?"

"Three years, minimum. I'll get you his PO's name as
soon as one's assigned. Since he was red level, it'll be
weekly at first."

"Let's tell him I retired in Europe."

"Wish I could, but I'm betting he can find you the same
way I did."

"Which was?"

"Called the Manceford County Sheriff's Office. They
gave me your business number. I looked up the number on
the Web, and Grandma Google told me everything else I
needed to know. Your company. Your bio. Home number
and address. Old news stories. A picture even. They call it
progress, Lieutenant."

"Yeah, really," I said. "Well, I appreciate the heads-up.
Maybe I should just wait out in the parking lot and mash
him with my pickup truck when he comes through the
gates."

"Then you'd take his place in here, Lieutenant. Trust
me, you wouldn't like it."

I thanked him again, hung up, and went to get some

coffee. All cops, especially retired cops, lived with this possibility. Bad guys locked up for years on end had plenty of time to stew up notions of revenge on the cop who'd put them away. Their being in prison was, of course, never their own fault, and, once out, they usually had nothing else to do, life having passed them by in terms of skills or capability. That meant they could be very dangerous.

I briefed my guys, who were all ex-cops. Tony Martinelli, Pardee Bell, and Horace Stackpole had all served on the MCAT with me back in the day. Now we worked court papers, found witnesses, and tagged the occasional philandering husband. I owned the company, and we all worked as much or as little as we wanted to. I didn't need the money, and the other guys were mostly filling up 401(k)s and staying out of their respective wives' hair.

"No problem, boss," Tony said. "You tell us who his PO is and we'll find a way to violate his ass right back to Alex."

Sounded like a plan to me.

I went out the next day to walk the property again, this time without the Realtor. I did take my two operational German shepherds, Frick and Kitty. Both were sable females. Frick was older and a bit smaller than Kitty, but they complemented each other nicely in the field. Frick was a busybody with an excellent nose who tended to scout ahead, while Kitty, with her strong sense of duty, stayed back with me at all times. The third member of my shepherd family, Frack, was a stay-at-home dog now, after losing a leg and an eye in the moonpool case. He was even older than Frick, and the role of senior citizen seemed to suit him just fine. As with too many aging German shepherds, his back end wasn't going to last much longer anyway. I dreaded that day, because when their wheels fall off, you have to do your duty.

The plantation's main driveway was a mixture of gravel and truly determined weeds. There were two brick gate pillars leaning at odd angles just inside the turnoff from the main road. One had a date inscribed, 1838, and the other the plantation's name, Glory's End. The numerals, antique characters partly obscured by ivy, were only faintly visible. The name's lettering, however, looked newer, which matched with the story of the name change at the end of the Civil War. As I turned into the drive I caught a glimpse of an even bigger house across the road behind its own aisle of oaks. David Oatley had told me that the neighboring plantation was called Laurel Grove and that the people who had built Glory's End had been related to the people across the road. I couldn't tell whether anyone was home, but the grounds did look maintained. Mr. Oatley had said the folks were eccentric, devoted to the past, and reclusive.

I drove almost a half mile to get to the house. The road was bumpy and needed crowning. The fields on either side were mostly overgrown with waist-high winter weeds. There were two tree-lined creeks running under the road and through the fields. It looked like someone had replaced the original wooden beam bridges with concrete culvert structures. As I got closer to the main house, a line of oaks began to flank the road, their overhanging branches creating a hazy green tunnel of spring foliage overhead. The road divided about a quarter mile from the front of the house, with the left branch headed down along the base of the homestead hill toward some barns and other farm structures behind the house. I took the right branch and drove up toward the house itself.

The building was well proportioned, with two stories built over another level that was half underground, half above. At the front there was a large white staircase leading up to the main level's columned front porch. Three tall windows bounded either side of double doors. There was a somewhat narrower sleeping porch above the columns. The semisubmerged ground level had smaller windows across its entire front, except where the twenty-foot-wide staircase obscured them. The bricks were obviously handmade, but some of the mortar had that floury look that indicated I'd need the services of a mason.

I let the two shepherds out and gave them a minute to desecrate the grounds. Then all three of us went up the staircase to the front doors, which were ten to twelve feet high and made of some heavily painted wood. The original nineteenth-century hardware was long gone. The doors were secured by a modern, brass-plated doorknob, to which I had a key. Except now the doors were partially ajar, and the shepherds were staring at the opening as if someone might be lurking in there. I tried to remember if we'd gone inside on the last visit, but we hadn't. So who was in there?

I stood on the porch and listened. It was a pleasant spring morning, with birds twittering in the nearby oak trees. The sound of insects rising in the unkempt grass provided a quiet hum in the background. There were no other vehicles in sight, so if someone was inside, he'd walked in. Kitty's ears went up, and then one door opened all the way.

A woman stood in the doorway, and for a moment I thought I'd fallen into a time warp. She was dressed in one of those black southern gowns I'd only seen in museums and movies, full length to the floor, flaring skirts, and full sleeves ending in white lace. She was handsome rather than beautiful, with dark hair done up in one of those *Gone with the Wind* hairdos, pulled back from her forehead in a tight bun that ended in long, luxurious, shoulder length curls clamped by an ornate ivory comb. She had brown eyes, under imperiously arched eyebrows, and a small, thin-lipped mouth. I could not guess her age. The shepherds sat down on either side of me to await developments.

"Good morning to you, sir," she said, inclining her head in the tiniest of nods. "Are you perchance the new owner?"

"Not yet," I said, "but we're working on it. And you are?"

"Valeria Marion Lee," she announced. "My mother,

Hester Lowndes Lee, owns Laurel Grove plantation, across the road." She looked at me expectantly as if all those names should mean something, and I supposed that they did in some southern pantheon.

"I'm Cameron Richter, and these are my helpers, Frick and Kitty."

She glanced at each dog in turn. "Kitty?" she asked.

"The folks who bred her did it as a joke. The guy's wife wanted to be able to call, 'Here, Kitty, Kitty,' if she thought she needed protection."

A very faint smile crossed her face. "How droll," she said. "I suppose you wonder what I'm doing here."

"Mostly how you got in. The Realtor told me the place was locked up."

She fished in a pocket and produced a brass key that looked identical to mine. She stepped out of the house, skirts swishing, and handed it to me. "We've had a key ever since Mrs. Tarrant became incapacitated by her advancing age. No need of that now, I suppose."

Standing closer, she was nearly my own height, although some of that was the Scarlett O'Hara hairdo. Her clothes smelled of lilacs.

"Thank you," I said. "Since you're here, though, would you care to give me a tour of the house? I suspect you know it better than Mr. Oatley."

She cocked her head for a moment, considering it, and then agreed. I left the shepherds on the front porch. She led me back into the house. She described the house's sty-listic elements—heart-pine floors, plaster and lath walls, fireplaces—and its basic history. The downstairs layout was similar to many large plantation houses of the prewar period: A central hall was flanked by withdrawing rooms on either side; a large, ornate staircase circled up both sides of the hall to the second floor, where there were four bedrooms giving onto a long hallway. What had become the master bedroom in more modern times now had a bathroom, which was a very obvious addition to the original layout.

The previous owner, Mrs. Tarrant, had set up a temporary bedroom on the main floor in the left-hand drawing room; there was a bed and some armoires, and over in one corner, a tiny bathroom had been plugged in. The ceiling was eighteen or maybe even twenty feet high. The paint scheme was strangely reversed: There appeared to be wallpaper on the ceiling and paint on the walls. The wallpaper design was filled with mythical animals, scrollwork, and numbers. Some of it was missing, leaving bare spots on the ceiling. I couldn't really make out the details, but it all looked to me like an astrologer's bad dream.

Behind the two large drawing rooms on the main floor was a long kitchen and pantry setup, with back stairs leading down to the in-ground floor. In the nineteenth century, this in-ground floor was where the food preparation area had been, as well as the main dining room, all situated half underground to provide a cool place during the summer. The original kitchen had been out behind the house, and its foundations were still visible, next to what she told me had been the smokehouse. The original springhouse was also still there, nestled in a grove of ancient oaks from which a brook escaped down the broad hillside toward the river. There was no period furniture, but there was a clunky-looking central heating system and some air-conditioning machinery out behind the house, surrounded by unruly boxwood hedges. I peeked into the main electrical box and found round fuses instead of circuit breakers. I was probably lucky to find electricity.

"This is known as a Thomas Day house," she said as we went back upstairs to the main floor. "He was a notable woodworker who specialized in moldings, fireplace mantels, and staircases. He was also a black freedman who himself owned slaves."

"Mr. Oatley took me to see the site of the train robbery,"

I said, looking out the back windows at the outbuildings. "Did the family have a cemetery here as well?"

"No," she replied. "There were Lees here for most of the house's history, but they're all buried in town in the St. Stephen's cemetery. Our family actually built the church in the first place."

"The disclosure statement says there's another burial ground on the place but that it's been lost."

"That was probably a slave cemetery," she said dismissively, as if to say, *Who cares?*

"Is your family related to the Virginia Lees?"

"So it is claimed, but I'm not entirely sure. My mother says we are, but only distantly."

We stepped back out onto the front porch. The floorboards were a little springy, and I noticed now that some of the railings had begun to sag. There were some little piles of sandy-looking mortar dust at the base of the front wall.

"There's a lot of land here," I said, looking out over the surrounding fields. "Can it be farmed?"

"Most of our land across the way is leased to local farmers. I'm sure there'd be people interested in leasing this. It's been lying fallow all these years."

"I'm looking forward to exploring it all."

"Mind where you walk, sir," she said. "There are undoubtedly some abandoned wells out there, and they can be fatally treacherous."

I heard a noise down the driveway, and then a horse and buggy appeared out of the oak aisle. A smiling black man was driving it. He waved when he saw us on the front porch.

"Your chariot?" I said.

She smiled again. "Its proper name is a governess's cart, but, yes, this is how I will get home." She inclined her head formally and presented her right hand. "It's been a pleasure to meet you, Mr. Cameron Richter. I hope you can join us for tea sometime."

I took her hand, not quite sure if I was expected to kiss

it or shake it. I gave it a slight squeeze and let go. "I'd like that very much," I said.

She went down the wide wooden steps, holding the hem of her skirt up with both hands as the little carriage pulled up.

*They're taking this living in the past pretty seriously*, I thought. Then I saw the cell phone in the old man's shirt pocket. He saw me looking at it as he got down to help Valeria Marion Lee into the carriage and gave me a wink. *Okay*, I thought, *they're not all nuts*.

I locked the front door, gathered up the shepherds, and drove into town for lunch. Afterward I stopped by the realty office, signed yet some more papers, and asked the ladies there if there was an established restoration company in town. Not exactly, they told me, but a Ms. Carol Lee Pollard ran a consulting business on restoring old houses. They said she volunteered over at the library, and gave me directions.

Carol Pollard was a shapely brunette, late thirties, maybe forty, five-seven with short flip-style hair, blue eyes, and a warm smile to go with a broad upland North Carolina accent. She recognized my name when I introduced myself.

"Oh, yes," she said. "Mr. Richter from Triboro. You bought Glory's End. That's wonderful. You're not a developer, are you? I mean, you will live there?"

"I hope to," I said, realizing not for the first time that there were no secrets in a small southern town. "Getting tired of city life. The folks at Oatley Realty told me you're the local restoration wizard. I think I'm going to need a lot of advice."

She asked one of the other librarians to take over the front desk, and we retired to the office, away from the library patrons. I noticed she walked with a slight limp.

"I basically offer a consulting service on restoration work," she told me. "I can recommend what should be done, what should be left as is, and who the local contractors are that I'd trust with a project like that. I can also act as the general contractor if my clients want me to."

"That's what I need," I said. "I'm not on some crusade to put it back to absolute authenticity. I'll want to address structural problems and then mostly make it livable."

"Great," she said. "Because if you try to take something like Glory's End all the way back to the 1830s, you'll never get there."

"So I've been told, repeatedly. I met one of my neighbors this morning. A Ms. Valeria Lee?"

"Oh, my," she said. "That's amazing. No one ever sees them except on important church days. You didn't just go knock on their door, did you?"

I told her the circumstances, and she shook her head. "Now that's really interesting," she said. "The Laurel Grove Lees and the Glory's End Lees haven't been on speaking terms apparently since the train robbery in 1865. Supposedly, if one mentions them in front of Ms. Hester—that's Valeria's mother—she will get up and leave the room in high dudgeon."

High dudgeon. I laughed. "I believe it. Ms. Valeria rode off in a horse and buggy after giving me a tour of the house. I thought she'd been putting me on with the antebellum getup."

"Not at all," Carol said. "They're both pretty eccentric. You should hear the stories. Candles instead of electric lights. The costumes, of course. Horse and carriage instead of a car. The obligatory crazy relative supposedly mewed up in the attic."

"Is there a Mr. Lee?" I asked. "Or would it be Colonel?"

"There is a Major Lee," she said, "but no one ever sees him. It's rumored that he's the one locked in the attic."

"Great local color, if nothing else," I said, "and my next-door neighbor. Are they going to be mad at me if I start messing with the house?"

"I don't know," Carol said. "They might, but they're such hermits I can't imagine they'd bother you, especially if you throw around the word 'preserve' liberally."

"Yet there she was this morning, wandering around in there like some kind of ghost."

"She probably heard about the place selling and wanted to see it one more time before the new owners knocked it down and put up a sacrilege."

"Not many secrets in this county, I take it."

"Not when it comes to big pieces of historical property, no," she said. "Especially one with the history of Glory's End. You know the story? Why there's a cemetery up there by the railroad bridge?"

I told her I did and said I thought that it needed some care. Then we talked a little business, made our arrangements, and agreed to meet out at the house the following day.

I drove back to Triboro. On the way I got a call from Pardee Bell.

"Alexander State called. They lied about the release date. They let your ghost out this morning."

"Terrific. Got a parole officer's name yet?"

"Yup. Already called her. Name's Arlanda Cole. I know her from before. Hard-core PO. She said he's already checked in by pay phone, and he's reporting to her office late this afternoon. I told her what was up, and she says you ought to join them. Get that shit right out in the open so Little Boy Blue knows we know."

"Works for me."

At five thirty that afternoon I was having coffee with Parole Officer Arlanda Cole in her office down on Washington Street. Kitty was sitting in one corner of the room, and Frick was sitting right next to me. Arlanda was a chunky black woman with meat-cutter arms and intense, glaring black eyes. She'd welcomed me and the shepherds, speaking to each one in turn but knowing better than to pet them. She'd read the mope's record and apparently knew the arrest history.

"What we're gonna do," she said, "is try to get him to act out. Make a threat or two. I got people downstairs can have his evil young ass back in Alexander State before lockdown tonight."

*My kind of PO,* I thought. Her phone rang. Security was escorting a "client" upstairs to see her.

Breen had aged a lot. He was still skinny as a rail, but his face had hardened into features that fairly shouted ex-con: ratty, slightly protuberant eyes, slicked-back hair, pasty white face, sneering mouth. He wore jeans, sneakers, and a red T-shirt underneath what looked like a pawnshop windbreaker. He looked slightly disgusted when he saw that his PO was a black woman. I spotted Aryan Nation tats on the backs of his hands. When he saw me and the shepherds, though, he stopped in his tracks.

"The fuck is this?" he asked, pointing with his chin at me. His voice was raspy and whiny at the same time.

"Mind your sewer mouth in my office," Arlanda said. "Sit your butt down and shut up until I've finished talkin', understand me, prisoner?"

He grunted when she called him prisoner, flopped down into the chair positioned right in front of her desk, and stared at the floor. Frick got up and growled low in her throat. He pretended not to hear it, but Arlanda did. "Good doggy," she said. Breen grunted again, trying to make like he wasn't afraid of anyone or anything in the room. I gave Frick a sign, and she sat back down again.

Arlanda got out his file and read the terms of his parole out loud. She enumerated all the restrictions on his activities. There were lots of them. He continued to stare at the floor the entire time.

"You understand all that, boy?" she said.

His nostrils flared at her use of the word "boy." It was

fun to watch her work, but so far, she hadn't provoked him to say anything. He just nodded.

"Look at me, boy. I'll ask it again: You understand what I've just read to you?"

"Yeah."

"Unh-unh, Mr. Billie Ray Breen. You answer me, it's 'yes, ma'am,' 'no, ma'am.' I ain't havin' none of that 'yeah' shit from the likes of some wife-beating piece of white trash like you. Try it again."

"Yes, ma'am," he said, but with an insolent sneer on his face.

"Much better. Here's your reporting rules. If you're late, I'll get a warrant to have them pick your ass up. Just like that, no warnings, no excuses. If you miss an appointment, I'll get a warrant. If you violate any of the other rules, I'll get a warrant. If you piss me off, I'll get a warrant. You hear me, boy?"

"Yes, ma'am," he said. Now he was trying to look bored.

"Now, then," she said. "Word from Alexander is that you been makin' threats, that you plan to get you some get-back on the lieutenant here."

Breen looked over at me and then shrugged.

"Well?"

"Cons run their mouth, ain't nothin to do with me," he said. He was back to staring at the floor.

"Well, lemme tell you something, boy," Arlanda said. "It don't matter whether you put an ad in the damn paper or you just thinkin' about it: We know. It's in your record here, and, more importantly, it's in my brain right here." She tapped a finger on her forehead. "This lieutenant even sees your ugly face on the street, he calls me, I get a warrant, and you're back on the red level before you can say love me tender."

His eyes flashed at her allusion to the prison sex scene, and he almost came back at her.

"I didn't hear it," she said, cupping one ear. Her expression said she wanted to come around the desk and whack him one. He was sitting there like a dog that was about to attack, eyes flitting sideways, his body tensed up in the chair. She was waiting for her "yes, ma'am." He wasn't going to say it.

"Here Kitty, Kitty," I said.

The big shepherd got up from the corner and walked over to where I was sitting at one side of Arlanda's desk. Frick joined her. I stood up and, together with the two shepherds, stepped over to where Breen was sitting.

"Find it," I said quietly, and both shepherds closed in on Breen and began to sniff his clothes. Standing over him I could see his fingers trembling and the pulse in his temple racing, but even this lowlife knew better than to move just now. Both dogs' hackles were up as they smelled his fear, but Breen still didn't move. He'd been inside long enough to know how to hold himself in readiness. He was tougher than I'd expected, and for the first time I wondered if I was really going to have a problem with this guy. I let the dogs get a good scent memory, and then I went back to my chair and snapped my fingers to recall them.

"I'm still waitin'," Arlanda said.

"Yes, ma'am," he said finally, his voice strangely neutral. He still wouldn't look at her. I stood up.

"I've got what I came for," I said.

She nodded. "You got my number, too, right?"

"Absolutely—and my friends here have his."

We left her office and went down to the parking lot. The cops at the security station admired the shepherds and wished me a pleasant evening. My Suburban was parked right in front. When we went out to my ride, I got a surprise. My entire crew was standing out there in the lot, waiting for me to come out.

"What's this?" I asked, as if I didn't know. Tony gave me a disappointed look, and then Pardee pointed with his chin. One of the security officers was bringing Breen out through the front doors. He shrugged off the officer's helping hand from his shoulder and then saw us. He stopped, reached inside his jacket, popped a pack of cigarettes, shook one out, and lit it without taking his eyes off of us.

There were four of us looking back at him. Pardee Bell, a tall, rangy black man, Tony Martinelli, as short as Pardee was tall but with his game face on, with a hit man's cold-crazy eyes, and Horace, who looked like an aging school-teacher in his birth-control glasses and rumpled clothes, until you realized just how big he was. Also, of course, my two furry buddies.

Breen took a single deep drag on his cigarette, burning down half its length, spat something onto the sidewalk, and then threw the cigarette in the gutter. He blew a plume of smoke up into the evening air, just to show us he could hold it, and then sauntered away without a word.

"At least now he knows," Pardee said.

"How often does he have to check in?" Horace asked.

"Daily for the first two weeks, then weekly after that if she allows it. It's up to her, and she hates the bastard already."

"One of us will be out here each day," Pardee said. "Remind him he'll be going up against a crowd, he tries some shit."

"Y'all don't have to do that," I said. "He's tough, but I don't think he's stupid."

Based on their expressions, they did not agree.

The next morning I went out early to have some time on the property before Carol Pollard showed up. Seven hundred acres makes for quite a long walk, but I knew the only way I'd ever see the whole thing was by tromping around on foot. I parked my Suburban at the house so Carol would know I was around and then set out with the dogs for the river bottoms below the main house. It was cool enough but with a hint of humidity, and my boots and trousers were soon wet from morning dew on the grass.

The Dan River was some two hundred yards wide as it passed Glory's End. The Dan is a substantial, muscular river. From the looks of all the snags and debris along the banks, it was capable of rising up from time to time. Across the river were rocky bluffs but no houses or other signs of habitation. I walked upstream for half a mile until I came abreast of the Confederacy-era railroad bridge abutments. There was a notch visible in the trees across the river, and out in the river itself I could see swelling whirlpools where I assumed the crossing pillars had been. On my side the abutment was still intact, fifty, sixty feet high with two rust stripes running down the face from some long-decayed truss pins. The defensive fortifications were crumbling badly.

I climbed the bank awkwardly amid a small avalanche of weeds, rocks, and gravel and reminded myself to bring a walking stick the next time. The shepherds passed me easily, scrambling up through the bushes, tails wagging. They loved to go out and just run. At the top I stood on the stone floor of the bridge abutment and surveyed my new kingdom. To the northwest, upstream, there was a low ridge, which Mr. Oatley had told me marked the western edge of the property, from the river all the way in to the road. To the southeast I could see the big house on its hill, surrounded by large trees whose heads were already filling in green with the new leaves. The rest of the property was hidden behind that hill. Three crows protested my sudden appearance.

I looked around for the shepherds and saw them nosing through the grove of cedars that marked the burial ground. I walked along the overgrown right-of-way, down the embankment, and then up the knoll. It was a peaceful place, overlooking the big river and the sleeping plantation. Glory's End. I could almost picture it—a platoon hurriedly drafted from the starving remnants of the gray armies, fleeing from Richmond as Grant tightened the vise, riding nervously behind a bottle-nosed steam engine. Coming into the watering station at dusk, feeling more secure now that they were across the river and safe from marauding Union cavalry, twenty-nine of them stepping down from the cars and their precious cargo to stack arms and go for a smoke or a water break of their own behind the trees.

Then the sound of hoofbeats in the nearby trees, a moment of terror as they scrambled for their guns only to stand down with a whistle of relief when the engine's headlight revealed graycoats on gaunt horses riding into the station. Even better—more protection. The engineer leaning out from the engine to greet the riders as they fanned out along the tracks, nodding to the soldiers who were restacking their rifles, and then the horrifying surprise as the riders pulled huge horse pistols and began firing, starting with the engineer, each rider calmly shooting down the man in front of him and then the one next to him, the scene dissolving into booming gouts of flame, plunging and rearing horses, and sulfurous puffs of gunsmoke until the train guard and the three-man crew were all on the ground and the last echoes of gunfire died out across the dark river.

Now all that remained was these rough stones, the weedy gravel, and the rusting bones of the water tank. It wasn't like some of the big Civil War battlefields I'd visited, like Antietam, where a walk at sundown would raise the hairs on the back of your neck as you contemplated the thousands upon thousands who had died there. This did not seem to be a haunted place, but rather more of a sad footnote to that tragic war, now sleeping comfortably in the morning sunlight. The shepherds were resting against the largest stone, which actually looked like a real tombstone. I bent down to read the badly weathered inscription.

### THOMAS HARPER, 1845–1865
#### GONE TO GLORY FOR NO GOOD REASON

*Got that right*, I thought. *Glory's End indeed*. As I stood up I caught a flash of light in the distance up on that ridge that marked the western boundary. It was a bright flash, as if a beam of sunlight had bounced off a mirror. Or some binoculars?

The top of the ridge was heavily forested, and I hadn't brought my own binoculars. I need glasses to read comfortably, but my distance vision is just fine. The shepherds, attuned to my sudden alertness, saw me staring and got up to look around. I walked deeper into the cedar grove to the highest point on the knoll, where there was a treeless clearing caused by an exposed rock ledge.

I stood behind a tree, however, just in case I'd caught a glimpse of a rifle scope instead of plain old binoculars. I was, of course, thinking of Billie Ray Breen, even as my brain was saying, *No way.* Then I caught a brief glimpse of a horseman up there in the trees, moving away from me and disappearing down the backside of that ridge. At that distance I couldn't make out whether the rider was male or female. The figure was wearing a dark slouch hat and what looked like one of those long western duster coats.

*Okay,* I said to myself. *Definitely not Breen.* Not on horseback. A neighbor, perhaps? I knew who lived across the road but not who lived on either side of the plantation. One more project for the to-do list. That was the whole point of my new home: projects, something to look forward to each day beyond yet another dreary court case. I craved an endless to-do list that could lead to tangible accomplishment. Restoration of the house. Bringing the farm back to life. Doing something about this forgotten graveyard. Meeting new and interesting neighbors. Maybe even learning how to ride a horse.

The shepherds were looking at me expectantly. "Okay, guys," I told them. "Let's go meet the pretty lady and get this show on the road."

Carol and I broke for lunch after two hours of inspecting the main house and its immediate surroundings. She drove me to a large, purple-painted Victorian-era house out on the main road. It had been the home of the man for whom the local town was named, and a couple from Chapel Hill had restored it and opened a restaurant. The place was full, and I soon found out why—the food was excellent.

"I didn't expect this out here in the country," I told her.

She laughed. "It's become quite well known," she said. "There's also a community college on the other side of town, and they have an excellent subscription concert program. We locals call it the Chapel Hill effect."

"Don't tell me suburban growth is pushing its way all the way out here, too," I said, noting the very mixed crowd of diners.

"Well, you're here," she pointed out.

*Touché*, I thought. *So I am.* My head was buzzing with all the details of our house inspection, and I was glad she'd brought a voice recorder along because I could not possibly have kept up with her.

"How can I find out who my adjacent neighbors are?" I asked.

"Courthouse," she replied. "Mr. Oatley can help you with that. You've already met the Lees across the road. The places on either side of you are even bigger than Glory's End. They won't necessarily have anyone living there, though. The really big tracts in this county are owned by just a few local families."

"Who 'never' sell."

"Generally, that's true. Everyone was really surprised when Glory's End came on the market."

"Who's everyone?" I asked.

"It's a really small town, Mr. Richter."

"How'd you get here?" I asked.

"I grew up here, went away to college and then out into the world for a while. Didn't care much for it and came back."

"Married?"

"Briefly," she said, looking away. I sensed she'd just as soon not pursue that subject.

"So what's next in our project planning?"

"Just that," she said. "Planning. I build a proposed restoration plan, you review and approve it, we set a budget, and then I act as the general contractor and start a bidding process. There's a sequence to these projects."

"Like doing electrical and plumbing before the wallpaper?"

"Exactly. First, of course, you have to close. How's that coming? Do you need some bank referrals?"

When I explained that I wouldn't need a bank, she whistled softly. "Wow. This has to be a seven-figure deal. Police work pays that well in Triboro?"

"If you let the right people bribe you, it does," I said.

She put up her hands in mock surrender. "Sorry," she said. "Didn't mean it that way."

"No offense taken."

"It's just that, in this county, when someone's considered to be rich, we're usually talking about land rich. Families who have been here since the 1700s, but they're riding around in Ford pickups, not Mercedeses."

I nodded. Then I told her about seeing the horseman on the ridge.

She didn't think it significant. "A lot of people ride in this county," she said. "There's even a fox hunt. Horseback's still the best way to get around some of the bigger properties. Do you ride?"

I told her I did not but might want to learn, among the many other projects I wanted to do on the property over the next few years.

"Few years?" she said with a smile. "Longer than that, I think. The house alone will probably be a ten-year project."

"It didn't take that long in that movie—at the end, where the crew comes in and swarms all over it?"

"*The Money Pit*? That's Hollywood. The truth comes in

two parts. One, you want to enjoy the process of bringing one of these places back to life. Two, getting the right people and materials takes forever—just the nature of the beast and the folks who do this for a living. The real craftsmen don't know the meaning of a schedule, and unless you're buying it to flip it and make money, you should just sit back and watch."

That sounded like the ground truth to me, and I had said that quality time was the objective. Now I knew why she hadn't mentioned a schedule when she'd described the project planning. I asked if it would take ten years before I could live there. She told me I could probably make a part of the house more habitable once the basics were done, and then just creep along with the project.

After lunch I went over to the courthouse to try my hand at researching the property title and possibly the surrounding parcels of land. An elderly gentleman wearing a wool suit and a bow tie greeted me in the records section. He gave me the immediate impression that I was disturbing him and asked if I was a lawyer. I said no.

He sighed and said that I would be wasting my time unless I happened to be an expert in deciphering old deed books, which he very much doubted I was.

I smiled patiently and told him that I was willing to try, if he would only do his job and get me the appropriate books.

"I do not work for you, sir," he said, laying on a little high dudgeon of his own.

"Are you paid by the taxpayers of this county, Mr. Clerk?" I asked.

"Are you a taxpayer in this county?" he retorted.

"About to be; I'm buying Glory's End. Then I'll be a voter, too. Imagine that, a landowner and a voter—and you in an elected position."

He glared at me and then said he would bring the books to the reading room, which was right through that door there, where normally only attorneys were allowed.

I went in and sat down, wondering about all this hostility. I'd dealt with minor bureaucrats all my life, and I knew some of them can grow a Nazi streak, usually in proportion to the insignificance of their job.

He came in bearing an armload of deed books. He informed me that I really meant the Oak Grove Lees, unless I was only interested in the time after the war.

"There's a magnifying glass in that drawer," he said. "Do you know how to read a deed book?"

I told him I'd muddle through, but if I had any questions, I knew where to find him.

"Well," he said, "I am fairly knowledgeable about the history of this county and the various important families. I myself am a Gaston."

"Wow," I said. "A Gaston."

He reddened, and then I decided to end the bullshit. I stood up, and we discovered that I was one foot taller than he was and quite a bit more substantial. "If I have a technical question," I said, "I will expect you to answer it truthfully to the best of your ability, and if you can't, I will expect you to refer me to someone who can. Clear?"

He put up his hands in protest. "I only meant that I am well versed in the names of various properties and the genealogy associated with them," he said. "I didn't mean—"

"Thank you," I said.

He backed almost out of the reading room, then stopped. He looked as if he'd gotten some of his courage back. "May I say something?" he asked.

I nodded.

"Glory's End and the Lees in this county have a troubled past," he said. "You need to be careful of what you go looking for, Mr. Richter. You just might find it."

I'd heard a variant of that expression before, as in, *Be careful what you wish for, you just might get it.* I didn't understand how that pertained to deed books, though—or a title search, for that matter. Before I could think of anything cute to say, he turned around and went back to his office.

There were six deed books piled on the table, and I was suddenly glad my own name wasn't Lee. One thing was clear, however: By taking on the house and the land, I was stepping into a rich vein of Carolina Piedmont history.

Thirty minutes and two deed books later I came to a decision: Much as I hated to admit it, the old man had been right. This little project was going to require an expert, specifically an attorney who did this for a living. I returned the books to the front desk and asked my new best friend to recommend someone.

"There's really only one," he said, trying to keep any hint of triumph out of his voice. "Hiram Whatley Lee, Esquire."

"Lee."

"Who better than a Lee, Mr. Richter?" he asked, cocking his head to one side.

*Who indeed,* I thought.


Arlanda Cole gave me a call at home that evening. They'd run a little con on Billie Ray that afternoon. They'd put him in a waiting room with two other "parolees" to wait for Arlanda to get around to him. The parolees had, of course, been undercover drug cops, and they got to going on the matter of getting back at some of the pig bastards who'd put them away. Billie had let them rant for a little while but did not join in. Then he made a single comment: There are people who talk shit, and there are people who do shit. Talkers were never doers. Then he clammed back up.

"Either he made 'em for cops," she said, "and was just messin' around, or that's exactly what he meant, that he was a doer and not a talker."

"I have to assume the latter, then," I said.

"Yeah, Lieutenant, I think you do. I'll keep irritatin' him, see if we can get him violated, but I believe this one's a crafty dog, you know what I'm sayin'?"

"Yes, I do. My guys are keeping an eye on him, for the moment. Letting him know we're watching him."

"Tell 'em to do it from a distance, okay? Don't want that little shit goin' and gettin' a lawyer, accusing you of stalking him. Co-vert, not o-vert, and you didn't hear that from me."

"Got it, and I really appreciate your help."

"You walk around strapped these days?"

"Not lately, but—"

"There you go. You have a nice evenin'."

I'd wanted to ask Arlanda where Billie Ray was staying, since he had to give his PO a physical address, but I knew she wasn't allowed to tell me that. I then called Horace and relayed the message about getting out of Billie's face. Horace said he'd pass it on and that he had a great rifle scope for doing distant surveillance. If I really wanted to find out where his crib was, my guys could probably manage it. From a distance, of course.

My visit to Lawyer Lee's office had been brief. He'd been out of the office. His assistant said that he could take on the project, but probably not for two weeks or so. I asked her to contact Mr. Oatley to get the precise property description in question. She gave me a smile not unlike the county clerk's and told me that Whatley Lee was fully familiar with Glory's End, formerly Oak Grove plantation. Apparently my input for the title search was going to be limited to paying for it.

Finished with my work for the day, I went home for supper, then got some single malt, and went into my study to read. The three shepherds came in, found their dog beds, and began to decorate them with dog hair. Frack, the oldest of the three, was showing a lot of gray in the muzzle, and even though he could get around on his three remaining legs, he was slowing way down.

I never thought it was possible to smell a moving bullet, but you can if it's close enough. Its vapor trail gives off a brassy, coppery smell, somewhat like ozone but with a distinct flash of heat. Also, if it's that close, the shock wave will press on your eyes.

The round that razor-cut the air in front of my face came through the window from the outside, but I didn't learn that until later. I'd been reading my book, not bothering anybody, when what turned out to be a .30-06 soft point clicked through the window, burned into the kitchen, and smashed six coffee mugs into ceramic dust inside one of the cabinets. I remember hearing a distant boom outside, but I was too surprised to do much more than blink as I rolled out of my chair onto the floor and pulled the table lamp over with me, breaking the bulb and putting the room in darkness.

I lay on the floor, wondering what would happen next, smelling expensive Scotch on the rug. A big piece of glass guillotined out of the window frame and crashed to the floor. A moment later I could feel a cool breeze from outside. I listened to see if anyone was coming up to the house, maybe to look inside, see if he needed to finish the job, but heard only the night wind. My nearest gun was in the gun safe in my closet.

Then I realized that this had to have been a warning shot. Somebody with a long rifle and a scope had just put one between my nose and my book, and I didn't think it had been Horace. If the shooter was that good, he could just as easily have put it in my ear.

Three cold shepherd noses were pushing into various places on my body, making sure I was okay. I crawled across the floor, found the phone, and called the cops.

"Okay," Horace said. "This doesn't compute."

"You mean Breen as the shooter."

"Yeah. What are the chances of an ex-con, out, what,

three whole days? Getting his hands on a thirty-aught and some ammo, finding your house, setting up a nighttime ambush, and then getting clean away?"

There was silence around the office conference table. I could see that my troops were as skeptical as I was. The sheriff's office had found where the shooter had set up in the construction site behind my house in Summerfield. They'd even found a single spent center-fire cartridge and footprints leading out through all the red mud to the gravel construction access road. After that, nothing. No witnesses, no tire tracks, no dropped calling cards saying the Shadow did it. Nothing. They were stumped.

"I mean," Horace said, "where would he get wheels? Did he buy the rifle? Steal it? Somebody just lend him one? Whatcha need a rifle for, Billie Ray? Not gonna murder some guy, are you?"

"And why the warning shot?" Tony said. "Guy like that, takes a baseball bat to two women 'cause the baby was crying? You're talking some kinda single-cell organism, does that kinda shit. Give a guy like him a rifle, put him in position, he wouldn't shoot a warning shot."

I nodded. "Yeah, that's what I think, too. Breen's definitely a POS, but I don't see him as a careful planner. It wasn't him."

"So," Pardee said. "You maybe got more than one ghost out there?"

I threw up my hands. "Would I necessarily know? It was a fluke that the people at Alexander State were able to warn me about Breen."

"Have they grabbed him up?" Horace asked. "Squeezed him a little?"

I nodded. Arlanda Cole had called first thing this morning after word got out downtown. Billie Ray had come in when called. He denied knowledge of any shootings, anywhere, anyhow. She'd said that, in her opinion, he seemed to have genuine parolee religion and that he was not about to put his freedom in danger just to scare me with a rifle. Besides that, his girlfriend could vouch for him at the time of the shooting. Of course.

That said, I couldn't think of anyone else who would do that. During my time I'd put more than one bad guy away, but so had all of us, and it was inevitably a team effort. The perps who came back as ghosts and acted on it usually did it by walking up in broad daylight, doing a remember-me, and then opening up with a barrage of some kind. They weren't thinkers, planners, or talkers. They were doers.

"Okay, then," Pardee said. "Let's assume we're right about that. So who—and why the warning shot?"

I drew a blank. Somebody from the hills, like one of the Creigh clan? Long guns were their specialty, but warning shots were not their style. If the hill people thought you owed them a death, they just flat took it. Fair's fair. And the vigilantes of cat dancer fame? I'd kept my part of that Faustian bargain and paid for it with my professional reputation. They had no reason to want my skin, assuming they were even still in business. There was another Billy, one with a *y*, down in Wilmington, who might qualify, but to the best of my knowledge he was in federal hands until the end of time for his part in the nuclear power plant sabotage case.

"How soon's that old house of yours out in Rockwell County going to be ready?" Horace asked.

I shook my head. "My ace restoration consultant says ten years to completion. I could get a trailer, I guess." A fleeting image of that flash of light and the disappearing horseman on the western ridge crossed my mind, but that didn't make sense, either. I hadn't been there long enough to provoke this kind of violence. Even the reenacting ante-bellum spinster across the road, strange as she seemed, had been friendly so far. "I don't know, guys, maybe I have to start sleeping days and then doing a little night recon for the next couple of weeks. See what we can turn up."

"We?" Tony asked hopefully.

"The shepherds and I. This guy comes back, I might miss him, but they won't."

They looked disappointed. The secretary told me I had a call. It was my old boss, Bobby Lee Baggett, high sheriff of Manceford County.

"Who'd you piss off this time?" he asked.

"I might have a ghost," I said.

"You probably have several," he said with a laugh. "Not to mention cat dancers and that wild bunch up there in the Smokies. But you said might—you don't think this is Mr. Breen?"

Leave it to Bobby Lee to have been thoroughly briefed. "It seems improbable that he could get something like this organized so quickly."

"On the other hand, he's had seventeen years to plan it and set it up. Getting out to your place and doing the deed would only take an hour."

He had a point there, I thought. "That means helper bees," I said.

"Yup, it does. Since it happened on my patch, I've got people pulling that string as we speak. You got someplace to go? I heard you'd bought a big plantation over in Rockwell County."

"Jungle drums alive and well, I see."

"Oh, absolutely. You know how it is—we keep track of our more notorious alumni. Seriously, give it some thought: We can work the cop side here, and you make it harder for the mopes to find you. You want me to talk to Sheriff Walker up there?"

"I was going to do that myself," I said, "but an advance call wouldn't hurt."

"You assume I'll speak well of you, Lieutenant."

"As well as you can, boss."

"You miss it?"

"I miss the people more than the job."

"You took a bunch of 'em with you, as I remember. Horace, Tony, Pardee. How's that going for you, your private snoop deal?"

"Boring," I said. "The Wilmington case was interesting, but the bulk of it is waste management, just like it was on the Job."

"Waste management," he said. "I like that. Slide your ass down a rabbit hole somewhere, Lieutenant. I'll be in touch."

"Thanks, boss. I appreciate it."

I meant that, too. The Manceford County Sheriff's Office was a tribe, and Bobby Lee Baggett was very much the chief. Their unofficial and often-denied motto was "Mess with the best, and die like the rest." I knew the sheriff would put a couple of tigers on this and dig hard.

"I guess I need to go out to my new county," I told my guys. "Find me some temporary housing."

"Make sure they take dogs," Tony said with a grin.

"Make sure you take a weapon or three," Horace said, ever Mr. Practical.

I drove out to the Rockwell County seat and made an office call on the county sheriff. His name was Hodge Walker, and he was a big-shouldered black man with iron gray hair, a deep baritone voice, and a wide smile. I'm no pygmy, but his hand engulfed mine like a gentle laundry press. I'd taken both operational shepherds into his office, and he thought that was just dandy.

"Bobby Lee Baggett called me earlier," he said. "Didn't know we had us a lawman celebrity up here in little ol' Rockwell County. You're the one broke up that terrorist deal down near Wilmington, right?"

"I had some competent help." I said.

He shivered. "Nuclear stuff gives me the heebie-jeebies," he said. "The North Carolina Sheriffs' Association toured the plant near Raleigh one time. We didn't see the reactors, of course, but they had 'em this big pool with some evil shit glowing down at the bottom."

"Moonpool," I said. "That's what the bad guys went after."

"I hear you've just bought Glory's End?"

I'd have been surprised if he hadn't known. I said yes.

"Beautiful old place," he said. "Some sad aspects to it, too."

"The train robbery."

"And the people who made it beautiful," he said, gently reminding me of the county's slave-soaked history.

"Yes," I said. "I'm fully aware of that aspect, too."

"So," he said. "Somebody took a shot at you over in Summerfield last night."

"Somebody did," I said. "Based on how it was done, I believe it was a warning shot. Did Sheriff Baggett tell you I've just acquired a ghost?"

"He did, and he also said you didn't think this was him."

I shrugged. "They'll find out, I suppose. In the meantime, I'm looking for someplace to go to ground up here while my restoration project gets under way. Any decent B and B's do long-term rentals here?"

"We've got two in town," he said, "but two big dogs like these are probably out of the question. Your new neighbors, now, the Lees? They have an old stone cottage on the millpond at Laurel Grove that they rent out from time to time. You want me to call Ms. Hester for you?"

I thought about it for a moment. It certainly would be convenient, but I wasn't all that anxious to drop back into the 1800s. He saw my hesitation and smiled.

"They're all right, those two," he said. "A little bit crazy, but of course I say that in the southern, which is to say complimentary, way. The major, now, is crazy in the medical sense, or at least that's what folks say. And I don't think they'd care about these two guys."

"Then, yes, please," I said, knowing full well the value

of a referral in a small southern town from the county sheriff. We talked law enforcement for a few minutes, and then I became aware that one of his officers was waiting to see him, so I made my manners and left.

I went back to the purple house for lunch. The sheriff called me there on my cell. He told me that the stone cottage was available and that I should go out there and speak to Ms. Valeria.

I drove up to the big house at Laurel Grove and found Valeria waiting for me on the front porch. She was wearing a different-colored version of the full-length puffy skirt and a blouse with long sleeves and lace cuffs. I got out of my Suburban and admired her for a moment. Standing on the veranda of the big house, she looked perfectly appropriate, if something of a stage prop.

"Ms. Valeria," I said, honoring the southern tradition of address. "We meet again."

"Why, yes indeed, Mr. Richter," she said in that throaty voice. "We understand you would like to engage the stone cottage for a spell?"

"I think so," I said. "May I see it first?"

"Of course, sir," she said, coming down the dozen wooden stairs in a rustle of silk and petticoats. "The cottage is a few minutes' walk from here. Shall we?"

I agreed and opened the door for the shepherds. They bounded out, took one look at Valeria, and went over to her with tails wagging and ears submissive. She bent down and addressed each of them, and they responded enthusiastically. "These are your guardians, Mr. Richter?"

"Precisely, Ms. Valeria. Where I go, they go."

"Just as it should be," she said. "It is their duty, if I'm not mistaken."

"Please, call me Cam," I said. "I'm not used to all this formality."

"It will grow on you, Mr. Cam," she said, granting me

half an inch. "Formality allows a certain distance, the better to make appraisals, don't you think? The cottage is just this way."

We set off down the circular driveway and then turned left onto a gravel lane that led down a gentle slope toward a dense grove of willow trees. The shepherds ranged ahead, happy to be loose in the fresh air after being shut up in the Suburban. I decided to be quiet and enjoy the scenery. This seemed to suit my hostess just fine as we walked apace down the hill toward the willows. At the bottom of the lane was a low stone dam, which backed up a millpond of about an acre. To our right were the foundations of what had probably been the gristmill. To the left, on the other side of the pond, was the stone cottage, partially screened by more willow trees.

It was a square building with a slate roof over gray stone walls. There was a low porch across the front and two large chimneys on either side. We went inside. The cottage smelled of wood smoke laced with lavender. There was a single large room just inside the front door and a small kitchen at the back left. On the right-hand side was a very spacious bedroom and bathroom, with a second, much smaller bedroom next to it. The cottage had two huge stone fireplaces, one in the main front room and a second in the main bedroom. The furnishings were all made of dark wood. Overhead were some antique chandeliers, and I couldn't tell if they were electric or perhaps gas lamps. Brass sconces were mounted on the walls, complete with candles. The floors were of polished pine with ancient oriental rugs here and there. I asked about heat and air-conditioning.

"There's no need for air-conditioning in the stone cottage, Mr. Richter," she replied. "These walls are solid stone, as the name implies. They are almost two feet thick, and the temperature in high summer is as it is now. Heat can be had from the fireplaces. The wood stores are out back on the porch. Unfortunately there is no telephone service, since we have not found a use for one here at Laurel Grove. There is a washing machine set in the alcove behind the kitchen."

I remembered the carriage driver's cell phone. "The lights: Are they electric?" I asked.

The barest hint of a smile crossed her face. "Yes, there is electricity. The cottage has its own well, as does the main house." She hesitated. "You must understand, Mr. Richter. We are not Luddites or ignorant of modern facilities. It's just that these buildings were built to be lived in long before electricity, telephones, and central, heat and air. We choose to take advantage of that fact."

"This all suits me just fine," I said. "I'll be spending most of my time across the road, and these days, the night-time seems best suited for sleeping. It's okay to have the shepherds?"

"Oh, certainly, Mr. Richter. We have two ancient dogs up at the house, and they keep us excellent company. A loyal dog is better company than many humans, in my experience."

I was suddenly curious. "Do you have significant experience of humans, Valeria? Out there in the big bad world?"

"It's Ms. Valeria, at least for now, if you please," she said, "and being both a Lee and a Marion, my family history is replete with experiences of all manner, past and present. Shall we go back now?"

Suitably chastised, I decided once again to be quiet. We walked back to my Suburban and I put the dogs on board. She said she and her mother would instruct Mr. Oatley to draw up a lease. She nodded graciously, looked forward to seeing me again, and then went up the stairs and back into the nineteenth century in a swish of voluminous skirts. I got into my ride and withdrew to the real world, wondering what the hell I'd gotten myself into this time. I had visions of the carriage man clopping into town with the draft lease, a piece of rolled parchment sealed in red wax that was still warm. Maybe that was why so many of the older buildings in town still had hitching posts out front.

Just for the heck of it, I pulled across the main road into the driveway of Glory's End—and got a surprise. There were now two tall iron gates suspended on those stone pillars, and a big bright lock and chain securing them.

Not knowing what else to do, I called Carol Pollard.

"Hey, there," she said. "Seen your surprise yet?"

"I believe I have—I'm parked outside the gates and was wondering how to get in."

"Come by and I'll get you the keys. Believe it or not, those are the original gates. I did some snooping in town and found this old boy who had them, and got them for three hundred bucks. They're wrought iron, and they're worth more than that, but he thought they should go home."

"Well, I'm delighted, Carol," I said. "Great job. FYI, I've rented the stone cottage across the way at Laurel Grove. Something's come up over in Summerfield, and I need to escape to the country. That seemed the perfect place."

"Well done yourself, Lieutenant. Those two won't let that place to just anybody."

"I had Sheriff Walker make a call," I said, "and I'd already met Valeria. Excuse me, Ms. Valeria."

"Don't you forget it, either," she said with a laugh.

"As she pointedly reminded me," I said. "How are we coming with contractors and other undesirables?"

"In a word, nowhere yet, but that's about par for the course. I always need to sweet-talk the good ones, and I'm working on that. I may have to go buy some flashier clothes."

"Last time I checked, you looked pretty good in what you've got, Ms. Carol."

"Well, thank you, kind sir. Let's do this: I'll put a key for that gate lock under a rock close by. You'll see it. As soon as you close, then we can write contracts."

"Got it," I said. "I'll let you know when I'm 'in residence' at Laurel Grove."

"No need, Lieutenant. I'll know, probably before you know."

"Jungle drums?"

"You have no idea. How were the crab cakes at the purple house today?"

The next morning I got up with the shepherds and went for a ramble. For some reason the dozers weren't annihilating the old farm this morning, and I wanted to walk the ground where my would-be assassin had set up on my living room. It was a typical subdivision-in-the-making: a moonscape of red dirt, lots of pink-flagged stakes, piles of drainage pipes and concrete forms, and a small mountain of dozer-mangled tree stumps from what used to be a pretty apple orchard. The old farmhouse was long gone, hauled off in dump trucks to fill in someone's blighted suburban ravine.

With all the trees gone, the field of fire from up on that hill was just about unlimited. I could clearly make out the piece of plywood where the window had been and could imagine the trajectory through the study and into my kitchen. It was about a two-hundred-yard shot, which was a piece of cake for a thirty-aught rifle. I found the pile of straw bales they were using for erosion barriers, and there was the bale he'd pulled out to use as a rifle rest. There were footprints in the mud around the bale, but also dozer tracks, loose gravel, and tire prints from a dozen construction vehicles. As a crime scene it was not exactly pristine. I had the shepherds go over the straw bale and then try to do some tracking, but there was just too much other scent up there. Like the cops had said, other than the single cartridge, there was no trail.

I wondered where he might set up if he came back to try it again. There were dense groves of Leyland cypress trees on either side of my property. I had originally bought three lots and forested the ones on either side of my house site. One stand faced the garage; the other, the bedroom side of the house. I took the dogs across the cratered landscape and eased into the bedroom-side grove. I'd planted this grove years ago for privacy, and now the thirty-foot-tall trees meshed their branches in a tight screen. The dogs went scooting under the lower branches, but I had to push my way through the aromatic thicket. Then the dogs stopped and began to sniff around a tiny clearing in the Leyland jungle. One of the trees must have expired long ago, because there was a dent in the ground and space enough for a single human to sit down in the ground cover. The shepherds were telling me that someone had done just that, and as I turned toward my house, I could see another perfect sight line into my bedroom window.

"Find him," I said, and Frick, old supernose, turned into the trees away from my house and started working a scent line. Kitty and I followed her until she led us out to the street, where she went one block and then lost the scent at the curb.

*Okay,* I thought. *He set up two locations, and he's used one.* I took the dogs back to the house and placed a call to Billie Ray's parole officer.

Two nights later the shepherds and I waited underneath my back deck. Kitty and Frick were curled up on carpet remnants, and I was sitting in one of those truncated beach chairs. Resting on the wooden latticework that ran along the base of the deck was the twenty-four-inch barrel of my rifle of choice, a Weatherby .270 Winchester stainless model, equipped with a Specter IR SP 50B Thermal Weapon Sight.

We'd been down there since 8:00 P.M. There was a carefully staged bedroom tableau in the house. I had pulled down the shades on the bedroom window facing the Leyland cypress grove and turned on the television. I'd positioned an easy chair with its back to the window and used the light from the television to silhouette a head-sized helium-filled balloon whose string was safety-pinned to the seat of the chair. Then I'd turned the overhead fan on low. The resulting air movement caused the balloon to move occasionally. From the outside, I hoped, it would look like someone sitting in the chair and watching the tube. I'd dropped the venetian blinds, just to obscure things a bit more, and put a ball cap high and tilted back on the balloon in case he wanted to play warning shot again. I'd obscured the windows into my living room with closed blinds, making any further shooting from the construction site impossible.

The distance between the shooter's hide and my bedroom window was about a hundred yards, maybe a little less. With the help of a milk crate, I could focus my sights on the exact position of the hide without having to hold the rifle, and I scanned it from time to time to see if we had a visitor. I expected one because of a little Kabuki I'd arranged with Arlanda Cole. With Billie Ray sitting in her office, she had faked a phone call that supposedly had me on the other end. The gist of the conversation was such that our suspect would know that I'd be in the house tonight, and then not for some time. If Billie was my shooter, I might get a chance to prove it, assuming he took the bait. She'd had him step outside the office during the phone call but had left the door open so he could hear. I still didn't think it was Breen, but it could well be someone he'd paid to do the deed. I had a thermos of coffee, a trucker's friend, and I was going to play the game until midnight.

He came just after eleven. When I took one of my periodic looks through the scope, there was an IR blob in the tiny clearing that hadn't been there before. I let my eyes relax and then concentrated. I should have been able to see his human form with that night-sight, but I couldn't. That meant he was wearing something thick enough to reduce his heat signature. Still, there was definitely someone there. I unlocked the safety on the rifle, pulled the stock into my shoulder, and settled my finger on the trigger. I thought about calling the cops, but I couldn't be absolutely sure that I, or my scope, wasn't imagining things. The dogs, alerted by my sudden attention to the rifle, woke up and watched me from their beds.

I heard a car coming down the street beyond the trees. It sounded like one of my neighbors pulling into his driveway, confirmed when I heard a garage door rattling up. A passenger jet whispered overhead in the night sky as it descended into Triboro's airport. I took a deep breath and forced my back and shoulder muscles to relax. I kept looking at that blob of color, then away to clear the image and blink. I looked back, and now there was a change. A beam of green light, no thicker than a pencil lead, was suddenly visible in the center of the shapeless blob. Then there was a bright flash as he fired.

I didn't hesitate. I squeezed the stock harder into my shoulder and fired one back, right below the middle of that green blob, which suddenly disappeared. The shepherds had jumped up with the first shot and got really excited when I fired. I made myself stay on the scope as I jacked another round into the chamber, suddenly conscious of the fact that I was taking shelter behind a flimsy wooden lattice wall. I was getting ready to put a second round up there when I heard a different car start up and accelerate out beyond the trees. My shooter could not have covered the distance between his hide and the street that quickly, which meant he'd had some help. Said help had apparently heard his boy's shot and then mine, no more than a second apart. The shooter's rifle and mine made two distinctly different sounds. The helper had correctly assumed that it might be time to vacate the scene of the crime.

I waited some more, watching the clearing. The blob was still visible in my scope, but it had subtly changed shape, or at least I thought it had. Trouble was, that didn't tell me much. Was he up there, scanning the house for my hiding place with his own night-sight? I moved the rifle back from the lattice about one inch. My night-sight was entirely passive, so, with the lattice, my own heat signature ought to be minimal.

If I'd hit him, nothing more would happen. If he was waiting for me to move and show myself, I wasn't going to accommodate him. Then I remembered my cell phone. I put the rifle back on the milk crate and called the internal operations number at the Manceford County Sheriff's Office, told them who I was, and that I had shots fired at my house. I asked them to come with sound and lights, hoping to make my attacker move, assuming he still could. If he did, I'd set the shepherds loose to take him into custody.

He couldn't move, as it turned out. My single round had hung what was left of his heart on the branches of the tree behind him. The new mystery was that it absolutely wasn't Billie Ray Breen.

I met downtown with the detectives assigned to the case the next morning. They had identified the shooter as a guy who'd been long suspected of being a contract killer over in Charlotte. He was a Guatemalan illegal who'd been in the country for six years. He'd been arrested and turned over to the federal immigration authorities on no less than three different occasions, and yet there he was. His rifle was a plain vanilla hunting gun with all identifying marks long since ground off. When I showed the investigating officers my little balloon rig, with the balloon deflated, by the way, we all made the obvious conclusion. This one hadn't been a warning shot.

Billie Ray, of course, was the prime suspect as the hit man's employer. The detectives had picked him up and put him through a long interview but got nothing of value. I fingered him for the driver of the unseen vehicle, but he had an alibi, again from his current lady-love, and he vigorously denied any connection to the two shootings. They were going to look at his finances, assuming they could find anything recognizable as his finances, but the chances were slim we could pin this on him. The good news, as one of the detectives pointed out, was that, if he'd paid for the hit, he'd probably blown whatever money he did have on this Guatemalan, so unless he turned bank robber or professional sniper, I would probably have some peace and quiet for a while.

Arlanda Cole put him on daily reporting for an additional ninety days, just to complicate his life. She also made arrangements to have him attend the shooter's autopsy. She told him she wanted him to see how contract killings sometimes came out, especially when it came to prison ghosts going up against ex-cops. I ended up doing a morning's worth of paperwork and an interview downtown with an ADA, even though it was pretty clear that I'd been the intended victim in this incident. One of the detectives wanted to bet me that the Guatemalan's live-in girlfriend would be able to exhume a lawyer to bring a wrongful death suit. I wouldn't take that bet.

I got clear of the police bureaucracy at noon and drove up to meet with Carol. I hadn't told her about the two shooting incidents at my Summerfield home, not wanting to color our association with violence before we even got started. I'd seen the police beat reporter for the local city rag hanging out in the lobby when I'd gone in to talk to the ADA, but hopefully whatever he wrote would stay down in Triboro.

Carol gave me a second key to the gates, along with my first bill—for the gates. I drove over to town and found a local bank so I could open a checking account for operations here in Rockwell County. Then I drove out to Glory's End. The two halves of the black wrought-iron gates fit perfectly on the hinge pins. The complete gate set was sixteen feet wide and about eight feet high in the middle. The padlock keys worked just fine, but I noted that the gates themselves didn't offer much actual security, as anyone could simply drive onto the edge of the open field on either side to get around them. I made a note to hire a backhoe to come out and make that harder. Leaving one half of the gate open, I drove up to the main house and turned the shepherds loose.

Nothing had changed, as best I could tell. A gentle spring breeze was stirring the trees around the house. I could see signs of bulbs sprouting in the garden beds among all the weeds. The view from the porches was very nice: rolling fields, dense greenery down in the river bottoms, and a few thousand trees beginning to swell their tops with a green haze. I heard a vehicle coming up the gravel drive. It turned out to be Sheriff Hodge Walker, rolling in his personal cruiser.

"Saw the gates open, thought I might find you here," he said, getting out of his vehicle. The shepherds greeted him, and he stopped to pet each one. "Heard you resolved your ghost problem the other night."

"After a fashion," I said. "I nailed a shooter, and the weapon was the same one that fired the warning round, but so far we can't tie him to an employer." I told him about the parole officer's little playacting with Billie Ray.

"I'll pulse the Manceford County system, see if we can find out what kind of ride your ghost is drivin' these days," he said. "Get that data up in our patrol division computers. One of my deputies sees your ghost, we'll get you some warning."

"I'd certainly appreciate that," I said. "I don't think he knows about this place, but there's no telling, these days. A deed gets recorded, and a Web search can find it."

"Maybe not quite yet, not in this county," he said with a grin. I remembered the old man down at the courthouse.

We chatted for a few minutes. I gave him my cell phone

number and told him I'd be staying across the road in the
stone cottage as soon as they got a lease drawn up. He took
it all aboard, wished me luck with the restoration project,
and left. I went inside the house to look around some more.

Some old houses are spooky by nature. This one wasn't.
I think there were simply too many tall windows to give
any self-respecting real ghost any privacy. I liked the way
the floors had become a little wavy here and there, and I
tried to visualize what it would look like with new paint
and furnishings. I reminded myself to get all that weird
wallpaper off the ceilings. The subground floor was a little
more gloomy but smelled pleasantly of a hundred-plus years
of fireplace smoke and old wood.

I noticed that the floorboards on the lowest level did not
feel as solid as I would have expected. Was there a basement? I went looking, and the shepherds followed me from
room to room, sniffing everything. The main kitchen was
on this half-underground floor. It was dominated by a huge,
nineteenth-century-style walk-in stone fireplace built against
the rear wall. Based on the layer of ashes in the grate, it
was still operational. The floor was made of random-width
pine boards, burnished to a mahogany color by years of
use and kitchen spills. The fireplace stuck out into the
kitchen a good five feet from back to hearth. It was flanked
by pantries on either side. I found what I was looking for in
the right-hand pantry—a trapdoor, which I assumed led
down into a basement. What surprised me was the bits of
fresh mud on the floor and the fact that the crack around
the trapdoor was clear of any dust and debris. Someone had
been down there, and recently, too. I wondered if it had
been Ms. Valeria, on that day when I encountered her in
the house.

I pulled up the trapdoor and latched it back against the
empty shelves. A set of surprisingly wide wooden steps led
down into complete darkness. I looked for a light switch,
but there wasn't one. I searched around the kitchen for a

flashlight, but the drawers were mostly empty except for some ancient cooking utensils. There was a single, well-used candle in a lead-colored holder in one corner, but no matches that I could find. Glory's End had electricity and relatively modern indoor plumbing, at least in the upstairs floors, but if Valeria had come over here to go into the basement, it was much more likely that she would have matches in her pocket, because candles were a way of life across the way. I fingered the wax at the base of the candle holder to see if it was freshly melted. It told me exactly nothing. The shepherds were looking at me as if to ask, *We about through? We saw squirrels out there.*

I went back upstairs and out the front door to get a flashlight from my Suburban. I turned the mutts loose to go chase squirrels and went back inside. When I got back downstairs to the kitchen, the candleholder was no longer there.

I stopped and looked around the room. I'd picked it up, felt the wax melted onto the base, and then put it back on the counter. Now it wasn't there.

Oka-a-a-y.

Was someone else in the house? The shepherds would have noticed another human lurking about. I looked around again. I hadn't been gone two minutes, but there was no getting around it—the damned candlestick was gone.

I went over to the trapdoor, which was still upright, the way I'd left it. I pointed the flashlight down the steps, looking for tracks in the dust, but there weren't any, possibly because there wasn't any dust. That, too, was a bit strange. The steps were made of rough-cut planks, smoothed and even hollowed out slightly in the center by generations of foot traffic. I went down the steps, wondering if I should go back out and get my SIG.

The basement was large, with almost ten-foot ceilings, a hard-packed dirt floor, and heavy, mortared stone foundation walls. It smelled of dust, mildew, and old dirt in

equal proportions. There was an expansive but unfortunately empty wine rack down one wall and floor-to-ceiling
bare shelves on all the others. There was no plumbing or
wiring in evidence, which made sense since the next floor
up was itself partially underground. The basement seemed
to match the footprint of the main house, and as I swung
my light around, I saw what looked like an open grave in
the floor, except that it was only three feet deep. I tried to
think of what they might have used that for. The shelves
would have contained provisions, perhaps, and possibly
weapons. There were meat hooks hanging from some of
the joists above, which might have accounted for the unusual
height. The temperature was cool, and the place seemed
to be perfectly dry. The shelves were empty except for a
single item: my AWOL candleholder.

I stopped and stared. That candleholder. The one I'd left
up in the kitchen when I went out to get a flashlight.

*Curiouser and curiouser,* I thought. *This is about the
point where the trapdoor goes bang up there at the top of
the steps and I start to hear rattling chains and ghostly
cackling.* Except nothing happened. No cold vapors, no
violins. Just the candlestick sitting there on that shelf, the
one that apparently had grown legs.

Obviously someone had been watching me in the kitchen
and had moved the candlestick down here while I was outside. The dogs hadn't sensed anyone in the house, which
implied that he'd been down here the whole time I'd been in
on the lower floor. So he'd been listening or watching from
the top of the stairs, heard me go out, went into the kitchen,
grabbed the candlestick, and then—what?

All right. Now: why? He'd grabbed it and moved it down
here. Logically, he'd wanted me to know that I wasn't alone
in the house. Then he had gone—where? Back upstairs? I
didn't think so, unless he was really light on his feet, because I think I would have run into him, or at least heard
him. There were back stairs from the lower-level kitchens

up to the main, public rooms floor, but they changed direction twice before coming out in the central hallway above.

I decided to test all my theorizing. I went back up the stairs and lowered the trapdoor while standing on the steps. Instant black darkness, with a tiny crack of light around the door edges. I then knelt down on the topmost step, hunched over underneath the door, and scanned the wall between me and the kitchen, using the flashlight. Nothing.

I turned off the flashlight and looked again. There: a tiny, pencil-sized hole between two studs. I peered through it and could see most of the kitchen. That solved the watching problem. I pushed the trapdoor back open and latched it back. The tiny peephole was under the counter, visible only if you knew where to look.

If he hadn't gone back upstairs, then he was down in the basement somewhere. Since the basement was empty, there had to be another way out of the basement. I went back down the wooden stairs and began to walk along the four stone walls, probing with my hands and the flashlight, looking through the empty shelves for signs of a secret doorway. There seemed to be nothing but solid stone. I checked the pit, but it was just hard-packed dirt and still about three feet deep.

I went back out into the middle of the basement, swinging the light every which way, looking for anything different about the walls, or, for that matter, the ceiling and the dirt floor. The only thing I noticed was that one set of shelves, at right angles to a corner of the wine rack, had a wooden backing. All the rest of the shelves were open at the back, built right up against the bare stones. I went over to that set of shelves and got down on the ground. Sure enough, there was a quarter-inch space between the bottom shelf and the cementlike dirt.

I looked for a hidden latch or activating mechanism, but I couldn't find a thing. I pulled on the whole assembly. It seemed to be firmly anchored. I also was wondering, if there was a hidden passage, where would it lead? The lower level of the house was already partially underground, maybe some four feet, which meant that this basement floor was about fifteen feet underground. I tried to visualize where the nearest outbuilding was at the back of the house. I thought it was the smokehouse, but I'd have to go out and see. Maybe I could find the way into the basement from its exit point.

"Anyone down there?" a woman's voice called from above. It sounded like Carol Pollard.

"Yeah, it's me, Cam Richter," I called. A moment later, a shapely pair of stockinged legs in a knee-length skirt came down the steps into the cone of my flashlight.

"What in the world are you doing down in this black hole?" she asked as she stepped onto the dirt floor.

"Just looking," I said, deciding to keep the mystery of the moving candlestick to myself for the moment. She joined me and blinked in the light from my Maglite.

"Checking out the woodwork?" she asked, indicating the hand-hewn floor joists above our heads. Then I realized they were whole tree trunks.

"Yes, and the general layout of the house. I didn't expect a basement with that lower floor halfway underground. Certainly not this deep, either."

"You're right," she said. "The whole point of the lower floor was 'coolth' in the hot summers. That's why the kitchens and the main dining room are down there. Look at that wine rack!"

"Missing one important commodity," I said.

"Can't have everything," she said with a bright smile. "I saw the front gates open and decided to come in to see who's here. Your shepherds are waiting at the front door, by the way."

We decided to go back upstairs into the daylight. I followed Carol up, exercising as much chivalry as I could with the Maglite. When I dropped the trapdoor into the basement, I saw an external latch, which I discreetly slid into the locked position.

In the light of the kitchen I noticed that she seemed to be dressed for a party, with a lot more makeup than I'd seen before. She caught me checking her out.

"A retirement party for Judge Corey," she said. "He's a kindly old gentleman who's been very nice to the library in town. Oh, and I have a lease for you to sign in my briefcase outside. David Oatley asked me to get it to you."

"Great," I said. "Does that mean I can move in across the way?"

"I think so," she said as we went up the front stairs and then to the front door. There were two sets of shepherd ears silhouetted against the wavy glass of the door's side windows. We went outside, and I executed the lease agreement.

"I was thinking," she said. "When you get settled in next door, perhaps you'd like to take a ride around the property. I've got a husband-horse I could bring for you, and it really is a great way to see the whole property."

"A husband-horse?"

She laughed. "That's a horse-world term for a perfectly docile horse that even the nonriding husband can ride. You would be riding on, as opposed to actually riding."

"Got it," I said. "Sure, why not? What could go wrong?"

She laughed again, and I found myself warming to her sunny personality, among other attributes. "Not much, actually, not on Goober, anyway."

"Goober."

"You'll see," she said. "I'll call you."

After she left, I considered the possibility that the stop-by had been dual-purposed. Get the lease signed, and give me a look at Carol when she cleaned up and invested in a little powder and paint. I also considered the possibility that the entire female universe might not actually revolve around me. God, I hoped that wasn't so.

I went back into the house with the mutts to pursue the matter of the light-footed candlestick. The first problem I encountered was that it was back on its table in the kitchen.

The trapdoor was still down and latched. I didn't remember bringing it back up, and nor had Carol.

*No way,* I thought. I went over and tugged at the handle of the door; it did not move. The latch held. So no one who could have been hiding in that basement could have moved the candlestick.

"C'mon, you guys," I said. "We're going exploring."

We went through the house, starting with another quick look down in the basement and then through every floor right up to the attic, which was accessed through a ceiling hatch at the back of the upstairs main hall. I'd found an antique wooden ladder stored in the hall closet, which allowed me to get up into the attic.

There was nothing up there but cold air, lots of spiderwebs, and a great look at the original construction timbers, which were, for the most part, more whole trees that had been squared off where needed and then fit into a roof truss structure with wooden dowels. There were no lights in the attic, but some light came in through air vents at the eaves, and it was fully floored. There were no chained trunks of hidden treasure, no wardrobes full of antique clothes, and absolutely no place for anyone to hide. The inside walls of the massive brick chimneys were exposed on four sides, and the mortar actually looked to be in pretty good shape. There were no water stains on the floor, so the roof was intact as well.

I climbed back down the ladder to where the shepherds were waiting and reset the hatch cover as I came down. We explored each of the main rooms, the few remaining armoires upstairs, and even the single bathroom grafted onto the drawing room downstairs. I'd taken some time going through the reception room on the main floor, which the old lady had converted to her bedroom in her declining days. As was customary in nineteenth-century homes, freestanding wardrobes and armoires were used in place of closets. There was a smallish canopied bed, two armoires, a ratty-looking oriental rug, and some chairs and tables.

I sat down on the edge of the bed.

I listened once again for rattling chains, low moans in the walls, or other ghostly noises, but mostly what I heard was the sound of two shepherds panting.

Someone had moved the frigging candlestick. Someone had been in the house when Carol and I had gone out to her car. That same someone had done his or her poltergeist thing and still managed to get out of the house, unseen and unheard, before I came back in and started looking around in earnest. The shepherds were relaxed, which told me that said someone wasn't here anymore. Ergo, no point in us sitting here waiting for something to happen.

We went back outside and walked around to the back of the house, which faced generally northwest. Here the bricks were in less good shape, and I could discern a definite starboard list on the back wall chimney structure. There was a set of stone steps leading up from the semisubmerged kitchen area, but they were covered in a thin film of moss and didn't bear signs of recent use. The backyard was actually a pebbled driveway area, surrounded by some ancient outbuildings. I reconsidered my mystery. There was one way it could have been done.

Someone hidden in the basement walls could have heard us go upstairs and then out the front door, grabbed the candlestick, come out into this back drive area through some secret passage, gone down those steps into the kitchen, replaced the candlestick, and then beat feet back outside to a hidey-hole before I got back inside. I had not looked outside once I started my tour, and I also had gone back down into the basement. If my mystery guest had heard me down there, he could have had time to get out of the secret passage and simply depart the premises.

So: Secret passage, where are you? It had to have something to do with that one set of shelves down there that had the solid wooden back. I decided to look through the old outbuildings to see if I could find any indications of foot traffic.

Thirty minutes later I'd discovered nothing useful. One building was indeed a smokehouse, a second looked like it had been a blacksmith shop of some kind, and the third was a long, low springhouse, complete with a pool of icy water laced with watercress. All of the buildings were made of the same handmade, oversized brick as the main house. All the fittings were wrought iron and looked original. A tiny brook headed downhill from the springhouse, but nothing else moved on the grounds except for an occasional and now respectfully distant squirrel.

Still and all, I thought, that had to be how it was done, excluding the duty ghostly spirit. Some kind of subterranean access had to be behind that set of shelves. The real question was why someone was screwing around in the first place. Was I supposed to be scared off? I decided to wait for further exploration until I had a crew here working, and then we'd disassemble that wooden shelf structure, with a backhoe if necessary, and find out where the secrets lay. In the meantime, I might still have a real ghost to deal with, back in Summerfield, if the demise of his hired killer failed to deter him. On that dismal possibility, I needed to get going on my move to the country. That meant a second visit to the stone cottage, and then a U-Haul operation.

By Tuesday of the following week, I was all moved in and now a semipermanent resident of Rockwell County. Cubby Johnson, the Lees' outside man, helped me move my stuff into the cottage and get my new digs up and running. Cubby was in his late fifties, maybe early sixties, and, except for a stint in the army, he had never really left Rockwell County. He and his wife, Patience, had worked for the Lees for most of their lives. He was a powerfully built black man, five-eight, with a fringe of graying hair around an otherwise bald pate, a round, intelligent face, and the handshake of a blacksmith. He had a low, mellifluous voice, and I assumed he was as curious about me as I was about the Lee family. It became clear during our first real meeting that we were going to observe a tacit agreement to let further details of our respective backgrounds unfold in the due course of time so as to maintain southern civility. It was also clear that he felt a certain responsibility to protect the Lees in their eccentricities in return for what had become absolute, lifetime job security for him and his wife. I let it be known that I was cool with the Lees' lifestyle, having seen far stranger things than Hester and Valeria Lee in my law enforcement career.

Cubby told me Ms. Hester was ailing, which meant that Ms. Valeria was attending, so I didn't see either of them in the course of moving in. Carol Pollard brought by a proposed restoration plan, and we agreed to get the thing going as soon as I closed the real estate transaction. David Oatley had hinted that closing could happen the following week if I was willing to forgo the due diligence. He'd shown me the four stone boundary markers, which looked like they'd been there since Washington was a surveyor. Being a stranger to these parts, however, I elected to go through the paper drill just to be sure.

The shooting investigation had faded to black, which often happened when the perpetrator got himself killed, thereby solving the major mystery. The sheriff's office had not been able to pin anything on Billie Ray, although he remained the logical suspect. The parole office forced him into a minimum wage job and then made him report what he did with his money, such as it was. The woman he was living with was a supposedly reformed crack queen, who, in the opinion of the detectives, was barely able to get herself from one end of their mobile home to the other. All of which left me with the lingering suspicion that my ghost problem might not be over.

In order to stay as far off the grid as possible in my new lodgings, I did not set up a landline telephone. I left the electricity and propane accounts with the Lees. I told the local post office in Summerfield to send all mail to my office as I was going to be in Europe for the next year. It was admittedly thin cover, but it might fool an ex-con for a while. I contacted a local Summerfield Realtor and made arrangements to rent my house, but not until after I'd closed on Glory's End. In the meantime, I needed to get some more folks on my side in Rockwell County.

Carol brought the first contractor out to Glory's End that Tuesday afternoon. He was the electrical guy, and he gave me a tour of the house's electrical system, such as it was. The wiring was from the 1950s and was the fabric-covered copper variety. There were only eight fuses for the whole house, and four of those had copper pennies underneath blown fuses. The only thing that had saved the house from a fire was that the old lady hadn't used much more than a few lights, an electric hot plate, and the furnace fan.

"So," I said. "A complete rewire?"

He nodded. "That's the safe way to go," he said. "This stuff hasn't met code for forty years, and the woodwork through which it's routed has zero moisture content. Plus, if you're going to live here, you're probably going to put a much bigger electrical load on the system."

He explained that he would disconnect the old wiring but leave much of it in place in order to avoid damaging the plaster and run all new, modern, meaning grounded, conductors. In some cases he could use the old wiring to fish the new cable up through walls and floors. "The good news is that there aren't any fire-stops in these walls," he said. "The bad news . . ."

He agreed to leave the current system operational until he was ready to proceed with the rip-out and the new installation. He then set about surveying the system so he could work up a bid, while Carol and I talked about the first few major steps to a renovation. As casually as I could, I asked her about the possibility of an underground passage in or around the house.

"Well, I guess it's possible," she said, "but what purpose would it serve? You've seen the covered walkways back to the service buildings, and it wasn't the plantation owners who would have to go out in the snow to fetch the firewood."

"The war, maybe? A place to hide themselves or their valuables if the Yankee hordes arrived?"

She nodded but pointed out that the Yanks had not come through this part of the South until the very end and that, beyond the house itself, the countryside was so impoverished by then that there'd been nothing much to hide or protect.

"The legislature and the governor were forever calling the citizens to arms and to fight to the last man and child," she said, "but the few remaining fighting men who'd survived to 1865 were with General Lee at Appomattox. It wasn't like Georgia when Sherman went through."

She was curious why I was asking, so I decided to tell her about the light-footed candlestick and my convoluted theory about how someone could have done it, if there was a passage.

"Great!" she exclaimed, happily. "A mystery, and maybe even a ghost."

"And that's good news—why?"

"Because every old southern mansion needs a ghost or two," she said. "It's traditional."

"Um . . ."

"Oh, you don't have to believe it," she said, "but if I tell that story in town, it'll simply make the place more interesting in everyone's eyes. Plus, the stranger now has a challenge on his hands beyond fixing up the house. Cool."

"You have to tell it, don't you?"

She laughed. "Absolutely," she said. "It'll be the first of many stories, Mr. Richter, and, as I told you, this is a—"

"Very small town," I finished for her. "Got that. If it's a human and not hoodoo, though, my cop instincts are not amused."

"Because of that shooting business over in Summerfield?"

I stared at her. She sighed. Sheriff Walker. It was a very damn small town.

"Yes, actually. Did you by chance hear how the second shooting came out?"

Her face sobered quickly. "Yes, we heard that, too. Seems only right. Some deranged guy fired a rifle into my house, I'd probably light him up if I could."

"Light him up?" That was a term I did not expect from a lady librarian.

"Okay," she said. "Truth in lending. I was a cop in Raleigh for eight years. I told you, I went away but didn't like it?"

I was really surprised. "Why did you leave?" I asked. "The police, I mean. If you want to tell me, of course."

"Seeing as you're a retired lawman," she said, "I think I can share. I was a little slow on the draw one time, and another officer was killed. I ended up taking out the perp, but not before yet another officer got winged, and me, too. It all washed up pretty well in the formal investigation, but I knew I'd screwed up. The blue wall started looking at me differently, and that was that."

"I know just what you mean," I said, remembering my own experiences after the cat dancers case. This probably explained the slight limp I'd noticed when I was checking out those lovely legs.

"You'll have to tell me that story sometime," she said, "but as to a secret passage and someone messing around, it's probably some local teenagers checking out the new guy."

"What, no ghosts?"

"Trust me, Mr. Richter. By six tonight you will definitely have a ghost out here. Now let's go see what Tim found out about the wiring."

She was wrong about that. I went into town around five to get some groceries and ran into David Oatley in the Food Lion. He stopped me in the cereal aisle and wanted to make sure that the presence of a ghost would not affect the sale of the property. He seemed sincerely worried about it, so I told him that the wailing and howling from the old well didn't bother me much, and as long as it didn't come across the backyard with that big-ass flaming torch and the dead baby again, I'd go through with the deal. I watched his eyes go round. *See what you think of that one, Carol Pollard,* I thought. As it turned out, what she thought of it was that it would be harder to get certain contractors onto the project.

*Ah, well*, I thought, *screw 'em if they can't take a joke.*

The next day we went though the same drill with a heating and air-conditioning guy and then a plumber and the local well digger. After they left I still had a few hours of daylight, so I went exploring again with the shepherds, this time down the service lane behind the big house to the barns and equipment sheds. It was another clear spring day with a brisk northerly breeze coming up the hill from the river. The smell of thawing earth and new vegetation was strong, and I reminded myself to pursue the leasing of the big fields.

There were two ancient tractors, dating from the 1930s,

up on blocks in one wooden shed, and some rusting agricultural equipment littering a long shed that had only a roof and a back wall, no sides. It was pretty obvious that no one had been down here for years, if not decades. So I was surprised when the shepherds suddenly started nosing around the ground and sniffing hard. There was obviously an interesting scent trail back here.

"Find it," I said. Frick put her nose to the ground, circled once, and then set off on a semistraight line through the weeds. Kitty followed, watching Frick. The dogs went about twenty feet, stopped at an area of discolored ground, walked around it, and then went over to explore what looked like a hatch cover. I saw a flash of red and then realized there was a ball cap wedged under the wooden platform. The shepherds, noses to the ground, hadn't seen it yet, so I went to retrieve it. Thinking that the discolored ground was probably the remains of an old manure pile, I went straight for it.

Big mistake.

Suddenly I was falling amid a small avalanche of dirt, sticks, and a brown tarp straight down into black, icy cold water.

I didn't have time to even squeak, or, for that matter, take a deep breath. I went under for what felt like several hundred feet and frantically clawed my way back up to the surface, scoring my knuckles on the rough stone wall of the well. I surfaced underneath the wet tarp, which didn't help my nearly paralyzing claustrophobia. When I finally got the tarp off and my breathing stabilized, I looked up to see two shepherd faces staring down at me from about twenty feet up against the late afternoon sky.

I was treading water in a stone-lined well, probably hand-dug back in the eighteenth century, from the looks of it. Close on the realization that I was trapped down here was the news that someone had set that trap, someone who knew I'd have the dogs with me, and what they and I might do when we saw the ball cap. The dogs had stepped around the discolored earth, and I'd missed that cue. What I had thought was the hatch cover was probably the well cover. I remembered Valeria warning me about abandoned wells.

Frick barked at me, as if trying to encourage me to get the hell out of there. I couldn't agree more, but there was the little matter of twenty vertical feet to overcome. The good news was that the walls were made of rough stones, not smooth concrete. That gave me a fighting chance.

I assumed the inchworm position in the water. There was barely room, and the first time I tried to move, my tennis shoes slipped off the mossy, wet stones. I kicked them off and then began heaving myself up the walls, pressing against my back and walking my feet up six inches, then pressing against my feet and shoving my back up six inches, while trying to stabilize my body with my hands. It's harder than it looks, especially when you get some daylight between you and the water below, and the rocks start making road-rash on the back of your shoulders. The problem came when I got to the top. There was nothing to grab onto.

I wedged my body and took a breather, while both shepherds panted impatiently for me to finish the job. I knew that if I tried to flip my body around and grab for the lip of the well I'd probably fall. I should have come up the walls belly down and not up, but even if I had, I wasn't sure I had the strength to do the final pull-up that would be required to get my center of gravity over the lip. There was nothing to grab.

Kitty solved it for me. She leaned over the lip and licked my face. Frick, ever the jealousy queen, came around to join in. I let go of the walls and grabbed a dog collar in each hand.

Both shepherds were surprised and almost came over the lip, but then they dug in. If you've ever played tug-of-war with a hundred-pound German shepherd, you know they can pull you over if they want to. The two of them were pulling hard, but with nothing on which to brace themselves, they began losing the war. As I was about to let go of them and drop back down into the water, Cubby Johnson's face appeared over the hole. He grabbed my right arm with both hands. I still had a hold on Kitty's collar, so between the two of them, they pulled me out. I skinned both knees and both elbows and was delighted to do it. Cubby ended up sitting down hard on the ground.

I flopped down on the ground myself and did some deep breathing exercises while massaging my legs, which had started to cramp up. Cubby explained that Ms. Valeria had told him to see if there was anything I needed down at the cottage. He said he found my vehicle, but not me or the shepherds, so he'd walked over here. He'd heard the dogs barking frantically and had come to investigate.

"Somebody set a trap," I said.

"Say what?"

"There was a tarp pulled over that well, weeds and shit put on top of the tarp. The real cover's over there."

He looked over at the wooden hatch cover in surprise and then back at me.

"Any idea of who or why?" I asked.

He shook his head. "This place been empty for a long time, 'cept for the old lady, Ms. Tarrant, and she bein' housebound and all. We got kids now, come out to the country, mess around on some of the big farms, but this here—this was nasty."

I started shivering, so I got up and walked around to restore my circulation. Nasty was the word, all right. If the dogs hadn't been with me I might have simply drowned down there once the cold water worked its lethal magic. Then all the trapper would have to do was pull the cover back over and declare victory.

Victory over what, though? The candlestick business had felt like the opening chapter in a head game of some sort. This was quite an escalation. *I'm going to make you go away, interloper, one way or another.* I got the message, but I couldn't think of anyone I'd met so far who'd been anything but friendly and encouraging about the project. Even the Auntie Bellums across the way seemed disposed to let me proceed without objection.

It was starting to get dark. It had been a spring day but not a warm day. I was cold, wet, and in my stocking feet. I had walked over from Laurel Grove, and now I was going to have to walk back on the gravel drive. I went over to the hatch cover and, with Cubby's help, tipped it end for end back over the dark hole in the ground. I put the ball cap in my belt. If nothing else, I'd acquired some physical evidence of my intruder. Tomorrow I would come back over here and see what the mutts could scare up in the way of a trail.

As we started back toward the house, I wondered if this could possibly be my hit-man-hiring ghost from Triboro. I didn't think so. Billie Ray did not have the resources to have found me out here this quickly. So either this was someone local, with a hate-on for strangers, or I had a new problem I didn't know about.

The back windows of the big house reflected the swaying branches of some of the bigger oaks, making it look like there were ghostly figures slipping past the windows inside. I think I would have preferred a couple of attic wailers to the sneaky bastard who had set the well trap.

My tracking exercise the next morning led to some interesting results. I followed the shepherds as they worked the barnyard area and then headed down toward the river bottoms. I had no way of knowing if they were on the scent I wanted them to follow, but we'd started with the ball cap, and Frick at least knew what I wanted. I had my trusty SIG .45 with me this time, and if the trail happened to lead directly to an operational human I was going to introduce myself by shooting him.

Instead, the trail led down to the river. The dogs lost the scent at the junction of a creek coming down from my property and the main river. There was a tiny patch of sandy mud on the north side of the creek, a clear sign that a boat had been pulled up on the bank. There were muddy holes where footprints would have been.

This told me a couple of things. One, I hadn't been indulging in paranoia about the setup in the barnyard. Someone had come by boat, beached it here, gone up to the barnyard, set his trap, and then come back. Two, my stalker was comfortable in the field. The Dan River is not a trifling stream. It's a good-sized river, fed from the mountains, with powerful currents and treacherous sandbars along its length in this area. It claimed a half-dozen humans a year, mainly kids who went playing along its banks, fell in, and were never seen again. A city boy would have come by car or truck, parked discreetly, and walked over the fields. This guy had come by small boat, and probably not from right across the river. He'd come looking to set up a trap that an unalerted ex-cop who always traveled with his dogs would not see. In fact, he'd used the dogs to lead me to that well.

I stood there, looking across the river. Billie Ray Breen was a red herring.

This was either someone from my personal past, someone who wanted to fuck with me for a while and then— what? Go away and leave me wondering when he'd be back? Or show himself and explain what his beef was? It pissed me off, especially since one of the reasons for coming out to the country was to get away from this kind of crap. The other explanation was that this was someone new, someone with an agenda I didn't know about.

I turned the dogs around, and we went back up the way we'd come. I scanned the ground, hoping, but not very hard, that he'd dropped something with his name and address on it. Something did catch my eye, over on that western ridge. Only the top line of the ridge was visible across the fields and behind the old rail line, but there was my horseman again, clearly silhouetted. I gauged that it was almost a half mile from me to the ridge, but I called back the dogs and changed course, cutting across the knee-high weeds of plowed ground and heading for the ridge. As soon as I did, he turned and disappeared behind the trees. I'd figured he wouldn't wait around, but his tracks might.

It took us forty-five minutes of hard going over the plowed ground and through the weeds, up and over the banks of the rail line, down across a troublesome creek, and then up the ridge on the other side through fairly dense pine trees and underbrush. I'd selected a tall poplar as my landmark and came up on that tree to discover three large boulders in a semicircle, with the smoldering remains of a small campfire in front of them. One of the boulders was shaped vaguely like a throne, and sitting on the throne, legs crossed and boots gleaming, was a Confederate cavalry officer, sipping something from a battered tin cup.

The shepherds closed in on me but did not seem to be very excited, which told me that this man wasn't emitting large volumes of adrenaline into the air. He was tall, and he looked like Valeria Lee, with the same aquiline nose and arched eyebrows over deeply pouched gray eyes. His dark hair was going to gray, and he sported a full salt-and-pepper beard that almost reached his chest, a gray wool jacket with two rows of buttons over gray trousers that had a single yellow stripe down their length, knee-high leather boots, and a broad-rimmed hat complete with a ratty feather pushed into the band. His saber was propped up on the rock in its scabbard, the leather and brass attachment straps dangling. He had a leather holster on his right hip that contained what looked like a period cap-and-ball pistol. Two gray gauntlets lay carelessly on the ground next to his boots.

He nodded at me when I appeared out of the underbrush but did not get up, possibly in deference to the two large shepherds who were watching him, although he didn't seem upset by the dogs. I spotted his horse behind the big rocks, standing to a ground tie and contentedly munching grass. I saw his eyes take in my own pistol strapped to my right hip, but he didn't seem bothered by it.

"Well, good morning—Colonel, is it?" I said.

"Major, suh. Major," he replied, lifting his hat with his left hand. I guessed that he was about fifty, but he had one of those tight, sallow complexions that make age estimation difficult. "Major Courtney Woodruff Lee, at your service, suh. Those are handsome animals with you."

"I'm Cameron Hartoff Richter," I said, unconsciously matching his own formality with some of my own.

"Had a cousin named Cameron," he said with a sniff. "Lost at Gettysburg, we're told. Not recovered. He was an adjutant with General Pickett, you see."

"I believe I saw you up here a few weeks ago."

"I reconnoiter daily, suh," he said, apparently not terribly impressed with the recitation of all my names. "General Sherman is reported to be at large in the low country, and we expect him to join Butcher Grant any day now. Any day."

I thought for a moment that this guy had to be putting me on, but then I caught the briefest glint of true madness in his eyes. Major Lee. Was this the crazy brother rumored to be locked up in the attic at Laurel Grove, and, if so, who'd let him out?

"You are armed but not in uniform, suh," he observed, looking me up and down. I was wearing khaki field trousers and a long-sleeved red and black Pendleton shirt over Bean boots. "Are you perchance a spy?"

"No, um, Major," I said. "I own this property." *Or almost own* it, I thought.

"Rubbish." He snorted. "The Lees own this property.

All of it, as far as the eye can see. Owned it for many score years. Who are you, suh? What are you doing here?"

I didn't know what to say, and he was now regarding me with a suspicious eye. I wasn't sure what I'd do if he reached for that horse pistol. There wasn't the slightest hint of humor in his eyes, and, if he was as nuts as he seemed, I could have a problem here. I tried some playacting of my own.

"Well, of course I don't really own this property," I said. "I'm the new overseer. We have a slave on the run, and we're in pursuit, my dogs and I."

"Ah," he said, visibly relieved. "I shall be on the lookout as soon as I've finished my coffee." He looked down into the cup, made a face, and threw the contents, a noxious-looking brown brew of some kind, into the fire. "Acorns, barley, moss, God knows what else," he said. "Haven't had decent coffee since '62. Damned blockade, you know."

I nodded, feeling faintly ridiculous talking to a lunatic as if this conversation were completely normal. I wondered what the gangbangers down in South Triboro would make of this guy if he came riding down past one of their corners.

"Well," he said, getting up and stretching to full height, which was impressive. "Get on with it, man. Watch the railroad bridge. That's where they go, if they're able. Can't abide water, you know. Those dogs, now, they look capable indeed."

He touched the brim of his big hat in my direction, gathered up his cavalry accoutrements, kicked some dirt into the ashes, and went over to the horse. He mounted in one easy, graceful movement, clucked quietly to the horse, and moved off into the trees. In a moment his broad, ramrod-straight back disappeared into the Virginia pines without a sound.

I blew out a long exhalation. Then I took the dogs over to where the horse had been standing, just to make sure I

hadn't been hallucinating. There were definitely tracks. I
went back to the campfire and kicked some dirt of my own
onto it, because the countryside was extremely dry. The
well-blackened stones indicated it had been used before.
As I looked around, I noticed that several of the nearby
trees had been blasted by lightning over the years and recognized what southerners call a lightning patch. Something in the ground, a concentration of iron, perhaps, invited
lightning to make repeat appearances, and the trees nearby
caught absolute hell.

I was pretty sure about who my horseman was, and either he was a consummate actor who enjoyed dressing up
and doing some horseback reenacting, or he actually believed he was a Confederate cavalry officer living back in
those dark days just before Appomattox and the end of the
Glorious Cause. The latter would fit right in with the Hester
and Valeria household, but not with deathtraps set in the
barnyard. I'd have to ask Cubby Johnson about the major.

"Okay, muttskis," I announced. "Let's go down to the
river and recapture Eliza."

I caught up with Cubby Johnson after lunch in the barns
behind the Laurel Grove house. The outbuildings were similar to the ones across the road, but in much better shape.
Cubby was head deep in the inner workings of a round baler
when the dogs and I showed up. He seemed ready to take a
break. I told him about my encounter with the major.

He smiled, shook his head, and then explained that the
major was something of an open secret in the local neighborhood. He was surprised that the rider had spoken to me,
as he had a reputation for not acknowledging the presence
of other humans he encountered.

"He's related to the ladies up there?" I asked, indicating
the big house.

He nodded. "Been like that since Patience and I've been

here. He don't bother nobody, closes farm gates behind him, that sort of thing, but he's well and truly gone around."

"This the crazy relative supposedly locked away in the attic I've heard about?"

"Yep, although he ain't locked up anywhere. Comes down of a morning, right after breakfast, all decked out, saddles up Henry, and then rides off into the back pastures, scoutin' for them Yankee rascals. Usually stays right here on the place, but sometimes, like this morning, he rambles."

"What happens when he encounters modern times, say, like a semi on the road?"

"Pretends he don't see it, I s'pect. Folks around here humor the man. He used to go out at night sometimes, but we put a stop to that after he rode across the road right in front of a state trooper."

"How'd you stop it?"

"Locked up the tack room at sundown," Cubby said. "Major won't ride without his cavalry rig. He complained some, but Ms. Valeria told him there was too much Union infantry abroad at night, and he settled right down."

"Wow."

He shrugged. "It's harmless, all this playactin'," he said. "They don't bother other folks, and there's plenty enough real craziness in this county if folks want somethin' to worry about."

I knew all about that. The seemingly peaceful countryside of most southern states presented a deceptively bucolic vista to travelers hustling by on the interstates. Go down to the very end of most dirt roads and you'll find dilapidated, rusting trailers and all the junk that goes with them, animate as well as inanimate. Far too many country folk, black and white, are indulging in the dangerous trades of marijuana, moonshine, and methamphetamine production, with all the attendant disasters of imprisoned parents and either addicted, brain-dead, or starving urchins left behind. North Carolina was no exception, as any county sheriff would be quick to tell you. They work it hard, but there's not much law enforcement can do about the resulting human wreckage. One politely demented southern gentleman riding around in costume paled by comparison.

I told Cubby about finding the signs of a boat landing down on the river, and my suspicions that it might be connected to my little "accident" in the well. He said that it was certainly possible, but there were lots of fisherman out on that river behind Glory's End. Sometimes there were calls of nature that couldn't be answered out on the river. I thanked Cubby for his insights, took the dogs back to the cottage, and then drove into Triboro to see what was shaking with my prison ghost and the investigation into the dead hit man.

As I had anticipated, the investigation had migrated to the way-back burner at Manceford County. The shooter had been eliminated, his identity and past verified, and the main suspect who might have hired him had an alibi, weak as it was. I'd been cleared by the DA's office. You know how it is, the detectives told me, and I surely did; they always had bigger and more urgent fish to fry. With the shooter in the ground, everyone was moving on to the next crisis of the day.

Everybody except me, of course. For one thing, I'd heard a car decamping right after the shooting, so there was at least one loose end still hanging out there. I sat down with some of my guys to brainstorm. We kicked around the idea of snatching up Billie Ray and squeezing him in ways the cops couldn't. Tony was enthusiastic; he said he wanted to see what this waterboarding business was all about. Horace and Pardee, however, were made of saner stuff. They reminded me of what I already knew, namely, that vigilante action would inevitably backfire and could get us all thrown in jail.

It was just a thought.

They were sympathetic but told me to concentrate on my Tara project, while they kept the occasional eye on Billie Ray Breen between their own cases. Business was brisk, and I sensed that they thought this thing was over, too.

I spent the night at my house in Summerfield. I met with the neighborhood dog-sitter to pay her for taking care of old Frack, who was increasingly quite content to lie about the empty house, dreaming of his action-filled past. Some of my neighbors were outside when I got there, and I asked around to see if anyone had anything on the mystery vehicle. Two people said they heard the rifle shots, but no one had noticed a strange car. I tried to reassure them that the incident was over and made sure they knew I'd taken up temporary digs somewhere else, although I left the somewhere rather vague. I got the sense that they were relieved. Two shooting incidents in the neighborhood had people worried and talking, and the newspaper article hadn't helped.

That night I sat out on the screened-in part of the back deck with Frick and Kitty alongside. Frack was down in the basement. My deck used to have a lovely view of my long backyard and the old, abandoned apple orchard on the other side of the creek. The orchard was now piled up in a nasty-looking heap of uprooted trees at the bottom of the field across the way. I'd wanted to sell my place once the moonscaping started, but a Realtor friend had told me to wait until the subdivision was in place. That would take at least a year.

My old-fashioned glass sat next to the SIG .45 on the metal table. I didn't think there'd be any more shooting through windows, but I was a bear for paying attention to recent history. I was trying out a new single malt whiskey and finding it most agreeable. Summerfield was growing up, with ever more development, mostly in the form of small, gated communities. Pretty soon the new people would be demanding that the state four-lane all our scenic country roads, and then it would be annexed by Triboro so that we could all take up our fair share of the eternal inner-city tax burden. I was mulling over how much of my stuff to move out to the stone cottage when the phone rang.

I picked up my portable and looked at the caller ID. PRIVATE CALL, it said unhelpfully. I answered. The male voice on the other end was definitely not Billie Ray Breen but possibly an older voice, disguised by some kind of sound filter.

"Nice shooting, Lieutenant," he said.

"What do you know about that?" I asked, figuring this was either a crank call, precipitated by the newspaper article, or a neighbor unhappy with nocturnal gunfire right down the street.

"I might know who sent him," he said.

"Well, ducky," I said. "You gonna tell me?"

"I just did," he said. "Relearned an old lesson, too. Never send a boy to do a man's work."

"Murdering someone with a rifle from behind a bush is hardly man's work," I said. "The word coward comes to mind. Was that you in the getaway car?"

"Probably," he said. "Salvo knew that was a balloon he was looking at, by the way. That really was supposed to be another scare shot. Our mistake was not thinking through what the balloon really meant."

He had my attention now. Either this was some sicko cop with an old grudge who had access to the file, or this was my real ghost.

"Balloon didn't survive," I said.

"Shit happens."

"So what's the beef?" I asked, unconsciously picking up the SIG.

"It's one of those eye-for-an-eye deals, Lieutenant. You owe somebody a death."

"Somebody? We all owe God a death, or so I'm told. You claiming to work for God?"

"Not hardly," he said. I was glad he was willing to keep talking. I couldn't do a trace, of course, but the sheriff's office had tagged the line for record keeping and maybe we'd get lucky. "But you're gonna think so, time we're done with you."

"You got a mouse in your pocket there, sport? You keep saying 'we.'"

"Nah," he said. "I just keep saying that to make you think I've got lots of help. What I've really got is lots of time and dedication. Serious dedication."

"Dedication or commitment?"

"What?"

"Well, which is it, dedication or commitment?"

"What's it matter?"

"There's a difference," I said. "A chicken is dedicated to the production of eggs. A pig is committed to the production of bacon."

"Oh," he said. "Then I'm definitely committed, just like you."

"Well, shit," I said. "Go up against a guy with a long gun, it's just a matter of time. Not exactly a contest there."

"If I just wanted to kill you, you'd be in the ground already. That's not my objective."

"Careful," I said. "You forgot to say 'we.'"

"Well, so I did," he replied.

I didn't say anything. I just sat there, fingering the grips on my SIG.

"So aren't you curious? About my real objective?"

"Actually," I said, "I'm getting bored. 'Bye now."

"Wait!" he said.

"What now?"

"You color-blind, Lieutenant? Can you see red and green?"

"Last time I checked."

"See the red spot on your chest, do you?"

I didn't bother to even look. I lunged sideways out of the chair practically on top of Frick. Just as I hit the deck I heard something snap and then what sounded like a cannon going off in my face. It was so loud and the flash so bright that I was literally immobilized, unable to even put hand and brain together long enough to fire back with the gun in my hand. The shepherds appeared to be equally paralyzed, if not more so.

It took a good ninety seconds for me to collect my wits about me. My ears were ringing, and my night vision was a maze of bright lights and floating green spots. I thought about getting up from the floor and letting off a few rounds into the darkened backyard, but that would be pointless. The stink of burned explosives filled the porch, overlaid with another, sweetish smell I couldn't recognize.

I found the portable phone by feeling around on the floor, but it was dead. No surprise there. Then I realized what had happened. He'd fired off a flashbang, one of those sensory disruptors we used to use in the SWAT world when entering a hot zone. I sat there on the floor with the dogs, blinking my eyes and trying to clear my ears. I finally saw the perforated grenade case lying in a corner. Then I thought I heard a cop-car siren, possibly two, coming down the street out front. An exasperated neighbor had called 911. They were probably getting tired of the war zone that had erupted around my house.

Me, too.

The next morning I sat in Sheriff Baggett's office in downtown Triboro.

"Thought you'd moved," he said as he read through the patrol reports from the previous night.

"I did."

"So how's this guy know you're there in Summerfield? And where's he getting a flashbang?"

"All good questions," I said.

"This business has gone a little bit beyond Billie Ray Breen, don't you think?"

"That's a fair assumption, but still an assumption."

He nodded. "I used to have a rule about assuming."

"Which you shared frequently, as I recall."

He grinned. "How's about this: we'll pull the string on the flashbang casing, and how he set it off remotely. Plus, I've already sent one of my surveillance nerds out front to sweep your vehicle. Your job is to come up with a motive. Tell me who might be doing this shit. We have to stop scaring the upstanding and increasingly vocal citizens of Summerfield."

"I sympathize," I said. I was probably shouting a little bit, as the ringing in my ears hadn't quite gone away. "I'll clear permanently out of my house there today or tomorrow, and then you can find me in the countryside. Can you brief Sheriff Walker?"

"I will, but I think we'd better be circumspect about all the lurid details—your new neighbors may ask you to leave. Rockwell County doesn't handle urban drama very well."

There was a knock on the door, and Maggie, Sheriff Baggett's secretary, announced that the surveillance tech was back. He told her to send him in.

Her in, as it turned out. She was a petite blonde who looked like she was at least fifteen. She was wearing plastic gloves, a hairnet, and a blue jumpsuit that bore signs of crawling around under a car in the parking lot. She was holding the frame from a license plate, which I presumed had come off my Suburban. Like most Americans, I couldn't tell you my license plate number if I tried.

"Sat-com," she said. "Same rig they use on semitrailers with sensitive cargo. GPS track report every ten minutes, location to fifty feet. Commercially available, or swiped at a truck stop. If that's what they did, they'd need RFID programming capability."

The sheriff frowned. "This isn't amateur's night."

"No, sir," she said. "Although it isn't rocket science, either. It's a matter of having the right gear and a little bit of specialized knowledge." She handed him the frame.

"For you, maybe," the sheriff said, turning the frame over in his hands. He looked over at me to see if I had any questions.

"On the off-chance that that thing is rough, did you look for smooth?" I asked.

She blinked and then shook her pretty blond head. The sheriff pointed to the door, and out she went.

"Hmmm," he said. "A flashbang, a penny-ante, semidisposable hitter from the barrios of Charlotte, and now this. What's all that sound like?"

"Someone in law enforcement, with a grudge," I said promptly.

"Yeah," he said, nodding slowly. "We'll have input from the phone company in a few days, but I'm not holding my breath. Your line was disabled at the street box, by the way, not up at your house. Not cut, but switched off."

"More specialized knowledge."

"Unfortunately, given the tag, they have to know about Rockwell County."

"He said I owed someone a death," I said. "Inferring that I got someone killed, and now it's payback time. Except I think he, or they, want to play cat and mouse first."

"I think you'll have a better chance out there in the country," he said. "Summerfield's like any other bedroom community. People get up in the dark and come home in the dark. Don't notice anything until Saturday morning, and then they mow their grass. New faces appear in the country, on the other hand, the locals notice and they talk."

He was telling me to plug into the local network as fast as I could, but that presented some problems. I was a new face, and if I was bringing trouble into the county, prospective helper bees might not want the hassle. I was very much still on trial out there. Maybe the major could keep an eye out, as long as I described my problem in Union cavalry terms.

"Keep close to Hodge Walker," he said. "He's good people, been sheriff a long time, and he'll know the ground out there in the sticks. Just lost his wife to some kind of cancer, I'm told. We'll work what we can here in town."

I thanked him for his help, while acknowledging the obvious: If Sheriff Baggett's people couldn't protect me from an ambush in Summerfield, they couldn't protect me at all out in Rockwell County. I left the building to go see what Blondie had come up with, if anything.

My stalker had been pretty good at his work. He'd been able to get into the house, or, now that I thought about it, the back porch, rig a flashbang for remote detonation, and then position himself where he could put a laser spot on me in the dark, which suggested night-vision gear. He'd been able to disable my phone remotely as well, because there was no way he could have gotten from his lasering position to the box on the curb in ninety seconds, unless of course he did have a mouse in his pocket, or a helper up on the street—and he'd disabled my phone but still made a call.

My license plate was lying on the pavement between two legs sticking out from under the Suburban. Two shepherds were trying to see what she was doing under there from the backseat.

"Any luck?" I asked.

"Not yet," she said. "I was looking for induction power supplies near the wheels."

"Can you say that in English?" I asked the legs.

"Tiny generators. You place them on the suspension, close to a wheel, and then use the rotation of the wheel to induce a current by placing a magnet on the rim. The generator then powers the tracking device transmitter, usually by charging a battery embedded in the plate."

"Sweet."

She hauled out from under the car on a mechanic's creeper and spit some dust out of her face. In the sunlight, she had aged somewhat. Seventeen, maybe. Two deputies walking by were giving me the once-over even as they said hey to her.

"Did that license plate thing go off the air when you took it off the vehicle?"

"Nope," she said as I gave her a hand up. "I'll go put it on a California-bound semi if you want, unless it's evidence."

"Yeah, it's evidence. Bag it and give it to the detectives working the house shootings in Summerfield, if you would, please. How esoteric is that device?"

"Ten years ago one of these would indicate CIA or one of the military agencies," she said. "Now, no big deal. DEA uses them extensively, as do trucking companies."

I couldn't stand it anymore. "How old are you, Deputy, if I may ask?"

She grinned and immediately looked fifteen again. "Twenty-six," she said. "I have a master's from NC State in double-E, and I've been here three years."

I shook my head in wonder. "I am definitely getting old," I said. "I made you for seventeen, which meant twenty-one."

"If it makes you feel any better, I get carded all the time. My husband thinks it's hilarious."

"Well, thanks for finding my bug."

"Like you said inside, I found rough. Smooth could still be inside, like integrated with your FM radio and transmitting through that antenna in the windshield. Bring her back to our surveillance lab and we'll do it right. Takes a morning."

"I'll try to do that," I said. "In the meantime, I need to keep in motion."

"One more thing," she said. "If we do find another bug, we can throw some shit in the game."

"You can spoof a GPS constellation?"

"No, but it's the bug that makes the report. We can make it lie."

"I'll keep that in mind," I said, wondering what else I didn't know about surveillance in this age of the Web and GPS satellites. Probably a lot.

I drove back to Summerfield, packed up some more of my stuff, including the contents of my gun safe, and headed back to the country. As I backed out of my driveway I noticed one of my neighbors staring at me from her yard. When I rolled down the window and asked if there was something wrong, she made a face and said something about my attracting a lot of unnecessary violence to the neighborhood. I told her I was leaving but once I was gone, the bad guys would be coming to see her instead of me. She humphed and turned away. Never did like that woman.

I would have to assume my vehicle was still being tracked until I had time to get it in for an extensive bug sweep. Or, I realized, I could simply trade it in and get a new one. There was a Chevy dealer right there in town, and this one was three years old. The damned things were the original gas hogs, and I suspected that I could get one for a song these days. Let my ghost follow one of the locals out to his deer camp and see what happened.

I spent the weekend getting situated in the cottage and taking some more long walks. My new Suburban looked a lot like my old one. On Sunday morning Carol called and asked if I wanted to go for a trial horseback ride. It sounded like a marvelous opportunity to embarrass myself, but I said yes. An hour later I was sitting atop Goober, who looked to me like a cross between a quarter horse and a camel. He was huge, and I felt like I was sitting on a moving Gel-Pak as he plodded along behind Carol's horse.

We rode around her place for a while as my lower legs slowly became paralyzed and I embedded some new finger grooves in the pommel of my western saddle. The shepherds trailed along on either side trying not to laugh at me. Frick had barked once at the massive beast, who'd responded a few seconds later with one enormous, ground-shaking stomp. Then it made a horrible noise in its throat and I found out why it was called Goober, as did Frick. After that, Frick, expertly slimed, kept her distance, giving both me and the horse reproachful looks from time to time. Carol managed to keep a fairly straight face through it all. Goober mostly seemed to be sleepwalking. I kept checking to see if my lower legs had fallen off.

Carol lived on a thirty-acre parcel outside of town. Her house was a restored eighteenth-century farmhouse, and she gave me a tour to show me what could be done. The before-and-after pictures were amazing. When she'd bought it, the four stone chimneys were mostly on the ground, the roof had fallen in, and the porches looked like wooden hammocks. Now it was spotless, standing on a small knoll surrounded by old oaks and boxwood clumps.

"Ten years?" I asked as we arrived back at the barn. I'd finally taken my feet out of the stirrups, and now my lower legs were improving to the pins and needles stage. My knees felt like they'd been screwed on and the threads stripped in the process. I dreaded the dismount and staggered around like a drunk when I finally did get off. Goober promptly went to sleep. Frick watched from about twenty feet away, clearly appraising her chances to run in and bite him.

"Just about," she said. "Basically we disassembled it, stacked all the useful bits on the grounds, and then rebuilt it from the stone foundations up. That's actually easier and cheaper than working from the inside out."

I wondered who the "we" was and where she'd raised the money to take on a project like that, but I was learning about country ways: They'll tell you when they're ready; if you press it, they shut down. We had a sandwich on the front porch and talked about the restoration trade and the state of the county's economy, which wasn't great. I remembered the Chevy dealer almost falling out of his chair when I said I'd take that one right there. He said he hadn't sold anything with eight cylinders in six months.

She asked how we were coming on the closing. I told her that the appropriate moles were digging into the stacks for the title search. I also told her what the old clerk had said. She was familiar with the issue.

"When you start talking about the big properties in this county, say, Glory's End size and up, way up, in some cases, the titles can become entangled."

"Entangled?"

"Well, the big planters, the families who came up from the coast or down from Virginia, didn't have a lot of respect for the land. They'd burn it out planting tobacco and cotton and then just move on to new land nearby."

I remembered Mr. Oatley mentioning this. "They'd just abandon it?"

"For farming, yes. It was easier to clear new ground than to invest a growing season and money in reconstituting old ground. Technically, they still owned it."

"Ah."

"Yeah," she said. "So when he says be careful what you wish for, you just might find out there are claims out there that go back a hundred fifty years."

"So why hasn't it been a problem before?"

"Because there are enough claims and counterclaims recorded in that courthouse to keep a dozen lawyers in court for a decade. As long as the 'right kind' of folk are on the land, usually meaning relatives, prominent landowners are satisfied to leave well enough alone."

"In other words, don't ask a question if you can't stand all the possible answers."

"You got it," she said.

I asked her why the Lees had fallen out.

"Woman trouble, is the way the story goes," she said. "The plantations were called Oak Grove and Laurel Grove back then, 1820s, '30s, or thereabouts. Nathaniel Carter Lee of Oak Grove, now Glory's End, supposedly stole away the sworn fiancée of Callendar Lee of Laurel Grove. Nathaniel was richer than Callendar, and in all probability, the lady probably followed the money. Her name was Abigail, and she was reportedly a great beauty, as is usually the case in these stories. They duly married, but then some years later, just before the war, Miss Abigail had an affair with Callendar Lee. Nathaniel called out Callendar, and they met with seconds on the Richmond-Danville railroad bridge one spring morning."

"Called out, as in a duel?"

"Exactly. Callendar was the younger man, something of a rake in the county, and known to be impetuous. He fired first, missed Nathaniel, hit the bridge steel, and the ricochet made a cut across Nathaniel's back. Then Nathaniel fired, and his ball hit Callendar in the head. Sixty-caliber ball, probably killed him dead right there and then. Supposedly his body fell through the trestle ties and was never found, the river being in full spate. The families never spoke after that."

"Damn. What happened to Abigail?"

"Nathaniel sent her away, of course. She went back to the coast to her own family, and nobody ever expected to hear from her again. The day after the duel he announced to one and all that his honor and family situation had been satisfied in all respects."

"That was the end of it?"

"Not quite. Abigail actually had the last word. She'd given Nathaniel four sons by the time of this duel. She left behind a letter for the local newspaper, saying that two of Nathaniel's four sons weren't really his, and that she'd leave the begats to the public's 'general interest and determination.'"

"Ouch. Even if it wasn't true, everyone would think it was."

"Yep. Then to top it off, Nathaniel's wound, which had seemed superficial, became infected, and a week later they planted him in Saint Stephen's burial ground."

"Which, like the Civil War," I said, "the Lees will never forget."

"That's the War of Northern Aggression, sir," she said with a smile. "Don't you forget that, either."

"Of course, the war didn't help with the property records. Maybe I should turn this project off."

"I wouldn't," she said. "The most probable claimants to that property, if there even is a claim, are right across the street. If they like you, and it seems they do, there won't be a problem. If they don't, there's no telling what they'd do, but you'd certainly know before you'd have to commit real money."

After lunch I thanked her for the ride and told her I'd try it again when and if my legs ever unkinked from trying to wrap around Goober's ample sides. She said that the only cure for that was more time in the saddle. As we walked down the front steps, I heard my cell phone chirping from the front seat of the Suburban. It was one of the detectives down in Manceford County. He wanted to know where I'd been last night at around midnight.

"What's happened now?" I asked, not wanting to step into something.

"Your boy, Billie Ray? He got clipped with a long gun while watching TV with his crack-skag last night. Head shot, deer caliber. Girlfriend finally has her some brains."

"I was asleep in my rental house out here in Rockwell County," I said, aware that Carol was listening. "Sorry I missed it, though."

He snorted. "Can you possibly corroborate that?" he asked.

"Not unless you can make my shepherds talk," I replied. "What kind of rifle?"

"Still waiting on that," he said, "but enough of a thumper to come through the trailer's window, do a through-and-through on Billie and another one on the refrigerator compressor. They found the bullet in a telephone pole outside. Any chance you can come down here and give us a statement?"

"Sure," I said, "but you've heard most of it already. I left Summerfield Friday afternoon. There's one neighbor who saw me leaving. Otherwise I've been out here, and, no, I can't prove where I was at midnight." I looked over at Carol, wishing she didn't have to hear all this.

"Well, I guess that'll do for now," he said. "Do you own any long guns?"

"Yup," I said, "and I emptied out my gun safe Friday before coming out here. You're welcome to test any or all of 'em. I did not shoot Billie Ray Breen. Thought about it, but it didn't seem worth the hassle."

"You understand we gotta ask, right, Lieutenant?"

"Absolutely. You have my number, and Sheriff Walker out here knows where I'm staying. Good luck with it."

I hung up and looked at Carol, who was giving me raised eyebrows. I knew I had to tell her what was going on. "Got any coffee?" I asked.

I drove back to the cottage after filling Carol in on what had been happening down in Summerfield. Sheriff Walker had already told her about the shooting incidents, but she did not know about the flashbang, and now our logical suspect had himself been killed. She seemed to have taken all this in stride, and then I remembered that she'd been a cop. She did ask the logical question: Was this business going to migrate out here to Rockwell County?

I wasn't sure what to say, but that telephone dialogue with the flashbang voice seemed to indicate we weren't done with each other. I told her about falling into the well at Glory's End, and that did bother her.

"Those damned wells are all over this county," she'd said. "One of my contractors dislocated both shoulders stopping himself from falling down one here, and that one had a brick walk over top of it."

"Is there a way to search for them?" I'd asked.

"Thermal aerial survey," she'd told me. "It's expensive, but they sometimes show up as black circles on IR pictures. Unless of course they're covered by a brick walk or a pile of grass clippings."

I hadn't elaborated on my theory of the scent trap, because I was afraid that might be the straw that broke the project's back. Carol might just back out, and without her, this was pointless. I put the question to her.

"Let's see what happens," she said. "I don't want to get in the middle of some revenge war, but, on the other hand, none of us should have to go around living in fear, either. That pisses me off."

Back at the cottage I put a call in to the Rockwell County Sheriff's Office and left a message at the operations desk for Hodge Walker to give me a call Monday at his convenience. I figured it would be better for him to hear about the Billie Ray problem from me if at all possible. I was introducing Frack to his new yard and surroundings when Walker called back. I apologized for disturbing his Sunday afternoon.

"When you're the sheriff, the days of the week all kinda run together," he said. "What's up?"

I gave him the gist of it, including the fact that Manceford County had called to get a statement and that I had not shot anyone since the Guatemalan hit man.

His tone became a tad more formal, as I'd expected it would. I proposed that I come in to see him or one of his detectives on Monday to lay out the whole history of my ghost problem. He thought that was a great idea.

"So this ain't over?" he asked.

"Unfortunately, I don't think it is," I said and told him about the tracking device that had been found on my license plate.

"This Billie Ray thing a red herring?"

"Maybe," I said. "I believe he truly wanted him some getback, but flashbangs, GPS-based surveillance devices, and now someone's popped him?"

"Yeah," he said. "Okay, let's talk tomorrow. I'll have one of my people get in touch."

"Sheriff?"

"What?"

"Do I have a problem with any of my neighbors that I don't know about?"

"Like the Lees?"

"Well, yes."

"Not that I've heard. What have you heard?"

"Ms. Valeria was all sugar and lace," I said. "I haven't met her mother, but they were perfectly willing to rent the cottage."

"There's always the major," he said.

"Met him," I said. "I don't think he's with us all that much." I described the circumstances.

"You're one of the few people's actually seen him, then," he said. "He really was in the army at one time. Vietnam, late stages. I believe he's medically retired."

"Medically as in mental illness?"

"Lots of those guys who went to Vietnam came home with damage. Some of it you could see, some of it you couldn't. I don't know, but everybody's heard the stories. There's a son, too."

"Oh, great. Another nutcase?"

"Nope, worse, from the Lees' standpoint. He did something that disgraced the family. They sent him away."

"Away."

"High drama. Banishment. Disinherited. The son, dead

to the parents. That sort of thing. He'd been in the service, too, and whatever it was, it involved the military. Doubly disgraceful."

"What happened to him?"

"No one knows. He disappeared. It's been years."

"Does everyone know everything about everyone else here?"

He laughed. "Absolutely not," he said. "We all just pretend we do."

"So in my case . . ."

"Yeah?"

"Well, I know it's a small town, but . . ."

"Gotcha," he said. "No more running my mouth."

"Appreciate it," I said. "I've got enough problems without scaring my neighbors."

"Or the lovely Ms. Pollard."

"Well."

"Unh-hunh. See you tomorrow, Lieutenant. Y'all keep those dogs close, you hear me?"

I called Bobby Lee Baggett's office and suggested one of the Manceford County detectives join us for the séance at Sheriff Walker's office the next morning. The desk officer said they'd take it under advisement.

At midday Monday I was sitting on the front porch steps of Glory's End with the shepherds, enjoying a greaseburger from the one and only fast-food joint in town. The shepherds had visibly high hopes for a fry or two. I told them there was no chance except for the ketchup packs; Frick loved ketchup.

The morning had been a lot like being back on the Job again, one meeting after another. No one had had any brilliant ideas, and the Manceford County investigations had produced nothing substantive in the way of evidence. The good news was that they didn't like me for the shooting. The only thing I did not bring up at the first group-grope was the goings-on in the house at Glory's End and my fall into an abandoned well. I had told Sheriff Walker about both, but he'd had the same opinion about the moving candlestick—probably some local kids screwing around. As to the abandoned well, he said that people often forgot that there'd been dozens of farms out there since the late 1600s, and every one of them had had a well. I didn't think he appreciated the significance of the ball cap, but I didn't press it because I might be making more of it than it warranted.

"The key thing is that phone call," he'd said. "That's your real ghost right there, and if he's serious, he probably will follow you out here. You need to go on the offensive."

I relented and pitched exactly one fry to each mutt, then threw the ketchup packs out onto the front lawn like any good redneck. Frick tore them up immediately, while Kitty looked at her fry disapprovingly. Kitty did not indulge in fast food. I was glad no one walked up just then; Frick's mouth was dripping ketchup, and she looked like a canine vampire.

Go on the offensive, Hodge Walker had told me. Great idea, but how? Billie Ray had been the traditional prison ghost—a dumb jailbird with a lot of anger but not many resources. The flashbang stalker was a different beast. I needed to do two things right away: First, learn my ground out here so that I knew it better than he did. Second, think long and hard about who this might be. He was using sophisticated surveillance techniques and careful planning, and he wanted to play a little before we got down to it. This ghost wanted a war.

Thinking and walking could be done simultaneously, so I called in the dogs and went back to the cottage. Fifteen minutes later we were back on Glory's End property and headed east this time. The two shepherds ranged ahead while I followed, pushing through knee-high grass and weeds in the plowed fields with a walking stick borrowed from the cottage. The main house was behind me, and ahead was a wooded creek, behind which rose another of those heavily forested ridges. The creek was about ten feet wide, filled with smooth stones, and running a foot deep. The shepherds jumped right in and turned into happy mudhens. I found a shallow area where one of the dirt farm roads had made a ford.

The road on the other side was badly rutted from rain washout. The trees along the banks were a bedraggled mixture of locust and straight-shanked poplars, rising sixty feet or higher out of the rocky ground as I climbed the ridge. At the top I could look back toward the house, now a half mile distant. It appeared I was at about the same elevation as the house. Ahead the farm road dropped down the back side of the ridge into wide meadows flanking both sides of the road. Farther to the left there was what looked like a stone quarry visible through the trees between the farm track and the Dan River. There were two beehive-shaped buildings at the back edge of the quarry, behind which rose steep banks of vividly red clay. At the far, eastern end of the meadow rose yet another ridge, which I believed marked the boundary of the property.

I cut left toward the quarry while crows in the trees warned the wildlife of my approach. The shepherds bounded right down the hill to the edge of the quarry but then stopped. When I got there I saw why: It was completely flooded. The quarry was perhaps two acres in size and roughly square, with straight stone sides dropping into dark blue water. A stone ramp led down into the water on the far side, and there was some rusting machinery along the eastern bank, including what looked like the drum of an ancient boiler. When I walked around I discovered there was a rail spur leading from the machinery area out toward the river in a long curve that suggested it had been joined to the old Civil War railroad at one time. Unlike up on the main line, the rails were still there, buried to their tops in dirt and

grass, the ties invisible. I could hear the Dan flowing behind a line of river oaks just beyond the rail spur.

The beehive-shaped structures were brick kilns, and I
wondered if they'd been used to fire the bricks used in the
big house. The black-mawed furnace boxes underneath the
structures were certainly big enough to have been wood-
fired. Scrub trees now grew up throughout what would have
been the work area around the kilns and the quarry machinery. Mounds of broken bricks surrounded the kilns, and
the overgrowth on the mounds suggested these works had
been silent for a very long time. Over to one side I found a
line of the tiny square depressions that in the South usually
indicate slave cabins. They were no bigger than chicken
coops. A weirdly leaning stone chimney guarded the tumbled remains of a larger log cabin, which was now home to
a mass of poison ivy, tiny birds, and at least one burrowing
animal. The shepherds both stuck their snouts into the hole,
and I waited for a retaliatory bite, but nothing happened.
The remains of a party gazebo occupied the corner opposite the brick kilns.

We walked around to the ramp leading down into the
flooded quarry. It had been cut through the raw stone, and
then the cut had been lined with cobbles for some reason,
possibly to give horses or mules better footing as they
dragged up their loads. I saw the rusting remains of beer
cans and other debris indicating that this place might be an
illicit local swimming hole in the heat of summer. Both
dogs ran down the ramp and jumped in. They paddled for
a moment, then seemed to sense that there was no bottom
within their reach and quickly came back out. I backed
away from them to avoid being soaked as they shivered off
the cold water.

Which is when I saw the hand.

At least it looked like a hand. It was about three feet
underwater, and the fingers were splayed out as if the hand
had been reaching for the light. I wasn't about to wade into

that icy water, but I changed position a couple of times on the edge of the ramp just to make sure it wasn't some kind of optical illusion. It wasn't; it was definitely a human hand, connected to a darkly blurred shape under the water. I took out my cell phone and found I had exactly one bar's worth of service. I called the Rockwell County Sheriff's Office.

It took a county SUV almost twenty minutes to find us down at the quarry. The vehicle pulled up at the edge of the water, looking like it'd had an interesting time down at the ford. Sheriff Walker got out of the right front seat; a deputy exited the driver's door, and another the backseat. I had the shepherds on a long down over by the rail spur: One of the deputies asked me if the dogs were going to be all right. I told him not to worry, that they'd been fed recently. He didn't look reassured, but Walker told him the dogs were okay. We all trooped over to the ramp, and I pointed to the fluttering white image. The sheriff stared down at it for a moment and then told one of the deputies to get the floater team out.

"You didn't try to pull that out, did you?" he asked.

I shook my head. "Made sure it was what I thought it was and then called you guys."

"Because you know what usually happens, you go pullin' on a floater."

"I do. The dogs jumped in just to get wet, but then they came right back out. I thought it was the depth that scared 'em."

"Could have been," he said. "This thing's easily a hundred foot down, believe it or not. There's a ledge along two sides, stickin' out five, six foot just below where you can see into the water. We've lost three kids here since I've been sheriff, divin' in and hittin' that ledge. Got two of 'em back."

"Could this be the third?"

He shook his head. "This is recent," he said.

I waited for him to explain that comment, but he seemed preoccupied. One of the deputies spoke into his shoulder mike and then reported that the team would be here in about an hour.

"Out exploring?" Walker asked me.

"Learning the terrain," I replied. "Just in case my ghost problem comes out here to play games."

"Good idea," he said, but once again he seemed distracted. "Deputy Baynes will take your statement now."

Sheriff Walker called me at the cottage that evening as I was finishing up a truly uninspiring TV dinner.

"We got an ID," he said. "Low-level gangbanger from Danville. We had some intel that somebody clipped a barrio capo and threw the body in the river three weeks ago. Apparently they chose the quarry instead."

"Which gangs?" I asked.

"The Salvadorians and some Crip wannabes here in town. At least that's the rumor."

"Crips? Out here?"

"Gangs are everywhere, Lieutenant. Even out here."

"How'd they do him?'

"The body was anchored to a piece of quarry stone with some fence wire. Divers said it looked like they slid the stone far enough down the ramp so that his head just went under. He went in alive, according to the ME prelim. Not a mark on him."

"Sweet," I said. "So they got to watch."

"As did he."

"All for what, some really bitchin' tennis shoes?"

"Or a sideways look at someone's special bitch."

We remained silent for a moment, each of us marveling at the human wastage that was the gang life these days.

"Lemme ask you something," he said finally.

"Shoot."

"Anyone ever called you a shit magnet?"

"What, three dead guys in as many weeks, and you think there's a pattern?"

He chuckled. "Look," he said, "you're reportedly not hurting for money. You might want to invest in a chain-link fence around that quarry as part of your long-range plan. Attractive nuisance, the lawyers call it."

"That thought had crossed my mind," I said. "Of course, it would help if they just stayed off my place."

"Seven hundred acres out in the country has a gravity all of its own," he said. "They know you can't patrol all of it. I'm talking now about the deer hunters, sex-crazed teenagers, hell, you probably even have a marijuana patch or three somewhere out there. And did they tell you about the abandoned coal mine?"

I groaned. "Abandoned coal mine?"

He chuckled again. "Oh, yeah, the coal mine. Back in the early 1900s, somebody thought there was low-grade coal under those ridges out there along the Dan. There was this cave, halfway up the ridge from that quarry. The Lees let some wildcatters come in and dynamite their way back into the cave, see what they could see."

"They find coal?"

"Nope," he said, "but they left an unstable tunnel going about six, seven hundred feet sideways back into that ridge. It's still there, although the entrance supposedly was covered by a rock slide. You might want to locate that and do something to seal it properly."

"Great. Any other little treasures I should know about?"

"Well, lemme see," he said. "The Lees lost all their slaves to cholera the last year of the war. There's a mass grave out there somewhere, nobody knows where for sure, but certainly someplace you do not want to put your veggie garden. Then, of course, there's your candlestick ghost in the big house. There's quicksand in the mouth of Bad Whiskey Creek. And did I mention that there's rumored to be a pack of wolves running that place? And—"

"Sheriff?" I said.

"Lieutenant?"

"Say good night now."

"Good night now, Lieutenant."

I hung up with my bad news bear and went to look for Carol Pollard's card. I called her at home.

"I think I'm getting cold feet," I told her.

"Oh, no—what's happened?"

I recounted my recent discovery at the quarry and then threw in the sheriff's joyous intelligence about a whole host of dangerous features at Glory's End. She was not impressed.

"I mean, it's terrible to find a body on your place, but that's hardly your fault. As to the rest, just about every big place out here has abandoned graveyards, brick and stone workings, and swamps where prudent people don't go walkabout."

"What about the abandoned coal mine?"

"If you can find it, and I suspect you can't, all you really have to do is post it and your farm's perimeter. I think the sheriff is messing with you. He likes you, by the way."

"Called me a shit magnet."

She laughed. "That's a new one, but undeserved. Let's meet for breakfast." She named a place in town, and I agreed to meet her at eight.

I hung up the phone and went for some Scotch. When I came back into the main room, both shepherds were at the side window and Frick was growling.

I put down my drink and flipped off the lights, having had enough of being shot at through the windows. I went over to the side window and looked out over the millpond. The night was hazy, but there was a moon. Budding willows framed the silvery water like a Japanese print. On my side of the dam there was a solitary figure on horseback, standing motionless in the moonlight. I felt a shiver go down my back, even as I realized this must be the major. He and the horse were silhouetted by the moon and totally motion-less, as if cast in silver and black granite. The visual effect was unsettling.

I went outside, leaving the shepherds by the door. They were not happy with that arrangement. I walked across the lawn toward the dam and stopped about ten feet away.

"Major," I said.

"Overseer," he replied, tipping his head slightly. The horse moved around a bit, but he did something with one knee and the beast stopped moving.

"Out late tonight?" I asked.

He looked over my head in the direction of Glory's End. "Those people," he said in a tired voice. "Those people are approaching from the east and south in their thousands. Sherman and his animal hordes. There's no word from General Lee. I think the end is near."

"Well," I said. "Perhaps it's time."

"Nevuh, suh!" he exclaimed. I held my peace, wonder-ing if I should even continue with this charade. Yet, surreal as it was, the setting rather supported it. Up to our left was the gray shape of the big house, looming among its protec-tive oaks, its ground-floor windows glimmering with can-dlelight. There was no traffic out on the two-lane to spoil the illusion. For just a moment, with the moon casting a broad ribbon of light across the millpond, it wasn't that hard to slip into the time warp.

His face was in total shadow, so I could not read his expression, but the horse moved nervously again, as if sens-ing that something bad was coming. He clucked to the ani-mal and then adjusted himself in the saddle. His long cavalry sword clinked against some part of his tack.

"Keep watch," he said. "If they come this way, they will hang people like you, suh, and the slaves will help them do it. Are you armed, overseer?"

"Well, yes," I said, even as I realized that I'd left my trusty SIG in the house. Had to stop doing that.

"Very good," he said. "Remain vigilant, then. Trust no one and report all strangers. These are parlous times indeed. I must return to camp."

I did not know what to say to that, but he had already nudged the big horse into a slow trot up the drive toward the big house, the horse's shoes snapping the occasional spark off the gravel. Once he'd gone I wondered if I hadn't imagined the whole thing.

An owl called from the other side of the millpond, its throaty hooting amplified by the still water. *Perfect,* I thought and went back inside. The shepherds kept watch by the door for a while, but there were no more night visitors, at least that I knew about. I kept the .45 on the bedside table, just in case, and Kitty slept in her now customary position, in my bedroom doorway.

Carol and I met at the local breakfast joint on the main street of town. It was a full house, and we ended up sitting at the counter, surrounded by a high volume of conversation laced with a surprising amount of cigarette smoke. This was tobacco-growing country, and the locals were apparently remaining loyal to that side. I told her about my encounter with the mad major, and she just shook her head.

"It sounds as if he's frozen in that one period of time," I said. "He keeps replaying it in his mind."

"Spooky," she said.

"I'll tell you what," I said. "It was spooky out there. It was like talking to a ghost, except he was real, and so was the horse."

She stirred her coffee for a moment. "You do know," she said, "that you're the only person I know who's actually seen the major?"

"Oh, c'mon," I said. "The sheriff told me about him. Cubby takes care of his horse daily. He told me he locks up the tack room at night to keep him from going out on the road at night."

"That may be what Cubby says, but I've never met anyone outside of the Laurel Grove estate who's actually seen the major. And what was he doing out there at night if Cubby locks things up?"

"Hell, I don't know. You think I'm seeing things?"

"No-o," she said, "but I'd be careful, if I were you, about telling people these stories about encountering the major. Most folks here in town think a lot of that is a tall tale, you know, the lunatic relative chained up in the attic at Laurel Grove, where, oh, by the way, they dress up in early Victorian clothes, ride in a horse and buggy, don't use electricity, and read by candlelight."

I sat back and looked at her. "Tell you what," I said. "Come out to Glory's End today and I'll show you where I first encountered the mysterious major. It's a campfire site, and it's obviously been in use for a long time. I can also show you the fresh pile of horse apples on the dam, from last night."

"Don't get upset, Cam," she said. "I believe you."

"Okay, then, come on out. Just let me show you. I haven't been on scene long enough to fake this, nor do I have any motive to make this stuff up. Like I said last night, I'm beginning to have second thoughts about the whole project."

She sighed audibly and looked around the crowded café. "I know this is difficult for you, coming up from the city," she said. "People here are mostly longtime residents. Their families have been here for generations. They think they know everything about everybody. Now there's a drug dealer pulled out of what has long been a county swimming hole, and you're having conversations with the legendary major of Laurel Grove. I'm just saying—"

"That since I've arrived in the county and acquired one of the historical properties, bad shit's been happening."

She looked uncomfortable, but then she grinned. "Yes and no," she said. "Some of us are, what's the word, rather fascinated? You're like a cue ball, cracking into the triangle

on a pool table, and everything that's been just-so for years
is crashing around."

"Is that a good thing?"

"It might be," she said. "This county's motto is 'Preserv-
ing the past, embracing the future.' Lots of people here are
all about the past, but not that many really embrace the
future. I guess what I'm saying is, please don't bail out
just yet."

"Then come with me to Glory's End. Seeing is believing."

"Will you stop talking about ghosts bearing dead babies in the grocery store?"

"If they stay away, I will."

She smiled and said okay.

We finished breakfast, and then she followed me back
to the plantation. An hour later and after an arduous climb
through the old croplands and up the ridge, we arrived at
the circle of rocks. The blackened stones were still there,
and even Carol could see that they had been used for a long
time. I was able to find hoofprints in the dirt behind the
boulders, and there were blackened coffee grounds in the
surrounding grass. Frick tried to eat some and then made a
bad face.

"I make my coffee in the cottage, and I don't boil the
grounds," I said. I told her about seeing the flash of reflected light up on this ridge, encountering the major, and
my indiscretion about claiming to own the place. "Now he
thinks I'm the overseer; that's what he called me last night,
too. Overseer."

"Well, you're at least the conservator. What happened
to all these trees?"

"I think it's a lightning patch," I said, and then I had to
explain that term to her.

"Great view from up here," she said. "Next time let's
ride it, though."

"My knees still haven't recovered from the last time," I
said. "I may get me a four-wheeler, though."

"Don't you dare," she said. "This land was meant to be ridden over, not torn up by one of those horrible, noisy things. The Lees would evict you if you showed up at the cottage with a four-wheeler."

"Gee, I wonder if I should stop using the electric lights in the cottage so much, too."

She gave me an exasperated look, and then Kitty woofed. We turned around, and there was the major in all his glory. Neither one of us had heard him coming across that carpet of soft pine needles in the forest, and Carol gave a little squeak when she saw him. He doffed his big hat and nodded politely at her. He looked older than the first time I'd seen him, but his eyes were in shadow under that broad-brim hat.

"Overseer," he said to me, "there's Union cavalry about. You should return to the house at once. They are burning the fields across the river."

"Yessir," I said, looking across the river, where indeed there was a column of smoke some miles distant. "We'll go right away."

He nodded again, tipped the brim of his hat at Carol, swung the horse around, and trotted off into the pines.

"Oh. My. God," she said when he was gone, a hand at her mouth. "You're so right—that was spooky."

"Try it in the moonlight," I said. "That old boy's truly down the road and gone around. See what I mean about the tape just replaying each day? Apologies accepted, by the way."

She shook her head. "That was amazing," she said, "and, yes, I'm sorry I ever doubted you. I can still hardly believe it. The uniform. That huge sword."

My cell phone rang. It was Tony, calling from the office. The connection wasn't wonderful. "Trouble in River City," he said.

"Who's dead now?" I asked and saw Carol blink.

"We had a break-in last night," Tony reported. "Nothing

taken that we can see, but whoever it was, he left you a message."

"I'm all ears."

"It's a single .30-06 round. Hundred eighty grain, at least. Somebody took the trouble to engrave your name on the cartridge. Left it on your desk."

"That's self-explanatory," I said. "How'd he get in?"

"Can't tell," he said. "We have that alarm system, which apparently he spoofed. All the computers were turned on, but it looks like he didn't get past the opening screen passwords. We had the city cops in, and you know how that went."

"Right," I said. "I'll be down early afternoon."

"What now?" Carol said after I closed up the cell phone.

"No more bodies, if that's what you're worried about." I looked around. It was a beautiful day in the country, and I would have much preferred to stay out there with Carol. "Something's come up," I said. "Let's get back to the house before that marauding Union cavalry shows up and hangs us."

A bullet with your name on it. I'd heard the expression, but this was the first one I'd ever seen. The guys had slipped it into a clear plastic bag, and I held it in my hand like a baby snake.

"Notice the rim?" Tony said.

I looked. There was a tiny dent on the back edge of the cartridge. "That's an extractor nick," I said. "So it's been in a rifle, but not fired."

"Maybe the same rifle that sent Billie Ray to the big trailer park in the sky."

"Quite a calling card you got there, boss," Horace observed.

We were sitting around our informal conference table in the coffee room. Tony, Horace, and Pardee were present for duty, along with my two fuzz balls, who were hoping for a doughnut.

"So some guy broke in here, without activating the alarm, and went around to all the desktop computers, looking for—what?"

"Your new address, maybe?" asked Tony.

"I took that tracking device out to the plantation, so what's he need an address for?" Then I remembered I'd sold that Suburban.

I asked them to tell me what they were working on and how things were going with H&S Investigations. There was nothing exciting to report. Then I filled them in on what had been happening out in the countryside, including the sheriff's fascinating inventory of dangerous features at Glory's End, and said that I was beginning to have second thoughts about life as a country squire. Tony didn't say *I told you so*, but he was clearly thinking it.

"On the other hand," observed Horace, "you can't stay in Summerfield, not after you whacked that Guatemalan guy. You might as well hole up in Rockwell County. At least there, a Guatemalan with a thirty-aught will stand out."

"Whereas in Triboro, he wouldn't?"

Everyone smiled except the mutts, who still hadn't detected any doughnuts.

Pardee picked up the plastic bag with the thirty-aught round in it. "This is personal," he said. "He told you that you owed him a death, remember? So who's died in the recent past who was tied to you? Or to whom you were important?"

I took a deep breath and let it out slowly. "My ex-wife and your favorite judge, Annie Bellamy, courtesy of a bomber or bombers unknown. Then, let's see, White Eye Mitchell, up in the mountains, when his pet mountain lion kicked his guts out after I wounded it."

"There's Allie Gardner down in Wilmington," Pardee

said, leaving unspoken the fact that we had almost added his own name to that list.

"Or that crooked sheriff whose daughter was all set to knife you, up in Carrigan County?" Tony said. "Except he died, too, when he and his partner shot it out with street sweepers."

"And Kenny," Horace said. "Kenny Cox."

That name rocked me. I could still picture his dying moments in that icy river up in the Smokies, his face getting whiter even as the water got redder. Kenny Cox. Probably my best friend on the Job, until I found out he'd become a vigilante cop.

Who had a brother. No, wait: His brother had committed suicide. I myself had heard the shot up there in that mountain cabin, and Bobby Lee Baggett had said he'd get Surry County to pick up the remains.

"Anybody know somebody out in the Surry County Sheriff's Office?" I asked.

Horace did.

"See if you can find out whether or not they ever picked up the remains of one James Marlor, who shot himself in a cabin out there."

The three of them looked at me. They all knew who James Marlor was, or had been, and it brought back some bad memories of the cat dancers case.

"I know," I said. "If they retrieved a body, then we can scratch him. If they didn't . . ."

"I thought you saw him ice himself," Tony said.

"I heard him do it," I replied. "From a hundred yards away, on a dark hillside, with snow blowing. One shot, sounded like a .45."

"You didn't go back to check?"

"It was dark and a blizzard was moving in. There was nothing I could do for him at that point, one way or the other."

"So he could have faked it," Pardee said.

"Or Kenny could have taken care of the body, once he found out."

"Go make the call, please," I said, suddenly hoping that I didn't have a Kenny Cox loose end here. If my ghost was James Marlor, I was in truly deep shit.

Pardee handed me the rifle bullet. "You ought to keep this," he said. "It might ward off the evil it represents."

I drove out to Summerfield after rush hour to check on the house. The lawn had been mowed, so my money-hungry teenager was still on the job. One neighbor waved as I went by; another just stared. I had half a mind to go into the backyard and unload the SIG into the hillside, just to keep them all on their toes. On the other hand, who could blame them?

I let the dogs out and told them to go check out the yard. They both went up on the porch and curled up. So much for canine discipline. There were no signs of forced entry or any other disturbance in the house itself. I'd left the power and the security service on. The mailbox was full, but it was all junk mail addressed to Current Resident or Dear Occupant. I told the mutts to get back in the Suburban, but now they decided to go check out the yard. I was getting ready to yell at them when the neighbor across the street, another retired cop, came over with a package in his hand.

"Messenger guy on a motorcycle brought this out, asked me to give it to you the next time I saw you."

The package was the size of a fat FedEx envelope, entirely covered in brown shipping tape, with my name and address handwritten on a stick-on label. I took it from him and felt the weight.

"Classic letter bomb is what that looks like," he said. "I kept it out in the potting shed."

"I agree," I said. "The messenger an older guy?"

"Nope. Young kid. Riding a Kawasaki crotch-rocket in spandex bike shorts and a T-shirt. All I could think of was the road rash, he ever had to lay that thing down."

"They're invincible," I said. "Thanks for taking this. I think I'll take it over to the bomb boys downtown."

"You know what?" he said. "You should have them come out here, pick that thing up. They got the gear for that."

"The bomb squad shows up in this neighborhood, I'll never be able to show my face again. I'm already getting stink-eye from Mrs. Jameson."

He laughed. "That's not stink-eye; that's her usual expression, caused by going around with a corncob up her ass. Let those guys transport it. That's the smart move."

I thanked him again and made a call to Manceford County Operations. I told them it was not an emergency, but this thing needed checking out. They said they'd send the boom box and a crew.

Forty minutes later the bulky truck and an operations van showed up. They hadn't arrived with lights and sirens, so most of the neighborhood remained blissfully unaware. I handed over the package, which the bomb guys treated with far more respect than I had. They had a portable X-ray machine in the van. A tech brought it out, and they examined the package right there on the front lawn. The tech set up the machine, and then we all backed away before he turned it on. He went back to the van to look in the remote monitor.

"Hello-o-o, Houston," I heard him call from the back of the van. "We've got wires."

I felt another little shiver go down my back, especially since I hadn't really expected it to be anything more than—well, what? Surely my ghost would anticipate that I'd recognize the profile and not just go ripping off a dozen winds of package tape, finally getting to the one attached to the pull cord. The bomb crew put the thing in the truck's armored transport box. The lieutenant came over as the truck pulled away. I didn't know him, but he greeted me by name.

"A little obvious, wasn't it?" he said, taking off his vest and face shield.

"That's what's odd," I said. I told him about the motorcycle messenger, and we agreed we hadn't seen any of those in Triboro. Everyone used one of the usual package services. Messenger bikes were for big cities with big traffic.

"Your ghost again?"

I shrugged. "Who the hell knows," I said. I showed him the thirty-aught round and told him about finding it on my desk downtown.

He shook his head. "We'll try to take that thing apart, see what's what. Although I have to warn you, with all that tape it's just as likely to go off."

"Well, don't put anyone at risk," I said. "I'm cool with just assuming it's exactly what it looks like."

He laughed. "Us chickens won't be within a hundred yards. Igor von Robot will do it, and we'll watch via remote TV. Sometimes these guys, you know, if it's their first device? They make mistakes and we can ID a component, maybe link it with a source. We'll let Bobby Lee Baggett know what we find; you can check with him."

I thanked him, and they took off. The shepherds were waiting back on the front porch.

"I should have considered that thing dog food, let you guys open it," I said.

They wagged their tails. I'd said the food word. Useless mutts.

I opened the back door of the Suburban, and they jumped in. As I walked around to get in the driver's side, I dropped the rifle bullet. I made a clumsy grab for it and ended up catapulting it into the air instead. It arced out on the concrete of the street, and I winced when it landed, but it didn't go off. When I went to retrieve it, I found that it had broken at the neck of the cartridge, exposing the smallest printed circuit board I'd ever seen. Then I started laughing.

It wasn't a bullet. It was another tracking device, and I'd been carrying it around in my pocket all this time. My ghost had a sense of humor. I drove back to the country.

The next morning I got up at six, made some coffee, and wandered over to the barns behind the mansion at Laurel Grove, looking for Cubby Johnson. I found him in the stable, grooming what looked like the major's big horse. The uncomfortable-looking cavalry saddle and a bridle were sitting on a saddle rack. There were two other horses in the barn, busily doing what they apparently do best. Carol had pointed out that the most active muscle on a horse was its jaw muscle.

"Morning, Cubby," I said. "I'm getting the impression that you must live here."

He laughed and told me that he got here every day around seven, but that he and Patience lived over on Mill Street in town, next to the abandoned textile mill.

"Major getting ready for another scout?" I asked. The shepherds snuck off, hoping I wouldn't see them grubbing for horse apples.

"Ain't no tellin'," Cubby said without looking up. "He rides out, he rides back in, and he don't tell me nothin'."

"Are there days he doesn't ride out?"

"Oh, yeah. Sometimes, Ms. Valeria, she'll come down here, say the major feelin' poorly. He gettin' old, you know."

"I saw him last night, as a matter of fact," I said. "Doesn't look that old."

Cubby looked up from his work. "You seen him at night? Over there?"

"Couple of times," I said. "You won't like what he calls me."

"What's that?

"Overseer."

"You shittin' me."

"First time we met, I told him I was the new owner of Glory's End. He said that was ridiculous, that the property belonged to the Lees, and that I must be the new overseer. I went with it."

Cubby nodded. "Overseer," he said, chewing on what had to be a highly charged word. The big horse moved around a bit and stomped at a fly. Cubby resumed the brushing.

"He seems locked into that last month of the war," I said. "Keeps talking about Union cavalry roaming the neighborhood, General Lee gone to ground, Sherman's hordes on the way up from the Carolinas."

"An' he's talkin' to you? Straight up?"

"Yup. Got that faraway look in his eyes, though. If he were to pull that hogleg of his, I'd be putting myself in motion."

Cubby nodded. "Yeah, me, too. Ain't nobody outside of us caught sight of the major, not close up, anyways, for years now. An' here he's talking to a stranger. Ain't that somethin'."

"Exactly how old is he, Cubby?"

Cubby thought for a moment. "Oh, sixty-something."

I was astonished. The man looked to be in his late fifties, maybe sixty. Which meant that Valeria had to be older than she looked, too. Cubby saw my surprise.

"Yeah, they can fool you," he said, putting away the brush. "They preserved. In more ways than one."

"Who rides these other horses?"

"Ms. Hester, she rides most every day, and Ms. Valeria, too. You talk about overseers—ain't nothin' goin' on they don't know about, the two of 'em."

Then he looked over my shoulder and grinned. The shepherds had encountered the duty barn cat, who was giving them some unmistakable visual cues.

"Better get them dogs up," Cubby said. "That cat right there? He'll tear their asses up."

The cat looked to me like he was enjoying the confrontation with the two circling shepherds. "They're German shepherds," I said. "There's only one way they learn anything."

A moment later the lesson was duly administered. One enormous hiss, a blur of fang and claw, stereo shepherd yipes, and then both dogs were running for the barn door with bloody noses. It was funny, although probably not to the shepherds. The cat sat back down in the barn aisle, licked a paw, yawned, and waited for a rematch.

I asked Cubby for his cell phone number in case I ever encountered the major in some kind of problematic circumstances. Then I took my unruly dogs back to the cottage and rubbed their snouts down with some hydrogen peroxide from my Suburban's first aid kit. That nearly got me bitten. Then my cell phone went off.

It was the lead detective on the Summerfield shootings. He had the bomb squad report. "Everything there but the bang," he said. "Wires, battery, trigger, just no explosive. The lieutenant said it was tailor-made for a sheet of Semtex. Guy apparently forgot to include the good stuff."

*Or,* I thought, *he was telling me that he could have if he'd wanted to.* I thanked the detective for calling me and asked if they had anything more on Billie's shooter. Nothing.

"Working it hard, are we?"

"Absolutely," he said. "Important guy like that. Hell, yes. His junkie girlfriend has disappeared, by the way."

"Displaying a moment of good sense, sounds like." I told him about the electronic bullet, and he asked that I turn it in.

"You think there's something you can learn from that?" I asked.

"Na-ah," he said, "but it'll give me an excuse to go see that little blond number over in forensics."

"She's married," I said.

"But reportedly not serious about it," he said, and hung up.

I got another cup of coffee and went out to a tree swing on the lawn to watch the sun come up.

What in the world was I going to do about this ghost? Shooting into my house, triggering a flashbang on my back porch, breaking into our offices, bugging my vehicle and then me, dropping Billie Ray, and now a messenger-delivered letter bomb, conveniently minus the bang.

Hodge Walker said I needed to go on the offensive, but against whom?

Suppose it was James Marlor? *You owe me a death*, he'd said. No—I owed someone a death. If it was Marlor, then he was seeking revenge for the death of his brother, Sergeant Kenny Cox. I hadn't killed Kenny, though—a mountain lion had done that, and then only after Kenny had provoked the encounter in that bizarre ritual of the cat dancers.

Perhaps Marlor didn't know that. If he'd gone off the grid after faking a suicide, he'd have had no access to the final police report regarding Kenny. Maybe some of the other vigilantes had gotten word to him that Kenny hadn't come back from the mountains and that I'd been with him. That might be sufficient to set a revenge plot in motion, but then, why all the screwing around? You want to take a man down and make sure he knows who did it, you show up in his face and get to it.

I decided to go over to Glory's End and do some more exploring. The shepherds' noses were swollen and they weren't feeling all that great, so I put some baby aspirins in a hot dog and then left them to sulk in the cottage. I did take my SIG, along with my hiking gear-belt and a walking stick. The day was shaping up to be sunny and even warm. I wondered if I'd encounter the major again, or if he'd stay on his own lands today. Depended on where the Union cavalry was operating, no doubt. The first guy who rode up in Union blue, though, I was out of there.

After two hours of tramping through increasingly assertive weeds and briars, I made a mental note to get some kind of vehicle for doing this, no matter what the Auntie Bellums might think. I'd seen a place over near Danville that sold golf carts that had been reconfigured as farm utility vehicles. Carol's protestations notwithstanding, I needed to be able to cover the ground more efficiently than by doing it on foot. I'd already dosed the dogs with Frontline, having picked three ticks off my own body.

I'd gone from the house down toward the river again, and then east, along the riverbank until I hit what I assumed was Bad Whiskey Creek, location of the reported quicksand. I didn't see any ground that looked like it would be treacherous. The banks were rocky and heavily forested, and the stream joined the river at an acute angle. I turned right, back toward the two-lane road, and walked up the west bank of the stream, pushing through lots of sprouting mystery bushes and causing many frogs to plop into the water. The long ridge rose up the other side of the stream; that was the one supposedly containing the coal mine. About a quarter mile back from the river I encountered a beaver dam, and there was a sizable pond behind it. When I tried to get around it I found the quicksand, or at least enough of a bog to cause my boots to sink almost to their tops before I was able to extract myself. I pushed my walking stick down into the muck and hit solid bottom at about three feet. Time to turn around.

I cut across what had been a large crop field and headed back up to the house. The next time out I'd stick to the farm roads and explore that coal mine ridge, and maybe see if I could find signs of a caved-in entrance. Once back at the house, I stood in the brook coming down from the springs and let the water melt the muck off my boots. Then I went up to the front porch, took the boots off to dry in the sun, plopped down in one of the ancient rockers, and did another tick check. When I looked up I saw two very large Dobermans walking calmly up the front steps, looking at me the way I look at a rare steak.

I froze in the chair, conscious of the fact that I'd never heard them coming and that now was not the time to jump up and run for the front door. They came over to my rocker and sat down about three feet away. Their coats glistened, as did their teeth. They didn't so much menace me as just make it clear that I should stay seated and not reach for anything, say, like my SIG, which was hanging on my field belt over on the railing. They were alert but not poised to attack. Yet. That's the big difference between a Dobie and a shepherd: German shepherds are typically friendly animals who can and will defend if their human charge is threatened. They're bred for defense. A Doberman was bred for offense. A shepherd can be taught to attack on command, but they don't take to it like a Doberman does. I was really interested in who might be nearby with the authority to issue that command. Then I heard the front door of the house squeak open behind me and found out.

"Don't turn around, Lieutenant," a man said. The voice sounded like my flashbang caller.

"Wouldn't dream of it," I said. "Not with these two lovelies in my face."

"They're not in your face," he said. "You wouldn't be talking if they were. As long as you sit still, nothing will happen."

"Got it," I said. "So what's the deal here, mystery man? Why are you and me at war?"

I heard another rocker being dragged over to a position right behind me, and then the sounds of someone sitting down. He was close enough that I could have kicked myself over backward and probably landed right in his lap.

The Dobermans read my mind and inched closer, peering intently into my face. They were both wearing red collars with what looked like ball bearings embedded in the fabric. I could see tiny clips where a muzzle could be attached to the collars. I heard the sounds of a cigarette being lit up.

"You don't know me," he said finally, exhaling his first drag. "I'm not James Marlor, by the way."

Now I knew why he'd broken into our offices. The thirty-aught round had been a distraction. He'd been there to place an audio bug or three, and he'd obviously listened to our entire conversation.

"Okay," I said, "and you're not Billie Ray Breen."

"That's right," he said. "Now, I want you to turn your head to the left as far as you can. Not your shoulders or your torso—just your head. Slowly, please."

He had something of a southern accent, but it sounded educated, not the sometimes nasal twang of the Piedmont. I complied, mindful of the sudden tension in the dogs' bodies as I moved. I kept my arms down on the chair's arms, my hands gripping the old wood harder than was probably necessary. I turned my head as far around as I could, and then he leaned forward in his chair so I could see his face.

I almost jumped. There was no face.

Instead there was an oval sheet of what looked like thin white rubber, stretching right up over his head. He looked like what happens when the Mafia ties a guy up and then puts a dry-cleaning bag loosely over his head, tapes it tight around his neck, and lets him slowly suffocate. The facial features were vague protuberances, but where I expected eyeholes there weren't any. The material simply thinned down to the consistency of semitransparent cling wrap. I could just barely see pupils behind the fabric. The material made his eyes look like they were equipped with nictitating membranes, like the eyelids on an alligator. The eyes were strangely immobile, looking past me with perfect parallax. I couldn't see how he'd be able to breathe or talk through that second skin, but then he moved his face out of my line of sight and told me to turn back around. The mask reminded me of one of those Roman marble death masks.

"How do you breathe with that thing on?" I asked.

"It's even harder to talk," he said. "Now, sit still. I'm going to put something over your head and around your neck. It won't hurt you." Then he spoke a sharp command in what sounded like Japanese, of all things, and both dogs stood up and leaned in my direction.

"Close your eyes," he said. I did.

What felt like a steel noose dropped down over my head and face and settled on my collarbones. I didn't care what he said—it felt like a garrote, but with those two Dobes hoping and praying that I'd so much as twitch, I remained still. I heard a latch click, and then I felt the full weight of the device. It apparently had a chain attached, because he tugged on it and pulled my head backward a few inches. It was a collar, not a wire. I was leashed.

"Here's the deal," he said.

"Finally," I said, still trying to keep my cool.

"You are responsible for the death of my wife. Responsible but, so far, never accountable. I'm going to rectify that problem."

My mind was racing, trying to figure out what I was going to do next, and then searching my memory for any case in which I'd done something fatal to a woman. With the exception of one woman up in the mountains, I came up blank, and this guy didn't sound mountain to me.

"Don't remember?" he asked.

"No," I said. "Sure you got the right guy?"

"Very," he said.

I shook my head slowly. It was hard to do with that collar on, and the Dobes were not pleased when I moved. One growled, and the other flashed its teeth, probably on signal from my captor. "Was this a cops and robbers deal?" I said.

"It'll come to you. As will I. What happened to her is going to happen to you, in a manner of speaking."

"I'm still confused," I said. "If I wanted revenge for something like that, some guy kills my wife, and assuming I couldn't hand the case over to the cops, I'd go find him and just do it."

"Would you?" he asked, tugging on the chain again just a little. "Just 'do it'? Or would you play it out a little, make your target suffer, experience some of the terror that she did? Make him go to bed at night wondering, when was it coming, how was it coming?"

I didn't answer. It was weird enough to be having this conversation in broad daylight, with a masked man holding me by the neck with a chain and two killer Dobes poised to share an eyeball appetizer. When I thought about it, though—well, yes, I just might drag something like that out.

"That's what I thought," he said as if he'd read my mind this time. "Either way, I don't care. I'm coming for you. We can have this little contest out here in the country, or downtown, or in Summerfield, or wherever. If you involve other people, they will share your risk. Make sure they know that."

"When did all this happen?" I asked. "I mean, I'm drawing a real blank here."

He ignored my question. "What do you think of my associates?" he asked.

"They do look competent."

"You have no idea. That's what's taken me so long to come for you. I needed something to balance out your shepherds."

My shepherds might be in big trouble if they had to go up against these two, I thought. "So what's the timeline? When do we start?"

"Sometime soon," he said.

"In other words . . ."

"In other words, you'll know it when you see it coming. If you see it coming. Remember, if you run, you'll just be putting off the inevitable."

He stood up behind me and dropped his end of the chain on the floor. There was a lot more chain than I'd realized.

"Stay right there," he said. "We're leaving. Me first, then my friends there. If you reach for that gun, they'll take a hand, so to speak."

"You walking or driving?" I asked, still trying for a little cool.

He laughed. "I'm going to vanish into thin air, smart-ass. The next time you see me, that's where I'll be coming from. Where we'll be coming from."

I heard him walk back toward the front door of the house, open it, go inside, and close it behind him. The Dobes did not move a muscle, and neither did I. He'd obviously given them another hand signal, which meant he knew what he was doing as a dog handler. Not good.

We sat that way for about two minutes, with me thinking furiously about what had just happened, and the Dobes still thinking about lunch. Then their cropped ears quivered and they both turned and ran down off the front porch and around the side of the house, probably in response to a dog whistle. I sat there, collecting my wits for a moment. I fingered the collar. It felt like hammered iron, a heavy metal but not smooth like steel. There was a latch at the back where the chain joined, and it was set tight enough so that I could not rotate it around my neck. I gathered up the chain and found out it was six feet long.

I wanted to get my gun and go into the house, but he'd probably just gone straight through and out into the back area, called for his dogs, and walked away. He had assumed I wouldn't try to chase him, certainly not with a dog collar on. He had assumed correctly.

So the game had begun. There was no point in my trying to run, unless I wanted to go overseas and disappear in some big city, like Rome. He'd already demonstrated enough in the way of sophisticated surveillance for me to know that running would simply delay the inevitable, just as he'd said.

I looked around the plantation, taking in the dormant crop fields, the budding woods, a few zillion bugs, birds, and squirrels starting up the new year out on the front lawns. *What the hell,* I thought. This place was as good as any. Now all I had to do was prepare myself. There was still a chance he had the wrong man, but as I got up and started back to the cottage, chain in hand, I had this bad feeling that he didn't.

Cubby was on a car mechanic's creeper, working under a tractor. He saw me come into his workshop, but since he was looking into the sun, he didn't see the collar right away.

"Hey, there, Lieutenant," he called. "Devil's been askin', where them brave dogs of yours?'

"Reflecting on their latest lessons learned," I said. "Don't ever let that cat wander out into the open, though."

"Oh, that cat? He'll ride one of 'em with his front legs and hook the snot out of the other with the back ones." Then he finally saw the collar, and his eyes widened. "Whoa!" he exclaimed. "Where did you get that damned thing?"

I was about to explain when the door at the other end of the shop opened and Valeria Lee stepped through. She had walked down the trellised brick rose walk from the big house and come in through the barn complex. She stared at the collar as she walked up to me.

"If that's supposed to be a joke, Mr. Richter, it's in exceedingly bad taste."

"Couldn't agree more, Ms. Valeria," I said. "It's certainly not my idea of a joke. In fact, I can't see exactly what it is."

She looked at me for a second and then understood. "Oh," she said. "Forgive me. It's a slave collar, of course. For runaway slaves. The pursuers would chain a group of them together to prevent further escapes."

That explained the hank of rusty chain hanging down my back. "I came to see if Cubby here could get this thing off."

Cubby had by now climbed out from under the tractor. He was clearly embarrassed by all this talk of runaway slaves but very much interested in the collar, especially the latch on the back. "Yass'm," he said to Ms. Valeria. "I do believe I can fix this," he said. "Hold on a minute."

I saw a cutting torch rig in one corner and was about to protest, but instead he left the shop and headed down between the outbuildings toward what looked like an old log cabin. Valeria stepped closer to examine the collar, and once again I detected the scent of lilacs and perhaps something more subtle in the way of perfume. She stood right in front of me, and her complexion was flawless, as was her makeup. The major might be in his sixties, but she was early forties, tops. I bent my neck so that she could look at the latch, and this had me staring down her bodice. She was amply endowed, and I was suddenly aware of her. I think she detected that sudden awareness, as mature women always do, and shifted herself slightly to my left side.

"Where did Cubby go?" I asked as her fingers lingered on my neck near the sharp edges of the collar latch.

"To the collection," she replied, then let go of the collar and stepped back. She had dark brown eyes and a long straight nose, and her lips were parted just ever so slightly. She was wearing another one of those period dresses that draped down to the floor, and I would have sworn I heard the creak of whalebone stays when she moved. "Cubby keeps a collection of relics he has discovered on the plantation over time. I believe he has gone to find a key."

Now that was interesting. A black man who had not only recognized a slave collar but who also thought he knew where a key might be. "This is somewhat embarrassing," I said.

"I should think so," she said with just the barest hint of a smile. She held her hands together in front of her, and I noticed how square her shoulders were. "It's a good thing you did not encounter the major wearing that device."

I nodded and hurt my jaw. "He calls me the overseer," I said. "This would have confused him even, um, well, I mean . . ."

She gave me a droll look. "Even more than he already is?"

I let out a deep breath. "It is pretty surreal when he appears out of the woods in that getup and goes on about Sherman and the inbound Yankee hordes."

"Surreal," she said. "What a charming way to put it."

I think she was going to say something further, but Cubby came back into the shop bearing a large, rusty iron key. "Yass'm, I believe this'll do it," he announced. He wasn't bowing and scraping, but he was definitely laying on some Uncle Tom.

The key was a cylindrical affair with what looked like a corkscrew on the end. He stood behind me, put it to the latch, and rotated the cylinder a couple of times until the collar suddenly dropped away and hit the floor with a surprisingly loud clang. Cubby picked it up and handed it to Valeria, who turned it over in her hands with visible distaste. The thing looked handmade, as did the chain.

I rubbed my neck and looked at Cubby, who was studiously looking at the ground. I thanked him and asked if he wanted the collar for his collection.

"Got three just like it," he said. "I'll hang it out there, though, you don't want it."

"I definitely don't want it."

Valeria handed it back to Cubby and turned to me. "I

assume you will want to deal harshly with the individual who put that hateful thing on your neck, Mr. Richter?" she asked.

"Harshly being the operative word, Ms. Valeria."

"I should think so," she said. "Mr. Richter, will you be so kind as to join us for tea this evening? At five, if that's convenient?"

"Yes, I can do that," I said, looking at my watch. First I needed to make some calls.

"Thank you," she said. She turned away in a swish of skirts and headed back up the walk to the big house.

"Yass'm?" I said to Cubby once she'd gone.

He sighed. "Got's to get in character when the main players come down to the barn," he said, tugging an imaginary forelock. "It's a job, Lieutenant."

"Thanks for getting that damned iron collar off me."

Cubby hefted the black metal object. "This thing here?" he said. "This isn't a real one. It's a new one."

"A fake, you mean?"

"Well, yes and no. It's handmade, and the smith knows his business. Cast iron, hammered true. The chain, handmade, too. The iron's too light, though. This here's modern metal." He handed it back to me.

"And you know this how?"

He smiled. "I'm a fair hand with a forge," he said. "Got to be, working here. Who you messin' with over there on that place?"

"A ghost," I said. "A bad one, too. Wears a white plastic mask and has dead eyes. I think I will keep this, after all. Maybe I can put it back on him one day."

"Somebody tryin' t' tell you somethin'."

"Perhaps," I said. "Or just a passing ghost, bored with life in the country."

"Ghosts," he said. "On the other hand, what's one more, I guess."

I started to leave and then turned around. "Yass'm?"

"Go on now," he said. "Don't make me sic Devil on you."

"This is a no-brainer," Horace said. "Just get your ass out of there. Learn Spanish, then go to Argentina. There's lots of Germans down there. They'll love the dogs."

I had the gang of three on a speakerphone downtown at H&S. I'd told them what had happened. None of them could make a connection with my killing someone's wife.

"Horace is right," Pardee said. "This guy's been watching and planning for some time. You go one on one with him, he'll take you down, especially out there in the bushes of Rockwell County."

"He did pretty well in Summerfield, too," I said. "But I see your point."

"Exactly," Horace said, "and he's a killer. I'll bet he's the guy who took out Billie Ray. Has to be, which means he's got it in him."

"So what was all that shooting through the windows shit? And why a barrio bang stick instead of doing it himself?"

"Who knows with these psychos?" Pardee said. "The point is, he's a sick bastard, and you need to get out of his line of fire."

"Well, supposedly whatever's going down is about to start. I'm not disposed to run, just yet. I just got here, remember?"

"Okay, boss," he replied, "but shouldn't some of us be out there? You bring a crowd, it may slow him down some. Complicate his planning."

"He mentioned that," I said. "Bring help, he said, and they'll get to play."

"Well, shit," Tony piped up. "You're not the only one bored with all this paperwork. Be fun to shoot somebody again."

"You brief the Rockwell County sheriff yet?" Horace asked.

"Very next call," I said. "Although he'll probably invite my young ass to get out of Dodge, too, especially if the Lee ladies weigh in and want me gone. I guess I wouldn't blame 'em."

"You need to listen to all those folks telling you to boogie," Horace said. "That's the best near-term option. Give us time to find out what he's mad about, regroup, and go chase his ass."

"I'll think about it," I said. "Lemme call the sheriff here, see what he says, and then I'll get back to you. First, though, I have to go to tea up at the big house with my Auntie Bellums."

"Tea?"

"Personal invitation. The hell of it is, I've got nothing to wear."

"Simplify your life," Tony said. "Go nekkid."

Sheriff Walker echoed the consensus from downtown. He still sounded friendly, but naturally he was concerned with the impact my stalker problem might have on his little county kingdom.

"Sounds like a wet-brain to me," he said.

"Agreed, but I'm not the running type. Makes my feet hurt."

"Personally? I'd probably want to go a round or two with him, too. Professionally? Your people are right. You're all alone, way behind the power curve, and there's nobody like a slate-eye for cold planning. You haven't closed on that land deal yet, have you?"

"Nope."

"Well, then, you won't have lost anything, except maybe your earnest money. Put your dogs in that new Suburban and get out of there. This evening. Go somewhere totally illogical. It might just be that you and Glory's End just wasn't meant to be."

His mention of the plantation surprised me. "You think there's a connection?" I asked.

There was the slightest hesitation before he answered. "That place," he said and then stopped for a moment. "That place has a bloody history. Some folks around here believe it's cursed, starting with the feud between the two families, and then what happened at the end of the War. It seems to attract blood violence."

"Kind of like I do," I said. "Maybe we're well suited after all."

"Your call, Lieutenant," he said. "And if you need police, we'll come anytime you dial 911. But my advice? Get out. Get away from this guy. Regroup, and then see what's what."

*Regroup,* I thought. *Everyone wants me to regroup.* "All good advice, Sheriff," I said. "Tell me, what does one wear to afternoon tea at Laurel Grove?"

"Oh, my," he said. "Aren't you the social climber. Is Ms. Hester Lee going to be pouring?"

"Don't know."

"Well, assuming yes, let's see. Gray wool trousers over polished riding boots. Long-sleeved, formal shirt, with ruffles. A narrow black ribbon tie and a satin waistcoat. A dark gray thigh-length afternoon jacket, gray gloves, and a walking stick. Don't forget your top hat and your calling cards. If you need to carry, it will have to be a derringer in your boot top."

"Unh-hunh."

"You did ask."

"Jeans won't hack it?"

"That's a big N-O. Or, better yet, take a rain check on the tea party. Tell them you simply have nothing to wear. Get the flock out of there. Your psycho-ghost doesn't sound like a tea drinker to me."

I thanked him for all the advice and said I'd think about it. Then I called the guys back at the office and reported what the sheriff had said. They waited for me to say that I was going to follow the consensus. I reminded them that consensus was not my style. That got me a chorus of ooooohh's, and one of them did a passable reprise of the whistle from *The Good, The Bad, and The Ugly*. No respect. I decided to go to tea.

I hate tea.

High tea at Laurel Grove was just about as surreal as encountering the major in the moonlight. I showed up promptly at five, wearing a blue blazer, a long-sleeved business shirt with tie, and gray slacks. I hadn't had a tie on in a long time. It felt like a noose, or a slave collar. Mrs. Johnson greeted me rather formally at the door and escorted me to the drawing room to the right of the main hall. There was another drawing room behind closed doors, on the left-hand side of the hall. A large formal staircase went up and around the entrance hall. There were two doors giving access to the middle landing, and then another flight of stairs to the actual second floor.

The house inside was absolutely locked in the time warp. Heart-pine floors were polished with what smelled like real beeswax. The carpets were oriental and thin from decades of use. There were unlit candles everywhere on tables and in wall sconces, and the furniture was covered in slipcovers and antimacassars. There was a small fire going in the fireplace, although it was easily sixty-five outside. A large if plain chandelier hung in the main hall, filled with candles. There were dozens of dark portraits on the walls, mostly of Lee ancestors, I assumed.

The ladies were in position when I arrived. That's what it looked like, as if they'd been set up as stage props in a Civil War movie. Ms. Valeria was dressed all in white, and Ms. Hester, whom I was meeting for the first time, was all in black. I was sure there was significance to the color scheme but didn't know what it was. The sheriff had been right: There was a silver calling card tray right next to the drawing room entrance. Unfortunately I was fresh out of calling cards. Mrs. Johnson showed me into the room, bowed slightly, then left.

"Mother, may I present Lieutenant Cameron Richter?" Valeria said. She did not stand up but continued to sit in the large chair with her back straight as a ramrod.

Ms. Hester looked to be in her early seventies, although it was hard to tell. As Cubby had said, they were both well preserved. There was a definite resemblance between mother and daughter, but the femininity had long ago drained out of Ms. Hester's face. I was reminded of that sepia-colored picture of the last empress of China, with her rigid hair, dark, almost black eyes under penciled brows, squared shoulders, and white, bony hands. Cubby had said she rode daily, and she certainly looked fit.

"Welcome to Laurel Grove, sir," she pronounced in a refined southern accent. "Please do sit down."

There was one chair that obviously had been positioned for me, and I sat down. There was an empty, slightly larger chair to Ms. Hester's immediate right, and I wondered if the major was going to join us. I noticed the portrait hanging over the fireplace. It displayed a handsome young man dressed in what looked like a cavalry uniform, and I wondered if it was an early portrait of the major.

"Mr. Richter was a policeman, Mother. He was a lieutenant in the sheriff's office, down in the city. Now he is retired."

"Are you retired, Mr. Richter?" Hester asked. "You seem much too young to be retired."

"Retired from active police work, Ms. Hester," I replied. "I run a company down in Triboro that does investigations work for private individuals."

"Ah, so then you are a private detective, is that it?" She

was speaking as if she were going through the motions, asking about me and my work but not really very interested. Valeria had an idle smile on her face, as if she were waiting for the real fun to start.

"In a manner of speaking, yes. We do investigation work for people who're unwilling to wait for the police to get around to it, or who are dissatisfied with what the police have already done."

"I see," she said. There was a clattering noise from the main hallway, and Hester frowned. Apparently the tea cart was supposed to make a more stealthy approach. She gave Mrs. Johnson a disapproving look when that worthy rounded the corner with an eighteenth-century wheeled tea trolley, complete with a silver tea service and the smallest cookies I'd ever seen. Mrs. Johnson ignored the look, which told me that there was probably something of a long-standing guerrilla war going on between the domestic and the madam of the house.

After we went through the one-lump-or-two drill, Hester asked me what I planned to do with Oak Grove plantation. I told her, while trying not to spill any tea from a cup that seemed to be made from a single eggshell. I hate tea in all its forms, which meant that I would be trying to balance a full cup for the duration of the call. I used the word "preserve" liberally, as Carol had suggested.

"Do you know, Mr. Richter," Hester said, "that there are many connections between Laurel Grove and Oak Grove? I do not approve of the new name, as you may have noticed. I believe it's rather like renaming a ship, which, tradition has it, invites bad fortune."

"I'm very new here, Ms. Hester," I said. "The history is what it is, I suppose. I wouldn't presume to rename it again."

She nodded at that. I think she liked that I-wouldn't-presume part.

"I've noticed that the gates have been returned," she

said. I then explained about Carol Pollard and how she was going to help me with the project.

"Valeria here knows quite a bit about that house, Mr. Richter," she said when I was finished. "She took care of Mrs. Tarrant for some years, and of course Valeria was born and grew up here on the plantations."

Ms. Valeria was studying her tea while Hester launched into a recitation about how long the Lees had been here and how much Valeria knew about all that rich and immensely interesting history. She was speaking almost as if her daughter were either somewhere else or an item being offered for sale at an auction. I took it all on board, slowly recognizing that Hester was, in a way, shopping her daughter to the new bachelor in the neighborhood. I almost laughed when I figured it out, until I caught a subtle warning glance from Valeria. I realized then that I really was a player in a carefully staged scene and that Valeria expected me to do my duty and humor the old lady. Patience Johnson had retired to the main hallway, where she sat in a hall chair, hands crossed in her lap, the servant in waiting. *How does she do it*? I wondered.

"I look forward to learning a great deal from Ms. Valeria," I said when Hester finally ran out of steam. "Carol Pollard has warned me that the restoration project will take some time, years probably."

"Do you already know what you want to do with the house?"

"Well, safety issues first, wiring, plumbing, that sort of thing. Then a repaint inside, especially those ceilings with all the occult artwork. I want to restore it to contemporary livability without hurting the historical aspects. Like I said, it'll take years, probably."

Hester nodded slowly. Suddenly she looked preoccupied.

"It took more than a few years to get it to where it is,"

Valeria said, rejoining the conversation at last. "Some of them more difficult than others."

"Yes, I can imagine," I said. "One of the first things I wish to do is to restore that cemetery up by the river bridge. I think those folks deserve a little more respect than an empty field."

"Rubbish," declared Hester. "They failed in their duty. They allowed some Georgia riffraff to steal the Confederate government's historical legacy. They did not fire a single shot. They are buried exactly as they should be, as discards, to be summarily forgotten."

"Mother," Valeria said gently, "Oak Grove will be Mr. Richter's to do with as he sees fit. We must trust in his good judgment now."

Hester gave me a semistony look. "I would hope that good judgment is indeed the governing rule," she said. "The weight of Lee family history will be sitting squarely on your shoulders, young man."

"Really?"

"Yes, really. In my opinion, you will hold that property in trust, and if the need arises, the Lees in this county can make your ownership of it a tenuous matter indeed."

"In trust? I thought it was going to be in fee simple absolute. At least that's what the deed's going to say."

There was a moment of strained silence. Hester fixed me with a stare that would have done an eagle proud.

"A deed, sir," she said slowly, "is only as good as the provenance of the title. The title to that property is a matter of complex history."

"I don't doubt that, Ms. Hester," I said. "That's why I'm having an attorney do a complex title search, all the way back to just before the carpetbagger era."

"Yes," she said. "So we understand. Whatley Lee, if I'm not mistaken?"

"Right."

"He is a cousin, sir."

"A good title search lawyer, I'm told. An officer of the court, and a man of principle. Is that the Whatley Lee we're talking about?"

"Without doubt, Mr. Richter," she said, putting down her teacup. She seemed suddenly tired of all the subtext. I wasn't backing down, and I think she'd decided to try another tack at another time. Valeria, looking concerned now, switched the conversation over to the farmland across the street and what might be done with it. I asked Hester how she rented out her lands, and off we went, veering quite nicely away from the contentious subject of how the new guy was going to behave, or not. At precisely thirty minutes, the call was over.

"It has been a pleasure to make your acquaintance, Mr. Richter," Hester said. "Please do proceed conservatively in your endeavors to restore Oak Grove. Some parts of that estate would be better left alone. Not everything that happened there brought honor to the families involved."

I stood up and replaced my teacup and saucer on the tray as gently as I could, hoping they didn't notice that most of the tea was still on board. "A pleasure and an honor to meet you, Ms. Hester," I said, with a bow of my head. "Please be assured that I will not do anything over there to cause either the neighbors or the history to be distressed."

"Ms. Valeria will see you to the door, then, Mr. Richter," she said and then looked away and sipped her tea.

Dis-missed, soldier.

We walked toward Mrs. Johnson, who had moved to the massive front door and opened it. She was standing to one side, staring into the middle distance, which I guessed was supposed to make her invisible.

"Thank you ever so much for joining us, Mr. Richter," Valeria said when we reached the door. I was struck again by her complete poise and extraordinary posture, as if nothing could ever shake her. I considered coming out of character to ask her what the hell that had all been about, but with Mrs. Johnson right there, I just murmured some more inane your-obedient-servant pleasantries and took my leave. The door shut behind me like a vault door, softly but with definite authority.

As I walked back to the stone cottage I marveled at how easily I had slipped into their stilted ways of speech and all the overdone formality. Ms. Hester had seemed to be sincerely in character, but I wondered if Valeria might not be on some soothing substance. Laudanum came to mind.

The mutts seemed glad to see me when I got back from high tea. Kitty's nose was still swollen, but Frick's had come down to a small furry clot. Frack thought they were both cowards to have left the barn with the cat still alive. Frack, on the other hand, had not met said cat.

I made a drink to wash the thin taste of tea out of my mouth and went out onto the porch overlooking the pond to watch the sun go down. There were decisions to be made. I really didn't feel like running. I'd bought this place to get out of the city and start a new phase in my life, however undefined that might be. I was looking forward to doing something different, and also something that would result in a tangible achievement, something beyond the usually hollow victory over assorted bad guys. Now here came some sumbitch with a lethal grudge, two powerful Dobermans, and a desire to play Most Dangerous Game.

So far he'd held the initiative, and if he'd taken the time to train two attack dogs, he'd also taken the time to plan this thing out. The one physical factor that was new to both of us was Glory's End. He couldn't know that ground any better than I did. Great. I guessed that we'd flounder around out there on seven hundred acres until we collided.

An evening breeze stirred all the willows around the pond. They looked like a circle of pale green hula dancers out there as the shadows lengthened over Laurel Grove.

I heard an engine start up behind the big house, run for a minute, and then shut down. Cubby must have achieved a victory over whatever it was plaguing the tractor.

I made my decision: Screw it. I wouldn't run. I'd get Tony and Pardee to come out here and camp out in the cottage with me, while Horace put his nose to the ground. Tomorrow I would go out to the county airfield and hire a plane. If my stalker was serious about getting it on out here, I didn't have time to scout all of Glory's End on foot, but from a small plane, I could assemble a collage of aerial pictures in an hour or so. Now I needed to make a list—weapons, survival gear, personal protection vests, tactical comms, and perhaps some even bigger perspective pictures from Google Earth.

"C'mon, fuzz balls," I said. "Don't just lie there and shed. We've got work to do."

From four thousand feet, Glory's End still looked like a green rectangle with three large ripples in it. The one on the western edge was the ridge above the old rail line where the major kept his morning coffee camp. The ridge in the middle contained the house and outbuildings, and the last one, on the eastern side, overlooked croplands on both sides as well as the flooded quarry. The Dan River showed a slate color on the northern edge, and the Laurel Grove plantation extended along the two-lane, overlapping my property by a few miles on each side. I could see the millpond but not the cottage.

I'd done this before, but not with the specific objective of aerial pictures. Tony and Pardee sat in the backseat of the four-seater we'd chartered, taking the pictures, while I just studied the farm's layout from the air, trying to make a tactical assessment of where someone could be hiding. I was also looking for ambush sites, and vantage points from which one man could see a lot of ground. The topography was clearly visible, but the pilot said that as the summer progressed and the trees filled in, treetops would become the dominant feature on the ridges, and whatever crops were planted would fill in the fields.

We circled the plantation for about fifteen minutes, and I paid particular attention to the eastern side of the last ridge, looking for signs of a coal mine. There was one area where the trees looked thinner than the rest, but nothing definitive. Then I had him fly us over to the Virginia side. I'd been wrong about the property directly opposite being devoid of habitation. There was a large plantation house, semiobscured by a dense grove of really big trees, about a half mile back from the river. The roof was gone, and it looked like there had been a fire. There were four walls, blackened wreckage inside, and four massive chimneys, two on each end. One of those had lost its top. The house was large enough for someone to hide in, but it certainly seemed thoroughly abandoned. The outbuildings resembled those on Glory's End.

Next I had him fly downstream for a few miles past the property. I wanted to see if there were signs of an encampment or a possible base of operations for my ghost. Nothing seemed to qualify. The adjacent farm to the east had its center of operations on its eastern border, leaving an expanse of fields and woods between their house and mine. On the western side there was a vast pine plantation with no houses visible except for a few mobile homes up along the road. We flew back upstream. The barely submerged channel pillar foundations for the Civil War–era railroad bridge were now clearly visible from directly above. I pointed out the site of the train robbery and its attendant cemetery to my two associates.

"Where's the nearest private airstrip?" I asked the pilot.

"Private? None around here," he said. "The regional airport is that way about ten miles. The FAA won't allow any private strips within its terminal control area."

"How about helicopter pads?"

"Wherever they want," he said, banking away from the direction of the airport as a small passenger jet hissed overhead, letting down for an approach.

An hour later we had lunch in town. Pardee had brought up one of the office portables. He said he could download all the pictures he had taken and then produce a mosaic. Tony was clicking through all the overhead shots on his camera's view-screen.

"Whole lotta trees going on down there," he said. "Those three ridges—more trees and big rocks."

"Your point being?"

"My point being that it would be pointless to go patrolling in that kind of terrain. I say we set up at the big house, make him come to us."

I nodded. I'd pretty much decided the same thing. We could go tramping all over that plantation and not find my stalker until we stumbled into an ambush. If we made him come to us, we could focus our defensive assets. The only problem would be if he decided not to play our game. He could always just walk away, for now, and see how long we were willing to hole up on the hill.

"Or," Pardee said, "we make it look like we're holed up in the big house but then set up on the perimeter." Pardee had been in the army and did not like the idea of being trapped in a house without any scouts out.

"He know that house?" Tony asked.

"I think he does," I said. "He caught me on the porch and then left by going back into the house, not around it. He's at least been inside, and maybe even knows stuff we don't."

"Then there's our plan," Tony said. "Let's get set up there and then go find all the secret passageways and hidden dungeons."

"How much help will we get from local law?" Pardee asked while the waitress cleared our table. As three obvious strangers sitting in one corner, we'd attracted some curious stares from the locals.

"Once we get set up," I said, "I'd like to invite Sheriff Walker out to the house, show him what we're doing. You see how these locals are looking at us. It's a really small town. Maybe he and his people can watch for strangers, especially ones with two big Dobes."

"What's the Rockwell County operation like?"

"Small," I said. "Nowhere near as big as Manceford County, but it's not Mayberry RFD, either."

"So no chance for round-the-clock assets?"

"I wouldn't think so. We're gonna be on our own unless it spills over into the community. Then I just don't know."

"We'll need comms with them, something besides 911."

"Right," I said, "and we need to be careful about what we say in both the house and the cottage. Have to assume they're both bugged."

"Where the hell does a civilian get surveillance devices, bugs, and all that stuff?" Tony asked.

"If he was in that business for a long time, he could have accumulated some shit," Pardee said. "Like I have."

"Did he sound old?" Tony asked.

"What, like me?" I asked.

Tony rolled his eyes.

"He didn't sound young, but he had that white film all over his face. He mostly sounded like a guy with a mask on."

"I can get us some commercial surveillance gear," Pardee said. "Is there power over there?"

"Some, if you don't mind pennies in the fuse slots."

"Electronics don't eat many amps," Pardee said. "I can get it swept. Then maybe rig a video system and I can set up a local cell phone network."

"One last thing," Tony said. "Who's gonna cook?"

While Tony and Pardee went back to Triboro to get more gear, I met with Carol at the cottage. I told her that I was going to suspend the renovation project for a little while in order to take care of a problem.

"This that stalker thing you were talking about?"

"Yup. He's followed me out here, and now we're apparently going to settle things."

"Brilliant," she said.

I looked at her.

"Why don't you just go on vacation?" she asked. "Give it to the sheriff and get out of the way? Then regroup and—"

I started laughing and then had to explain it to her. She shook her head, and I had the sense that she was a little disappointed in me. I told her about my meeting of man and beasts on the front porch. "Look, Carol," I said, "this is no dumb-ass jailbird. This guy is educated, probably ex-military or even a cop, and he's really determined. He as much as said I could run wherever I wanted to and he'd just be waiting whenever I came back."

"Running's not your style, right?"

"Exactly right. I'll back out of any tactical situation that's impossible, but if someone's determined to rumble, then I can do that."

"You know you sound like just any thirteen-year-old, don't you?"

"Perhaps," I said, "but you know what? My business for too many years was dealing with strong, aggressive, violent men whose development had pretty much terminated at thirteen. Besides, you know what they say: The difference between the cops and robbers is a piece of tin."

She waved her hands in an I-give-up gesture. "I'm sorry," she said. "I have zero right to lecture you. It's not like I made a success out of being a cop."

"You made a mistake. We all make mistakes, and I'm no exception. Unfortunately for you, it was the kind of mistake that the brotherhood won't forgive, so you also made the right decision to give it up. Essentially, though, this is what

I do, Carol. I came out here for some new directions. Guess what?"

"Yeah," she said. "I get it. How can I help you?"

I grinned then. "That's better," I said. "You can help me, or us, actually—I've summoned some backup. You can help by paying attention to new people in the area. New faces, people mentioning a guy going around with two big Dobermans, a vehicle you see running down that two-lane out there more than once. Like that."

"Do the Lees know about all this?"

"Valeria knows something's up. She was there when Cubby took that collar off."

"That's Ms. Valeria," she reminded me.

"Oh, right," I said, although, based on Valeria's body language at the tea party, it might not be. Carol, ever the attentive female, gave me an inquiring look. "Careful, big guy," she said. "That's very deep still water."

"That or superbly medicated," I said and described the tea party.

Her cell phone went off just then. It was the Realtor calling, asking if she knew where I might be. Apparently the title attorney was available to take the job and asking if he should proceed. She handed me the phone, and I told him to go ahead with it. Oatley said this would delay closing, because Whatley Lee did not do anything quickly. He proposed the alternative of my buying title insurance, but by now I was more than a little curious.

"The survey bring-up and the title search have become important," I told him. "I'm willing to wait. With a cash buyer in the offing, I suspect the sellers are willing to wait, too, right?"

He agreed with that notion and said he'd take care of it. I switched off the phone and handed it back to Carol.

"Does anyone do reenactments around here?" I asked.

She shook her head. "There weren't any real battles

here," she said. "The anniversary of the train robbery is coming up in a few days, but the people most associated with that sad business would rather just forget it."

"Got that right," I said and told her what Hester had thought about my cleaning up the graves on the hill, perhaps turning it into a historical site.

"Just remember," she said, "if you do that, you must grant perpetual access to any and all descendants of any of the men who died there. That could mean a lot of strangers tramping through your property."

I hadn't thought of that. For that matter, I hadn't thought of a lot of things when I made the decision to buy this piece of property. The history could cut both ways, apparently.

"I've got my guys working back through Manceford County Sheriff's Office records on the wife-shooting conundrum," I said. "My bad guy kept saying that it would come to me, but damned if I can remember anything like that."

"You've talked to him?"

"In a manner of speaking," I said and elaborated on the porch encounter.

"That's scary," she said. "Especially the Dobermans."

"Well, I guess I can't complain. I run around with German shepherds, don't I? The real problem is that, so far, he's holding the initiative. That's what's scary."

"Maybe it means that you locked him up, and his wife then killed herself out of despair. Something like that?"

I hadn't considered that. It would certainly widen the scope of possibilities.

We talked about other, less frightening things for a few minutes, and then she had to go. She said she'd be in touch and left.

I called Horace and asked him to expand his search to look for dog trainers who specialized in Dobermans, again statewide. I needed to find a guy who'd had two dogs trained in the past five years for attack work. He said he'd get right on it. Then I passed along Carol's idea. He groaned. That would make a really big search effort. I told him to forget it unless nothing else panned out.

Once Carol left I grabbed my SIG, the two operational shepherds, and a walking stick. We headed out into the forests and fields of Laurel Grove this time. I dropped by the shop behind the big house, but Cubby had already gone for the day. The sunset was bright yellow, and I wished I'd brought some sunglasses. I thought I saw movement behind the curtains in one of the upstairs rooms, but it was probably just my imagination.

"C'mon, you hairballs," I told the shepherds. "Let's go find that cat."

At the mention of the word "cat," they both gave me a look that said, *Let's not and say we did.*

The Laurel Grove plantation was quite different from Glory's End. For one thing it was an active farm, so there were many more dirt roads, and the fields were all either in crops or being readied for planting. The terrain was rolling, but the ridges of Glory's End subsided into the ground on this side of the road. We walked for an hour into early nightfall and then returned to the cottage. I walked the dogs around the building to see if they alerted on anything, but they did not react. The moon was low in the sky, and the night was going to be clear. I checked the Suburban, locked it, and went inside. I put Frick on the front porch on her dog bed, and Kitty came in the house with me. She was not only bigger than Frick but seemed to have a more developed protective sense. Frick was getting a bit independent in her old age.

Once inside we went through the rooms and generally checked the place out. If someone else had been in the cottage since we'd left, Kitty would have been following scent trails, but she appeared to be mostly bored. I checked on Frick, who'd not been happy being left outside, especially when Kitty got to come in, but she was on her dog bed, watching the lawn. It had been much easier to train Kitty with Frick around, because dogs learn best from other dogs.

I turned off all the lights in the cottage except one in the bedroom and closed the curtains in that room. Then I found the bottle of single malt, sat on the couch in the living room, and called Pardee at home. His wife, Alicia, was a trial lawyer in Triboro and one tough lady. She asked if he could call me back as they were sitting down to dinner. Pardee was back to me in twenty minutes.

"Sorry to intrude," I said.

"She's a little pissed that I'm going camping again," he said, "but I'm not."

"Joys of married life," I said. "Get the stuff?"

"Pretty much. Tony's working on a couple things. Horace is tackling the dog trainer business."

I remembered then my own caution about the cottage possibly being bugged, but I didn't want to step outside. "How's the hive?" I asked.

"The hive" was a code word we'd decided on to indicate that we thought there was a bug or two within range of the conversation. Hive, as in many bugs. It took Pardee a second to get it, but then he did. "We're working on that, too," he said. "I talked to the young blond lady down at the ranch. She said she could get us something to deal with that."

"Great," I said. "She knows her stuff, actually. I'm staying here for the night, and then I'll contact one of you in the morning to see what's next, and where."

"Got it," he said. "Or you could come down here for the night, stay with us, and then catch your plane to the Seychelles."

*Factor that*, I mentally told any listening devices. "Thanks for the invite, but I'll wager Alicia is giving you that serious trial lawyer frown, as we speak."

"Well . . ."

"Yeah, right. Hasta mañana, Detective Sergeant."

From the couch I was able to see out onto the front lawns and down to the millpond. There was still enough moonlight to see pretty well outside, and I had a good view of the dam and the road that crossed it. Old Frack was a dark furry ball in the corner of the living room. Kitty waited by the bedroom door so she could assume her sentry post. I called her over to the couch and gestured for her to curl up next to me. It took her a good second or so to make a decision about that. I had her on one side, my SIG on the other, and the world's supply of Scotch. I waited for something to happen, and within minutes fell sound asleep.

The next morning I awoke with a start and a stiff neck. Kitty wanted to go outside to piddle, so I let her and the elder statesman out with Frick. I made the dogs' morning chow, put the bowls out on the front porch, and then went into the bathroom to take a shower. I took the SIG with me, although I felt a little foolish with a loaded .45 parked on the towel rack. When I came out into the bedroom, showered, shaved, and partially awake, I opened the curtains. There were two windows in the bedroom, and when I opened the second curtain, there was the guy in the white mask staring back at me. I nearly jumped out of my skin and was bringing up the SIG when I realized what it was: Someone had taped a life-sized picture of that white rubber face to the glass from the outside, looking in.

I went to the kitchen and made some coffee, trying to think whether I'd actually looked out those windows last night before I closed the curtains. The bedside table light had been on, and I couldn't imagine that I would not have seen that bright white face staring at me. That meant that he'd come in the night, without alerting the German shepherd out on the front porch. My stalker must be an expert creep. There'd been a very slight breeze, and it had been coming across the pond, which was on the opposite side of the cottage, so he would have been coming up into the wind. Still—neither Frick nor Kitty had heard anything to cause them to alert, and their hearing was a damn sight better than mine.

So: Elvis was in the building, or at least in the neighborhood. Not great. Not great at all. It also meant he'd had time to rig anything he wanted to over in the deserted mansion at Glory's End. Hell, for all I knew he was holed up there, using it as his base of operations. First order of business, then, would be to sweep the environs of that hill very thoroughly, but not until my partners arrived.

Pardee showed up an hour later, and Tony was right behind him with a minivan. I stepped outside to avoid listening devices and told them what had happened overnight and what we had to do. Pardee got out some sweep gear and went through the cottage, finding no bugs. He suggested we do the same thing to the old house at Glory's End, but I said no. I remembered what the young blond tech had said about how a listening device could work for two masters.

We took all three vehicles and both shepherds with us, leaving Frack to guard his dog bed in the living room. We started with the house itself, and I again put Frick on watch outside and took Kitty with us into the house. We went room by room, checking walls, floors, and windows on all three floors, then the attic, and then we tramped down into the basement. I showed the guys where I thought there might be a false wall, and Tony went outside to get some tear-down tools.

It turned out to be much harder than we'd anticipated. Tony's crowbar and claw hammer were no match for 160-year-old, two-inch-thick oak boards. We then searched for the secret latch, because by now we were convinced there was something behind this damned panel of shelves.

"Maybe it only opens from the other side," Pardee said. "No latch or key on this side."

"Then what's the point?" Tony said, trying once more to pry something loose. The wine rack next to this shelf moved easily.

"Ultimate bolt-hole?" Pardee said. "You keep the door wedged open in times of danger and then close it behind you if you have to run?"

"Let's go outside," I said. "We'll start with the smoke-house. It's the biggest outbuilding."

It was pretty ingenious once we finally found it, and it was in the smokehouse. The building was a tall brick structure, maybe fifteen feet square, with heavily blackened beams overhead and a dirt fire pit right in the middle of the earthen floor. There were two cradle-shaped wrought-iron andirons in the fire pit. A few dozen badly blackened bricks were stacked on one side of the smokehouse. Tony was the one who figured it out. He grabbed the andirons and pulled up. The bottom of the fire pit was actually a wooden hatch, balanced on two thick pins, so that it came up like a trap-door. Once we had it open we could see that the top of the hatch was a sheet of hammered metal. A few inches of baked-on red clay concealed the metal surface. Underneath the hatch a crude wooden ladder emerged from the cloud of fireplace ashes. It went down about ten feet into a brick-lined tunnel. The direction of the tunnel pointed right back to the big house.

"Bingo," Pardee said. "Who's up for a tour?"

Tony shook his head. He was claustrophobic and said he would stand guard on this end while we explored.

Pardee went down first, and I followed. The tunnel was lined with the same handmade brick out of which every-thing seemed to be constructed. The mortar looked even more floury than the exterior bricks, and as we walked, our footfalls produced faint wisps of white powder out of the arched ceiling. The air was cold and dry, and the floor was hard-packed earth. Our flashlights lit the tunnel up pretty well, but it was narrow enough that we could not walk side by side. The floor seemed to slope down as we proceeded, and the tunnel bent around to the left before we finally came to an alcove, which required a step down. I noticed that the right-hand wall near the alcove was actually a huge outcrop of granite, which had probably been the reason for the bending in the tunnel.

"Bingo number two," Pardee said, hunched over now because the ceiling was much lower here. We were facing a dogleg turn in the tunnel, first to the right and then to the left, all within four feet. "Somebody thinking tactical," he said. "Nobody could stand in the basement and shoot down the full length of the tunnel while folks were running."

There was a heavy wooden door in the alcove, latched by a solid bar of black wrought iron encased in two brackets on either side of the doorway. The door was hinged at three levels with more black iron. Pardee pulled out the bar, and the door swung quietly on obviously oiled hinges into the tunnel, revealing the darkness of the basement on the other side. Mystery solved: It was a one-way escape door, opening only in the direction of safety.

"You guys cool down there?" Tony called. The tunnel was nearly a hundred feet long, and his voice was muffled by that dogleg turn. Pardee told him we were okay and relatched the door.

"Actually," I said, "let's close it and wedge it with something that will allow us to open it from the other side. This was a bolt-hole, and we may need one."

Pardee looked over at me. "You really think so?"

"We're playing dumb defense right now," I said. "Until we can change that, we're the ones who need options."

He pushed the big door back into its frame and wedged it by crushing a ballpoint pen in the crack. We left the bar on the floor and went back to the smokehouse access ladder. Tony was staring down at us from the hole above.

"You find the door?" he asked.

Pardee described it to him as we climbed out.

"Okay, now what?" Tony asked.

"We look for a second one," I said. "This was too obvious."

We closed up the hatch cover in the smokehouse fire pit, smoothed out the ashes, and went back into the kitchen through a set of steps leading down from the back courtyard. Kitty greeted us as we stepped through the door. The access to the basement level had been through the right-hand pantry room in the kitchen. I hadn't yet examined the left-hand pantry, where we found the electric fuse box, a rusty-looking hot water heater, a blue pressure tank, and what looked like an electric water pump. As the electrician had described, some of the fuses had failed at some point and were now sporting copper pennies under their bases. The box was ancient, and there were only ten identifiable round slots for circuits. The wiring was thick copper, covered in black fabric instead of vinyl.

"Why a pressure tank and a water pump?" Pardee asked, ever the techie.

"Big house?" said Tony. "System needs a booster?"

"Or," I said, "there's no operational well and the water comes from that old springhouse on the hillside."

Tony looked at his watch and announced that it was lunchtime. Tony kept track of such things; he was thin as a rail but ate more than both of us. We went into town for a sandwich. I took Kitty with me and left Frick in the house this time, promising her some fries and ketchup if she was a good girl. Over lunch we kicked around other possibilities for a second escape tunnel and decided to just go back there and do a hand-over-hand search of that whole lower floor. We stopped by the Realtor's office, and I signed a professional services contract for Lawyer Lee, which devoted one line to the title search but covered his fees in exquisite detail. Mr. Oatley gave me the name and contact information for the surveyor he recommended and said it should not be a difficult job because the plantation was essentially a rectangle.

Once back at Glory's End, we searched again for a second passage. If finding the first one was too easy, finding the second was too hard. We gave up after three hours and went back out to the front porch. Tony had a six-pack in his truck cooler, so we each cracked one and watched the afternoon subside. Frick was out on the lawn hunting for any ketchup packs she'd missed. Kitty sat on the front porch next to me, getting an ear rubbed.

"I don't know, boss," Tony said. "Guy says we'll get it on any day now, and then, shit, he could go off to Disney World for the week. Leave us high and dry."

"Somebody put that mask picture on my window last night," I said. "Can't do that from Disney World."

"Still," Pardee said. "Assuming he's been watching, he knows it's three against one now. That's what I would do—wear us out with waiting."

I thought that Pardee was hinting at something besides the fact that we did not have the initiative here. He could only stay out here for so long before Alicia started to complain.

"That's true," I said. "So we need to do something to change that equation. Something he doesn't expect."

"You mean something dumb," Tony observed.

"Probably," I said. "He'll expect us to take up a defensive position. So let's don't. Let's leave here, go three separate ways, meet somewhere else, and then come back tonight after dark with our gear."

"But return separately," Pardee said. "Come from three

different directions, converging eventually here at the big house. Maybe we get lucky. Surprise him. Flush his ass out."

"If he's even here," Tony said.

"I think he is," I said. Then I heard the sound of hoofbeats coming up from behind the house.

"Pardee, get inside," I said. "Now."

Pardee gave me a funny look but moved quickly to the front door and went inside the house. A few seconds later, the major came around the corner in full regalia, silhouetted for a moment in the lowering sun. Both dogs reacted and I called them down before they spooked the horse. Tony silently mouthed the words "holy shit."

"Major," I said, surreptitiously hiding my beer bottle.

"Overseer," he replied, reining in the horse and leaning back in the saddle. The cavalry saber swayed at his hip after the horse came to a stop.

"What news, Major?"

"Spies," he said. "I've seen Yankee spies. I observed one over at the brickworks an hour ago. Lurking amongst the kilns. Wished I'd had a rifle."

That piqued my interest. A lone individual at the brickworks? That could be our guy.

"Perhaps I'll saddle up and go have a look," I said. "I do have a rifle."

"Excellent," he said. "Who is this gentleman?"

"An agent from Richmond," I said. "He's a spy hunter. Looking for Pinkertons. Richmond is very concerned."

"As well they should be," the major said. "Very well. Report what you find, overseer. Do not be circumspect. If you see one of those bastards, gun him down forthwith."

"I'll do it, Major. I surely will."

"Then good day, sir," he said to me. He nodded at Tony, who was staring at him in total amazement, and rode off down the driveway toward Laurel Grove.

"You can come out now," I called to Pardee.

"Mo-ther-fuck," Tony said quietly. "That guy gonzo or what."

Pardee walked back out on the porch.

"Sorry about that," I said, "but a black man sitting up here with the 'overseer' would probably have produced that hogleg he carries."

"So that's the major," Pardee said. "He doesn't look all that crazy."

"Yeah, he does," Tony said. "You see those eyes? Dude's out there, guys; w-a-a-y out there. And what's this 'overseer' shit?"

I explained it to him. "He said he saw a lone individual at the brickworks," I reminded them. "That may be our guy."

"Wanna take a shot?" Pardee asked.

"Yes, I do—but first, let's set the scene a little bit."

It was full dark when we jumped off. Before leaving the house, we'd gone back in and pretended to search for the passage some more. Then I'd announced to whatever bug might be listening that I was getting tired of this shit. On cue, Pardee had suggested that he and Tony go back to Triboro for the night and come back out next morning. I'd argued but then agreed, and we'd left. End of Kabuki.

Now, with field gear and weapons in hand, we executed our plan, beginning from the two-lane. We started up at the western boundary of Glory's End. I would go out first, with my objective being the area above the railroad bridge. From there I would go along the river to end up near the brickworks. Pardee would then let Tony off just past the main driveway. He would approach the house from the front, check out the near perimeter, and then set up behind the springhouse, where he could watch both the house itself and the approaches from the barn area. Pardee would continue down the road to the eastern ridge, park, and come in along the meadow that contained the quarry and the brickworks. We'd gone over the aerials and decided to keep it as simple as possible. Once Pardee and I met up at the brick-works, if there was no action, we'd notify Tony and head for the house.

We had two things to worry about: our target and those Dobermans. One of the things I'd asked Pardee to acquire was a set of police dog trainer's arm and leg pads as defense against dog bites. Additionally, we all carried the latest pepper spray pencils, which were mounted on the backs of our tactical gloves. All you had to do was point your hand, make a fist, and squeeze; the pencils would emit a stream of incapacitating cayenne pepper juice six feet in front of you. We would communicate via text message, using a repeating local cell network box mounted on the top of my Suburban. Combat knives, single-optic night-vision gear, SWAT suits with Kevlar pads, compact head gear with amplifying ear lenses, and a sidearm of choice.

"The Dobes won't bark," I'd reminded them. "They'll just come at a run and go for either an arm, the throat, or the crotch, depending on who trained them. Stand fast, feint one way, and then jump the other way as they spring. They'll land, turn, and that's when you shoot them, spray first, gun second."

"What if we don't see 'em coming?"

"They'll knock you down, so throw up a padded arm or leg and let them bite it. They'll bite and hold on, and it will hurt, even with all that padding. Let that arm go limp, and then use the knife or the spray, whichever you can get at. If you even think they're close, get your back to a tree and ball up. Forget the gun: Get a knife in one hand, pepper spray in the other."

I had brought Frick but not Kitty. I told the other guys that she wasn't ready for this yet, but the truth was, while Frick might or might not win a fight against a Dobe, Kitty was too new at this to have even a chance. Frick, eight going on nine years, would give me precious warning time, and if I was going to lose one, I wasn't going to sacrifice the youngest one. Plus, there would be one less dog in the way if I had to start shooting. I had to keep telling myself that that made it all okay. Frick seemed up for it, but then she always did.

She and I bailed out at the appropriate moment and slipped into the woods. The Suburban's taillights disappeared around the corner. It was a cool, clear night, and we moved off into the trees quickly. The forest here was chiefly pines, which meant we could move quickly across a bed of pine needles without making noise. In twenty minutes we were up on the road end of the western ridge, where I'd first caught the flash of the major's telescope. Frick was ahead, casting for scent, and I could now see down across the cemetery meadow to the remains of the river bridge in the moonlight. The distant house was a grayish shape on its hill, sleeping in the shadow of all those big trees. The outbuildings behind it were clearly visible, so I sat down on a rock and surveyed the house, outbuildings, and barns through my binoculars.

By now Tony should be moving up the line of trees and underbrush along the driveway toward the house, but since the main driveway was sunken below the level of the adjacent fields, it was entirely in shadow. The plan was for him to text me when he reached the springhouse. That would be my signal to come down off the ridge and head for the riverbank. If he hit trouble, I could come downhill rather than uphill to back him up. I continued to sweep the near hillside with the binocs, the slaughterhouse scene of the train robbery, and then the intervening fields surrounding the house on its hill. Frick sat down next to me and kept watch on our close-in surroundings. I didn't fancy the idea of two big Dobes bursting out of the pines behind me at a full run like sleek black torpedoes. My ghost had had a long time to think about this caper, and he'd done the one thing that neutralized my biggest advantage by arming himself with Dobermans.

After twenty minutes of binocular watching, my cell vibrated in its chest holster. I hauled it out.

Tony. IN POSITION, it read. Pardee had rigged the network so that every text call went to both the other phones.

MOVING OUT NOW, I sent back, and then I put it away.

We started down the moonlit hillside, moving from tree to tree as much as possible. I mentally apologized to the sleeping soldiers as we walked over their graves. A screech owl started up back in the pines, and even I could hear the rustle of field birds and startled rabbits scuttling out of our way through the knee-high grass.

I stopped when we got to the railroad embankment. There was no way to cross that while staying concealed. Even with the iron rails long gone, the right-of-way provided a sight channel for a few hundred yards in either direction. Then I remembered the fortified stone bridge abutment to my left. If I went left, down to the river, I could cross under that sight line where the meadow fell off down to the riverbank.

My climb down to the river at the base of the bridge abutment was not entirely graceful. We both ended up at the bottom pursued by a small avalanche of stones and old gravel, some of which rolled into the river itself with what sounded like a lot of noise. *So much for stealth*, I thought, as I picked myself up and brushed the burrs and dirt out of my clothes. The river was flowing silently by, glossy black in the moonlight. The pale face of the opposite bank abutment looked like a tombstone. Frick had her nose down and was headed upriver. I had to snap my fingers to get her going the right way. A big turtle plopped off a snag as I went under the rail line, and a snake took off into the tall grass at the speed of heat, causing Frick to jump straight up in the air.

It was much slower going along the riverbank because of all the debris from floods past. There was the usual American riverbank decor of beer cans, tires, plastic bags of all description, an occasional sodden mass of bedding, and more tires. What was it about a big river that made people want to dump their trash? After clambering over snag after snag, I realized that the river bottom was terraced. There was the immediate bank, then a three-foot terrace inland of that, and another one beyond that, perhaps a hundred feet back from the current banks. Most of the debris was littering the first two terraces, so I elected to move right and up. I could still see the actual riverbank, but I could now make some time in my trek downstream to the brickworks.

I had to detour around that creek mouth where previously I'd seen the evidence of a boat landing. First I went down to the water to see if there were any more signs, but I found nothing but yet more tires. Then I walked inland until I found a place where I could get across the stream on a downed tree trunk. Frick wasn't having it. Ever the water-baby, she went down into the creek, splashed her way across, and then shook off on the other side. Then back we went to the edge of the first terrace and continued downstream. My phone vibrated again.

Pardee this time.

HALFWAY TO BRICKS, it read. SLOW GOING.

ON THE RIVER, I sent back. SLOW GOING.

SOMEONE IN THE HOUSE, came up on the screen from Tony.

I stopped in my tracks, and Frick came back to where I was crouching over the little green screen. Some famished gnats began to gather around the tiny light.

I turned around to look across the field and up the long, grassy slope that led to the house, which was maybe a half mile away. I couldn't see the house itself, or even any of the outbuildings, just the big grove of oaks and a smaller blob that might be the springhouse.

I waited for Tony to elaborate, but nothing came.

I'M BEHIND YOU ON THE RIVER, I texted. WILL COME TO SPRING.

No reply.

BRICKS OR HOUSE? came in from Pardee.

He would have to turn up and over that eastern ridge to get to the house, and there would be no cover at all once he came down from that ridge and got out into the cropland.

BRICKS, I texted back. NO ACTION, RETURN TO ROAD.

GOT IT.

I gathered Frick back from the riverbank, and we turned uphill toward the house. I had the same problem Pardee would have: no cover if I went directly up that long, grassy slope that provided such a magnificent view from the house. There was a single line of smallish trees along a field boundary that led back up to the barn area, but I had to backtrack along the river terrace to get to it. I kept watching my cell screen for anything from Tony, but there was nothing. He wouldn't actually have much cover up there at the springhouse unless he got down into the cooling pool itself. The exterior walls of the springhouse were lattice boards, and the stone foundations stood in two feet of icy water.

I hurried along the river. Once I turned left and started up that tree line, I'd have to proceed very carefully—and quietly. Hopefully, someone in the house didn't automatically mean Dobermans on the grounds. If it wasn't my stalker, then who else would be in the house this late at night? The major? Sex-starved teenagers?

I got to the river end of the tree line, where it merged into the general scrubland along the banks. I turned left, uphill. I kept Frick close in, worried now as much about loose Dobes as making noise. When I got to a tractor break in the line, I hunched down and texted Tony.

STATUS?

No answer.

Not good.

I had a frightening vision of him fighting off two Dobermans in the springhouse while my ghost watched from the lawn. Should I create a distraction? Fire off a gun?

Then the phone vibrated. It was Pardee.

WHERE TONY?

NOT ANSWERING. GOING TO SPRINGHOUSE.

NOTHING HERE. I'LL MAKE NOISE ON DRIVEWAY—
DRIVE HIM INTO YOU.

AGREED.

Pardee had the right idea. He'd always been the tactician on our MCAT cell. If he came up the driveway in my Suburban, lights on, gunning it up the hill, whoever was in the house might bolt in my direction.

Along with his toothy friends?

I took a deep breath. *Well, somebody has to deal with them*, I thought. I patted Frick on the head and then scooted across the tractor break and back into the cover of the tree line, which now featured a tumbled-down stone wall. It wasn't a fancy wall, more like an organized pile of unwanted field rocks, but I got on the side away from the house for additional cover.

When I finally made it to the top of the hill, and about fifty yards from the springhouse, I tried texting Tony again. Still no answer. The springhouse was just a dark blob on the lawn under the big trees. The lattice showed gray in the moonlight. The tiny brook generated by the spring passed under the stone wall right in front of my feet. I waited. If Pardee thought no one was out there, he would make much faster time getting back to the Suburban.

Ten minutes later, I heard a vehicle out on the two-lane. It slowed down and then accelerated noisily onto the gravel driveway. Pardee had the high beams on and was coming as fast as the rutted road allowed. I chose that instant to make my dash for the springhouse, hoping that whoever was in the house would be looking out the front windows or headed for the basement.

The basement, where we'd left that door unlatched.

I veered away from the springhouse and ran across the back lawn to the smokehouse. Just outside was a stone bench next to a sundial garden. I dropped behind the bench and pulled Frick in close to me. I sighted my .45 at the smokehouse door and waited.

Pardee arrived at the front of the house and shut down the engine but kept the high beams pointed into the windows on the ground floor. The light was strong enough that I could see right through the house.

I texted him: STAY PUT, SEE WHAT HAPPENS.

Then I waited.

Absolutely nothing happened. No one came bursting out of the smokehouse door. There were no shadows moving in the house. Tony still wasn't answering. I got a whiff of road dust as the cloud Pardee had generated swept around the house in the night breeze.

Where was Tony?

I turned around slowly, keeping my back firmly against the stone bench, so that I could examine the utility buildings and barn area behind me. There were no black torpedoes headed my way, and Frick seemed relatively relaxed, although alert to the tension I was exhibiting.

I texted Pardee: GONNA SHOOT, SEE WHAT MOVES.

R, for roger.

I made Frick lie down and then pointed the SIG at the barns. I fired four careful rounds, aiming low at each building so as to blow wood bits onto anyone hiding back there. My ears rang when I was finished, and I had to pat Frick on the head again. She hated gunfire.

Then from the area of the springhouse I heard someone making the noise of a submarine Klaxon. A moment later, a dripping wet Tony climbed out of the springhouse and called my name.

We regrouped at the cottage a half hour later. Tony sat in the living room in a bathrobe while the ancient dryer restored his clothes to usefulness. He had a glass of some kind of horrible dago grappa, while Pardee and I had Scotch.

Tony had filled us in on his excellent adventures. He'd seen a dark shape move past one of the windows in the back of the house, on the main floor. He'd gotten off that last text message and then moved to one end of the springhouse to get a better look.

"You said they'd come fast, but you failed to define fast," he'd said. "Those bastards came in like bullets."

"And everything I told you went right out of that pointy little head."

"No," he said. "It went right out my bunghole. Thought I heard something. Turned my head around. Saw two sets of teeth coming through the darkness about a foot above the ground. Coming from the house. Point and shoot, you said. My grommet did just that. I damn near fainted."

What he'd actually done was to push backward through one of the lattice panels and fall into the spring pool. Fall was the wrong word: Reverse belly flop was more like it, as the pool was only three feet deep, at most. He'd heard the Dobes slam into the lattice, and then the whole panel disintegrated and fell into the pool on top of him. He lay on his back in the pool, gripping the lattice with his fingertips to keep his nose and mouth above water.

"Guess what?" he said. "They don't like water. They knew I was down there, and I sure as hell knew they were up there, but they ran back and forth along the stone edge, whining like frustrated puppies."

"No bad guy?" Pardee asked.

"Fortunately, no. I had my gun out by then, but I wasn't sure if the barrel was clear. The dogs stayed around for a minute, then both of them looked across the yard at something and took off in the direction of the house. I stayed at periscope depth until I heard you shooting."

"Water cold, was it?" Pardee asked.

"That's an icehouse, not a springhouse. Considering the alternative, though, it felt wonderful."

The dryer buzzed, and Tony went into the laundry alcove to retrieve his clothes.

"Well," I said. "It's good to know they don't like water."

"It's not so good to know that he was out there tonight, with his assassins, and in that house."

"He seems to be comfortable in that house," I said.

"Yeah, he does."

"So maybe the thing to do is to set up some kind of trap in there."

"Or at least some kind of surveillance system. Some minicams on a twenty-four-hour loop, maybe."

"Can those be detected electronically?"

"Only if we make them wireless. Hardwire the network, and he'd have to dig around in the woodwork to physically find them."

I'd put all three dogs outside when we got back to the cottage. One of them whoofed from the front porch. Pardee turned off the standing light by the couch while I went to the window. Tony came back into the sitting room with his gun drawn.

Out on the dam a familiar sight materialized. The major on his horse came at a slow trot across the dam, passing the cottage without so much as a glance, and then disappeared up toward the manor house.

"Awfully late for that theater, isn't it?" Pardee said softly.

"I'll bet he knows that property over there like the back of his hand," Tony observed.

"And that house, too," Pardee said.

I didn't know what to say. It surely was quite a coincidence that the major was out and about this late at night, just an hour after Tony saw someone in the house and then was attacked by the pair of Dobermans. Cubby had said they didn't let him out at night, hadn't he?

"It doesn't compute," I said finally. "I saw that masked

face—wrong shape. I heard his voice. Wrong voice. That wasn't the major."

"Maybe somebody working for the major, or the whole family?" Pardee said. "Don't want you there. Don't want anyone there. They like things as they are and as they always have been."

"That computes, sort of," I said, "but then why let me stay here? Why encourage me to proceed with the purchase?"

"Keep your friends close and your enemies closer?"

I pulled away from the window and went back to the couch. The timing didn't quite work to support that theory. I'd had guys shooting at my house before I'd gotten involved with Glory's End. Then I thought about it: Was that true? I had already walked the ground with Mr. Oatley on the day they'd called me about my prison ghost. I'd been looking at the place for two months before that. I hadn't met the Lees before then, but Oatley could have been talking in town. When had I taken that house tour with Valeria? The very next day?

Pardee was yawning, which got me started.

"There's a couple beds in that room over there," I said. "Let's declare victory and call it a night."

"Works for me," Pardee said. "Should we set a guard?"

"That's what those guys are for," I said, pointing to the front door.

The next morning we teleconferenced with Horace down in Triboro to see if he'd found out anything. No progress. He'd searched Manceford County records using search strings for female homicides or suicides in the police records statewide. No hits that could be connected to me or the MCAT.

Pardee talked to his wife and was reminded of soccer games this weekend, so I told him to go on home and take care of family business. Tony didn't care one way or the other what he did for the weekend, and my stalker problem seemed more interesting than his current girlfriend. I did ask Pardee to get some surveillance cameras together for installation at Glory's End. Then I called Carol Pollard and asked if she could meet us at the house later that morning with her structural reconstruction expert. I still wanted to find that second passageway, assuming there was one.

Tony and I went over to the house after making breakfast. I took all three shepherds. We put Frack in the house. He couldn't do much, but he would bark if something or someone showed up. We did a quick sweep of all the rooms and floors, including the attic, and then deployed the two shepherds out back while we searched the grounds. We began at the springhouse, and the dogs caught a scent, probably of those two Dobermans.

"Which way did they come from?" I asked Tony.

"Don't know," he said. "They came so fast I didn't have time to look. I thought it was from the house, but . . . I was too busy diving into that water." He shivered, remembering how cold it was.

From the springhouse, which was about fifty feet down the hill from the main lawn, we had a clear view of the old barn area and all the outbuildings closer into the house, such as the smokehouse. I cast the two shepherds out on a big loop to see if they cut the dog scent between the outbuildings and the house, but they didn't seem to react. Then I sent them out toward the barns in an expanding loop, looking for any trails coming from that direction. I hoped there weren't any more wells out there along that farm road leading to the back buildings.

It was a clear, sunny morning with a promise of some heat later on. I asked Tony to check the close-in buildings one by one, especially to see if the fire pit in the smokehouse had been disturbed. I went toward the back, passing the stone bench next to the sundial. I had my SIG out, and Tony had his Glock. I wasn't really expecting trouble, either human or canine, but it was better to be ready. Then I realized I hadn't reloaded since last night when I fired those four rounds. I stopped, extracted that magazine, and replaced it with my spare. I made a mental note to clean the weapon once I got back to the cottage. This was no time to be sloppy about my firearms.

I checked the two barns that faced the house. I'd aimed low last night, mostly to ensure I didn't send 230-grain bullets out into the night and injure some fisherman out on the river. The barn on the right had the ancient farm machinery parked inside, on mostly flattened tires. I recognized some of it, but not much. I found what looked like a fresh bullet hole on the back wall, round on the entry side, splintered on my side. The boards were old and dry as paper. Then both Kitty and Frick barked.

I turned around and saw them backing away from the other barn. Kitty was growling, but Frick was more upset than alerted, based on her body language. I moved carefully across the barnyard road to the nearest edge of the barn, SIG at the ready. Both dogs were staring inside. Kitty was showing impressive hackles, and Frick had her ears flattened. I waited for a moment to see what, if anything, would happen. Tony was not visible, and I didn't want to call out.

Finally I crouched low and swung around the corner of the barn pointing the gun where I was looking. Inside this barn there were five bays, separated by steel farm gates. The first and nearest bay held a moldering stack of hay or straw. The one next to that contained an antique tractor that was a solid mass of rust. The dogs were looking into the third bay.

"If somebody's in there, I need to see you right now," I called.

No response. Kitty barked again. It was an impatient bark, not a warning. As in, get over here.

I stood back up and walked across the front of the first two bays, stopping at the edge of the third. This one was a workshop with several benches, vises, a table saw, a drill press, and the body of a woman sitting up against the back wall on an overturned wooden crate. She had a big hole just under her left cheekbone and a small lake of blood between her legs.

I called for Tony, and he heard me on the third try from inside the smokehouse. I walked over to the body, careful where I put my feet. I knelt down in front of her to feel for a pulse, but it was pretty clear she was gone. There was the one black entry wound, extensive bleeding from the mouth, and a skin bulge high on the other side of her head where the bullet had almost exited.

She was just sitting there, with a surprised expression on her face. There was a scoped hunting rifle on the ground next to her, but her hands were empty and her fingers curled in, as if she'd been holding it when she was shot. I could not guess her age, but her face was leathery and seamed with too many years of cigarettes, whiskey, and hard, lean living. She could have been anywhere from fifty to sixty-five. She was wearing a long-sleeved tan Carhartt shirt, tight faded jeans, and plain cowboy boots. She had a utility hunting belt that carried a small canteen, some ammunition pouches, a first aid kit, and a fair-sized knife. Tony arrived.

"Whoa," he said.

"You got your phone?"

He did.

"Call 911, report a shooting with one fatality. Tell 'em who you are, and our location behind the big house."

"Shit, boss—you do this last night?"

"Sure looks like it," I said. "I was firing low to keep the rounds down, and I fired into these barns. She must have been hiding in here."

"With a thirty-aught and a shooting hole," he said, pointing to a hole in the back wall I hadn't noticed. It had been recently gouged out, based on the splinters on the ground. "Not your basic peeping Tammy."

"Make the call," I said, standing up. "We need to back out of their scene."

We sat on the front porch of the house while the incident response team did their thing back in the barn. Tony had stayed with them; the sheriff and I plus one detective had gone to the house so I could make a statement. The detective had produced a recorder and had me sign the appropriate warnings and waivers, and then I told them the entire history of this mess from the day that the first shot had come through my window back in Summerfield.

The detective asked an occasional question for clarification but otherwise simply let me tell it. The sheriff sat there in a rocking chair with his head resting on his left hand and his eyes closed. He looked asleep, but I knew he wasn't. When I was done, the sheriff looked over at the detective, who nodded, then turned off the recorder and got up to take a smoke break out on the front lawn.

"You've closed on this property?" he asked.

"Not yet. Waiting on the title search and a survey."

"So, technically, you're not the owner."

I nodded again. He sat there for a long minute, staring out at the front lawn. The shepherds were on the porch with us, watching. I felt this cold pool of guilt growing in my belly. I've shot people before, but always in the course of a hot pursuit or a gunfight. There's always a sense of revulsion when you see the results, but it's usually tempered by the knowledge that you're standing and the other guy isn't, which typically isn't what he intended. This was different.

"I can play this a coupla different ways," he said finally, "but, on the face of it, before any forensic reports are made, the county prosecutor is probably going to charge you with reckless endangerment and involuntary manslaughter, for starters."

I couldn't think of anything constructive to say.

"I mean," he said, "you don't own the property. You have been threatened with murder. You were searching the grounds for intruders. There were intruders, at least in the form of two killer Dobes, who attacked one of your helpers in the night. You fired four rounds as a distraction, and one by terrible chance caught the human intruder, who was armed with a long-range rifle, in the head. Serious gray area there."

"Except she's dead with a bullet in the head."

"Yup."

"Anybody recognize her?"

"There was no ID on the body, and the guys are still sifting the scene. Unlike on TV, that's gonna take all day, maybe two. Coroner says time of death corresponds to when you fired those rounds, more or less."

I sighed. "I feel like shit," I said. "Seeing her there, looking so damned surprised. Maybe she was part of this, maybe not, but this was an accident."

"Copy that," he said. "Which is why I'm not hauling your troublesome ass downtown to the hoosegow. Lemme talk to the county ADA after we get that statement transcribed. I'll call you in later today to sign it, and then maybe we'll know more from the scene."

"Seems pretty cut and dried to me," I said.

"I know," he said, "but we have to dot the *i*'s, cross the *t*'s. We're a small operation out here, but we do know how to do this."

"Never thought you didn't," I said. "Dammit. All I was trying to do was make some noise, maybe spook one of 'em."

"Worked," he said.

"We'll need that weapon," the deputy called from the front lawn.

\* \* \*

Carol Pollard showed up at the cottage at two thirty, sans restoration expert, which was just as well. A deputy at the end of the driveway diverted her to the cottage. She asked what had happened. I gave it to her in highly abbreviated form, and she was clearly taken aback.

"You're saying you shot randomly into the barns to make someone move and hit this woman in the head?"

"Looks that way," I replied. "Nobody else was shooting last night."

She sat down on the couch and rubbed her cheeks. Tony came in then and reported that crime lab people had been called out from Triboro to assist their country brethren. "It'll be a while before they close it up over there."

"Find anything newsworthy?"

He shrugged. "They wouldn't tell me shit, which is as it should be. You have to go in?"

"Just to sign my statement," I said. "At least that's where we stand so far. The sheriff's on my side, but the lawyers may view it differently."

"Lawyers view everything differently," he said. "I'll stick around, get you some bail if it breaks that way."

"Bail?" Carol said.

"I'm an ex-cop, Carol," I said. "They have to be very careful about what they let me do and not do. If you shoot someone in this county, and the routine procedure is to lock up the shooter until they have a clear picture of what happened, they'll have to lock me up."

"Oh, great," she said. "But it was an accident."

"Maybe it was, maybe not. I did aim at those barns. I wasn't trying to hit anyone, but I was trying to hit the barns. It's not like I dropped my SIG and it just went off."

She told me her restoration expert had forgotten the appointment and gone to the beach. "Par for the course in this business," she said. "Plus, he's almost seventy."

"Just as well," I said. "That project may go on indefinite hold."

In fact, I was wrong about that. Tony and I sat around the cottage after Carol left and tried to figure out who the victim was and what she'd been doing there. Tony asked if I wanted something to eat, but I declined. My stomach already had a rock in it. You fire a bullet, be it from a rifle or a pistol, and you're supposed to think about all the possible targets downrange. I knew that.

I went out to the porch to drown my sorrows in some early Scotch. My cell went off. It was Sheriff Walker.

"Need me to come in?" I said, wondering if I was over the limit to drive.

"We have preliminary results," he said, "thanks in part to the forensics crew up from Manceford County. Those guys are pretty good."

"She's dead, right?"

He grunted, not amused. "Yes, she's dead. Single bullet wound to the head. Time of death estimated to be coincident to your little hide-and-seek exercise last night. Plus, we have an ID, from AFIS of all places."

"She was in the system?"

"Yup. One Elizabeth Craney. Know her?"

"Nope."

"Charlotte cops do. Biker connections. One DUI, a couple of drunk and disorderlies, and one conviction for assault with a deadly weapon, namely a Doberman, which resulted in a year in jail and a euthanized Doberman. Apparently some of the meth mobsters are into having savage dogs around, and she was the supplier, as well as the duty punch for a crew over in Charlotte."

"She looked the type," I said. "Dried up and used up."

"Yes, she did. Here's the important part: You didn't do it."

I sat up in my chair. "I didn't?"

"Not unless you went behind the barn, pulled out a silenced Glock nine, tapped her on the shoulder, waited for her to turn around, knelt down, and shot her in the face. You do all that?"

"Nope."

"Right. Your weapon squares with the four holes we found in the buildings, plus one intact round retrieved by the squad from a support pole. Our guys noticed the angle of her wound, couple of other inconsistencies, said you didn't do it. I waited for the Manceford forensics crew to have a second look. They came up with the same thing. She was shot by someone standing behind her, and probably by someone for whom or with whom she was working, in that there were no signs of a struggle or an attempt to avoid the hit."

"Wow."

"Feel better?"

"Much."

"Thought you might. Take the weekend off. Come see me Monday morning, with your sidekicks, human and otherwise."

"Sounds like changed circumstances to me."

"There's good news and bad news," he said. "The good news is you now are going to have some official help with your stalker."

"The bad news?"

"You now are going to have some official help with your stalker."

"Meaning we're gonna do it your way."

"Bingo."

"That actually sounds good to me, Sheriff."

"You don't have a reputation for being much of a team player, Lieutenant."

"That was then. I'm older and wiser now."

"For now, I'll believe half of that. See you Monday."

I put a call in to Carol Pollard and told her my good news. She was very relieved. She'd made it clear before that she didn't have a problem with my shooting someone who was laid up in a back barn with a rifle at night, but she knew that the legal hassle would be onerous. I told her that the restoration project was still on hold until we resolved this problem, and she understood. She invited me to come over to her place later and said she'd burn something in the kitchen for me.

I went over to the shop to look for Cubby. He was, as usual, working on some machinery, this time a riding mower.

"How does one get an appointment with the grande dames up in the big house?" I asked.

"You tell me, I tell Patience, and she tells Ms. Valeria. By'n by, word will come down from the throne."

"You can't go direct?"

"I don't go in that house," he said. I waited for him to amplify that, but he didn't.

"Okay," I said. "If you would start that process, please."

He crawled out from under the machine with a handful of crimped fence wire and threw it into a barrel. "You gonna let me in on what happened over there last night?" he asked while wiping grease off his hands.

I gave him a quick rundown, and he nodded solemnly when I was finished. He told me that was what he had heard in town, all except the fact that I hadn't shot the woman in the barn. That was news. I asked him to keep that news to himself, because the sheriff might want to use it to catch this killer. "Finding this guy's important, Cubby, and not only to me."

"Meanin', don't stand too close to you once the sun goes down?"

"Yup. Although you may not have to worry about it, once the ladies hear the story. They'll probably ask me to find somewhere else to stay."

He shook his head. "That ain't their style," he said. "You'll see."

He tossed the greasy rag into the barrel and then stopped for a moment. "You know," he said, "there's something about that place over there, draws blood. Ever since them Georgia boys threw down on all those soldiers up there at the bridge. There's been other stuff, too."

"Like Abigail and Nathaniel."

He looked surprised but nodded. "Yeah," he said. "Like that. Sometime, if you can, get Ms. Valeria to talk about all that. You may want to reconsider buying that place."

"I'll be at the cottage until about seven," I said.

He looked at his watch, nodded, and then went up the walk toward the big house.

I found my way over to Carol's house a little after seven. I took Kitty with me, as well as one of Tony's many guns, since my SIG was still in lockup over at the county. He'd gone back to Triboro for the weekend but said he'd be available if anything came up.

Carol appeared in the doorway when I drove up. She was wearing a loose, knee-length flowing skirt, topped with a long-sleeved, modestly low-cut peasant blouse. The lights from the house backlit the skirt, revealing that she was, indeed, a very shapely lady. I was going to leave Kitty in the Suburban, but she insisted that I bring her into the house. Her own dog, a Heinz 57, took one look at Kitty and slunk off to the back of the house. Kitty went into the living room and lay down by the fireplace as if she owned the place.

I sat in the kitchen with a glass of wine while she worked on a primavera. There was warm French bread, some Port Salut cheese, and a small brick of pâté on offer. I asked if she cooked like this all the time.

"There's a Whole Foods down the road in Hillsborough," she said. "If I did this every day I'd be two hundred pounds."

"Well, obviously you don't," I said. "I've been letting

my own exercise program lapse, and damned if my clothes haven't started shrinking."

"Clothes do that," she said. "Okay, we're there."

After dinner we sat out on the side screened porch in deference to the mosquitoes of spring. She'd produced a bottle of single malt, much to my delight. I can drink wine, but I'm not a big fan. She switched to Scotch to keep me company, and I noticed she drank it neat, as I did. Kitty joined us on the porch, calm as always.

"She keeps you in sight, doesn't she?" Carol said.

"That's her job," I said. "She's not as aggressive or knowledgeable as Frick and Frack, but she's learning."

We talked about the shepherds for a while, and then about the restoration business. I finally asked if she'd ever been married.

"Briefly," she said. "How about you?"

I told her about my marriage history, how it had ended early in my career, when my wife, an up-and-coming trial attorney, had stepped out. Then I described how we'd re-started, with my ex now a state judge, and then how the rematch had ended with a boom in Triboro one night when someone put a bomb in her car.

"Jesus!" she said. "What was all that about?"

I told her the story of the cat dancers, and how it had ended in professional ambiguity. She asked if that case could be the origin of my current stalker.

"It's possible," I said, "but what he says, that I killed his wife, doesn't track. I haven't killed anyone's wife. I've got one of my guys going through records to see if anyone we put away could be connected to known suicides, things like that, but that's a real long shot."

She was sitting on the porch swing, legs crossed, and rocking the swing just enough to make me notice. She wasn't overtly flirting, but she was definitely letting me know what was possible in the great scheme of things. I was sitting in a large wicker chair that looked big enough for two people, and the view was enticing.

"I lived with another cop for almost a year," she said. "Until our sergeant found out. He pulled me in one day and told me what a bad idea that was, and why. How relationships between cops usually blew up, and all the subsequent problems with discipline, watch assignments. You know all this, I suppose."

"I do," I said. "He was mostly right. Even the marriages between cops often blow up."

"Well, after that some of the guys thought I was just stuck-up, you know, here I was, on street patrol with a college degree. Then that terrible night, after which none of this mattered anymore. Since then I've just been—lazy, I guess, is the best word."

"I've met too many women who are out there husband-hunting," I said. "They're kind of scary."

"I think it just has to happen. At my age, anyway, I think we'd have to be good friends before anything else could develop. I'm forty-two, by the way."

"I've got eleven years on you, and you don't look forty-anything."

She smiled, and she really didn't look forty-anything when she did that. There was a period of comfortable silence. She rocked, and I tried not to look.

"Don't you just love it?" she said. "Beginning the dance. Pretending we're talking about other people, or just people in general."

I laughed then. That was exactly what had been going through my mind. "This is the point where I clear my throat and say I have a big day ahead of me tomorrow, and thanks for a lovely dinner."

"Or," she said, reaching for my glass, "you could have another Scotch, and then you'd be over the legal limit, and then you'd have to stay for a while. Maybe go for a walk or something, work off all that alcohol."

"Work off."

She tilted her head and smiled again. "Said the spider to the fly."

"Well, shucks," I said. "If I really don't have any choice here, I guess I could go for just one more."

"Scotch?"

"That, too."

I got back to the cottage at midnight, feeling much better. Carol had had her moves pretty much all planned out, and the whole thing had been delightful. She'd gone back into the house with the glasses, then come back out onto the porch, stood next to my chair for a moment while she let her hair down, and then slipped onto my lap and gave me a long, lingering kiss. After that we made love right there, as if we'd been doing it for years. She dozed for a half hour or so afterward, opened one eye, and then told me a really funny joke. A married couple was in bed after dinner, watching TV. The wife was surprised to feel her husband's hands start in on her body, surreptitiously at first, but then with a lot more purpose. It had been a long time. She was enjoying all the sensations when he suddenly stopped. She opened her eyes, told him that that had been lovely, and asked why he'd stopped. Found the remote, says he.

After that she'd sent me on my way with a go-cup of black coffee and an invitation to come see her again whenever I was ready to start that exercise program. I'd driven back to the cottage, trying to analyze my feelings. Then I gave up and just savored the evening. There didn't seem to be any strings or subplots, just two grown-ups enjoying each other's company. Said the fly to the spider.

I let the rest of the mutts out when I got back and then took that nightcap that had never made it to the porch down to the swing set by the pond. The resident owl greeted me from across the still water, and Kitty whoofed back at it. We hadn't had owls in Summerfield, and I wondered what she thought it was. Then she whoofed again, and I turned around to look. There, along the driveway, came Valeria, carrying a tiny handbag over one arm, a small lantern in one hand, and a dainty parasol in the other. She looked like a ghost coming soundlessly down the gravel drive, dressed all in white. I stood up as she approached the swing set.

"Ms. Valeria," I said in greeting.

"Mr. Richter," she murmured. "May I join you, sir?"

"Absolutely," I said. "Should I go in and get another glass?"

She sat down primly in the long swing and said that that would be very nice. I was back in a flash. She had put the parasol down now that she was under the canvas cover of the swing and safe from the evening dew. She was sitting back, her long black hair in a twisted coil over the front of one shoulder and her legs out in front of her, barely touching the ground. That's when I noticed what she was wearing: It was a long-sleeved dress made of what looked like layers of thin white gauze that reached all the way to her ankles. In terms of womanly flesh on display, it was modest in the extreme, except for the fact that sometimes, if the humidity is just right, gauze clings. That old rule about less being more applied in spades, as every aspect of her decidedly lush body was on perfect if circumspect display in the starlight. I felt guilty about even looking, especially considering the earlier part of the evening. We clinked glasses, and I waited to see what she'd come down for. At that moment I would have been content to just sit there and look at her.

"Cubby informs us that you wished to confer?" she asked. The royal "we" came through loud and clear.

I said yes and then told her in broad terms about the events across the road of the night before, and how the major issue had been resolved. I admitted that I was worried they might want me to find accommodations elsewhere and said that I'd completely understand if that was the case.

"Nonsense, Mr. Richter," she said. "You are now the rightful owner of Glory's End?"

"Actually, not yet. I've put down some earnest money, and we're waiting for a survey and a title search."

"A title search? I heard Mother mention that. What is it, exactly?"

I told her.

"How interesting," she said, sighing. "Mother's right. Defining the legal title to Glory's End may be more than you bargained for, Mr. Richter."

"So people keep telling me," I said. "I keep wondering why."

She was silent for a moment, but then she answered me. "A title search sounds like a history of power," she said. "An effort to identify those with the power to claim and hold a property, as opposed to those who either can't or who lost it."

"Or sold it," I reminded her. "Ownership of property is not always about a power struggle between the strong and the weak."

"It is here," she said, "and in most of the South, I would expect. The Recent Unpleasantness was all about property."

"I thought it was about slavery."

"Precisely," she said, sipping some Scotch and then exhaling in pleasure.

*Whoops*, I thought as I caught her meaning. Good thing Cubby wasn't around.

"In any event," she said. "It is outrageous that someone would come onto your property in the middle of the night with guns and vicious dogs and expect you to just run away. Of course you would fight back. We would do the very same, I assure you."

"I guess I have to warn you, this isn't over. In police parlance this guy is known as a ghost, as in someone who comes back to haunt you because you took some law enforcement action against him. I believe he'll keep trying until one of us is in the ground."

"Ghosts are nothing new to this part of the county," she said with a wry smile. "There have been people living, loving, fighting, and dying around here for three hundred years. Of course there are ghosts. What's one more?"

"Well, I'm relieved. The cottage will be a perfect base of operations, but I'll try to keep any real warfare across the street."

"Do not do that on our account, Mr. Richter," she said. "We have weapons in the house, and anyone who tries conclusions with either of us will find out why the Recent Unpleasantness took four valiant years to resolve."

"Not to mention the major," I said, not wanting to point out how the Recent Unpleasantness had been resolved, with the utter destruction of southern society and all its many twisted mores.

"Indeed," she said.

Our glasses were empty, so I did the honors. She managed her whiskey very well, without any signs of intoxication.

"Must you stare so, Mr. Richter?" she asked, again with just a hint of a smile.

"You are quite a sight in the starlight, Ms. Valeria. That dress is—something." I felt weird—an hour away from Carol Pollard, and this very strange woman was turning me on. Plus, she was absolutely doing it on purpose.

She arched her back slightly, finished her Scotch, and then stood up in front of me. She ran her hands down the opposing sleeves of the dress, smoothing the fabric while tightening it at the same time across her front. "This dress," she said, continuing to run her long, elegant hands over the fabric, "takes about an hour to get right. There are forty-eight buttons on the back alone, can you believe it? Velvet buttons, which are difficult to manipulate. One requires help, you see."

I almost hadn't noticed, but she'd moved directly in front of me and close enough that I could catch a trace of her perfume. She definitely wasn't wearing lilac water to-night. Then she did a graceful pirouette, extending the hem of her dress out with one hand while placing her other on her hip. The extension of all that fabric rendered her body in a lovely silhouette. She executed another one, and then I realized she was moving away from me now, out into the lawn in front of the swing set, not dancing exactly but just wheeling to the soundless memory of a waltz some-where back in time.

"Come calling, Mr. Richter," she said from about thirty feet away as she turned to go back up to the house. "I've lots to show you."

"Count on it," I replied, trying not to squeak. That's the thing about the country: When it rains, sometimes it pours.

We met the sheriff in his personal office at ten, as requested. Horace Stackpole, Pardee, Tony, and I sat on one side of his conference table. Frick and Kitty guarded the under-side of the table at the end nearest the doughnuts. Sheriff Walker had all three of his detectives present. Horace had gone to school with one of the detectives, so we had an im-mediate in with the gold shields.

In addition to the D's, their Major Crimes boss, Captain Hildegard Hapsburg, was in attendance. She was built like the proverbial fat lady of the opera, lacking only the winged helmet. She viewed us outsiders with deep suspicion. I won-dered idly what would happen if she showed up in a German customs hall with that last name.

I was still thinking about the night before when Tony had first arrived. He'd given me a couple of speculative looks, but I pretended not to notice. In the world of boys and girls and the games they play, Tony is a player. I didn't doubt for a moment that he knew something had happened. If he only knew.

"Dearly beloved," the sheriff began. "We are gathered here in the presence of edible doughnuts to figure out how to save Lieutenant Richter's butt from being shot off by a person or persons currently unknown. Lieutenant, how's about you start off with a five-minute summary of what's happened so far, up to the point where we got involved."

It took ten, but the sheriff was indulgent, seeing as I didn't make anyone look at slides. The detectives were a mixed bag. The two older white guys, maybe five, six years from hanging it up, listened dispassionately, their faces displaying the permanent skepticism that comes from a few decades of listening to people lie to them. The third detective, an attractive black woman in her late twenties, was taking notes and listening very carefully. When I said I was finished, she raised a hand and asked a question, which is when I realized that her notepad contained a whole list of questions. Captain Hapsburg was also taking notes, but so far she hadn't said anything at all.

"This guy said you killed his wife," she said. "Have you killed any women or anyone's wife in your career or afterward?"

"One," I said. I then explained what had happened up on Spider Mountain, when one of the Creigh women had pointed and fired a .357 at me. She was, however, not anyone's wife, nor would she ever be.

"So it's possible that he doesn't mean that literally?"

"Explain, please."

"It's possible that he means you destroyed his wife in some other way. Like putting her in prison for a life sentence."

We hadn't thought of that. As I'd told Carol, I'd had Horace trying to build something on that under the assumption that it involved a dead woman. The detective had a good point.

"Yes, that's possible," I said. "Or she committed suicide because I put him away for a long jolt. Horace Stackpole here's been digging along those lines in the records down in Manceford County."

"You were head of the Manceford County MCAT, right?" she asked. "So it was a team effort to take the assholes off the street. Any individual make a big deal about that being personal?"

"I've been searching for just that, Detective," Horace said. "In theory, that should narrow the search field considerably, but sometimes the boss is the guy they focus on."

"Plus," I said, "we're looking for someone other than just your average B and E guy or corner pusher. He's killed two people so far, mostly for becoming loose ends."

"What was your MOS in the Corps?" one of the other detectives asked.

"Sniper."

"Any possibles there?"

"None living," I said. The detectives smiled at that.

"You seem to attract a lot of trouble, Mr. Richter," Captain Hapsburg said. "Why should we be helping you here?"

She had a strong accent, and the "here" came out more like "hier." The sheriff intervened.

"Because we're working a homicide, Hildy," he said. "You know, like murder? Helping Lieutenant Richter is incidental to catching a bad guy."

The lady detective had several more questions, but none that produced any sort of clarifying moments. Captain Hildy went back to taking notes, but clearly she still disapproved of the entire proceeding.

"Okay," Sheriff Walker said. "Here's my plan. We're gonna work the victim in the shooting out at Glory's End. Pull the string on her and everyone she knew, the bikers, the meth world, her dog-training thing, like that. With any luck someone will say, hey, yes, I remember a guy she trained for who bought two dogs and here's his license plate number."

Chuckles all around. As if.

"Sergeant Stackpole, sounds like you still have a reliable pipe into Manceford County. Keep at it. I can call Sheriff Baggett if you ever need some top cover."

"We're good," Horace said.

"Mr. Richter, I'd appreciate it if you would spend as much time as possible at the plantation, with whatever support your guys can give you. I'd like to develop how this guy got there and got away, and whether or not he has a base of operations out there on Glory's End somewhere."

"Right," I said. "Detective Sergeant Bell here is our electronics wizard. He's going to wire the house for video. If you're amenable, he'll get together with your people and arrange secure comms for us. Now that we're all retired and working private, we have access to some fairly spiffy toys in that department."

"Absolutely," he said, "and we'll give you the code for our jungle drum system, and also the secret smoke signals."

*Ooops,* I thought, *there I go, stepping on toes again,* but the sheriff was smiling. I decided to stop talking before I got in any deeper.

The meeting broke up, the detectives talking to my guys, the sheriff and I discussing possibilities out at Glory's End, and the shepherds sitting now at the end of the table, unashamedly pointing the two remaining doughnuts on the plate.

"How are you and the Lee ladies getting on?" Sheriff Walker asked.

I almost blinked when he asked that. I was still digesting the unexpected meeting with Valeria the night before. I told him we were doing fine, so far. He asked if he needed to drop by and explain what all the ruckus had been about across the road. I told him that I'd done that, and that their reaction had been to encourage me to shoot the bastard the first chance I got.

"Yeah," he said. "That's sounds like Hester, anyway. I would never go creeping around that house at night. She reputedly can shoot the ear off a squirrel at a hundred yards."

I asked him about his Major Crimes boss.

"Hildy?" he said. "She's okay, most of the time. She disapproves of civilians, and I think she wouldn't be entirely averse to bringing back elements of the secret police to our business. You should see her do an interview."

"I think she doesn't like me."

"Hildy doesn't like anybody," he said. "Even me. She was here when I got here, and she has the admin situation in her own personal vise. That's valuable, but it makes us all somewhat dependent."

"You let her go operational?"

"Not if I can help it," he said with a laugh. "She's good people, just a little bit too serious most of the time."

I wanted to ask him how he knew about Hester's ability with a rifle, but at that moment a deputy came in and told the sheriff that the homicide victim's husband was out front.

"Husband?" the sheriff asked.

"Says he is," the deputy replied. "There's five of 'em. Bikers. Said they rode up from Charlotte. Uglier'n stumps, every one of 'em."

"Bikers," mumbled the sheriff. "I hate bikers."

"Except when they give me shit while they're on their bikes and I'm in a cruiser," Tony said. "Then I can give them a physics lesson. That can be real fun."

"These here aren't posers, you know, lawyers and doctors?" the deputy said. "Front desk told the 'husband' he could stay; sent the rest outside to keep their hogs company. They started up with him, and he had to send for Willard."

"Willard?" I asked.

"Willard is our uppity manager," the sheriff said. "Okay, I'll go talk to this guy. Deputy Smithy here will take you out the back way. Make sure my D's have all your numbers, and we'll get up with you as soon as we have something."

I thanked him for all his help and said we'd be over at Glory's End for the rest of the day. As we left, he noticed that the mutts were still pointing the doughnuts.

"Oh, for God's sake," he said and tipped the plate in their direction. Two audible snaps and then they joined the parade to the back door. The sheriff was now a designated softie, and they would always remember that.

As we went down the hall, we passed, or rather stepped aside for, a huge, round-faced, glary-eyed black man in a straining khaki uniform. He was six something tall, the same wide, and he had to lean slightly back as he walked so as to counterbalance his sumo-sized paunch. His fingers were curled in a grab-it-and-hurt-it posture, and his arms hung out at his sides like two Smithfield hams. He walked like a Hollywood robot, one leg followed by the other, and the walls literally shook as he went by. Even the shepherds were cowed.

"Willard?" I muttered as we headed for the back door.

"Willard," the deputy said. "Specializes in anger management."

*Uppity manager*, I thought. *Got it.*

I thought about Carol as we drove back to Glory's End, followed by a fleeting image of Valeria, excuse me all to hell, Ms. Valeria of the moonlight, as we drove past the entrance to Laurel Grove and headed up the driveway to my new home. I had to force myself not to look up that long drive just before we turned in. I did glance in my rearview mirror and saw Tony grinning. I tried to ignore him. Where was Willard when I needed him?

Just for the hell of it, I'd left Horace back at the sheriff's office, ostensibly to visit with his old friend, and perhaps get us some information on the suddenly bereft "husband." We were in an anomalous position with the local gendarmerie. As retired cops, there would be a certain amount of professional courtesy. On the other hand, we were technically outsiders in a homicide that had happened on Sheriff Walker's patch. I didn't have to tell my guys how to behave, but we were operating on split objectives. Walker and his crew had themselves a homicide. This guy had said he was going to kill me. Their efforts would not necessarily prevent my problem from happening, so I certainly wasn't going to sit around and wait for the long but legally shackled arm of the law to do its thing, sympathetic as it might be.

Horace showed up a little later and told us about the husband and his supporters. Apparently, the grieving spouse's main interest had been in getting his dead wife's monthly Social Security check transferred into his name, and for that he needed a death certificate. The sheriff had informed him that the certificate would give "pending investigation" as a cause of death but that that was not sufficient for the Social Security Administration. This led to a display of anger management issues, at which point the sheriff had Willard escort the deeply bereaved biker out of the office without his feet ever touching the ground. Horace said it was quite a scene, especially when Willard deposited the biker on his hog, lifted the rear tire and rider off the ground, swung it around so that the bike pointed in the away direction, and then pushed the bike forward. One of the would-be desperadoes had given Willard yet more static, which inspired the big guy to plant his legs astride the guy's front wheels and turn the handles 180 degrees, which did amazing things to control wires. Everyone concerned apparently got the message. They eventually departed in good if really noisy order.

The sheriff had asked Horace an interesting question as he was leaving: If the dead woman was the dog handler, where were the Dobermans? That question had been on my mind, too. They'd attacked Tony in the springhouse, then disappeared right around the time I shot up the barns and my stalker shot down his associate. Had the dogs gone with him? Or had they fled when their trainer had been killed? In which case, were they now somewhere out there on Glory's End, looking for something to eat?

Pardee and Tony set up the private cell net for us on the front porch of the house, and then Pardee swept the house for bugs. He didn't find any. I asked Pardee and Horace to go back to Triboro, Pardee to get that surveillance gear for the house, and Horace to see if he could get a line on the bikers from Charlotte. One of them, maybe even the devastated husband, might know who had hired our late Doberman trainer. Horace asked if he should do that or casually mention it to his buddy in the Rockwell County office. Horace was thinking straighter than I was. He then asked what our plans were.

"Tony and I are going to start looking for coal," I said and then explained what I meant.

"Suppose you guys find him?" Pardee said.

I made that whistling sound from the spaghetti western. They all grinned, but I knew that had been a valid question. Assuming he didn't get me first, I needed to decide if I was going to hand him over to the cops or take care of business.

They left for Triboro. Tony and I went into town for something to eat and then up to Danville to get us some ground transportation. An hour later, the golf cart dealer followed us down the drive at Glory's End with a Club Car model 1200 XRT utility vehicle on a trailer. It was a four-wheel-drive number, complete with canopy, Plexiglas windshield, camo paint job, headlights, two rear-facing seats in the back in place of a dump box, and two outlets for charging cell phones or other equipment. It weighed about a thousand pounds and had a noisy gasoline engine and seriously knobby tires. I would have preferred all that with an electric drive motor, but only the smaller golf carts had electrics. One option would have to be special-ordered, and that was a couple of heavy square nylon netting panels that went on both sides of the cab, which would keep occupants in during rough-and-tumble off-road going. I wanted them to keep attacking dogs from being able to jump into the cab long enough for us to get our weapons out.

Tony and I set out in our new chariot just after three, headed to the eastern ridge where the coal mine tunnel was supposed to be. I had the shepherds running ahead because I wanted them to be able to hear. Our own hearing was clobbered by the noisy engine, which put us at a tactical disadvantage. On the other hand, we could really cover the ground compared to being on foot. Tony drove while I watched the farm road ahead and what the shepherds were doing. If they stopped, we stopped. We went down that dirt road that went east-west across the center of the property, crossed the creek, climbed the ridge, and stopped in the gap overlooking the next valley. The brickworks were off to our left down by the river. With the engine off, we could hear a truck going by on the two-lane to our right, but it was out of sight behind the trees fronting the cropland.

The ridge lifted steeply about a hundred feet above the farm road on either side and then ran due north toward the river, dropping down to the bottomlands only at the far end. It was covered in trees and some good-sized rock out-croppings. The sun was behind us, headed for sundown in about three hours, so the eastern slopes of the ridge were already in shadow. The shepherds had gone on down the road but returned when they realized we'd stopped. Frick spotted the two seats in the back and hopped in; Kitty fol-lowed suit. No more running down the dusty trail for them— they were going to ride with the gentry. The doughnuts were taking their toll.

Tony had brought along Pardee's collage of aerial pho-tographs. He looked up at the boulders and seams of gran-ite hanging above us. "Great place for an ambush," he said. "So where's this coal mine?"

"Don't know, but I'm guessing the entrance overlooks this set of crop fields in front of us. Sheriff Walker wasn't too clear about the where, or even if the story was true."

"There's this one area, maybe two-thirds of the way to the river, which might be a tailings pile. Hard to tell with all these trees."

We drove down to the bottom of the hill, turned left on the dirt path that led down toward the river and the brick-works, and began to scan the hillside on our left. To our right were crop fields, overgrown with tall weeds and grass. The highest point of the ridge was above where the central road came through. From there it descended toward the river, devolving into wooded bluffs. While Tony drove I tried to match the aerials with the terrain, but it all looked pretty much the same. Then, about a quarter mile from the river, I saw what looked like a spur path leading off to the left and up the hill. It was more like two ruts in the dirt than a road, but I noticed that it was covered in large gravel.

Tony took the vehicle off the path and pointed it upward into the trees. We got maybe fifty yards and had to stop because of all the new-growth scrub trees in the way. The two ruts were still visible, and they led into those trees. We shut the vehicle down and took stock. Tony got out and scuffed the ground. The shepherds jumped out and began sniffing around.

"Something must have been up here," he said. "This gravel is two, maybe three inches deep, and hard-packed."

Frick suddenly stiffened and looked up the hill. Kitty stopped her examination of the ground and also looked.

"Down!" I ordered, and Tony hit the deck, rolling swiftly behind the vehicle, where I was already unlimbering my SIG. The dogs kept looking up into the trees, and I expected gunfire in the next few seconds.

Nothing happened. The sounds of the country intruded, birds, insects, a couple of crows raising hell about something in the distance, a jet flying high overhead, the ticking sound of the engine as it cooled in the late afternoon air.

"What ya got?" I asked the dogs. Frick looked back at me but then resumed her scan of the hillside. Somewhat to my surprise, Kitty moved slowly to her left, away from Frick, and then began to creep up the hill. As she got about thirty feet up the hill, two black shapes came out of the trees above us.

The Dobermans.

This time, however, they weren't attacking. They were coming down the hill in a submissive posture, not quite slinking but displaying zero aggression. I heard Tony rack his weapon. I told him to wait, that something had changed. Frick went forward, hackles up, but Kitty did not seem alarmed. That confirmed to me that something had indeed changed.

The Dobermans came on down to the vehicle, with the shepherds closing in from both sides. They got to about ten feet from us and then sat down, ears back, heads down, their sleek bodies actually trembling. When they stopped, my dogs stopped.

I stood up and came out from behind the vehicle. "Watch the tree line above us," I told Tony.

I approached the Dobermans, who wouldn't look at me. They were a pair of males, beautifully conditioned, with cruelly cropped ears and shiny black coats. They were still wearing their collars. One of them was slightly larger than the other, and I spoke to him.

"Down," I said. No reaction. He still wouldn't look at me.

"Heel." Nothing.

I tried German. No response. I didn't know any Japanese. So I sat down in front of the larger male.

"Boss," Tony said.

"I think they're here to surrender," I said. "I just don't have their language."

I put out a tentative hand, fingers down, to the bigger male's muzzle. Finally he looked at me, crept forward, licked my hand, and then lay all the way down. I massaged his head and rubbed his ears while making comforting sounds. The second one then approached for some of the same treatment, and then they were both alongside, pressing in as Dobes do, demanding affection and orders at the same time.

"What the fuck," Tony said.

"Their master has been killed. I'm guessing they saw it happen, and now they don't know what to do."

I continued to rub their heads and mutter sweet nothings to them. The words didn't matter as much as the tone of my voice and the feel of my hands. Finally I stood up. I called my dogs into the vehicle, and they both jumped in.

I told Tony to get in, and then, after he had turned the vehicle around, I called to the two POWs, and they dutifully followed us back down the hillside and all the way back to the big house.

Sheriff Walker and his animal control van showed up an hour later, and I explained what had happened. The animal control officer was a female, and I wondered if there was going to be some drama between her and the Dobes. Turned out she knew exactly what to do, and in five minutes, with the assistance of some dog treats and a few dominance maneuvers, she had them in the back of the van and was petting them through the access hole while they wolfed down some food.

"Nice work," I said.

"Piece of cake," she said. "Dobies are respectful of dominant females. These are really gorgeous dogs."

"You should see them with their game face on," Tony said.

"Yeah, I know," she said, "but I had a Dobie bitch one

time? If you put both arms out in front of you with your palms up? She'd jump into them and lick you to death. A bad Doberman simply reflects a bad human."

"Those dogs have been trained to attack people," I said. "If they're going to the county shelter, they can't go home with just anyone."

"In that case," she said, "I may take them myself. Surprise the hell out of my asshole ex one day."

The sheriff and I watched her drive off with her prizes. "So maybe your ghost didn't run those guys himself," he said. "Maybe the lady dog trainer was along for all the operations."

"Then why would he kill her?" Tony asked. "That cost him a real asset."

"Thanks be to God," I said. "I was more afraid of them than him."

"Two possibilities come to mind," the sheriff said. "Either he didn't kill the woman, or he did because they failed to nail your associate here, when they had him dead to rights at the springhouse. Your opening fire on the barns meant that those dogs, and by definition their handler, weren't up to the job."

Tony and I looked at each other. That was a sobering observation.

"Unforgiving ghost," I said.

"Very," the sheriff said.

It was almost sundown by the time the sheriff left. We still hadn't found the entrance to the abandoned coal mine, and neither of us was especially enthusiastic about going back up there in the dark. We were standing by my vehicle out in front of the big house, swatting at the year's first mosquitoes.

"So," Tony said. "We try it again? Hole up here tonight, see what happens?"

"He figured that out last time," I said. "Once the dogs came back without some meat scraps, then Pardee's headlights, and then my firing into the barns, he had to know we'd been waiting."

"So let's try a variation," he said. "I'll hole up in the cottage with the vehicles, you walk over here with the dogs and hide here, in the house this time. I've got some night-vision gear in my truck you could use."

"You're assuming he recons the cottage before he starts anything."

"I would," he said. "Or we missed a bug in the sweep and he simply interrogates it before making any moves."

"So, what then? We leave here, together, go back to the cottage, settle in for the night, and talk whatever trash is required to set the stage that we're in for the night?"

"Right."

"What if he comes for you instead of me?"

"Bring it," he said. "Those dogs scared the shit out of me last night. I owe him one."

That became the plan, in the absence of any other brilliant ideas. I didn't like the fact that we were still reacting to whatever this guy might do. On the other hand, his Dobermans were off the board, and the Rockwell County Sheriff's Office was on his tail now instead of just us chickens.

I went out into the yard after dinner to use my cell phone and called Carol. I told her I needed her electrician to meet me at the house tomorrow so that we could rig some power on all the floors for Pardee's video surveillance system. She said she'd make it happen and asked how it was going. I told her that we'd made a little progress today and that the sheriff's office was now officially in the game, which ought to help. She wished us luck. I told her how much I'd enjoyed our time together the other night.

"I think I surprised myself," she said.

"Maybe just horny? I mean, did you still respect me the next morning?"

She said something rude, laughed, and hung up.

At a little after ten, I took the shepherds over to Glory's End. Once inside, I wrestled the mattress off the old lady's four-poster on the ground floor and humped it up to the second floor. I had brought one of my rifles as well as my SIG .45. Before securing myself upstairs I'd sent the dogs down into the lower level and then the basement just to see if they had any reaction. They did not, so I locked the doors, told the dogs to stay on the main floor, and went upstairs. There I set up a watch station at the back windows of the larger bedroom. I had a night scope on a tripod, a thermos of coffee, and a blanket and pillow from the cottage. I'd been careful to show no lights once in the house, and I stayed back away from the windows in case my stalker had his own night-vision gear. Now it was a matter of waiting and keeping awake.

I failed the keeping awake part. I don't know when I fell asleep, but it was sometime after midnight. I'd gone down once to check on the dogs, who pretended to be wide-awake when I showed up. They undoubtedly went back to sleep as soon as I went back upstairs.

The waking up part turned out to be a breeze, as I bolted upright to the sound of screaming. Really loud screaming, a woman's voice, and she was being drawn and quartered by the Inquisition on a rack somewhere in the house.

I jumped off the mattress, SIG in one hand, flashlight in the other, trying to gather my wits while the poor wretch screamed, desperate, bloodcurdling screams of mortal agony. It was coming from everywhere, but it was louder downstairs. I ran down the stairs and nearly tripped over the shepherds, who were beside themselves, running around in circles and barking.

The moment I hit the lower landing, the screaming got louder upstairs, and it seemed to be coming from the lower level, too. The woman was truly shrieking now, and I had visions of babies being torn out of living wombs. I ran into the back of the house, using the flashlight now, and the screams were definitely coming from the lower level.

But also from upstairs.

I stopped and thought about that. The noise on this level was nothing compared to what I was hearing from the other two levels.

Motion detectors and speakers.

Fuck.

I ignored the awful racket and went around the rooms of the main floor until I found a small white cube sitting on a white mantel, practically invisible unless one was looking for it. The cube was heavier than I expected, and there was a tiny glass eye on the front. When I waved my hand over the eye, the dying woman stopped screaming in my face from the embedded speaker. The shepherds backed away, totally confused by what they were hearing and not seeing.

I went back upstairs and found the second speaker, and then down to the lowest level for the third one. In each case, the speaker stopped its noise the moment I came into the room. I carried all three in my hands to ensure the eyes could detect motion, and the house went blessedly silent. I went back up to my mattress and popped out their batteries to end the disturbance once and for all.

*Not bad,* I thought. Somewhere nearby there was a transmitter that had been activating these devices. It was amazing how much noise these innocuous looking four-inch cubes could generate. Once again my ghost had flushed out his quarry, and once again he'd been in the house while we'd been out beating the bushes for coal mines. His ready access to the house had to mean that he had a hide somewhere not too far away—or more accomplices. Or maybe not, given this guy's predilection for shooting accomplices who disappointed him.

I called Tony and told him what had happened. I said I was going to come back to the cottage. He pointed out that that might have been the objective of the screaming barrage: to get me to come out of the house into the darkness. I thought about that and then told him I was going to try a gambit of my own. I hung up, gathered up the dogs and my gear, and went to the front door of the house. I opened it and then slammed it again, loud enough that if someone was listening, he might think I'd gone out the front door. Then I took my buddies downstairs to the kitchen, unlocked the trapdoor, and went down into the basement. I used the flashlight freely down there until we were right in front of the escape door. It had a red lens that could be rotated over the clear lens, and I did so. Then I switched it off and pushed gently, hoping that our guy hadn't discovered our fake door latch.

The ballpoint pen dropped and the door swung open. A wave of cool air came in from the tunnel. We stepped through, and I left the door ajar. Keeping the shepherds right behind me, we crept to the dogleg turn and then stopped and listened. There was no sound in the old tunnel, just the smell of ancient mortar, dirt, and mold. I stuck a gun around the dogleg and followed it. The red light would have been useless outside, but in the absolute darkness of the tunnel it worked just fine and also preserved my night vision. We hurried down the tunnel to the point where the fire-pit access hatch was right above us, stopped, and listened.

This was going to be the tricky part, so I decided to wait and listen for a few more minutes at the base of the ladder. My plan had been to go out the tunnel and up into the yard, where I hoped to get behind my tormentor. I'd forgotten the dogs: There was no way to get them up that ladder.

Then I heard a sound, a heavy clunk down at the other end of the tunnel.

The door had closed.

I tried to remember the bolting arrangement. There had been a black iron bar and brackets, but they were on my side of the door. The other side had been a bare wooden wall. I looked up at the trapdoor underneath the fire pit. Tony had lifted the trapdoor by pulling up on those andirons, but there'd been no latch. So either way, I wasn't trapped down here.

Or was I?

I went up the ladder and pushed on the trapdoor. It moved a quarter inch, but there was something really heavy on it, and I couldn't get the leverage I needed to lift it.

I went back down the ladder, checked my SIG, and then went back into the tunnel to the dogleg turn. I sent the shepherds around the corner, but nothing happened, so I followed them to the basement door. It was shut, but that black iron bar was still lying on the floor. I went up to the door and listened and then pulled gently on the edge board. The door didn't move.

What the hell? There had been no latches on the other side, no bars, brackets, or any other way to keep that thing shut except from this side.

Three powerful bangs on the other side made me jump and the dogs bark. I quickly retreated to the dogleg turn.

"That you in the box, Richter?"

It was that same throaty voice I'd heard behind the mask, sounding more like a prolonged cough than a voice.

"Good job on the screaming woman," I said. "Those are some speakers."

"Made you move," he said.

"So it did," I replied, still staying out of the line of fire in case he decided to put a few rounds through the door. "Now what?"

"Now you're buried alive," he said.

I wanted to say, *No I'm not. Tony will be out here at daylight.* Instead I tried to draw him out. "Why'd you shoot the biker mama?"

"She failed me," he said.

"Will you please tell me what this is all about?" I asked. "I mean, since I'm buried alive, now's the time, right?"

"I've already told you," he said.

"We've looked back. It's not true."

"True to me, and that's what matters," he replied.

"How'd you get into the house?"

"There are two bolt holes, just like you thought. Only I know where the second one is, and you don't."

"So I guess it's not the smokehouse, then."

"Remember all those bricks stacked in there? They're all oversized, handmade. Weigh about eight, nine pounds apiece. Push hard, maybe you can lift them. Except, perhaps, for that pole."

"Pole?"

"Yeah. The one that wedges the trapdoor shut. It'll move about a quarter inch, enough to give you some air when you need it, and you are going to need it. Got your dogs with you, do you?"

I still wasn't too worried. This was a big tunnel, relatively speaking, and there was plenty of air. "Always," I said. "We captured yours."

"They were useless when it really counted," he said. "You're welcome to them. I had high hopes, but you can't find good help these days."

"I've got lots of good help," I said.

"You think so?" he said, and those were the last words I heard from him.

I did try to lift those bricks, and he was right—I managed about a quarter of an inch before the dead weight of several hundred pounds pushed back. I'd tried the door again, but it still wouldn't move—and, of course, there was the pole.

*You think so?*

Had he done something to Tony? Had we missed a bug and somehow revealed that I'd be in the house and Tony would be alone in the cottage? I'd called Tony and he'd answered immediately, which meant he'd been awake. I'd left Frack over there, so he should have had some warning if someone hit the house.

The shepherds were worried and showed it. I'd turned off my flashlight to conserve the batteries. Daylight up above would not do anything for the absolute darkness down here. Assuming I couldn't force my way out of this tunnel, I'd be dependent on one of the guys, Tony or Pardee, who knew about this tunnel. I couldn't remember if I'd told the sheriff about this place. Carol knew, I reminded myself. Would any of them think about the tunnel if I disappeared? The only one I'd told I was going to try something had been Tony.

*You think so?*

That didn't sound so good.

"Okay, guys," I said. "Time to go night-night. See what happens in the morning."

I went back to the basement door and lay down on the cold earthen floor. The shepherds curled up beside me. The air still seemed serviceable, and the tunnel was at least a hundred feet long.

Some water would have been nice. Some Scotch would have been better. Some frantic tapping on the door from the other side would have been best.

I woke up and checked my watch: seven thirty in the morning, not that it was morning down in the tunnel. My watch light looked like a tiny night-light in that blackness. The shepherds stirred but didn't get up. They were completely blind in that darkness.

I pulled out my cell phone and opened it. It still had battery, light on the screen, and, of course, absolutely no signal. Tony should have been over here by now, so the fact that he wasn't led me to believe my ghost had either attacked him or somehow diverted him. I turned the phone off to conserve its battery and then used the flashlight to explore the tunnel. It hadn't changed much over the night: earthen floor, brick walls, curved, arched brick ceiling, which dusted my face with old mortar each time I looked up. The ladder at the far end was about ten feet high, and the ceiling was maybe seven feet from the floor. Had they dug a long trench, built the walls and arched ceiling, and then just backfilled it?

When I went back to the door I tried to move it again. It budged, but not much. I stubbed my foot on the iron locking bar. Four feet across, three inches wide, a half inch thick, forged iron, and weighing about twenty pounds. I thumped the door with it and made a suitably loud noise. Maybe I could batter the door down with the bar, except that the door was made of two courses of oak boards running cross-grain with one another and reinforced with iron strapping material. Then I remembered the smokehouse trapdoor, and the fact that I could move it just a little.

"C'mon, muttskis," I said. "Let's try the world's simplest tool."

I climbed the ladder, leaving the flashlight, on white beam now, on the floor pointed up. The dogs looked up expectantly, tails wagging in encouragement. I positioned the edge of the bar up against the crack, spread my legs on the ladder, and pressed my upper back against the boards. Then I heaved upward with all my strength. The trapdoor moved maybe a millimeter.

I relaxed, did some deep breathing, and this time repositioned the bar into one corner of the trapdoor. I'd tried to lift the whole thing the first time. Maybe I could lift one corner. All I needed was a half inch in which to wedge that iron bar.

One more deep breath, and push. The rung of the ladder on which I was standing cracked and then broke, nearly dumping me off the ladder and down onto that hard earth floor. I dropped the iron bar trying to stay on the damned ladder and only narrowly avoided beaning one of the dogs. Fortunately the next lower rung held, but I was now too low on the ladder to get much pushing leverage.

I went back down and retrieved the bar. The shepherds were giving me reproachful looks for throwing heavy objects at them. Back up I went, and this time to the next rung up from the new gap on the ladder. This had me bent way over, but it was the best I could do. I positioned the bar into one corner and then, using my legs this time, tried to stand up.

The hatch moved and the bar slid into the resulting crack, just barely. I heard that familiar cracking noise, so I took the strain off before I broke another rung. I relaxed with my head up against the rough bottom of the trapdoor and did some more deep breathing. There was no fulcrum on which I could use the bar as a lever, but I felt the tiniest wisp of air coming through that crack. Progress.

I went back down the ladder and did some back-straightening exercises. I had a feeling I was going to hurt in a little while. The dogs were looking at me with their good-job, now-what expression. Good question.

I turned off the flashlight and turned on my cell phone. When the screen lit up, I went back up the ladder, put the phone up against the crack, and, lo and behold, there was a single bar of signal. The bar was probably acting as an antenna. I dialed 911 and hit SEND. A badly garbled voice answered me, and the call went dead the moment I spoke. Then I remembered what a deaf paralegal had taught me: You can text to 911 if for some reason you can't talk.

I crouched on the ladder and thumbed in a message. Then I redialed and sent the text. Fifteen seconds later MESSAGE RECEIVED appeared on the screen.

I exhaled in relief and went back down the ladder. Now it was just a waiting game.

Thirty minutes later I heard someone banging on the

wooden door from the basement side. I yelled back and then waited for them to do something on the other side that involved cutting metal. Finally the door pushed open in my direction and light blazed in the doorway from two powerful flashlights. As fresh air flooded in, I realized that our air supply in the tunnel had not been as good as I thought it was. The dogs went through while I was still getting my wits together.

Two deputies welcomed us into the basement and showed me the chain arrangement that had been used to keep the door from moving. They said Sheriff Walker was on his way over. I told them I was okay and did not need EMS. While one deputy canceled the EMS dispatch, the other asked what had happened. I told him I'd debrief to the sheriff and then asked if they could check on my associate over at the Lees' stone cottage.

Sheriff Walker showed up fifteen minutes later, and we met on the front porch.

"At least we know he's still in the area," he said, coming up the steps.

"And he still has the initiative," I replied, and then told him what had happened last night. We went inside to see the little speakers, but, of course, they were all gone. The second deputy came back about then and reported that Tony was not at the cottage, nor was his vehicle. The old dog in the house appeared to be fine.

I tried his cell phone. He answered.

"Where are you?" I asked.

"I'm almost to Charlotte," he replied.

"Charlotte?"

"You told me to go to Charlotte, first thing this morning, meet with some guy who oversees kennel clubs in the city, and get him to identify people who know the Doberman scene down there."

"Fascinating," I said and then told him where I'd been all night. I asked him how he received those instructions.

"Text," he said. "On my cell phone—from your cell phone."

"Turn around," I said. "That's all bogus. I never sent any text messages."

"Well, okay," he said, "but I talked to that guy in Charlotte. He's real, and he says he knows the Doberman scene. I'm almost there—what could it hurt?"

I asked him to hold on and asked the sheriff what he thought. "Why not?" he said. "We pulsed the city cops down there, but the biker world doesn't talk to cops. The dog show people might."

"Sheriff says proceed," I told Tony. "Then we have to figure out how this guy got into our comms."

"Ask Pardee," he said. "He's the data-dink."

The sheriff said they'd been tracing back on their victim and had developed a small list of known associates, but so far, no leads on a lone ranger who'd wanted two dogs. He asked about our efforts to recon the plantation.

"Interrupted," I said. "We thought we were homing in on that old coal mine tunnel until the two Dobes came down the hill and put us at general quarters."

"How convenient," he said.

"Yeah, wasn't it. Let's take a walk."

When we got out under the big trees, I told him that I thought this guy still had the house under audio surveillance, and maybe even our vehicles and the cottage. "He anticipates our every move, and he's able to deflect us at will."

"Which means he didn't run after popping the dog trainer," Walker said. "He's in the area, so he's got a base."

"That's what we were looking for, something like that old mine, or a deserted building out there in my seven hundred acres of weeds and trees."

"Maybe we should try aerial," he said.

"We did that. Took pictures, even. Pardee put together a

composite, and we've been over it with a magnifying glass. Nada."

"And yet . . ."

"Yeah. I've been trying to put together a picture of my ghost. He has technical ability and access to tech toys. This whole thing's about his wife and something I supposedly did, but he won't tell me what it is. That's all he'll say. Maybe we need a profiler."

The sheriff snorted. "Might as well read the horoscope in the newspaper," he said. "Those pogues all trained up at Delphi." He assumed the pose of a mystic. "Your perpetrator," he intoned, "will be a male, somewhere between twenty and sixty, with two arms and two legs, capable of extreme violence and yet also able to plan in detail. He'll prefer rifles to pistols, he likes or at least respects dogs, I'm getting black dogs in particular . . ."

"Okay, okay, I get the point—but maybe we could profile the tech toys?"

He nodded. "That's more like it. His surveillance tags, his ability to send text messages from a clone phone, a flashbang, that sort of stuff might narrow it down."

"Do you have assets?"

"No, but the SBI does. Get your Mr. Bell to send us a laundry list of what you've come up against so far and I'll take it up with Raleigh."

"And we will go back out into the back country here and see what we can dig up. Or at least I will, until Tony gets back."

The sheriff looked up the hill toward the big house. "You sure he's not holed up in that thing? Some more secret passages, or a priest hole in the walls somewhere?"

"I guess I could burn it down, see what scuttles out," I said.

He laughed. "Try another search first, why don't you?"

\* \* \*

After the cops left, I called Carol and suggested she bring lunch over to the big house here at Glory's End. "You fly, I buy," I said.

"Deal," she said.

I thought she and I might take another look at the house with an eye toward finding possible hiding places and maybe even that second escape route. Even my ghost had mentioned it. She was an expert in old houses and might be able to see something that we'd missed.

We sat up on the front porch to eat a somewhat elaborate picnic she'd acquired at the purple house restaurant. I was hungry after missing breakfast. The two shepherds had been banished to the steps, but they were begging shamelessly anyway. In their defense, Carol had failed to bring along any dog chow.

She looked good and obviously felt good, and I was comfortable being with her. In contrast, my run-in with the nighttime version of Valeria Lee had been disconcerting, almost a little scary. Yes, I'd reacted, but there'd been that little voice warning me to check out her canine teeth, just in case.

I told Carol about what had happened the night before and said that I needed to go through the house with a fine-toothed comb to see if I could find any more hidden places. She agreed to help, although she thought it was somewhat surreal for us to be sitting out there in the sunlight while my ghost might be crouching under the porch floorboards, listening to us. I said I could put a few rounds down through the floorboards if it would make her feel better. We pitched the scraps out onto the lawn for the shepherds and went inside to begin our search.

We started in the attic and worked our way down. The rooms were still mostly empty, and all the walls seemed to match up with the walls in the adjacent room. We thumped the built-in bookcases in both drawing rooms to no avail. I did look under the front porch, but it was just bare earth and lots of spiders. We poked around the kitchen and checked the base of that giant fireplace. It had a single lintel stone, which must have weighed two tons. It was covered in blackened plaster. Carol asked about the water supply to the house. I showed her the pantry alcove where the pressure tank lived and pointed out the window to the backyard area where there was no wellhead.

"That tank indicates a modern system," she said. "In the old days, the slaves would have carried water to the house from that springhouse."

"The pump is usually in the ground, though, down in the well. I don't see a well."

"Well, then, there has to be a connection between the water source and the house, maybe something to do with a cistern. Let's go look at the springhouse."

We did, and when we got to it I noticed something I hadn't seen before. I'd always assumed the spring was lower in elevation than the main house, but when I lay down on the ground and tried a sight line, I could see that it was actually higher than the partially submerged level of the house.

"Then this is the reservoir," she said. "They didn't need an outside cistern as long as this spring kept running."

She examined the broken latticework where Tony had gone through to escape the Dobermans. The water below was visibly flowing. The end wall that faced the house even had some decorative brickwork, with a flat lion's head medallion right in the middle. The other end had a set of steps leading down into the water, which Carol told me was used for retrieving cooling milk, meat, and eggs, which would have been stored in metal containers in the fifty-degree water.

"So somewhere back there is a pipe or other conduit that sends water back to the kitchen?"

"Yes," she said.

"And we care—why?"

"Because there ought to be water storage in the house, something larger than that little pressure tank. I didn't see one or even a place for one."

We went back to the house, down to the partially underground floor, and into the kitchen area again. I could just see the top of the springhouse from one of the windows, and it still looked like it was lower on the hill than where I was standing, even though now I knew it wasn't.

Carol found it a few minutes later, after banging the handle of a screwdriver on the interior walls of the walk-in cabinets. An entire set of shelves was hinged and latched to the wall. When we unlatched it, it swung back to reveal a doorway, behind which was a set of stone steps leading down into darkness.

"Just what I want to do, after last night," I said. "Go down into another damned tunnel."

I brought in both shepherds, put them on a down at the entrance, and told them to eat anyone who touched that swinging shelf. They lay down on the floor and watched attentively. After last night, they weren't coming with me no matter what I said.

I still had my flashlight, and Carol came along with me. This tunnel was very narrow, so much so that my shoulders almost touched the walls. It was straight, with no doglegs, and I was pretty sure it pointed in the direction of the springhouse. The walls were stone, not brick, and the ceiling was made up of heavy planks sheathed in what looked like copper. The floor was pounded red clay, and it was wet. A plain steel pipe ran along one side of the floor. When we got to the other end, there were five stone steps leading up to a short metal door. When I shone the light on that door, we could see that the bottom one-third of the door was perspiring.

"That moisture would indicate that the door opens into the spring," she said. "What good is this?"

"Something for a real emergency," I said. "Or they had a way to dump the spring from in here." I looked up and saw a badly rusted lever high up on the right-hand wall alongside the stone steps. "Like that."

I got down on one knee and shone the flashlight along the earthen floor. I could see our footprints, and what looked like other prints underneath ours. This was how my ghost had been getting in and out of the building, once we'd discovered the other tunnel.

We walked back to the house end of the tunnel, where I discovered tiny bits of wire and a bent connecting clip beside the steps. The shepherds were watching us now from the top of the steps, but they still weren't coming down. The debris was further evidence of my stalker: He'd probably wired the speakers down here before setting them out in the house. I still could not find any internal water storage system for the house, but maybe one old lady living here didn't need that much water. We went up the steps and back out into the kitchen.

"Okay," I said. "That's two tunnels. Suppose that's it?"

"That's two more than I expected," she said. "The question is, how in the world did your ghost, as you call him, know about these?"

"Excellent question," I said. "I think I'll ask Ms. Valeria Lee if she knows about any tunnels in this house."

"Why her?"

"She apparently had been taking care of the old lady who lived here, and she grew up here, according to her mother."

"Okay, that makes sense."

"I'll just pose the question about tunnels casually," I said. "I want to watch her reaction."

"Why?"

"If she knows all about them, I learn nothing. If I sense that she's evading the question, then I'll have to assume a connection between my stalker and the crazy ladies across the road. It would sure as hell explain how this guy has been able to move around here so easily."

"That doesn't track," she said. "I thought this whole thing started as a prison ghost, back in Summerfield."

"I'm beginning to think that was all coincidental. Billie Ray kept denying that he had anything to do with any shootings, and even I thought it unlikely that he could acquire a rifle and set up a hit that quickly."

"Then someone shot him."

"Correct," I said. "So now I'm thinking more about the timing than the location. All this stuff started after I came out here and started making inquiries about land and then, specifically, Glory's End."

"What about the you-killed-my-wife stuff?"

"Beats me," I said. "One mystery at a time, I guess. Right now I'm going back out there to see if that coal mine's up there."

Carol had to go meet another restoration client. Before leaving, she gave me a quick kiss. I turned it into a slower one and then brushed my hands across her bottom. She giggled but backed away. "Not in front of the shepherds," she said with a grin, and then she left.

I called Pardee. He had acquired most of what he needed and asked if the electrician had set up power. I'd forgotten all about the electrician and said I'd have to look. Pardee said that he'd be out in the evening and that Tony had debriefed him on the events of last night. I told him about finding the second escape route and explained my theory about the Lees and a possible connection to the land. He had an interesting question: How had the Lees found out that I was going to buy the plantation? That was easy, I said, having already seen the county grapevine in action. It had to be Oatley or someone else in town, I said. He suggested I chase down that connection, see where it led. I told him that first I wanted to go find that coal mine, hopefully without distractions this time.

I went back to the cottage, fed the starving mutts, and got my field gear. Then I drove the utility vehicle over to the barn and told Cubby that I needed to see Ms. Valeria again but it wasn't urgent. He thought the vehicle was a great idea but advised me not to drive it up to the big house where Ms. Hester would see it.

"You don't think she's already seen it from one of those windows up there?" I asked.

He grinned. "Ms. Valeria? Yeah, she's seen it, and you in it. Ms. Valeria, she sees everything. But Ms. Hester? She's takin' a nap right about now. Thing is, she's got a hate-on for those four-wheelers, and that's what's she's gonna think this is. Might shoot at it, even."

When I drove back over to Glory's End, I got a surprise. Carol Pollard was waiting for me. She'd changed out of her town clothes into jeans, boots, and a long-sleeved shirt-blouse. She was carrying a Smith & Wesson .357 Magnum side gun in a holster. I asked her about her client.

"They forgot the appointment," she said. "Clients are a lot like contractors sometimes."

"And?"

"And I thought about you going out there on your own," she said. "I'm not a cop anymore, but I have had the training, if you'd like a hand."

"Absolutely," I said, eyeing the hand cannon and wondering if she could use it. "Backup is always welcome. Hopefully we won't need artillery."

"If we do, though, there's no acceptable substitute—is there?"

Carol and I rode in my trusty new chariot back out to the cut through the eastern ridge and then left up the hill to the spot where we'd acquired the newly disgraced Dobermans. The shepherds rode along in the back compartment as a concession to the fact that I'd just fed them. I was glad to have Carol along, but what really made me feel more confident was the fact that the other guy's dogs were no longer in the game. He'd made a mistake doing that. The first of many, I hoped.

Carol asked me about the so-called coal mine, and I told her what Walker had told me. She'd never heard that story, or that any coal had ever been found in Rockwell County.

"They didn't find any here, either," I said. "Sounded to me like someone came along and scammed the owners in a get-rich-quick scheme."

We stopped at the same place we'd stopped when the dogs alerted. I looked back at them to see if they were interested in anything up in that tree line. Frick burped. Good deal.

I pocketed the keys. Carol and I got out and started up the hill. I'd brought a walking stick, so I made better progress than Carol, who was being careful not to turn an ankle in all the loose rock.

Loose rock?

I looked down and saw that we were climbing up what had to be a tailings pile, hidden under a carpet of weeds and small trees. I sent the dogs ahead, but they couldn't make quick progress, either, due to the sharp footing. Carol swore behind me, and I turned around to see her hunched over, both palms on the ground and her legs out behind her. She couldn't straighten up without falling, so I went back down and rescued her.

"What is it with all these rocks?" she said. Her hands were bruised.

I told her what I thought it was, and we both looked up into a line of scrub pines that seemed to mark the top of the rockslide. The shepherds disappeared into the trees.

"Great place for a shooting gallery," she said softly, staring into those trees.

"Let's split up," I said. "Separate by about twenty, thirty yards. Divide the targets."

"Right," she said. I gave her my walking stick and then went left across the rocks. I had heavy-duty field boots on, which gave my ankles a whole lot more support than her L.L.Bean day hikers gave her. She went right, far enough to force two shots, but stayed near enough that we could still see each other. I was counting on the shepherds to give us some warning if there were bad guys up there.

In the event, there weren't. We climbed through the pines and found both mutts waiting for us in front of what had been the entrance to a smallish tunnel or natural cave in the side of the ridge. There had been two massive vertical beams for the side of the entrance, and one even bigger, tree-trunk-sized beam for the lintel. All three beams were smashed into a collapsed mass of shattered wood and rocks. The tunnel had either caved in or had been dynamited down. Either way, there was no access here, and the entire pile of rocks and crushed timber was studded with dozens of small cedars.

We poked around the entrance area just to make sure that someone hadn't staged a cave-in, but it seemed real enough. The dogs weren't picking up any interesting scents, which was comforting. I did wonder why the Dobermans had come from this direction and mentioned this to Carol.

"How about air vents?" she said.

*Good question,* I thought. Even if this hadn't been a real coal mine, they might have cut some air vent shafts farther up the ridge. The problem now was that the ridge went almost vertical at the face of the tunnel entrance, rising up maybe two hundred more feet to the top. There was a surprising number of trees growing off this face, slender, spindly specimens in survival mode, trapping water by putting roots down into cracks and crevices along the face.

"I'm trying to figure out how the tunnel would have gone," I said. "Straight in here, but then where?"

"If they kept going straight, they'd come out the other side of the ridge," Carol said. "If they turned it, they could go along the drift of the ridge for almost a half mile."

"I would think it would go down, not horizontally, if they were looking for coal. They wouldn't find coal in the top reaches of a ridge."

"They're finding it that way in West Virginia today," she pointed out. "They're strip-mining by taking off the tops of mountains."

She was right. Now that I thought about it, the sheriff had said they'd taken the tunnel sideways down the ridge for six or seven hundred feet.

"We need to get up top," I said. "Look for any air vents, or even another entrance on the back side of the ridge."

"I thought your interest in this was a safety issue," she said, eyeing that near vertical face. "This looks pretty much closed up right here."

"My interest is in seeing if this tunnel, assuming it hasn't collapsed, too, is a base of operations for the guy who's after me. I don't want to go underground. I just want to rule it out."

"That's good," she said. "I don't like heights, and I hate going underground. You have no idea how hard it was for me to go into that escape tunnel."

I looked at her to see if she was serious about all that. She was.

"Okay," I said. "I don't want to go all the way around to the other side of this ridge and make another long climb. It'll take too long. Let's do this: You take the shepherds and go back down to the vehicle. Take it back to the dirt road that goes along the bottom of the ridge and head toward the river."

"What are you going to do?"

"I'm going to climb hand over hand, using those trees, get to the top, and then walk the top of the ridge down toward the river. I'll keep you in sight, and you should be able to see me. I'll come down off the ridge when I get near the river. That should put you near the quarry."

"I don't know, Cam," she said, looking up at the ridge again. "If something goes wrong, I can't help you from down there."

"I guess you could always call the cops," I said and gave her the keys.

The plan fell apart as soon as the shepherds realized I wasn't in the utility cart. I'd begun my climb only to be interrupted by Kitty barking down at the base of the cliff, while Frick ran back and forth around the collapsed entrance, trying to find a way up. I could see Carol in the distance, standing by the vehicle, her hands up in an I-tried gesture. There was nothing I could do about the shepherds, and I now had my hands full, literally, with staying on the cliff. The smaller trees were shaky as handholds because they were rooted in their imagination for the most part. I pulled a couple out and then had to slide back down until I could grab a more substantial tree trunk. Each slide produced a baby avalanche of gravel and loose rocks. I also found myself puffing more than a little and vowed to get back to daily runs and a lot more exercise, just as soon as I got off this damned cliff.

A half hour later I reached the top of the ridge. I could no longer see the dogs down below, and I hoped they'd gotten tired of being rained on by my clumsy climbing efforts. The view was pretty spectacular from the top. I could see the big house in the distance to the west, and I could clearly see Carol and the vehicle rolling down toward the river and the quarry area to the east. As I watched, two dusty shepherds came out of the woods along the road and caught up with the cart. Carol stopped, invited them to climb into the back, and then looked up toward the ridge. I waved, and she waved back. Okay, back on track.

The very top of the ridge was solid rock, which looked

like granite to me. The scrubby trees began on the nearby slopes, but the backbone of the ridge was like a paved road, maybe twenty feet wide. I was looking for signs of ventilation shafts, but wondered, now that I beheld all this granite, if they'd really run any shafts down to that tunnel. Sheriff Walker had said the tunnel began in a cave, and that almost didn't compute: Caves were usually found in limestone, not granite. Maybe the whole thing was BS, with the efforts of the alleged coal miners confined to blowing up a perfectly good cave. Either way, the ridge didn't seem to be a very promising place for a hidey-hole.

A blur of motion to my left had me whirling and reaching for my SIG when two deer came bounding past me in those exaggerated leaps they make. They'd come out of a clump of hardwoods down to the left and about thirty yards ahead of me. I put the SIG back and veered off the clear rock path and went down into that grove of trees, where I found a spring. The water looked cool and inviting, but I was mindful of giardia and other parasites, so I washed the sweat off my face but did not drink. There were three game trails leading away from the spring, which was the source of a pretty brook that went splashing down the hillside. A hawk launched out from the side of the ridge below me, screaming indignantly at something.

Then I froze. I'd been above the deer, and yet they'd come in my direction. The hawk had blasted out of the trees farther down the same side of the ridge. Maybe I wasn't the cause of all this spooked wildlife. I was keenly aware that I could no longer see Carol, or she me, now that I was off the top of the ridgeline.

I listened but heard only a mild breeze sloughing through the trees and the musical noise of the brook dropping down into a baby waterfall, which seemed to echo.

Echo?

I started grabbing small trees again as I let myself down the western hillside, following the course of the outfall from the spring. After about forty feet of going tree to tree, I came to a real cliff, a sheer wall of solid rock. Then I realized it wasn't a cliff at all but a crack in the ridge. It was perpendicular to the ridgeline and about twenty feet across where I was standing, narrowing down to almost nothing about a hundred feet down. It was as if the part of the ridge that sloped down to the river had broken off the main stem of the hill, like a ship whose bow gets too heavy for its keel. There were decent-sized trees on both rims, which is why I'd never noticed this formation from down in the crop fields below. Even more important, directly opposite from where I stood, there was a rope, anchored to the edge of the crack, dangling down into the shadows below.

Gotcha.

We held a council of war at the local pizza joint over beers and some surprisingly good pie. Tony was back from Charlotte, and Pardee back from downtown. I'd invited Carol Pollard to come along. She wanted to help, had local knowledge that we needed, and wasn't afraid to go out in the woods. The fact that she carried a .357 was a plus.

Tony had mixed results to report from the world of Charlotte Dobermans. There was an active breed club in the city, but no one remembered anyone asking to acquire two working Dobermans. There was one breeder who said he'd supplied four Dobes to an individual who'd claimed he was an estate manager out in the Asheville area about a year ago. Tony didn't think that sounded like my guy. None of the club's breeders had ever heard of the biker gang's dog supplier, but they did acknowledge that there could be other breeders out there who did their own thing and didn't come to the AKC shows, weren't members of the Charlotte DPC, etc. Otherwise, he'd drawn a blank.

Pardee had managed to acquire the components he needed to put up a video surveillance system at Glory's End, including both the house and the grounds. He had designed the system so it could be monitored from within the big house or from the stone cottage. I asked him to send a list to Sheriff Walker of all the high-tech widgets we'd come up against since my stalker started his thing, so that he could get the SBI going on providing a possible profile.

Then we talked about the mysterious rope. Tony immediately suggested we saw three-quarters of the way through it. Next time the guy started down, he'd get a courtesy drop test. I wanted to climb down it and see what was at the bottom. Pardee said that the bottom of that chasm would make a perfect place for my stalker to finish the game. That rope, he suggested, might have been put there for me to find.

He had a point: My ghost had been ahead of us all the way up to this moment, and there was no reason to think we had the initiative now. Then Carol had a question.

"Is the bottom of that crack in the rock level with the entrance to the tunnel on the other side?"

I tried to picture the elevations. "I think it's higher, not lower," I said. "I guess we could find that out with a GPS set. Why?"

"Because that might be the other way into the old mine," she said. "Or maybe even the back of the original cave."

"Then one of us has to go down that rope," I said.

"Or we go down our own rope," Tony said. "Or maybe even use two ropes, so you have backup at the bottom."

"Or," Pardee said, "we send down a video camera and some portable lights, have a look around at the bottom before anyone goes down a rope."

"Now we're talking," I said.

"You guys going to cut the sheriff in on all this?" Carol asked.

Of course we were.

"Before you go jumping into the void?"

"I really want this sumbitch," I said, "but I guess you're right. If they've got a rope team, all the better."

Tony and Pardee said they needed to get back to Triboro and spend a day in the office, catching up on the things they'd dropped to come help me. I told them I'd get up with Sheriff Walker. If the county guys did take over, we might have to wait for them to get their plans in order.

"And?" said Tony.

It took me a moment. They were both looking at me. So was Carol. "And," I said, "no Lone Ranger stuff on my part."

"There you go."

We went our separate ways. I took the mutts and my tired ass back to the stone cottage. I fed them, as they'd only managed to cajole Carol out of one piece of pizza between them. Then I got a glass of single malt, my cell, and a hat against the rising gnats and went out to the pond swing to call the sheriff. Pardee had assured me that the house was clear of listening devices, but I wanted to be damned sure that whatever the sheriff and I set up remained secret.

I dialed the nonemergency number for the sheriff's office. The sheriff was busy and would call back, which he did. I told him I needed face time with him, tomorrow if possible, and described what I'd found up on the eastern ridge. I also described the second escape tunnel in the house and the bits of wire. He said he'd drop by the cottage when he was done with his next phone call. He showed up thirty minutes later and said yes to a Scotch, and then we went back out to the pond. The shepherds followed.

"I didn't mean tonight, Sheriff," I said. "Tomorrow would be just as good."

"No matter," he said. "It's not like I have any reason to go home at night these days."

"No lady in your life?"

"Lost her to cervical cancer a year ago," he said with a sigh. "Took the fun right out of this job, if you really want to know."

"Damn," I said, remembering Bobby Lee Baggett's comment. "My ex and I had gotten back together after a lot of years, and then some bastard put a bomb in her vehicle. I know precisely what you mean about the juice going out of life."

"She refused to get an annual physical," he said. "All the women in her family went out relatively early, and she said she wasn't going to mess with God's will."

"Wow," I said. "What will you do?"

"I'm thinking of hanging it up when my term's over next year," he said. "Maybe go somewhere else. I don't know. You ever thought about being sheriff of a county?"

"Me?" I said, surprised. "I guess I could be sheriff, but I could never get elected. For one thing, I can't stand the thought of kissing babies."

He laughed. "What's wrong with kissing babies?"

"They emit noxious fluids at both ends, usually when you get near them."

"Think about it," he said. "You're going to be a prominent landowner, you've got the background, and you've run a company."

"There's no one at the House ready to step up?"

"One or two," he said, sipping his whiskey, "but if I campaigned for you, they'd back off. Plus, I can bring you the black community vote. Sine qua non, if you get my drift. Think about it."

I didn't say yes or no. The idea was much too sudden. I decided to get back to business. "First I have to get this spider off my back," I said.

"Our spider," he reminded me. "So tell me: You think you were supposed to find this mysterious rope rig?"

"Entirely possible," I admitted. "If it was my only escape rope, I'd have hidden it in the bushes."

"Me, too," he said. "I keep coming back to it: If this guy wants you dead, why hasn't he just used a long gun, taken you out on the front porch?"

"He wants me to 'pay' for something I supposedly did that involved his wife."

"Pay, as in blackmail?"

"No, as in mental anguish. Fear of stepping out the door. Always watching my back. He does shit. Pasting the scary mask to the window. The screaming woman trick in the empty house over there. Rifle rounds into my house. He wants to get me so rattled that I can't function. He wants me sitting in bed at night, waiting for him to come. Then he'll use the long gun."

"Is that how you feel right now? Fearful?"

"Right now I'm mostly pissed off. I'll take precautions, but I'd sure like to hunt him for a change."

"He might have anticipated that," the sheriff said.

"Put something like a climbing rig out in full view, in the hopes that I'd lunge at the chance to get him."

"Unh-hunh," he said. "That's how I'd read it."

"You keep saying I need to go on offense here."

"Why don't you set a trap or two?"

"Like where?"

"How's about that second tunnel? You said you found bits of wire and footprints that weren't yours. I can get you a real concussion grenade, not a flashbang. Hell, paint glue all over it, cover it in bird-shot or finishing nails, rig it to a trip wire. Then you and your guys stay the hell out of that tunnel."

"I like the way you think," I said. "Can you get me two?"

He laughed. "You never heard that idea from me," he said. "Now, as for the rope: Go back there, with your helpers. Cut through the rope, maybe one-third of the way. Do it right where he'd see it as he was coming up, but not enough to make it break. Let him know you found it, and that you, too, can play fuck-fuck."

"It's a start," I said, "but what I want is a finish."

"What'd your people find out in Charlotte?"

I told him. Then I asked him what he'd found out about the biker woman.

"We added some depth to the ID," he said, "but nothing about who may have hired her. Her name was Elizabeth Craney. The bikers called her Betty Boobs. The Charlotte metro cops had never heard of her other than for the Doberman assault case, and Mecklenburg County hasn't had any trouble with her other than a couple of misdemeanors. Her biker buddies, of course, told my guys to pound sand."

I finished my Scotch. "So we're nowhere, really," I said. "I know he exists and that he's serious; you guys know the dead woman's name."

"As long as he wants to make a game of it," he said, "you still have a chance at him."

"I feel so much better."

"Like I said, set some traps. Vary your routine. Use these dogs. Walk over to that crack in the hill at two in the morning and drop five sticks of dynamite down there. Throw some shit in the game."

After the sheriff left I continued to sit out by the pond with the dogs. Maybe Valeria would come out to dance for me again, or even the major. It was so peaceful out here on these big tracts of land. No neighbors in sight, no traffic, no sirens. It was exactly what I wanted, but I couldn't have it until I took care of this wee little problem.

Where was he now? Holed up in some cave, waiting for us to come do something about the climbing rope? Over in my house next door, planting the next nightmare? Or was he up at the big house behind me, having a drink with the Lees and telling them about his adventures? I looked over my shoulder and saw the dim glow of candlelight on the second floor. I'd promised the guys no Lone Ranger stuff, but going over to my own house couldn't be that dangerous. What could go wrong?

* * *

Thirty minutes later the mutts and I were pushing through the pine plantation on the western side of the house, headed for the back barns. I'd left a message on Tony's cell phone that I was going to hole up at Glory's End tonight. I'd brought a short-barreled, semiauto twelve-gauge along with my SIG. The night was clear and cool with sufficient moonlight to see where I was going in the trees. I had no specific plan other than to go over to Glory's End, set up in a place where I could watch the house, and hope that my stalker decided to do something similar. I knew there was a fifty-fifty chance that he might do the same thing over at the stone cottage. Maybe we'd meet on the road in the morning and do a rerun of the O.K. Corral. The Earps had used shotguns, hadn't they?

I came up from the river side, going slow, approaching the house through the barn aisles, checking each building with the dogs and taking my time, conscious of that abandoned well. The shepherds jumped a rat in the hay barn, but I quickly brought them to heel. They were both interested in the spot where the woman had been shot down, which told me their noses were working. We ended up in the barn to the left of that one, where the ancient tractors were busy oxidizing. This shed had three windows in the back wall, so I climbed up onto one of the tractors and sat down on the bare steel seat frame. From there I could see the smokehouse, the springhouse, and the back courtyard and garden areas. The shepherds lay down on either side of the tractor. I'd brought along a small thermos of leftover breakfast coffee, and I sipped some of that while watching out the windows. It was horrible, as all leftover coffee is. I propped the shotgun up on the steering wheel and waited.

After almost an hour of listening to mice scurrying around in the moldering haystack, I was getting pretty sleepy. I set my cell phone to vibrate a wake-up alarm in an hour and stuck it back in my pocket. I was just settling into the backrest of the tractor when both dogs got up suddenly and stared back out into the barnyard area behind us. I turned around slowly, shotgun in hand, and tried to make out what they were looking at. The buildings behind us were all gray in the moonlight, and I realized that some mist had crept up the hill from the river bottoms.

There.

Next to one of the smaller sheds, about a hundred feet away, I could just barely make out what looked like a large human figure, decked out in some kind of flowing black robes. It had a pale gray oval where its face should have been. It looked like one of those movie theater lobby cut-outs, until it moved.

The hair rose on the back of my neck. Kitty growled deep in her throat, and Frick put her head down as if about to charge it. I kept blinking my eyes, trying for more detail, when suddenly the figure levitated off the ground and flew right at me, the pale gray oval becoming a horror mask, and then I woke up, the cell phone humming against my right thigh.

There were no death monsters, the shotgun was still wedged into the steering wheel, and both very special guard dogs were out like lights under the tractor. My neck was stiff, my mouth tasted of coffee grounds, and I felt like an idiot.

This was pointless.

I had started to slide down off the tractor when something really did catch my eye through one of the back windows. Something had moved out there. Then the moon slipped behind a cloud and it got really dark. I couldn't see anything through the windows anymore, but I was sure I'd seen movement over by the smokehouse. It looked like it had been coming toward the barn area.

I continued to slide down off the tractor. Both shepherds got up and gathered around. I tiptoed to the open doors of the shed and went down on one knee. Then I motioned for both dogs to close in on either side, which they did.

I put an arm around each one and cupped a hand over their muzzles. Frick knew what this meant, and Kitty was about to learn. I stayed motionless on the ground, watching and listening. The moon was still obscured, and my eyes hadn't yet adapted to full darkness. The only sound was that of the dogs' breathing through my fingertips. I would look at a spot and then look off to one side, trying to see the peripheral image. Then I felt Frick tense up, and I knew she'd seen it.

I waited, and then Kitty saw it, too. I increased the tension on both dogs' muzzles. I didn't want any growling or barking. I tried again to see the thing that was out there, but the image just wouldn't come. The dogs' muzzles were slowly traversing to the right, and when I was pretty sure it had come past my building and was about to go between the next two sheds, I launched Frick, who went out like a bullet, then Kitty, hot on her tail. I reached back for the shotgun about the time they made the hit.

There was a thump, a yell, and then a lot of shepherd intimidation barking. Then, mercifully, the moon came out. I walked out of the shed, checked to make sure he didn't have help, and then walked over to the large figure that was prostrate on the ground. The two shepherds were standing over him and giving him absolute hell as he covered his head with his arms. Then I saw the uniform.

"Get 'em off me, please," Sheriff Walker said.

I gave a command, and Frick jumped away and sat down. Kitty wasn't sure she shouldn't just go ahead and eat him, but then she reluctantly backed away and looked at me for further instructions.

I helped the sheriff up off the ground and pointedly did not look to see if he had embarrassed himself, although my nose told me he may have. He brushed the yard dirt off his uniform and then bent down to retrieve his service weapon, which he'd apparently been carrying in his hand when the two shepherds hit him from behind.

"Goddamn, Lieutenant," he said, rubbing some sand out of his mouth. "Those sumbitches hit pretty hard. I heard 'em comin' at the last moment, but then I was down and having me a dirt sandwich."

"Sorry about that, Sheriff. You said to vary my routine, so I decided to come over here and just see who or what showed up."

"I should have told you I might come around," he said. He ran one hand over his head and then spit some more dirt out of his mouth.

"I'd just about decided that I was being stupid," I said, "sitting out here in the damn dark, and then I saw you coming out of the smokehouse."

He shook his head. "I came by the smokehouse, not out of it. Parked right out front, walked around the house like I owned it."

*That's funny,* I thought. I hadn't heard a car coming up the drive. Of course, I might have been engaging the flying banshee right about then, too. I apologized again for knocking him down, and the shepherds closed in to make friends. He had the grace to pet both of them and tell them they were good dogs. They recognized their doughnut touch and wagged enthusiastically.

I took him into the shed to show him where I'd been set up. We strolled around the working area of the barns, and I pointed out where my favorite abandoned well was lurking. Then we walked over to the springhouse, where I showed him the back wall that doubled as an escape door from the main house. He took it all on board without comment, and I wondered if I was telling him things he already knew. He was holding one elbow, which I'm sure was hurting after he'd been taken down by the dogs. The sheriff was a solidly built man, but he'd be hurting all over tomorrow morning.

We stood by the springhouse, taking in the moonlit view down the wide lawns and out over the crop fields between the house and the river. The moon went back behind a cloud, and it became dark as the proverbial well digger's behind. The air was perfectly still. Then I heard a clunk in the distance.

I looked sideways at the sheriff, and he had cocked his head to listen.

"Recognize that?" I whispered.

"Paddle on the side of a johnboat," he replied.

Exactly what I'd thought. It's an unmistakable sound, and it had come from across the fields from the river bottoms. Maybe my ghost had just screwed up.

"We wait or we go down there?"

"How long would it take us to walk to that crack on that ridge over there?" he asked softly. "To get to the side with the rope on it?"

"You don't think he's coming up here?"

"Maybe," he said, "but if he comes here, finds nobody home, he'll go to his hidey-hole, if that's what it is. We wait by that rope, maybe we get him."

*What the hell,* I thought. It might work. "Backup?" I asked.

"Too much noise," he said. "Besides, we got four against one."

I couldn't argue, and I wouldn't be Lone Rangering anymore, either.

It took us almost thirty minutes. The sheriff's definition of walking was just a hair slower than my definition of a comfortable jog. I didn't want to deal with that slide of rocks and scree in the dark, so we turned left in the entrance to the pass itself and went up the backbone of the ridge instead. I knew our target might be going directly to the rope from the river side, which meant we might just collide on the ridge. The sheriff didn't seem to care, but I had Frick and Kitty cast out ahead as scouts, which should give us a little warning if we were approaching a head-on. The clouds had disappeared, so we could see much better. That was a good news and bad news deal: so could he.

I took the sheriff to the side from which I'd seen the rope the first time. It was still there, twenty, twenty-five feet across the shadowy defile. We worked our way back up the hill to the top of the notch and then back down the other side, being as quiet as possible now in case this had been his destination and not our playground over there on the big hill. The dogs found the rope and its anchor first. The sheriff pointed silently to the anchoring arrangement to make sure I recognized that it was professional climbing gear. Lots of stainless steel and complex knots. Then we backed out of the immediate area and into some trees uphill of the rope anchor. The sheriff said we should separate.

"We want to take him in, or just take him?" I whispered before we took up our positions.

"I'm here to apprehend a suspect," he said, "but if it turns into a gunfight, I'm gonna be standing when it's all over. What you got in that shotgun?"

"Heavy game load."

"Can you hit him from here with that .45 if you have to?"

"Yup."

"Me, too," he said. "I'll go down the other side, set up directly across from the rope. He shows up, I'll light him up with my Maglite here. Then I'll do a standard yell-down. He just stands there, take him down with the dogs. He pulls, oh, well. Okay?"

"Works for me."

I kept the shepherds with me while the sheriff went down the hill about fifty feet and faded into the shadows of the tree line lining the cut in the hillside. Tactically, we were set up correctly: If any shit started, our guy would have two separate shooters to deal with, one he knew about, one he hopefully didn't. We might have to wait a while if he was headed first to Glory's End or the stone cottage. Of course, it could have been a poacher we'd heard down on the river, some guy running his trotlines after dark. I didn't think so, though, and neither did the sheriff.

I settled into the weeds and put my back up against a tree trunk. I'd put Frick on a sight line between me and the rope anchor, about halfway down. I kept Kitty with me. Even though it was a pretty fair ambush setup, it was comforting to have that big warm furry thing right at my side. Besides, I knew that Frick would give warning with her ears, while Kitty, still new to hunting games, might bark.

An hour passed, an hour during which I changed position against the tree trunk, sat back, sat forward, knelt on one knee, stood up, and did everything else I could to stay awake and alert. Kitty was curled in a ball, but with her head pointed down the hillside and her eyes on Frick, whom I could no longer even see. The moon traversed the sky and began sinking toward the western ridge of the property beyond the big house. *At some point*, I told myself, *I'm going to fall asleep*. I think my body knew that we had made a lot of assumptions about where the man who'd gone thump in the night might be going. He might even have been getting back into his boat, having been up in the barnyard listening to us.

Then Kitty was rising to a standing position, her ears forward and her body starting to tense up. I put a hand on her neck just to let her know I was watching.

Something moved down the hillside. A figure, man or woman I couldn't tell, but definitely human. I got ready to fire the dogs at him. For an instant, the figure stood at the edge of the rock face. Then it knelt down. I heard a loud click of metal on metal, and the next moment, it was gone.

Where in the hell was the sheriff?! Why hadn't he lit the guy up and made his noise? Had my stalker taken him out first?

I couldn't see Frick, but Kitty was relaxing, which probably meant that Frick didn't know what to do. Neither did

I. The sheriff solved it for me a minute later, coming down the hillside from behind me, making just enough noise that both the dogs and I could hear him approaching. He raised a hand as he walked up.

"I know," he said softly. "I changed the plan. I thought about what you'd said, about backup. He could have done the same damn thing the moment I lit him up—dropped down that rope where neither one of us could get a shot at him. This way, we know where he is. Now I'm going to get me some backup."

*Get me some backup.* Not "us." I realized that what had really happened here was that the sheriff's professional standards had reasserted themselves. It might sound good to say *take the perp out*, but in reality, the law was different. Also, it wasn't like I could argue. As far as he was concerned, this was probably the guy who'd shot the Craney woman in the barn. He had every right to tell me what I could and couldn't do as long as he was pursing a murder suspect in his exclusive jurisdiction. Still, I wouldn't have minded putting a few rounds down the hillside. It might have caused the guy to drop into that gorge without the benefit of his rope. Frick rejoined us, looking annoyed that she hadn't gotten to bite anybody.

"Right," I said. "It's your patch."

"You're thinking like a sheriff's office lieutenant again," he said approvingly. "When in doubt, bring a crowd."

"Absolutely," I said. "I'll wait here with you until your guys show up, but after that, you don't need me here anymore, do you?"

He hesitated for just a second. "No," he said. "We'll get set up and then send some SWAT people down that gorge to see what they find."

There was an unspoken question there, as in, *Don't you want to know what we find*? The truth was, I was really tired. I knew that it would take a few hours for them to get set up properly and get more people in position along the ridge to watch for a second way out. They'd be polite, but I also knew I'd just be in the way.

I let him do his thing on the radio with his operations center while I walked back down to that rope anchor. The gorge was at least a hundred feet down, maybe more, and very narrow, perhaps only man-wide at the bottom. The sheriff might have had a shot, but the moment he slipped onto that rope, I would not have been able to get a bead on him. The shotgun might have worked, but I didn't really have cause to shoot the climber without knowing who he was.

We'd been speaking as quietly as we could, so I didn't think our ghost would have been aware of us down there, unless he'd put some more electronics in place up here on the rim. So what had he done: clipped on his descenders, kicked off the rock rim, and gone down in one smooth descent, applying some brakes only as he neared the bottom. Then stepped off the rope and into—what? An old ventilation shaft? A breakthrough collapse in the cave walls? I knelt down at the edge of the crack in the hillside, experiencing a mild wave of vertigo as I looked down into the deep darkness below.

Once I saw the blue lights flickering out on the two-lane, I told the sheriff I was going to take my dogs and go back to the stone cottage. He nodded, but he was preoccupied with getting his people in position. I climbed up the ridge to the granite road to watch for a few minutes and then headed down toward the farm road. Then I stopped.

What if we had it wrong? What if this guy had not gone into the alleged ridge tunnels but had instead run for it? It was a simple matter of his turning downhill at the bottom of the chasm and then heading back to the river and his boat. If he'd tumbled to the potential ambush up top, he wouldn't deliberately go into a tunnel from which there might be only one way out.

*You're pushing it*, my tired sensible brain told me. The lizard half, however, wanted to get this guy.

I turned around, called the mutts, and headed back. I wanted to tell the sheriff what I was doing, but the first deputies had already arrived at the top of the gorge, so I drifted to the right along the top of the ridge and retraced my steps of the afternoon, aiming for the river bottoms at the north end of the ridge. I could see more blue lights coming into the main driveway of Glory's End. The sheriff must have indeed summoned a crowd.

The backbone of the ridge began to tilt down, but it was still pretty clear sailing along all that smooth rock. If I was correct, my ghost was headed in the same direction, only he'd be working his way down in the creek bottoms to my left. That would be slow going compared to this relatively paved road up here, so I kept to the east side and moved as fast as I could, shotgun at port arms, shepherds out in front. When the ridge tipped down at a fifteen-degree slope, I had to slow way down. The moonlight was getting dimmer now, but there was a cool breeze rising from the river, dispersing the mist. I could smell pine trees the closer I got to the water, along with the first hints of mud. I slowed to a careful creep through all the flood debris along the banks and brought the shepherds closer in.

The question now was, where was his boat? It had sounded like he'd been messing with it from somewhere upriver, but the directionality of sounds carrying across the country night could not be trusted. I turned upriver, aiming for the point where that creek that ran the western side of the ridge finally joined the Dan. I was hoping for a clean crossing, but instead I found myself stepping through increasingly gooey muck. I hoped this wasn't the quicksand people talked about. The shepherds were now following me instead of me following them. Their pointy little feet were going deeper than my size sixteens. I had to stop.

There was an enormous tree root ball lying parallel to

the riverbank. I hoisted myself up on that and then dragged both dogs up onto it with me. The ambient light down here in the bottomlands was minimal. I could both hear and feel the river flowing by, and I could see pretty well across the water. Something substantial plopped into the water from the root ball. A snake?

Now what, as Tony would have asked. Was this a wild goose chase? The guy could also have gone inland instead of back to his boat. All he would have to do was wait by the road for all the cavalry to go rushing by, and then scamper through the crop fields to the two-lane and beat feet for—where? It kept coming back to that: Where was my stalker holing up?

At that moment there was some frantic thrashing in the darkness upstream from our tree trunk, and then two deer came bounding awkwardly out of the darkness, headed downstream. Frick held. Kitty, unfortunately, did not. She bounded off the tree trunk and went after the deer before I could grab her. Worse, she barked. The next thing I heard was the wasp noise of bullets in the air punctuated by repeated bangs from a gun somewhere in front of me. I went flat against the tree trunk, swung the shotgun out, looked for and caught a dim red flash in the trees ahead, and fired three times at a point just above the flash. I thought I heard a muffled cry, and then I definitely heard a loud splash.

I slid down off the tree trunk, followed by Frick, who'd been startled by the shotgun blast and was pressing hard against my leg. I shoved some more rounds into the shotgun and began to scan the surface of the river. If I'd hit him and he'd gone into the main river channel and not the creek, he'd be coming by almost immediately. Every time I looked directly at the water, all I could see was the bloom of the shotgun blasts. If I looked sideways, I could just make out the surface. Kitty and the deer were long gone, which was a separate problem because a deer can run an inexperienced dog to death.

There. Something.

No. My eyes were playing tricks.

I looked away, then back. Something. Metal. Shiny metal.

A boat. Thirty feet away, at most.

I lifted the shotgun and fired into the boat. It was close enough that I could hear the loads shredding metal sides. When my vision recovered, the boat had disappeared. Then I saw blue strobe lights approaching as two cruisers arrived at the brickworks behind me in search of the fire-fight they'd heard from up on the ridge.

I'd been tired when the previous evening had begun, and now, at 2:00 A.M., I was well and truly whupped. I'd tromped over to the brickworks to meet the deputies, who came out with guns drawn until they saw Frick. They'd given me a ride back to the cut through the ridge, where we'd met the sheriff coming down off the hill.

Turned out they'd sent three roped climbers down the side of the gorge opposite where our ghost had dropped into the gloom. At the bottom was a tiny creek running through a space no more than one man wide. Uphill was a crack in the rock from which water was weeping, and downhill the gorge widened until the brook joined the larger creek on the western slope. No cave, no tunnels, no secret entrances. Flashlights had revealed fresh footprints leading down the hill, not into the mountain. A careful search of the top area near the rope anchor had produced two motion detectors, each with tiny transmitters. The rope had indeed been bait.

While I debriefed the sheriff and his people on what I'd been doing down by the river, Kitty came bounding out of the woods with white deer tail hairs stuck to her muzzle. She seemed to be no worse for wear, and I was too tired to reprimand her for her egregious breach of discipline. The deputies took us back to the stone cottage. When I went inside I found out why there'd been a delay between when we'd heard the oar clank on the boat and when my stalker had shown up on the hill. There was another of those white-face pictures pinned to the couch, only this one had a note. Frack was watching me with his one good eye when I picked up the piece of paper. He'd been left in the cottage when I went out, which meant he'd let the guy in. *That should mean something,* I told myself, but my brain was too dulled by fatigue to bring it up.

The note said simply, *It's been fun.*

*Fine with me,* I thought. Then I went to bed. As I drifted off to sleep, I wondered if tonight's gunfight had changed my stalker's schedule.

The following morning I took my utility vehicle over to Glory's End to meet the sheriff. Once it was daylight, he had sent a full forensics team up into the crack in the ridge from where it opened on the lower creek. They confirmed that there were no hidden entrances or other signs of tunnels or ventilation shafts. Rock sides, sand bottom, a spring-fed brook leading down, and, of course, my stalker's roping gear. They took one footprint cast out of the creek sand that didn't seem to match with the SWAT guys' footgear, the stalker's climbing equipment, and the two motion detectors back to the lab for a workup.

"You think you hit him?" the sheriff asked again.

"I fired three shells, heard what sounded like a grunt, and then a big splash," I said.

"So he could have just been real surprised and made a noise when he jumped into the water?"

"That's possible, and what I saw of the boat as it went by was a peripheral image. I know I hit the boat."

"So that should still be out there," he said.

"That'll depend on the current, but yeah, if it was in-shore, it should still be there."

He raised some deputies on the radio, and we went down in his car to take a look. I left the shepherds up at the main house, not wanting any more deer chases. One of the deputies found the boat a hundred yards downstream from where I thought I'd been last night. He'd climbed a tree and looked down into the water, where he spotted the glint of metal. It took all four of us to grapnel the thing onto the riverbank. We confirmed that I had definitely hit it with the shotgun. There were seven holes along its starboard side and six more on the other where the shot had gone all the way through. There were no traces of blood or anything else in the boat, nor was there a boat license with my stalker's name and address, either. I felt relieved that we'd found some physical evidence from the night before to back up my story of a gunfight down here, but there was no way to tell if he'd been in the boat or had just lost it to the current.

"Let's go check the bank upstream of that cross creek," the sheriff said, and we did. Either the river had come up during the night or no one had been running that way. We found nothing but the usual riverbank debris.

"Well," said the sheriff, "we might get lucky and get a floater in a couple of days, but right now, besides the boat, this here looks like another dead end."

We went back to the main house. At the sheriff's request I took some of his detectives through the house, pointing out the two escape routes and showing them the smokehouse and the springhouse exits. We walked the barn complex, where I showed them the abandoned well. I didn't see fit to tell them about my encounters with the major, as I didn't believe that had anything to do with my night stalker. We discussed the events in Summerfield and the pictures of the mask taped to my windows at the stone cottage. They speculated as to the meaning of the latest picture postcard, but I pointed out he'd said something like that before and we were all still playing fuck-fuck. Horace down in Triboro still hadn't come up with anything useful. We went back out to the front porch.

"Well, damn," one of the detectives pronounced, as we tramped up the brick walk behind the house. "What do we have?"

"One dead Guatemalan hit man, one dead biker skank, and one dead ex-con," I said. "Rifle rounds in my woodwork, a flashbang on my porch, scary faces taped to my windows out here, a climbing rope hanging on a cliff to nowhere, and now a love note hinting that the fun and games are over."

"You want protection?" he asked.

"I want to kill the sumbitch," I said. "With any luck I got a start on that last night."

We kicked it around some more on the porch, and then I said I planned to go to town, get some lunch, go back to the cottage and get a nap, and then come over here tonight with guns and dogs and see what or who showed up.

"We can assign some people here," the other detective said. "Give you a little backup."

"You know," I replied, "I think at this juncture I'd just like to see if I can flush him out and get it done. No offense, but so far, as long as I've had help, he keeps putting off the showdown."

"That may be no accident," he said. "You know, keep jerking your chain until you finally lunge—into something bad."

"I've hunted humans before," I said and watched their expressions change. "Sometimes you simply have to go into the woods and stir shit up. He's out there, somewhere on these seven hundred acres. He's mobile, he's got sensory equipment, he's got weapons, and apparently he has a demanding motive. It's time."

They shrugged and said they'd report that back to the sheriff. They warned me he might have a different take on the matter, the biker woman's murder having taken place in his sandbox.

"I'll take him alive if that's possible," I said.

"Or he'll take you."

"That's also possible."

"Oh, by the way," the first detective said. "Sheriff said to tell you he saw a box, back where you were sleeping last night."

I thanked him. Once they'd left, I walked back to the barns and began looking. I nearly missed it, because he'd put it up in the tractor seat where I'd waited the night before. It was a metal U.S. Army ammo box, olive drab, the size of a shoebox turned on its side, with all sorts of army serial numbers, marks, and mods stenciled on it. Inside were two concussion grenades, which were far more powerful than flashbangs.

Set some traps, the sheriff had said. These would do nicely.

Before setting out for Glory's End, I walked up to the barn area looking for Cubby. He wasn't around, which wasn't too surprising since it was the end of the working day. I eased around to the horse barn to see if the major's horses had been put up for the night and the tack room locked, which they were. As I was headed back toward the cottage, I spotted Patience Johnson apparently leaving for the day. I intercepted her and asked if Cubby was still here. She told me he hadn't come to work today because he was home sick with an ear infection that was driving him and everyone else crazy.

"Old fool's gonna learn one day," she said. "Somethin' you need?"

"I'd asked to speak to Ms. Valeria. He said he'd relay the request to you."

"You asked Cubby?"

"I did."

"Didn't tell me nothin' about it. I'll speak to Ms. Valeria first thing in the morning if that's all right."

"That'll be fine," I said. I went back to the cottage to

gather up the dogs and my weapons. When I got into the cottage, my cell phone was ringing. It was Hiram Whatley Lee, Esquire.

"Mr. Lee," I said. "Pleased to meet you, if only telephonically."

"Mr. Richter," he said. "Hope I'm not intruding at this late hour."

I sat down on the couch. "Not at all," I said. "How can I help you?"

"I was calling to see if you really wanted a title search of the Glory's End property, and by that I mean all the way back to the original land grants."

"I need a title search that will satisfy me that I'm not buying into a nest of liens and that the heirs of Mrs. Tarrant have a legal right to sell it. You know, that she left it to them in her will, and the will passed probate, and so on."

"I see," he said. "I'm glad you mentioned wills, because therein lies a possible sticking point."

My heart fell. "How's that?"

"Well, nowadays, wills are recorded, if the people making them know enough to do so. In the distant past, that wasn't always the case. This means we have two collections of wills at the courthouse, the ones done by attorneys and duly recorded, and the others."

"Others?"

"Yes, like when an individual passes away and his heirs or family go through his files and then hand over deeds, mortgage paperwork, trusts, and other important-looking paperwork to an attorney. They get deposited but not necessarily recorded."

"I would have thought that stuff like that wouldn't ever be orphaned, so to speak."

"Nowadays, with most everything being recorded, it's rarely an issue, but I'm talking about the nineteenth century, and, of course, the effects of the war. Whole families were destroyed, sometimes thrown off their properties, and these documents don't resurface until years later when someone finally ventures into the attic."

"Okay," I said. "I can see that."

"It bears on your request because I can do a fairly simple title search of the recorded papers. That would reveal any lurking liens or judgments. Or I can do the full Monty, which would entail archaeology in the special records."

"You know, counselor, the clerk warned me to be careful what I wished for in that regard. What do you think about that?"

"I think he knows more than anyone else in this county what's been gathering dust for decades in that courthouse. He may have a point there, Mr. Richter. Plus, of course, it will be pretty expensive if I have to go into the special collections. Did he mention title insurance?"

"Mr. Oatley did, and I haven't yet done the math to see if the premium for a two point five mil price tag is less or more than a title search."

"That might be worth investigating, for two reasons. First, the money. Second, we don't know what might be in the special collection. There could be things in there, especially considering the history of that property, that could undo any chances you have of acquiring it, at least in the short term."

"Sounds like you know more than you're letting on, Mr. Lee."

"Not at all, sir," he said. "It's just that I do know a thing or two about the two families whose history is intertwined with that property, and not always in a pleasant manner."

"I've heard a bit about that," I said. "Let's do this: Let's go back to the very end of the Civil War, 1865. The following decade brought the carpetbaggers, and I understand that's where a lot of title problems begin. How's that sound?"

"I can certainly do that, and I'll start this week. I would

request a three-thousand-dollar retainer to begin the work, if that's all right."

"That's fine," I said. "How about calling me next week so I can get an idea of what you're finding?"

He agreed to that and told me where his office was. I made a note to take a check by tomorrow. The clerk had said Mr. Lee worked slowly. Hopefully I'd have my stalker problem resolved before he got done.

I got out the collection of aerial photos. I didn't want to just go over there and bang around in the weeds until something happened. I had to assume that his little love note meant that we were done playing games and from now on any collisions would be for real.

He'd been messing around with a boat. That meant his base of operations might be across the river and not here. We now had the boat, which might also mean that he'd have to start using a vehicle. I focused on that ruined plantation house across the river. Behind it there was a two-lane road that paralleled the Dan. To the east and north was the regional airport complex. To the west that two-lane intersected a four-lane highway maybe eight, ten miles upstream, and the four-lane had a bridge.

"Let's go hunting, dogs," I said.

The ruined house was actually bigger than Glory's End, but ruined was the operative word. There was a five-acre park of trees and grass surrounding the house. The trees, all huge, spreading oaks, were doing fine. The grass was four feet high and choking on itself. The driveway was dirt, not gravel, and there was a chain across it about twenty feet onto the property. I'd parked the Suburban in the high grass, stepped over the chain, and walked the third of a mile into the grounds. The shepherds stuck to the driveway with their noses down, while I followed them slowly into the gathering darkness.

The house had burned and essentially collapsed into

itself. The facade was intact, as were two of the four big columns, but the remains of the roof were down in the underground floor. One chimney had kept one side of the house from falling in, but the other one stood all alone, the fireplaces for two floors gaping like empty wisdom tooth sockets in a long red jaw. I circled the house as quietly as I could. There was no way anyone could hide in the remains of the structure, because there was a large pile of burned debris, dirt, and weeds within the walls.

Out back were the familiar outbuildings of the era, a smokehouse, a summer kitchen, both of which were tumbling down, a large, covered well, and a carriage house with four stable doors. It was still intact. There were signs that amorous teenagers had been coming back in here for some time. I saw Frick stop, then retrace her steps around to the front of the house. Then she came back, obviously following a scent trail, and this time she went to the carriage house. She stopped again nearest the right-hand door, and Kitty joined her.

I crept up to the front of the building. Up close it didn't look quite so substantial. The lintels were sagging, and three of the stable doors had been nailed to their frames a long time ago. Each door also had a separate chain and padlock stretched across it. The locks were antiques, and I suspected they were frozen with rust, but I wasn't ready to show a flashlight yet. I could hear cars coming and going down the two-lane out front, but I could no longer see their lights because of the high grass and all those oak trees out front.

I walked around the carriage house to see what was out back. There was still some afterglow on the western horizon, and the moon was rising across the river, which was a good half mile behind and below the burned-out house. The back of the carriage house had windows, but they were so covered in dust and vines that I couldn't see into the building. Frick went back around to the front and hovered around that right-hand-most door.

I examined the lock and chain and made a discovery: The hasp on the lock had been lifted out of its case and was resting right on top of the flat metal. More important, I could smell the familiar odor of WD-40. As quietly as I could, I twisted the hasp out of the way and took it off the two parts of chain, which I slipped down onto the dirt. I checked the hinges and found more WD-40, so I put my fingers into the crack and pulled gently. The door opened outward without a sound. I pulled it just far enough so that the shepherds could fit and then vectored Frick through the opening. I kept Kitty with me.

Frick was back in thirty seconds and didn't seem alarmed by anything, so I went in and pulled the door shut. Then I opened it again and grabbed that padlock before pulling the door shut again. I'd had enough of being trapped in confined places.

The carriage house was empty inside except for what I'd hoped to find there: an old pickup truck parked in the right-hand bay, its nose pointed toward the door. It was a full-sized Ford F-150, and the back had a low-rise camper shell in the bed. The sliding windows in the camper section were open and covered with fine screen against insects. I checked the plate. It was a Wilmington license with a current sticker. I wrote down the plate numbers. There was a pile of trash in the corner indicating someone had been camping out back here, and I was pretty sure I knew who it was: my dedicated stalker, who was probably across the river right now, laying out the next ambush.

*Well now,* I thought. *Two can play that game.*

I extracted one of the concussion grenades and went to work on that truck. As I set the booby trap, I wondered how he was getting across the river now that we had his boat. For that matter, with the current in the Dan as strong as it was, I wondered how he ever managed to get a flat-bottomed johnboat across the river without ending up two miles downstream of Glory's End.

When I was finished in the carriage house, I withdrew with the dogs and reset the fake lock and chains. It was much darker now, but I could discern a faint trail through the grass leading down to the river, so I decided to go down there and see what we'd find. Interestingly, the trail didn't go straight down to the water but angled to the right across a big, gently sloping field. Once we got down into the bottoms, I could see that it pointed at the old railroad abutment that faced the one across the way on Glory's End.

At the bottom of the stone pier-wall I found the answer to how he'd been getting across the river: There was a wire leading down into the water. The current was strong enough even here inshore that the wire, which resembled a metal clothesline, was leaving a small wake in the water. When I lifted it, I discovered that it was bowing downstream and probably lying quite close to the bottom. To get across, all he'd have to do was clip the boat onto that wire, pull hand over hand to the other side, and not lose any ground.

I used the flashlight on red beam to see if there were fresh prints near where the wire was anchored to a tree with a bolted pad eye but couldn't find any. I knew that the water level in the Dan rose and fell capriciously as a function of upstream hydro dams and passing thunderstorms. There could be plenty of footprint evidence six inches underwater right in front of me. I wanted to undo that wire rig but didn't have any tools. The wire strengthened my conviction that I'd found the bad guy's hidey-hole. Finally.

The smart thing to do now would be to let the sheriff know what I'd found here, so he could liaise with the Virginia authorities and whoever owned this property to see if they could surprise him here. First, though, I wanted him to find my own little surprise, so I decided to simply back out and go back to the cottage. Let him prowl the grounds at Glory's End tonight if he felt like it, while I got a good night's sleep. Tomorrow I'd run that plate through Sheriff Walker's office, and maybe we could finally find out who this guy was and why he was determined to kill me.

Wilmington. Was there a connection there?

My guys and I had disrupted a sabotage effort at a nuclear power plant down near Wilmington, but there hadn't been any wives involved. Who could be in Wilmington who thought that I'd done something to his wife?

Back at the cottage, I parked my Suburban out behind the Laurel Grove barns. If he'd already taken a look at the cottage, I wanted him to think I was still out for the night. Then I set the two operational dogs up to watch outside, leaving Frack to sleep in the living room. I called Tony's cell and left him a message describing what I'd found and what I'd left behind. Then I got myself a Scotch and sat down to study those aerials some more on the dining room table. I chided myself for not having looked over there before this.

Round about ten, Frack lifted his head and whoofed quietly. I doused the reading light and went to a window. The moon had been waning, so there wasn't very much light outside, but there was enough to see the major walking his horse off the dam and up toward the house and barns. His head was down almost as if he were asleep, and the horse was just plodding along. Both outside shepherds were out in the yard, sitting down but watching him go by. Once he'd passed, I turned the light back on and resumed my study of the aerials. Cubby had said they didn't want him going out at night, and the barn had been locked. He sure seemed to do it often enough, though, and why was he walking?

After looking through all the pictures for good ambush places, I realized that there were too many good sites. I decided that I'd move over to the big house on Glory's End and make him come to me. Time I had, and now that his base of operations had been busted, he'd have to do something. He'd also probably realize that I'd seen the license plate, which meant there was going to be an identification made. The local cops wanted him for a homicide, and that would make his capture a priority. He could either run tonight, and go back to Wilmington, or try to finish it in the next twenty-four hours. Having put so much effort into his campaign, I was expecting him to take one last hard shot. On the other hand, if he set off that concussion grenade tonight when he got back, he'd be in no mood for any hunting for several hours.

Tomorrow we would probably finish this matter, one way or the other.

I refreshed the Scotch and called Carol. She answered but sounded sleepy.

"Hey," I said.

"Back at you," she said. "Where are you?"

"In the cottage, surrounded by incompetent mutts."

"What's up?"

"He's probably out in the woods, beating the bushes for his target, but his target has decided to get a good night's sleep and deal with his evil ass mañana."

"What if he doesn't want to wait?"

"My shepherds will eat him."

"Why don't you come here," she said. "In a manner of speaking."

I grinned. "Don't want to expose you to danger."

"Bring the shepherds."

"They make too much noise."

"I'll drown them out."

"That's not fair."

The next morning I called the Ops desk at the sheriff's office and gave them the plate number. I asked them to have Sheriff Walker call me as soon as he could. Then I went to retrieve my Suburban. I looked into the shop area for Cubby, but he wasn't there. I saw Patience hanging some sheets out to dry behind the big house and went up there. She said Cubby was still down with his ear infection and would probably be out for the rest of the week. As I walked back to the cottage, I wondered about Patience. She'd been unusually voluble, as if my inquiries were making her uncomfortable. I'd had earaches when I was a kid; they gave you some stuff and it usually went away in twenty-four hours. Now that I'd asked twice about Cubby, Patience was suddenly nervous.

I parked the Suburban and went into the cottage to check my cell phone. No messages yet. I let Frack run around in the front yard for a bit and had another coffee. Tony called, and I filled him in. Then I asked him to entertain a theory. When I was done he said he and Pardee would be out later this morning. I called the sheriff's office and asked if the boss was available yet. They told me the office was all spun up over a robbery-homicide out on the major east-west road through the county, where a couple of teenagers shot and killed a shop owner for the forty-two dollars in the register.

I asked for the sheriff's voice mail. The deputy said I was talking to it. I told him that my stalker had been holing up in the ruined house directly across the Dan River from Glory's End, and that his detectives had the guy's plate number for a possible ID. I gave the deputy my cell number as the callback. Then I piled the shepherds into the Suburban, and we went into town.

A couple of stops later, I was parked at the intersection of Mill Street and Main. Down the block, just beyond a row of small houses, was a large concrete warehouse. It had an old-fashioned water tower and a brick smokestack and was surrounded by truck parking lots and a chain-link fence. There was a rusting sign that read SPRINGMAID on a billboard above the factory. Behind the houses was a generous creek, which had probably supplied water and power to the mill way back when. The textile industry in this part of the world had long gone the way of most manufacturing in this country, that is to say to rice country, and the buildings had that abandoned look about them.

The town phone book had listed two sets of Johnsons on Mill Street, which was in what the locals openly referred to as the black part of town. Not knowing Cubby's real name, I couldn't determine which house was his, so I'd decided to just park across from the entrance into Mill Street and see what showed up. I saw some faces watching me after a while and figured that a white guy with dogs sitting in a Suburban was fairly shouting "cop" to the neighborhood, but no one came out and openly challenged me. The sheriff finally called while I was waiting.

"You found his spider hole?"

"I think so," I said and then described what I'd uncovered the night before.

"So if we go over there with some of the Virginia guys, we need to watch for that grenade?"

"I'm hoping he took care of that all by himself last night," I said. "Although I didn't hear any boom."

"We'll have to get a warrant and then get with the Virginia Highway Patrol to execute it. The plate was no help."

"Stolen?"

"Yup. Little old lady down in Wilmington. Belongs on a '98 Caddy."

"I knew it was too good to be true," I said. "I'm going to hole up at the house at Glory's End with my buddies for the next twenty-four. We'll see what happens when you make your roust."

"Hopefully you won't hear us do it," he said. "Prepare to explain where that thing came from, by the way."

"What thing is that, Sheriff?" I asked innocently. Then I saw Cubby Johnson.

He was coming up Mill Street toward the main drag,

and he didn't have an earache. The whole left side of his head was bandaged, and the bandaging hadn't been done by any doctor or hospital. He was walking with a slight limp, and he did not look all that healthy just now. No wonder Patience had been nervous.

Well. Well. Well.

I waited until he'd turned the corner and headed toward a group of stores three blocks up from the intersection. I got out of the Suburban and let the two shepherds out. They had their game faces on, and I had my SIG in a holster on my right hip. Three teenagers on a nearby porch had been building up the courage to come over and ask me what I was doing around there, but when they saw me start down the sidewalk with two big shepherds at my heels and a big black gun on my belt, they vanished, and I heard other doors closing along the street. I stayed on my side of the street, about a hundred feet behind Cubby, who was on the opposite sidewalk. After one block, I saw him slow down and then stop. There was no traffic, so I crossed the street and walked up to within ten feet of him. I told Kitty and Frick to watch him. They advanced to half the distance between us and sat down.

"So now you know," he said, not turning around.

"*Now* I know," I said. "A minute ago I was just guessing. You had a doctor look at that mess?"

He shook his head, and I could see that the movement hurt him. "They'd ask too many questions," he said.

"Where else are you hit?"

He pointed to his left side with his right hand, where I saw a bulge of bandages under his T-shirt. I took my cell phone out to call the sheriff's office. A car filled with black people went by going the other way, all of them staring at this tableau of a large white man with two police dogs behind a black man sporting bandages. It occurred to me that we needed to take this little drama off the streets and out of the 'hood, and that now would be nice.

"I can call the cops now, or you can come with me and tell me what the fuck is going on," I said.

"Okay," he said.

"Wait right here," I said. I left the shepherds and went back to the Suburban. I drove down to where he was standing and picked him and the dogs up. Then we drove out to Glory's End in silence. There didn't seem to be any fight in him, and his slumped posture told me that he probably had an infection going.

"You taken any antibiotics?" I asked.

"Patience had some old stuff," he said. "Ain't workin'."

"I've got a Z-pack in my first aid kit," I said. "We'll get it when we get to the house."

"Don't bother," he said. "I'm done anyway, all this gets out."

"Maybe, maybe not," I said. "Depends on what you actually did."

We pulled into the driveway of Glory's End. The gates were still open from my last visit. *Need to start using those,* I told myself, *and to schedule that backhoe.*

We drove up to the house, and I put Cubby in one of the rocking chairs on the front porch while I went fishing in the Suburban for the first aid kit and some water. I punched out one of the three big pills and gave it to him, along with the water bottle. He took it immediately and then drank all the water.

"Okay," I said, sitting down across from him. The shepherds were still on watch. "I assume you've been the helper bee?"

"Didn't want to," he said. He still hadn't been able to look me in the eyes. "This goes way back."

"I am all ears," I said, checking to make sure my cell phone was on and still had a signal. I put the SIG in my lap just in case he was faking his debilitation.

Cubby, it turned out, had been telling the truth when he

said he'd done a stint in the army. He just hadn't finished it. He had deserted from the army in 1970, toward the end of the Vietnam War, when they had told him they were going to send him back for a second one-year tour as a Long Range Reconnaisance Patrol shooter. He'd had enough of spending weeks in the bush with two other guys, cut off from any friendly front lines, shooting itinerant Viet Cong and the occasional main force NVA officer from five hundred yards away.

He'd come home to Rockwell County and disappeared into the town's black neighborhoods, which were at that time hugely disaffected as the racial tumult of the sixties in North Carolina still raged. He'd met Patience while hiding out from the army CID, who had come looking for him. She had begun working for the Lees at Laurel Grove, and she got him work there as the outside man. Neither of the Lee ladies had actually inquired about his draft status, but they accepted Patience's statement that he'd been drafted, done his time, and now was out and done with it. She had showed Ms. Hester Cubby's military ID card, and that had closed the matter.

"Somehow, 'bout ten years later, Ms. Hester found out," he told me. "Wanted my ass off the place that day, but by then Patience was so much a part of the house that when she said she'd leave, too, Ms. Hester had to let it go. You from the South; you know how that goes."

I did indeed. So-called domestic servants often became utterly indispensable in southern homes. "Hester told somebody, though didn't she."

He said yes.

"You rig that well as a trap?"

He said yes again. That explained how he'd been there to rescue me. It also explained how he came to have a key to that slave collar—he'd made it.

"So it was you, putting the paper faces on the windows?"

He nodded. "He said he wanted to scare you out of the

land deal, and that he'd kill you if he had to. I told him, I wasn't killin' no one. He said that didn't matter; he liked to kill people."

"I believe that," I said. "What's he look like, this guy?"

"Ain't never seen him," he said. "He gets behind me, out on the farm. Whispers."

I could relate to that. "What about those two Dobermans?"

"He got 'em from that biker woman," he said. "That night he shot her, I was supposed to be along. I'd said no, 'cause I figured he was finally gonna do what he'd been sayin' he was gonna do."

"Which was shoot me."

He coughed. It sounded like his lungs were in trouble. "That's right," he said. "That's why she was along. I wouldn't go. He got all pissed off, said he didn't have time to deal with me right then, but he'd be back. Said he'd take care of me once he was done with you. Said I'd become a loose end, and he'd get me, or maybe Patience. Fucker's crazy, scary crazy."

Now I understood some of his despair. "Is Valeria part of this?"

"Don't know," he said. "Ms. Valeria's got a streak in her. Ol' Hester, she's a damn snake, but Patience? She says Ms. Valeria's got two women inside of her. That's why she don't want me talkin' to neither of 'em. She says she never knows who she's talkin' to with that one."

"What about the major?"

"He just gone," Cubby said, coughing again. His hands were starting to tremble.

"You knew all about the underground passages out of this house?"

He nodded. "That's not all I know," he said. "Lemme show you something."

"What's that?"

"Reason why Ol' Hester don't want nobody in this

house." He pointed to the dogs with his chin. "They gonna let me up?"

"They'll watch you until I tell them something different," I said. "Where we going?"

"The kitchen," he said. "I'm gonna need me a hammer."

Like I was going to give him a hammer. On second thought, watching him move was pretty painful. I went out to the Suburban, got the toolbox, and extracted a small hammer. He was waiting at the door when I got back up on the porch, but he couldn't open it. There was now a small red stain on his side. Z-pack or no, I was going to have to call EMS.

He shuffled through the house to the back stairs, and we went down to the lower level of the house. He put out his right hand for the hammer, and I gave it to him. He walked over to that huge colonial fireplace that took up most of the back wall. He moved to the left edge of it and then stepped sideways twice, to not quite the center. Then he whacked the front of that plastered, monolithic stone lintel stone, blasting a big chunk of plaster right off it. He did it again, and suddenly I saw that there was writing under the plaster. When he was finished knocking the plaster off, there were crude block letters that spelled out the name CALLENDAR.

He gave me back the hammer and then had to sit down in one of the creaky kitchen chairs. His forehead was covered in perspiration.

"Okay," I said. "Who's Callendar?" I pronounced it Cal-en-*dahr,* but Cubby shook his head. "Calendar," he said, pronouncing it like the familiar noun. Then I remembered the story Carol had told me, about the young buck from across the road who'd stolen away the affections of Nathaniel Lee's wife. She'd pronounced it like that as well, now that I thought of it.

"You mean the guy who got himself invited to a duel on the river bridge and all that?" I asked.

"That's it," he said. "See, Callendar Lee's come back for his inheritance."

"You mean his ghost," I said. "It's been over a hundred fifty years."

"When the Lees run Ms. Abigail off, she went on back to Wilmington," he said. "This here's her many-greats grandson, or so he claims. Patience told me that old Nathaniel had him a will, leaving everything to Ms. Abigail, when things was still good between them. Callendar came sniffin' around, got Ms. Abigail to run off with him, and then he and Nathaniel Lee had 'em their duel. Nathaniel's wound rose up to proud flesh and killed him before he ever changed his will."

"What would that matter to Callendar?" I asked. "He died in the duel."

"Unh-unh," he said. "He got shot, yeah, but he wasn't killed. He went into the river, got carried down a ways, and then got hisself out. Made it down to Wilmington, where he ended up with Abigail. She knew all about that will, so when she was dyin' some years later, she made up her own will, and she left Oak Grove to Callendar."

"Did he make the claim?"

"Hunh-unh," he said. "By then Nathaniel's sons had the plantation, and Callendar knew if he ever come back to Rockwell County, those boys would kill him for sure, 'cause he'd put their daddy in the ground. Then the war came. Nathaniel's sons died at Gettysburg. Then they got cholera on the place. Wasn't no Lee womenfolk left, so the whole place was abandoned, then went for the taxes."

"How do you know all this, Cubby?"

"Patience," he said. "Those women over there? They talk about stuff. They talk a lot, 'specially 'bout the old days. Remember, now, that's where they livin'. Most time they act like Patience ain't even there."

"And this talk was all about this supposed will?"

"Long as they had some say in who lived there, like ol' Ms. Tarrant, they could pretend like they owned it."

"Well, hell, I'm not sure such a will would have any standing today, but why didn't this long-lost descendant just hire a lawyer to find out?"

"Hester don't want nobody over here," Cubby said. His voice was losing strength. I knew I had to get him medical attention, but there was also a lot more I needed to know.

"Why is that?"

"Somethin' to do with that," he said, pointing to the lintel. "It was Ms. Hester had me plaster over that, long time ago."

I considered that.

"How did Hester and Valeria find out about my buying the place?" I asked.

"Somebody at the courthouse," he said. "Lotta gossip over there."

That was for sure. "This is important, Cubby," I said. "Would you be willing to help me get this Callendar guy?"

He nodded and started to answer, but then his eyes closed and he slumped in his chair. I felt his pulse. It was weak and thready.

I called the Rockwell County Sheriff's Office and said I had to speak to Sheriff Walker.

In a meeting.

Get him out.

Why should we?

"I've got the shooter in the Glory's End homicide."

Wait one.

Then Walker came on. He started to ask a bunch of questions, but I cut him off. I told him I needed EMS out here immediately to attend to a gunshot wound case, and I needed him out here to handle the turnover of the individual to the EMS team. There was a moment of silence, then he agreed. Smart guy that he was, he knew better than to ask a bunch of questions in front of his people.

The ambulance showed up fifteen minutes later, with Sheriff Walker and one of the detectives right behind them. They hooked Cubby up to IVs right there in the kitchen and then rolled him outside to transport. Sheriff Walker personally signed the dispatch paperwork so the hospital would not need to file any police reports over a GSW patient.

The sheriff, the detective, and I retired to the front porch, and I brought both of them up to speed. I then suggested that the detective go across the road and get Patience, so she could get to the hospital. Once he'd left to do that, Walker raised his eyebrows, as in, *Okay, what's the real deal here?*

"I believe Cubby Johnson was forced into this by Hester Lee and this Callendar guy from Wilmington," I said. "They know something about Cubby, and they're holding it over him."

"Blackmail?"

"Yes, but again, not for money. He's been helping this Callendar fella. That's why he could move around as well as he could."

"Cubby Johnson."

"Yep."

He thought about that for a long moment. "I've known the Johnsons for some time now," he said. "This is way out of character for either of them."

"Thought so, too."

"Did he tell you what the something was?"

"He did, but for now I'd like to pretend he didn't. If I can tell him I haven't revealed his secret, I may be able to get him to come over to my side of this fight."

"This is not like him at all."

"I know," I said. "I think Callendar used him mostly for

local knowledge and access. The escape tunnels. The well trap and the really convenient rescue. Putting stuff on the cottage windows. The dogs didn't react because they knew him."

"How about shooting the Craney woman?"

"He said he backed out that night when he realized the guy meant to do more than run me off. Callendar apparently then told him he, Cubby, had become a loose end, and that there would be payback, possibly for both him and Patience."

"Okay, but then what the hell was he doing out there on that rope? And shooting at you when you caught up with him?"

"Don't know," I said. "Unless he thought I was Callendar. Or he's lying, and he was the boat man, waiting for Callendar, the rope man. I surprised him, and he opened fire. Unfortunately, it was a handgun against a shotgun. No contest."

"We need to find out his medical status before we go over there," he said.

"Right," I said. "If he's in ICU, there's no point. Otherwise, here's what I'd like to do."

When I had finished, he nodded agreement. He had two conditions: He had to be there, with an assistant district attorney, when I made my proposition to Cubby, and his people had to be involved when we went after this mysterious Callendar.

I grinned at him. "You think I might just shoot your prime suspect?"

"You didn't hesitate to shoot his accomplice," he said. "I want to interview this fuck. Then maybe you can shoot him."

"Deal."

Tony and Pardee arrived an hour later at the stone cottage. I brought them up to speed on the Cubby revelations and then sent Pardee over to Glory's End to set up the video surveillance system. Tony stayed behind.

"I think I know where this bastard's been holing up," I told him.

"Right up the hill there?"

"Yeah, I think so. The spider hole across the river would be convenient for night ops and stashing shit that might upset the Auntie Bellums, but that house is bigger than the one across the street. If this is all about scaring me off the property so he can inherit it and Hester can rule it, then they're all in on it. Except maybe the major."

"Is that what's keeping Sheriff Walker from getting warrants and tearing shit up here at Laurel Grove? Because it's the Lees?"

"It may well have a bearing," I said. "This is a small town and county. It's full of goddamned Lees, and it is the S-O-U-F, South, after all."

"Well, hell," Tony said. "Let's us get strapped and go on up there, search the fucking place, collar his hateful ass, and hand him over."

"I promised the sheriff he would run that side of it. This Callendar guy is his prime suspect in an open homicide. We bag him, some liberal judge will just have to throw it out. No, what I want to do is get him out of that house for one last play session."

"You think he knows Cubby's talked?"

"I told the deputy to tell Patience that Cubby checked himself into the ER because his ear infection wasn't getting any better. I also told him to get her to use her car to go get him, as opposed to going in the cruiser. So right now, she'll think the cops think it's still just an earache."

"How about the fact that a cop car came with that news?"

"He knows Patience. They're neighbors. He made some shit up about being in the ER for another problem and talking to Cubby, who was on eternal hold at the front desk while they took care of last night's cutting and gutting."

"The sheriff can't just go get a search warrant and go through the big house here?"

"He apparently feels he can't," I said. "I don't know—maybe the judge in town is yet another Lee, Hester's brother or something."

"So what he really wants is for you to front him."

"Yeah, I think so. I told you, he suggested I run for sheriff out here because he's going to retire. This may be his way of showing me how shit really works in this county."

"Ah, the lovely countryside," he warbled. "Where fangs are long and the maws are wide."

"Yeah, well, I think I'll go make a call on Ms. Valeria Lee. Hold the fort here. If I don't come back, call the sheriff."

"Don't come back?"

I looked up the hill toward the big house. For the first time, even in the daylight, it looked just a bit sinister.

There was no doorbell near the front door, so reluctantly I lifted the heavy knocker and let it drop twice. It sounded like the crack of doom on the huge door. I knew that Patience wasn't there, so one of the ladies would have to answer, assuming they would perform such a menial action.

It took almost two minutes, and I was just about to knock again when I heard footsteps approaching in the hall. The door opened and Valeria stood there. She was in costume, with a pair of antique round eyeglasses, suspended by thin black straps, hanging on her bosom.

"Mr. Richter," she said. "To what do we owe the honor today?"

"I'm looking for a man named Callendar," I said, figuring that this wasn't the time to beat around the bush with delicate pleasantries.

Her eyebrows went up, and I caught just the faintest intake of breath before she regained her customary equanimity. "He's right over there," she said, pointing into the drawing room to the right. I stepped in and saw that she was pointing to the portrait that held the place of honor over the fireplace.

"That's Callendar, the original?"

"That's Callendar Jackson Lowndes Lee," she replied, closing the front door. "I'm afraid he's been dead for over a hundred fifty years, though, so if you're really looking for him, we cannot help you. No one can."

"Because he went into the Dan River after Nathaniel shot him?"

Another eyebrow twitch. "That's correct," she said. "Or, more accurately, that's the tradition as told down through our family, Mr. Richter. Is this another one of your mysteries? Are you, what's the word, 'detecting' today?"

"The Callendar I'm looking for is of a more recent vintage. I believe he's been staying in this house while conducting a guerrilla campaign to drive me away from Glory's End."

"Why, that's preposterous," she exclaimed, her voice rising. "There's no one in this house besides Mother, the major, and me, and Patience, of course, during the day. Where did you get such an idea?"

"So you won't mind if the sheriff comes by and conducts a house search?"

"There'll be none of that!" snapped Hester Lee, emerging from the other drawing room. She was brandishing an antique short-barreled shotgun. Those guns were heavy, but she was managing just fine.

"So he is here," I said.

"You, sir," she said. "Sit down in that chair right there."

"Mother," Valeria began.

"Do not interfere, Valeria. This man is dangerous to us. Sit down!"

I sat. Shotguns will have that effect.

"For what it's worth, I've already called the sheriff," I said. "He may not care for the sight of that coach gun."

"Sheriff Walker will pay far more attention to what I want than what you want, Mr. Richter," she said. "Valeria, go to the front door and keep watch."

"What *do* you want, Ms. Hester? What's so vital that all the Lees are suddenly afraid of me?"

"Afraid of you, Mr. Richter? We're nothing of the kind. You should be afraid of me."

"Did Valeria tell you I'm having a title search done on Glory's End?"

"Why should I care?" she asked. To my great relief, I heard the sound of a vehicle crunching up the driveway outside.

"Because old Whatley Lee is supposed to be quite thorough. Slow, but thorough."

Valeria opened the front door. A moment later Sheriff Walker stepped past her, took in the tableau in the drawing room, and stopped.

"Ms. Hester, whatever are you doing?" he asked in a casual, even conversational tone of voice.

"This man is a trespasser. You must arrest him at once."

"That's funny," I said. "I thought Valeria let me in. Why is Valeria doing door duty, by the way? Where's Patience?"

"What?" Hester said.

"Where's Patience? Is this her day off?"

Hester looked confused, then glanced sideways at Valeria for an explanation. "Patience had to go to the hospital, Mother," Valeria said. "Cubby has some sort of infection, and she had to attend to him."

"Why wasn't I told?" Hester said. "The servants do not just leave this house without permission."

"Because Cubby's got more than just a little earache," I said. "Cubby's in intensive care for gunshot wounds, which he received in the course of a gunfight. With me, actually. Apparently he's been helping your star boarder here. Now it seems he's had a change of heart. He was telling me something about an old will?"

Her face froze, and then she wasn't brandishing the shotgun anymore, she was pointing it right at my head. "You horrid man," she hissed. "I ought to shoot you right there, in that chair."

"Ms. Hester," the sheriff said. "Put that thing down before you do something you'll regret forever."

"There are already things I will regret forever," Hester said. "What's one more?"

"Mother, for God's sake," Valeria said.

"Be still, girl," Hester said. "This concerns the family. Mr. Richter here knows something he should not know."

"Ms. Hester," the sheriff interjected. "Put that gun down right now. You shoot this man, the Lee family name will be destroyed. Let me take care of this. I will arrest him and take him to jail. Then we can sort things out."

It was interesting, if not downright exciting, to watch the play of emotions on the old lady's face. One moment she looked as if the family name could go screw itself, the next, she was hesitating, and then the word "jail" penetrated.

"You will put him in jail?"

"And throw away the key, Ms. Hester. If he's frightened you so much, there must be something terribly wrong about him."

The shotgun began to waver just a little. I decided it was okay to exhale.

"Take him away, then," Hester said. "Forthwith, before the major sees him. The major will not hesitate to take direct action, as you well know." Valeria was trying to look indifferent over in one corner of the room, but she was also fanning herself with a folded lace hankie.

"You know you can depend on me, Ms. Hester," the sheriff said. "If I take him, I can protect you and the family against any further disturbances. You must distance yourself from actual acts of violence. Think of the family name."

Hester looked like she was still considering shooting me right there and then, and the Lee family name be damned. She didn't say anything for a very long moment and then she lowered the shotgun. "Very well," she said. "Now take him away."

The sheriff stepped forward and told me to stand up and put my hands together. Then he cuffed me.

Valeria opened the front door so he could march me out. Hester followed us out onto the front porch, still holding that coach gun. The sheriff pushed me roughly into the backseat and slammed the door. As I leaned back into the seat, I could see Hester standing tall on the porch, looking resolute and perhaps a bit disappointed in not getting to use the coach gun. Valeria had disappeared back into the house.

I wondered if Callendar was watching this little drama through one of the many curtained windows above the pillars. Then the sheriff got in and shut his door. He turned around in his seat, got himself all glary-eyed, and started yelling at me, letting go with all sorts of fulminations about not trying to escape, how I'd be shot down like a dog, and more ranting along those lines. In the midst of all the noise, to which Hester, watching from the front porch, was listening with fiery-eyed approval, the cuff key came flipping between the seats and landed in my lap. Then we drove off down the driveway.

And I thought I did good Kabuki.

"She had me worried back there for a moment," I said as I got the cuffs off. He turned right onto the two-lane, drove a half mile to one of the farm roads, and then turned left into one of the Glory's End side roads.

"Had to get your interfering ass out of there," he said. "I believe she was serious about taking you downstairs to the basement and doing a Romanov on you. You think he's there?"

"Valeria protested like it was all a figment of my imagination, but Hester went bipolar when I mentioned the will.
If he's not there now, he has been."

"Okay," he said. "I guess you've lit the fuse. Now let's
go see if we can talk to Brother Cubby."

In the event, Cubby was still in ICU and not available for
questioning. Sheriff Walker sat down with Patience and
explained the situation while I, her husband's shooter,
made myself scarce. He did know them both and confined
the discussion to the problem at hand, finessing the real
reason why the Lees had been able to force him to help our
mystery man. He also set up security precautions in the
hospital until we knew we had our guy, because Callendar
had threatened both of them. I called Tony to come pick
me up at the county hospital, and the sheriff went back to
his office. He was going to set up surveillance on the ruined
plantation house and have one police boat with night-vision
gear out in the river after dark in the vicinity downstream
of the railroad bridge. I was to call in at six to brief them on
the surveillance system we had set up and to discuss our
movements for the night.

Back at the cottage, Pardee was wiring in a single video
camera to put surveillance of the lawns between the big
house and the road over the millpond dam. The house at
Glory's End had cameras set up to cover the back barns,
the smokehouse, the springhouse, and the kitchen access
to the basement. The central monitor would be set up in
the cottage, where Pardee would be on watch tonight. He'd
also replaced the batteries on the cell net transponder so
we would have our private cell phone network back up.
Ms. Hester hadn't actually evicted me yet. She'd need the
sheriff to do that in any formal proceedings, and that wasn't
going to happen tonight, if ever.

Our plan was based on some assumptions, as most
plans are. Hester Lee knew that I was onto the will scam.

She was also aware that I, at least, believed she had been helping Callendar do his thing in the area, including gunning down the dog trainer across the way. That would make her an accessory to a homicide. We couldn't prove that yet, nor did the sheriff have sufficient grounds for a search warrant at Laurel Grove, but if we could spook Callendar into moving, we had a shot at catching him. He'd been using two bases that we knew of, but he might have another, like that mythical coal mine.

I called Whatley Lee and asked how things were going with the title search. Slowly, he reported. There were many associated files and books he had to explore to cover the badly confused era right after the war. I decided to take a chance. I asked him about the will, describing the circumstances as best I knew them. I halfway expected him to laugh and say forget about it, but he didn't.

"It would depend," he said. I groaned mentally; my lawyer friends were always saying that.

"There are state and federal reconstruction laws that may have a bearing on such a document, assuming it exists and the Lees can prove the provenance. Many of the ante bellum plantations ultimately were abandoned by their owners because they either no longer had the wherewithal to work them, or because the bulk of the men had been lost in the War. Women, as you know, rarely owned land in those days."

"So if this fella, Callendar, could prove that his ancestor, Abigail, actually owned the land, then he'd have a claim?"

"In my opinion, he would have a basis for bringing an action. Whether or not he could prevail is another issue, but it would make your purchase of the land moot for as long as it was in court."

"What would that be worth to the Lees?" I asked.

"In monetary terms? You yourself have defined that, Mr. Richter."

So I had.

"For that family, Mister Richter," he said, "Control of Glory's End might mean more to them than the monetary value. At least that's my general impression."

"Are you related to them, Whatley?"

"Me? No, sir. My family is descended from the Virginia Lees." His tone of voice made it clear that his ancestry was far superior to the strange crew out there at Laurel Grove. I asked him to keep plugging and hung up.

Lawyer Lee might be onto something with his comment about the money. Hester and company didn't appear to be suffering from a case of genteel poverty. Cubby seemed to think that the name engraved into the kitchen mantel had a bearing on why the Laurel Grove Lees had such an abiding interest in Glory's End.

We sent Tony into town to get some takeout while Pardee and I set about preparing our equipment for the evening's festivities. I tried not to think about the possibility that Callendar had already flown the coop. It would depend on whether or not he knew about Cubby's revelations to me. If he and Hester were in cahoots, and he was there, then she'd probably told him what I'd said about the will. On the other hand, if he ran, then they couldn't put the alleged will in play. Neither Hester nor Callendar seemed shy about removing obstacles. If I wouldn't back out gracefully in deference to my social betters, then I could join the dog trainer woman in the cold, cold ground, just like those contemptible train guards buried up on the hill.

There'd been no sign of anyone leaving or entering Laurel Grove by the time the sheriff checked in with us. He had a surveillance team watching the place across the river, and I described for him the coverage of our video cameras. He told us he was on his way to execute the second phase of our plan, namely to inform Ms. Hester that a judge in town had forced him to release the notorious blackguard Cameron Richter for lack of evidence of any crimes committed.

He would amplify that by telling her he had transported said Mr. Richter back to Glory's End, where he had said he was going to conduct a search for something he believed was secreted in or around the house. Mr. Richter had been ordered to stay away from the Lee ladies at Laurel Grove.

"Now you realize," he said, "that none of that makes a whole lot of sense if they think it through."

"Yeah, but consider the context," I said. "That old lady is living somewhere back in the past, and now I've come on the scene and threatened their noble existence."

"I wish we knew what it is she's so exercised about," he said. "Anyway, I'm about to turn into the drive. When we're done here, we'll drive our way over to that quarry area and then walk back to the big house."

"We?"

"Yeah, I brought me along a little help. Case someone gets uppity."

Willard.

We watched the driveway to the big house up the hill light up with the sheriff's headlights. The windows in the mansion were glowing with their usual candlelight, but the big front portico was completely dark. As I watched, the front door opened as the sheriff was coming up the stairs, revealing a figure in the doorway carrying a small hurricane lamp. Then the door closed. I could see Willard sitting in the right front seat; he looked like a tree in there.

The cameras over at Glory's End were showing still lives of their objective areas, with nothing moving. Pardee had set up portable infrared floodlights from the house's porches, and the cameras were set for night vision. Our display was a study in greens and whites. All three shepherds were curled up in furry balls by the cottage fireplace. If they sensed our own tension, they weren't reacting. We had lights on in the cottage, so anyone watching would have to know someone was there. I told Tony to go outside and walk around in hopes that someone would see him when the sheriff left. There were three vehicles parked outside, so this should alert them to the fact that I was not alone.

Ten minutes later the sheriff came out, turned around to say something to the figure with the lamp, and then drove away. I watched the windows of the house until I saw a new glow behind the curtains upstairs. Someone being given a debrief?

My cell phone went off. It was Sheriff Walker.

"How'd they react?" I said.

"They were not pleased," he said. "My chances for re-election have been severely damaged."

"Who took the message?"

"Ms. Hester," he said. "No sign of the other one, Valeria is it? Hester still had that coach gun, sitting right there on the coffee table. All candlelit inside; just a little bit spooky."

"Do we know they don't have a phone in that house?"

"I can find that out from the central office in town if they have a landline, but probably not until tomorrow. Cell phone will take longer. Why?"

"If Callendar's not there, she'll want to get a message to him. No phone, they might use the major. I'm going to go out and watch that back barn where they keep his riding stuff. I'll keep my guys here in the cottage; they can reach me if they have to."

"Roger that. Our guys are watching that house on the other side of the river. I'm going to the office until I hear something."

I explained my plan to the guys, rousted the two operational shepherds, and went out onto the front porch to get my vision adapted to the darkness. I'd set my cell to vibrate for any text messages. I wore the SIG on my belt and carried my autoloading shotgun. Pardee had rigged some SWAT Kevlar helmet liners with night-vision goggles, so if I ended up across the road I could take advantage of those IR floods.

I kept to the shadow of the big trees as the mutts and I went up the hill and then slanted across one inside paddock to reach the back of Cubby's shop and the horse barn. There was some weak moonlight, and the occasional flicker of what I hoped was just heat lightning way out to the west. The back windows of Laurel Grove were dark, but there was still some light in that side window. It could have been Hester's bedroom for all I knew, and she was up there reading a book. I'd asked Tony to text me if he saw any new lights come on in the big house.

We took up a position underneath a large apple tree whose limbs hung down almost to the ground. From there I could watch the shop, the horse barn, and the walkway leading up to the house. Behind the horse barn I could hear the horses making soft noises, but that didn't mean the major's horse was out there. He could already be inside in a stall, already saddled and ready to go. Or he could have left an hour ago. The dogs were now aware that something was going on. Frick had assumed the down position I'd commanded, but Kitty refused to lie down. She'd decided to sit and then fidget. Lots more training was in order for Kitty, but I couldn't indulge in that now without making a lot of noise. I just hoped that damned barn cat didn't make an appearance, because if he did, there was going to be lots of noise.

My phone vibrated. The text read LIGHTS DOWNSTAIRS. I acknowledged and then pushed Kitty down into the grass. When she made to get up again, I flicked my finger against her ear and told her to lie down. This time she obeyed. Moments later I heard a door up at the house open and then shut quietly. There were no lights, but they didn't need any. A single figure appeared out of the gloom and went into the horse barn. A cloud passed over the moon about the time I should have been able to see his face, but it looked like the major. The difference was that there was no hat or cavalry saber that I could see.

We waited under our tree. I got both shepherds up and ready. There was no way I could follow the major with him on horseback and me on foot, and our utility vehicle wasn't suitable for following anything but another utility vehicle. My plan was to step out and confront him and try to find out where my bad guy was holed up. Then I'd call the sheriff and we'd muster up a posse to take him down. I was strangely disappointed that the major was in on all this; I think I liked him better fully crazy.

Ten minutes later the barn doors swung open and a horse came out. The rider had to duck to get under the door frame. When the horse reached a spot about twenty feet in front of me, I sent the dogs out with a command to bark. Kitty was new to this, but Frick wasn't, and the noise was amazing. Once Frick lit off, Kitty got the idea and joined in. To my amazement, however, the rider didn't panic or even stop. He swung that horse around 180 degrees, which allowed the big animal to start kicking out at the dogs with lightning snaps of its hind legs, any one of them powerful enough to take a dog's head right off. That I couldn't stand, so I stepped forward and fired two blasts from the shotgun straight up into the air. The horse reared, and the rider went down with a thump and a distinctly female grunt of pain.

Female?

The dogs had scattered when my gun went off, and the horse was now dancing around the figure lying on the ground, who still, amazingly, had hold of the reins. Finally she let go and the horse trotted right back into the barn, where it began making long snorting noises through its nostrils. I approached the figure on the ground, and then the moon came back out. It was Valeria, and she was definitely not pleased to see me. She was even less pleased to see my shotgun, because she'd opened her mouth to yell at me and then snapped it shut again when she saw the gun.

"Where is he?" I asked, dispensing with the usual formalities.

"You go straight to hell," she spat as she struggled to sit up and catch her breath. She was dressed in what looked to me like a gaucho outfit, all black, with blousy-legged pants and a short dark jacket. The shepherds were watching from a semisafe distance, eyeing the shotgun the whole time.

"Listen to me," I said. "You and your mother are accessories to murder. That means you will both get the same sentence he does for shooting that woman."

"What woman?"

"The one who provided the big black dogs," I said. "He shot her in the back of the head when the dogs fucked up."

"That's not true!" she shouted. "He sent her away, her and her dogs. She was useless!"

I went down on one knee so that I was right in front of her. "He sent her away, all right, but with a nine-millimeter pistol. She had a surprised expression on her face and a bullet pushing the skin out on the side of her head. He turned the dogs loose, and we captured them over by the brickyard. He's a homicide fugitive, Valeria, and if you've been harboring him, guess what? Now: Where. Is. He?"

"Not true," she muttered, wiping the dirt out of her hair. "None of it. You're lying."

"Why should I?" I asked.

She looked at me, blinked, but couldn't find an answer. At that moment I saw movement up on the path. Someone was coming. I hoisted Valeria off the ground just as Hester came to a stop halfway down the path, screamed out an unintelligible epithet, and then fired off that damned coach gun in our general direction.

She was at least a hundred feet away and the coach gun was probably more than a hundred years old, as probably was its ammunition, which is what saved both of us. It didn't entirely save Valeria. I actually felt some of the pellets hit her, and she cried out and then slumped in my arms. Something tugged at my sleeve, and then I felt the sting along my upper right arm. The back of Valeria's head was suddenly all wet, and she was moaning.

"Where is he?" I asked her again.

"Who?" she asked in a faint voice. She was trying to stand up, but it wasn't happening.

"Callendar."

"Oh, him," she said. "He's in the bridge." Then her eyes rolled back as she fainted.

Up on the walk I heard the unmistakable sound of the coach gun's action being closed. She'd reloaded.

"Hester, you damned fool," I yelled. "You've shot Valeria. Put that goddamned thing down!"

"You lie, you godforsaken Yankee bastard!"

"Come see for yourself, Hester. Come see her body. Come see what you did!"

"Body?" Her voice changed all of a sudden, transitioning from banshee to mother. "Body?"

I heard the shotgun drop to the ground, and then she was there, an old lady now, immediately starting up with the hysterical wailing and crying. I actually didn't think Valeria was dead or, for that matter, even that seriously injured, given the range, but she'd been pincushioned pretty good and there was a lot of bleeding. As I backed away from the suddenly anguished mother, I heard a horse go blasting out of the barnyard paddock behind me. I whirled around and caught just a single glance, but the hat was unmistakable: The major was away.

*Holy shit,* I thought. Had Valeria been just a decoy?

An hour later the grounds of Laurel Grove returned to some semblance of normalcy. The EMS crew had packaged Valeria up and transported her to the hospital. One of the techs confirmed that she had mostly flesh wounds, with some of the pellets still visible right under her skin. Lots of pellets, though, so there'd definitely be some surgery and then some really good drugs required. I'd alerted the sheriff, and he now had Hester up in the big house for a combination of consolation and some embarrassing questions. My guys had come running when I'd fired the first shots and then had wisely taken cover halfway across the lawn once Hester opened up with that ten-gauge antique. The shepherds were cowering safely back under the apple tree, probably wondering why any of us ever left it. I realized I had yet another training issue: guns and their noise.

With the major on the loose, there'd be no chance of catching up with Callendar, if that's what he was doing. We pretty much had to assume now that they were all in on it. When we did catch this little shit, some prominent people were going to be in the dock with him. The problem now, of course, was catching him. At this juncture he had every motive to hit the bricks and get out of the county.

*He's in the bridge.* Not at. Not by. Not on, but in? Not possible: There was no bridge.

"So what now, boss?" Tony asked. He was holding Hester's coach gun, which I reminded him was still loaded— and cocked. He gingerly let the hammers down, broke the action, and pulled out two ancient shells.

At the moment, I was fresh out of answers. I was hoping the sheriff could convince Hester to let him search the house, just in case our boy had gone to ground there and never left. If Valeria had been a decoy, then the major could be doing the same thing: riding around the countryside at night to make us think he was in contact with Callendar. Or, having heard gunfire, he could be chasing the ghosts of the Recent Unpleasantness across the empty fields of his aging brain.

Then we heard an interesting noise. It came from across the fields of Glory's End and the Dan River, and it carried well on the night air: the satisfying sound of a concussion grenade going off with a truly authoritative boom.

*Well now,* I thought. *Who set that off?*

A minute later we heard gunfire, the rapid-fire pop-pop-pop of an untrained shooter, interspersed with the steadier booming of a larger caliber gun being deliberately aimed and fired. There was a pause of about thirty seconds, and then it started up again. Finally there were four more shots from the big gun and then a growing silence from across the dark fields. It was amazing how sound carried out here in the peaceful countryside.

"Sounds like the O.K. Corral going down over there," Pardee said. The shepherds had heard the distant gunfire and decided to rejoin us.

Then the sheriff came hustling out of the house and onto the drive with his cell phone jammed to one ear. I thought I could hear radio traffic crackling from inside his cruiser, so we walked across the lawn to see what was up.

"Okay, I'll wait here," the sheriff said, then snapped the phone shut and turned to us. "Goddamn Hildy!"

"What happened?"

"Hildy is what happened," he said, shaking his head. "She made a command decision. Decided to go bust the carriage house. Bad guy had put some kind of booby trap in his truck, and it went off when she climbed in to search it."

"Booby trap?" I said with a straight face. He gave me a suspicious look, then remembered, and then grinned, despite himself.

"Anyways," he said. "One of the outside deputies thought he saw someone running down toward the river, so he yelled and then fired some warning shots. Boy runner sent three back at him and disappeared down by the bridge tower. By the time they all got down there, they thought they saw him swimming across, although it was pretty dark. He helped them decide by putting another couple rounds in their general direction, so Willard, who's a crack shot, by the way, put four rounds from his .44 Mag all around the guy, and he disappeared."

"And of course they think they got him," I said.

"Of course."

"In fact . . ."

"We don't know jack shit," the sheriff finished. "He was using that wire you told me about, which explains how he could shoot and swim at the same time."

"Another Callendar disappears into the Dan River," I said. "Fancy that."

The next morning we met at the sheriff's office in town. I'd sent Pardee and Tony back to town and their day jobs, as the immediate threat seemed to be over. The sheriff had invited an ADA named Lee Davis from the county prosecutor's office to sit in. I'd left the shepherds in the car. I told them there wouldn't be any doughnuts, but I don't think they believed me, based on all the resentful looks. There were cops all around; had to be some doughnuts in there.

Captain Hildy showed up looking like a raccoon. She'd been wearing protective glasses when the concussion grenade went off, and they had imprinted their circular lens covers around her eyes, complete with dark rubber smudges. Everyone pretended not to notice, which was the safe thing to do. She arrived at the meeting carrying the expended grenade case. I suspected that she wanted to know how that little piece of police equipment had ended up in the bad guy's truck. The sheriff and I had entered into a mutual conspiracy of absolute omertà.

"Okay, people," he said. "Here's where we stand: Our prime on the Craney killing has apparently disappeared into the depths of the Dan River. He might be dead. He might be wounded and holed up. He might be down the road and gone. We have no way of knowing which until either we find a floater or he pops up on the radar again."

He looked through his notes for a moment before going on. "Subject Cubby Johnson remains in the ICU, unable to talk. The quacks say his infection is responding to treatment.

Patience Johnson, his wife, states emphatically that she knows nothing about nothing, and she is obviously terrified that both of them are going to lose their jobs at Laurel Grove."

"Are they?" I asked.

"I tried to gloss over Cubby's role in this case when I talked to Ms. Hester. She was mostly focused on her daughter's condition and how she was going to get to the hospital. I offered to have one of my people take her, but she refused to ride in a cop car. I called out the pastor at Saint Stephen's, and he came and got her."

"It vas dis Hester voman who shot her own daughter?" Captain Hildy asked.

"Indeed it was," the sheriff said. "The current theory is that she was shooting at Lieutenant Richter here, but Valeria stood up at precisely the wrong moment. She has eleven puncture wounds in various parts of her anatomy, some of them fairly personal, but nothing life-threatening. The major damage seems to have been to her memory: Ms. Valeria also knows nothing about nothing, just like Mrs. Johnson. Lot of that going around out there."

"Except she does," I said. "She told me that Callendar sent the dog trainer lady away because she and her dogs were useless."

"Away?" one of the detectives asked.

"I explained that to her. She was in total denial about Callendar murdering the woman. But she's definitely part of this deal."

"Oh, man," the sheriff said.

"And the major?" I asked. "What happened when he came back?"

"He came back in at dawn in full regalia, saw the cops, told them there was Union cavalry afoot and that they should be extremely vigilant. Then he put up his horse and went inside, looking for breakfast."

"He knows nothing about nothing, too, right?"

"Absolutely," the sheriff said. "Just another pleasant night ride in the country."

"Vell, someone knows somezing," Captain Hildy said. "Zis vas no phantom explosive zat went off in zat truck. Zis is police equipment."

The sheriff eyed the raccoon circles. "What prompted you to go into that truck?" he asked. He had to raise his voice because she couldn't hear very well.

"Someone vas zere," she said. "Ve couldn't see him, but Deputy Barnes heard a noise in zere. I assumed he'd been varned and vas preparing to drive zat truck out of zere."

"How is the truck?" I asked as innocently as I could. Sheriff Walker seemed to be having trouble controlling his expression.

"No more vindows," she said, looking at me suspiciously. She just knew I had something to do mit zat.

"Sheriff," I asked, anxious now to change ze subject, "you got a look in the house at Laurel Grove?"

"A look is the right word," he said. "Not a search by any means. Hester maintained that the only people in the house were the family members: the major, Valeria, and herself. She showed me all the rooms. I also got to look into the attic, where there's nothing but old timbers. I didn't get into the basement, if there even is one."

"No signs of use in the guest rooms?"

"There aren't any guest rooms, best I could tell. Place is a damn museum. It's all late 1800s, the furniture, the bric-a-brac, lace doilies, stuff like that. Wall sconces with candles instead of lightbulbs. Portable lamps with glass chimneys. Fireplaces in every room, and all still in use, from the look of them."

"I wonder," I said. "Could Hester be telling the truth? Maybe Callendar never was in that house?"

He raised his eyebrows.

"Well, look, that's not the same as saying Hester and this guy aren't mixed up in some scheme to acquire Glory's End, but it is possible that he's not physically been there."

"Then how are they communicating?" Hildy asked.

"That crazy old man who rides out night and day, and God knows where he goes."

"On horseback," the sheriff said, "he could go damn near anywhere."

That's what Carol Pollard had told me, I remembered. "Could he cross the river?"

"I guess he could swim the horse if the river was fairly quiet."

"Or," said one of the deputies, "there's one of those Civil War era fords. Some of 'em were natural shallows, some they made by layin' down slate and gravel so that cavalry could get away by crossing the river at secret locations."

"You think the major is in on this, then?" the sheriff asked. "You're the one who's really met him, talked to him."

"I do not," I said. "Not in the sense that he is a co-conspirator. I do think Hester could tell him that he had to meet one of Jeff Davis's spies down by the river and deliver a written message, and he'd do that."

"Holy shit," murmured the second detective, shaking his head.

"That's where he lives," I said. "If he's faking it, he's awfully good at it."

The ADA looked at his watch. "Sheriff, is there a case to be brought here?"

"Well," the sheriff said, "I'm guessing that Ms. Valeria isn't going to prosecute her mother for peppering her with a ten-gauge, and Cubby Johnson is a deal prospect when he comes out of ICU. So I guess, for now anyway . . ."

"Right," Lawyer Davis said. "I'm due in court in thirty minutes, so I'll excuse myself. I have just one question: Why was Mrs. Lee trying to shoot Lieutenant Richter here?"

*Great question,* I thought. I explained the sequence of

events that led up to Hester's unintentional ventilation of Valeria's backside. ADA Davis looked over at Sheriff Walker, as if to confirm that the sheriff had himself a genu-wine Lebanese goat-grab on his hands with this one, then left.

"Zo, now vhat?" Hildy asked, suddenly eyeing me like a piece of meat. "Ve haff a crime, or no?"

"Ve haff a hairball, is what," the sheriff said. He rubbed both sides of his face with his hands. "Okay, everybody," he said. "No further action until all the wounded have been restored to duty and we can get some more statements, assuming they'll make some. Lieutenant? You are going to have to move, I understand?"

"In the works," I said. "I'm going to move over to the house at Glory's End. Save all the Auntie Bellums the trouble of evicting my ass."

The detectives laughed at the Auntie Bellums comment, but Hildy was not amused. She vas still trying to pin zome high crimes and misdemeanors on zomeone, hopefully me. The sheriff got up.

"Sometimes," he said, "we just have to wait and see what develops. I'll be in my office, should the president happen to call."

"How about zis little problem?" Hildy asked, holding up the expended concussion grenade case.

The sheriff looked at it. "It appears to have been expended," he said. "Throw it away."

I took the mutts back to the cottage and began the process of packing up my stuff for the move across the road. The big house up across the lawns was silent, what with Cubby and Patience gone, Valeria in the hospital, and Hester probably with her there keeping watch. I wondered if anyone had fed the horses in all the excitement but then realized that the major was probably up there. Surely he would realize that the barn creatures had not been cared for. I was tempted to go up and remind him but then decided against it: If he'd witnessed the altercation with Hester and Valeria the night before, he might just answer the door with his own coach gun.

As I was packing up the Suburban, Carol Pollard came down the driveway in her pickup truck. Apparently the word hadn't gotten out yet about the night's events, so I had to fill her in. She helped me carry out the rest of my stuff, such as it was.

"You can't live there," she said.

"Old Mrs. Tarrant managed," I said. "Besides we've got the place wired up a bit, and there's reliable electricity. I certainly can't stay here."

"So this thing's over?" she said. "This guy who said he was going to kill you? He's gone?"

"Well," I said, "he might be. He might not be. He can't present a will to the court without exposing himself to local law, and after last night, they've got a fair laundry list of charges."

"Except they can't prove it was Callendar who was shooting at them. Like you said, they never saw his face."

"True," I said. "That's why it may not be over yet. Either way, I can't stay here, and I at least have some surveillance gear over there. Plus these three fuzz balls here."

"I've got three bedrooms in my house," she said. "You're welcome to hole up there if you'd prefer. It might be safer."

I smiled at her. She'd tended to her powder and paint this morning and looked very nice. She'd been doing that a lot lately. "I'd like that," I said, "but it would also put you in the line of fire. This mess has been between him and me since the beginning. I still don't entirely understand it, but if he's alive, he'll be back."

"John Wayne to the very end, hunh?"

"Remember, Carol, his specialty is a long gun through the window. Me first, then anyone who happens to be with me."

"Well, at least let me make you dinner on your moving night," she said, getting back in her car. "You remember how to get there?"

"I think so."

"Oh, good," she said. "I was afraid you'd forgotten."

"Not likely."

"So?"

"I've been busy," I said. It sounded weak, even to me.

"That busy," she said, in fake amazement, as she smoothed the fabric of her jeans around her hips.

I made a bleating noise. It was all I could muster.

"I get home at five thirty." Then she drove off.

I watched her go. The shepherds watched her go.

"She's pretty nice," I told them.

Frick barked at me, which I took as an invitation to provide early chow.

I got back to the stone cottage at ten thirty, pulled into the parking space, and only then did I realize I was at the wrong place. As I was turning around, the sheriff called on my cell, so I stopped in the driveway.

"Went to the hospital this afternoon," he said.

"Worth the trip?"

"In a manner of sorts," he said. "I saw Hester. She was there in Valeria's room, along with the pastor's wife. She's going to stay with them in town until Valeria can come home."

"So you didn't try to get a statement?"

"I'll let the detectives handle that when she's better able to focus," he said. "Besides, they weren't exactly friendly. Then I checked in on Cubby Johnson."

"How'd that go?"

"He's not doing all that well. They got the first infection under control, then moved him to a room, and now he's got something else going, one of those damned hospital bugs. C-something. They're hitting it pretty hard. But Patience ran into Hester in the cafeteria, and she told her she had to get back to Laurel Grove to take care of the major."

"That must have been a relief for Patience."

"Indeed. Visible relief. I did talk to Cubby, but mostly to tell him everything was going to be okay. He's been babbling about having no choice, they made him do it, stuff like that."

"He was out of it?"

"I couldn't use it even if he gave it up," he said. "Again, I'll let the system work, let my D's do their thing. That's how it works when you're the high shareef: You stay above the details and let your people do it, legal-like."

"I knew that."

"Of course you did. But if your buddy the major goes walkabout tonight . . ."

"That house will be empty."

"I didn't say that."

"Right. I'm at the cottage now. I've moved my stuff over to Glory's End, drove back here out of habit. Maybe I'll hang around, see what happens."

"Good a place as any, Lieutenant. Watch yourself, now."

I took all the mutts into the cottage. I mostly wanted to make sure I'd not left anything behind. I'd had to call Pardee to find out how to take down and then reassemble the TV monitor system over in the other house and where to place the extra camera. He volunteered to come back out, but I told him to hang loose, that I expected a waiting game. He said he'd be up on his cell all night, and he'd get Tony alerted to do the same. Then I sat down in one of the big living room chairs, turned out the lights, and wished I hadn't taken the Scotch next door.

I woke up and looked at my watch. It was a little past midnight. The shepherds were at the windows. I reached for my SIG and then remembered I'd left it in the Suburban. I went to a window and looked out in the direction of the big house. Here came the major, his horse at a slow walk, going down the drive toward the millpond. I decided to go out and talk to him.

"Evening, Major," I said. I was standing next to the Suburban just in case I did need that SIG. The major pulled up and touched the brim of his hat.

"Overseer," he said.

"What's the situation, sir?"

"Tenuous in the extreme," he said. "We've had to send some of the womenfolk south to the city. Many slaves have run away."

I had an idea. "I saw the guards at the bridge firing at a spy last night," I said. "Someone was returning fire from the Virginia side."

"Did you, now," he said.

"I couldn't tell if he was swimming or on horseback," I said. "He may have been trying for the secret ford."

"The ford's not near the bridge," he said. "It's further downstream, near the quarry. They took the tailings from the quarry at Oak Grove at the beginning of the war to fill in the bottom holes."

"Well, there certainly was a bit of shooting," I said. "Right around the bridge."

"Perhaps I'll go scout that out tonight, then," he said. "You are to remain on the grounds here, overseer, in case more spies appear."

"Yes, sir," I said. "I'll do it."

"Very well, then," he said and rode off across the dam.

Now the house should be empty.

I gave the major twenty minutes to clear the plantation and also to make sure he didn't change his mind. Then I grabbed my SIG, called the dogs, and went up to the back door of Laurel Grove. There was no light in the house, as one didn't leave candles burning in an unattended house. I had my small Maglite, which I switched onto its red lens. I took the shepherds in with me, and we prowled that house like any good cat burglar.

It was spooky, just as the sheriff had said. The chairs and sofas were enormous compared to contemporary furniture. The rooms smelled of beeswax, wood ash, and the stale odors of sachets left here and there. The floorboards creaked when I stepped off the carpets. I felt for the shepherds—their sensitive noses must be overwhelmed by all the different scents. I spent some time in the rear kitchen areas looking for a basement access but didn't find one.

Upstairs there were four rooms, almost identical in size. I didn't go into the rooms, just examined them from the hallway. I figured out that one was for Hester and the major, a second for family visitors, since it had personal items on the vanity, and a third for Valeria, although that one had two large beds. The fourth appeared to be a sewing room with no beds but lots of fabrics, dresses, a mannequin, and a foot-pedal-operated Singer sewing machine that had to be from the early 1900s. There was one spacious bathroom, which had obviously been added to the house at the end of what had been the long upstairs hall. It contained a single commode, a large freestanding bathtub, a vanity with a washbasin, and three armoires.

There were no light fixtures nor electrical switches in any of the rooms upstairs except the bathroom, where there was an electric heater. Apparently the nineteenth century had its limitations. There was also electricity in the kitchen, which ran a single large refrigerator. The stove, however, was one of those British Aga cast-iron wood burners, complete with a wood box next to it. The fireplace in the kitchen resembled the one in Glory's End, big enough for a man my size to walk into and turn around, but with a wooden mantel instead of one made from a single enormous slab of granite. There was a bed of ashes in the fireplace and a second wood box, complete with logs and splinters of hardened pine sap. I hadn't seen any telephones anywhere. There was a maid's room off to one side and a large pantry that gave access to the adjacent dining room through a swinging door.

The ground floor pretty much mirrored the arrangement upstairs. It contained the two drawing rooms, which were nearly identical and opposite each other across the spacious central hallway. A third room appeared to be a library, and the fourth was the dining room. No light fixtures or switches here, either, but there were chandeliers and wall sconces in every room.

Most important, there was no sign that anyone other than this happy little band of antiquarians had been living there. Now I regretted the events of the night before, because it was pretty obvious I'd been wrong. Valeria's injuries were my fault, and I was going to have to apologize. The only positive result from all of that had been her probably unintentional revelation that Callendar did exist—and something about the bridge.

I was standing in the hallway, trying to figure out if I should really toss the place or just get the hell out, when I noticed the shepherds were missing. Then I heard the scratch of a wooden match and saw a flare of light in the library doorway.

I drew the SIG and walked toward the doorway, which consisted of two ten-foot-high mahogany doors that swung back against the wall. I found the shepherds.

I also found Patience Johnson.

She was sitting in one of those big chairs next to a reading table. There was a smallish hurricane lamp on the table with a lit candle inside. It threw off a surprising amount of light in the dark room, illuminating the gilt lettering on several books. She was dressed in normal clothes, not her high tea uniform. She was smoking a small brown cigarillo, and she held a snifter of what looked like brandy in her hand. The shepherds were lying on the rug in front of her, looking altogether too comfortable. I felt a little dumb, standing in the doorway with a .45 in my hand.

"Mr. Richter," she said, ignoring the hand cannon. "Good evening to you. Exploring, are we?"

"In a manner of speaking," I said. "How's Cubby?"

"Funny you should ask," she said.

"He started it," I said.

"No, he didn't," she said. I couldn't tell if she was mad at me or just depressed. "He worked here, just like me. It was that damned old woman who started all this."

"I meant he shot at me first, that's all. I shot back in self-defense. I had no idea it was Cubby, and I don't think he knew it was me over in the dark."

"She knew."

"Look," I said. "There's been a guy hunting me ever since I signed up to buy Glory's End. I think she's behind that, too. I'd sure like to hear what you know about it."

She gave me a long, thoughtful look. "Get you some of this cognac," she said. "Then put that gun away and sit you down."

I did that. It was pretty good cognac. "I was looking for evidence that they have been harboring a man called Callendar."

"Oh, him," she said, blowing out a long plume of smoke.

"Strange," I said. "That's exactly what Valeria said last night."

"She ought to know," she said, looking right at home in the candlelight, which, I guess, she was. "She and her mother. They've been brooding over that insane plot for years. The glorious lost will and all that."

"So this isn't new?"

"Those other people tried to sell Oak Grove some years back. I'll bet the Realtor didn't tell you that, did he."

"Nope."

"Well, they did. Ms. Hester wasn't too pleased. She let them know it, too."

"So what happened?"

"They had 'em a summer party, down at the quarry. It went on all afternoon, like they do. Lotta white folks drinkin' a lot more than they should. It was August, and really hot. Some silly damn girl decided to go swimmin', went in wearin' her party clothes, then they all went in. The owners didn't happen to come out."

I remembered the ruined party gazebo by the side of the ramp. "They drowned?"

"Ain't no one knows," she said. "The paper said they was 'both seized with stomach cramps.' In all the splashing and shrieking, no one noticed them go down."

"I'll bet Hester did."

"Could be, Mr. Richter, could be. I did the cookin', 'cept for one plate Ms. Hester was passin' all by herself."

"What was that?"

"Don't know. Covered plate."

"And the heirs?"

"Took that property right off the market."

"Fancy that."

She shrugged and sipped her cognac.

"So you're saying that Hester knew about the will and the potential claim even then?"

"I work here, Mr. Richter," she said. "Been workin' here for years and years. I won't say I know what they know, but I'm damn sure I know what I've heard. I believe the family has known about the will from the very beginning. That's why Hester and them believe that Oak Grove is theirs."

"So who is this Callendar? What's his part in all this?"

"Callendar is Hester's son."

"What?"

"That's right. The one the major threw out of the house, declared him dead, and all that foo-raw. That son. The oldest child. What he forgot was the way it is between mothers and their sons, just like it is between daddies and their daughters. He may have been dead to the major, but he and his mama stayed close over all these years. The major, he bein' crazy and all, had no idea."

*Wheels within wheels,* I thought, but it was beginning to make sense. Callendar had a stake in Glory's End, however tenuous.

We talked for another half an hour, just sitting there in the gloom of the library by the light of one lamp. It all seemed fairly natural, given the surroundings: the old house with its eighteen-foot ceilings, the library, the smell of leather-bound books and cigar smoke. Electric lights would have almost been out of place.

I told her what had been going on and said that Callendar was now wanted for a homicide, among other things. She, like Valeria, said she'd heard differently about the dog woman, but I think she believed my version of it. I then pointed out that Hester and Valeria would be considered accomplices to the Craney killing, given that Hester was the guiding spirit behind the lost claim to the property and that Valeria had knowledge.

"They big girls now," she said simply. "My concern is Cubby."

"If Cubby comes clean and will help us to trap Callendar, I'm pretty sure he'll be in the clear."

"Pretty sure."

"Let me rephrase. He will be if that's the deal he makes."

"You makin' promises you can keep?" she asked.

"I can only promise to make it so. You know that."

"You help him make that deal?"

"I will."

"Why? The man shot at you."

"He was being played, just like I was. I don't believe Cubby is a killer."

"He was at one time, over there in Vietnam. That's why he ran off. That ain't why I'm scared."

"Okay, what?"

She took another drag on the cigar. "This family," she said, "has 'em a long history. They don't hold with folks who make mistakes or don't do their job. They git 'em for that, and if it's family, they really git 'em. You understand what I'm sayin'?"

"Cubby is family, as much as you're family. So Hester and Callendar will get him for talking to me?"

"Damn right they will. His job was to help Callendar run you off. Now they all in trouble, and they be lookin' for someone to blame, 'cause none of them ever make mistakes."

Somewhere out in the hall, a large clock began to chime the hour.

"If Callendar fails to run me off, one way or another, will Hester go after him?"

She smiled in the candlelight. It was not a pretty sight. "You'd better git on now," she said, "before the major comes back."

"Is he part of this, Patience?"

"Hell no," she snorted, "but he come back, find me talkin' to a Union spy or a Pinkerton, right here in the house? We both dead."

"He was a real major at one time?"

"Yeah, he was. Came back from Vietnam, he wasn't right in the head anymore. Question was, did he go over there that way—but, yeah, he was in the army. His boy, Callendar, too. Something he did there was the reason the major threw him out."

*That computes,* I thought. "Can you tell me what he looks like, Patience?"

"Who—Callendar?"

"Yes."

"You go look in the drawing room, right there over the mantel. Looks just like that, only he a dead-eye. Hester's baby boy. Liked to kill things, growin' up."

*Still does,* I thought—but she was right. It was time to

get the hell out there and do some of that regrouping everyone wanted me to do. I thanked her for talking to me. She gave me a wave of her hand and then poured some more of the master's cognac. As I went toward the doors, I saw one of those military medal shadowboxes on a low bookshelf. The name on the brass plate read MAJOR COURTNEY WOODRUFF LEE, AUS. Besides the army's usual present-for-duty awards, there was a Silver Star, a Bronze Star, and a Purple Heart. He was indeed a real major.

The mutts and I went back to the cottage for one last walk-through. The night was humid, and the sky was running a low overcast. Once again there were flickers of heat lightning over on the Virginia side. I decided to leave the Suburban at the cottage and take the utility vehicle. It had lights, and I wasn't going very far. Frick, being senior, rode on the seat next to mine. Frack sat on the deck in front of her seat. Kitty was relegated to the back compartment but seemed to enjoy it just the same. Nothing much fazed that dog, and I was beginning to really like her. Frick, too, was getting old, and I needed Kitty to take aboard some more of Frick's tactical spirit.

I made a camp of sorts in the house at Glory's End. I kept all three shepherds inside with me, and we severally conducted a recon of the house from top to bottom to make sure we were alone and that the various doors and secret passageways were all secure. The television monitor showed nothing afoot outside, and, it being past two in the morning, I turned in. I made a mental note to get Tony to research Major Courtney Woodruff Lee, AUS. As I lay there, watching the heat lightning caress the distant Blue Ridge Mountains through the wavy glass of the back windows, I still wondered if Callendar might not be a figment, and perhaps my real stalker had been riding around the countryside right in front of me. Patience might tell me anything to get Cubby out of the crack he was in.

* * *

Sometime just before dawn I was awakened by a rumble of thunder. I got up to look outside and was rewarded with a sharp stroke of lightning hitting down by the river, followed by a thunderclap that had all three dogs wrapped around my ankles in two seconds. Then the rain hit, and I watched as the trees writhed in the wind and tiny, bright pellets of ice danced on the brick walks below. I wandered through the rooms, looking outside as the lightning flashed and illuminated the lawns, the big oaks, the springhouse, and the smokehouse. My brain kept looking for the image of some lurking bad guy to imprint on my vision, but if anyone was out there, he was hating life right about now. I couldn't remember if the house had lightning rods, but if it didn't, it soon would have. It was a really impressive storm, and it took over a half hour for it to dissolve into just plain rain. I went back to my mattress and waited for sunrise.

I woke up to cold noses touching my cheek and a blast of sunlight coming through the freshly scrubbed windows. It was almost nine. The mutts wanted chow, and I needed coffee. I got everyone back into the utility vehicle and rambled back over to the stone cottage to retrieve the Suburban and go to town. I threw the dogs in back and went to sit down in the front seat. There, on the passenger seat, was another of those white death-mask faces that I'd discovered taped to the cottage windows. Written in black Magic Marker ink across the forehead was a message. *Enjoy the day. It will be your last.*

I drove on into town, focusing on first things first. I don't drink a lot of coffee, but I really do need that first line of caffeine to get my brain going. I hit the local Waffle House for breakfast and then carried three doughnuts out for the piranhas in the back of my Suburban.

So today was my last day, and of course the mask picture was confirmation that Willard was not the great shot he thought he was. While driving back to Glory's End, I called Tony and gave him his research assignment. I added Callendar Lee to the slate because Patience had said he'd been in the army, too. Tony's contacts in the Manceford County Sheriff's Office could get access to military personnel records if it involved a homicide investigation. If Tony hit any walls, I'd get Sheriff Walker to give it a try. Which reminded me: I needed to talk to the sheriff.

Another call revealed that he was at the county hospital, so I diverted from my trip home and went to the hospital to see the Sheriff. He was visiting Valeria Lee, so I wrote out a note and asked a nurse to pass it to him. He came down to the hospital cafeteria twenty minutes later, where I was indulging myself in a second cup of coffee and listening to the night shift people talk about their lively Friday night in the ER. It had been a payday, with the usual consequences.

"Mr. Richter," he said as he slid into a chair. He was in full uniform, and he looked tired.

"Sheriff Walker," I replied. "Does that 'mister' mean something? As opposed to 'lieutenant'? Am I in hot water again?"

"Absolutely," he said with a grin. "Ms. Hester wants your skin. Ms. Valeria wants your skin, stretched and salted. Apparently she will have to lie on her side for a while and stand up a lot."

"I didn't shoot her," I said. "That was Mommy."

"Yeah, but you started it," he said. "What did you find out last night, if anything?"

I filled him in. He was as surprised as I had been that Callendar, the son who'd been "banished" for so many years, was probably our guy.

"Do you believe Patience?"

"I do, if only because she wants a deal for Cubby."

He nodded. "I guess I need to call Ms. Hester into the office," he said. "Formally. With her attorney."

"I explained the notion of an accomplice to Patience last night," I said. "I'm guessing that wasn't exactly news."

"Problem is, Hester hasn't been home since Valeria got her ass air-conditioned," he said. Three young nurses sitting nearby had been eavesdropping, and one of them started laughing. He gave them a brittle look, and they decided to finish their breakfast and go in the away direction.

"Hester claims you caused Valeria to come off her horse," he said.

"True. I thought it might be Callendar trying to escape, so I got right in the way. I sent the dogs in first, but when her horsie tried to kick their heads off, I fired my scattergun."

He rubbed his eyes. I wondered if he'd slept at all last night.

"Well," he said. "What fun."

I told him about my theory that Callendar and the night-riding major might be the same person. He shook his head.

"I asked an old friend in the SBI to run a check on Callendar, who I assumed was a Lee. He's real enough. He was a Citadel grad. Went into the army and got cashiered after a training accident that killed three of his soldiers. They fired him for lying about what happened, not for what happened."

"I wonder how that sat with the major."

"Not well. He came home in disgrace; the old man declared him a nonperson, threw him out, never to darken the doorway at Laurel Grove again."

"What's he do for a living?"

"That gets interesting," he said. "His credit records give his employment as a hunting guide down east of New Bern."

"Hunting guide."

"Yeah, but one who lists his income for the past year in the low six figures."

"Pretty good for a hunting guide."

"I asked my contact if he could access his tax returns, and he said no, he couldn't, but what was my question. I told him. Next day he told me he'd discovered some more information that might be pertinent."

"You, of course, did not ask him where or how he got it."

"There you go. Anyway, some of his income was tax free. Now you tell me: Whose income is tax free?"

"Military guys in a war zone, for one," I said.

"And some of those security contractors, say, like in Iraq and Afghanistan?"

"Wow," I said. "He's one of them."

"That was my contact's general impression, based on records he did not see."

"That would explain some of the toys and methods he's been throwing against me. Any local records?"

"The local sheriff knows him but says he's never been a problem. He has a driver's license, so I've requested a photo from DMV."

"Be interesting to see that," I said. "That little white mask on my front seat would indicate that Willard missed."

"Willard will be sad to hear that," he said, "but yes, that's what I would conclude."

"The major could have put that there," I said.

"The major is gonzo."

"He was in the army, too, though. I saw his medals in the library last night. It might be interesting to know what he did for a living in the Green Machine."

"It wouldn't matter," he said. "Just feature the major in court. Even if he's been helping his son mess with your mind, which isn't likely, is it, we couldn't touch him, other than maybe to commit him."

"What do you want me to do?" I asked, suddenly out of answers.

"Chain yourself to a tree out in front of the big house at Glory's End tonight. Turn on some spots and bleat like a goat. We'll be up on the porch, watching for the tiger. How's that sound?"

"Not great."

"We've got to flush him," he said. "He has to know the will scam won't fly anymore, but if he is still around, I'd assume he wants your ass dead."

"So either way, I'm bait?"

"Any other suggestions?" he said. "I mean, this thing's murky enough right now. I'd be satisfied with a righteous self-defense shooting."

My brain still wasn't working on all eight cylinders, even after two coffees.

"I've set up camp in the house at Glory's End," I said, "but if you put guys out on the perimeter, he'll just wait until you run out of overtime money."

"Yup."

"Goat, hunh?"

"Yup."

"Will you come when I call?"

"You bet," he said. "Hopefully just in time, too."

Then his cell phone went off. He looked at the screen and said he had to boogie. As he went out the door, Carol Pollard came in. She saw me and waved, and I motioned her over to my table, since the cafeteria was pretty full. I had a third coffee that I didn't need and filled her in on the events of the past few days. She laughed when she heard the part about the goat.

"We've tried to find a way to take the initiative from this guy," I said, "but it keeps coming back to waiting for him to make his big move."

"So far it's been mostly talk, hasn't it," she said.

"So far," I said. "It's not like he didn't have some opportunities."

"Yet it was Hester who actually raised a shotgun and tried to shoot you."

"What's your point?"

"My point is that she's the driver in this game. He's doing what she tells him to do, because it's really Hester who wants you off that property. You want the initiative, squeeze Hester."

"How?"

"Oh, I don't know. How about this: Tell her you're going to dismantle the house. Take it apart, pile up the pieces, and then rebuild it stick by stick—like I did with my house. If there's something there she's afraid of, something hidden in the house, I don't know, some deadly secret? She'll act, or she'll push Callendar's go button."

I thought about that, and the fact that the Lees cared an awful lot about the family's reputation. They also tended to act decisively when someone failed them, like Callendar's shooting down the dog lady. It might work.

"Okay," I said. "How do I get this message to Her Hestership? She sees me, she's likely to reach for that coach gun again, and Valeria will hand her the ammo."

"Let me do it. I'm a volunteer here, too. I'll go upstairs, run into the Lees somehow, and positively bubble over with excitement about your plans to dismantle the house. How interesting it will be to see how the house was built, and all its historical secrets."

"How do you know she won't fold you into the goat pen with me?" I asked.

"You need some help out there?" she said. "I'm not all that bad with that Mag."

"Plus, you're bored."

"A little bit, yes. It's a very small—."

"Town," I finished for her.

She smiled brightly.

"It would mean you'd have to spend the night," I said. "Think of your reputation in this very small town."

"What can I tell you," she said. "A local creep tried to break into my house one night. I surprised him, and he ran for his truck. The truck ended up with a blown engine, two shattered axles, no window glass, and smelling like a sewage treatment plant. Since then my reputation and my Magnum have been married, so to speak."

I spent the rest of the day setting up for something of a siege at Glory's End. I acquired two real beds and some other stuff from a seedy-looking furniture store that was desperately in the "huge sale, limited time only" mode, on the condition that it all made it out to the house by three this afternoon. The store manager promised fervently that it would. Then I loaded up on groceries, some more Scotch from the ABC store, a coffeemaker, and some fresh ammo for my various guns. The shepherds gamely rode around in the Suburban for the whole shopping expedition and were very glad to get out back at the house. Frick surprised a squirrel, and then all three dogs got into a fight over the carcass. Being in the car all day makes them cranky.

Tony called in around three with the news that he had not been able to find out anything at all about the major or Callendar. Since 9/11, the Defense Department had put up some pretty big walls around military personnel data. I told him it was okay, that the sheriff had found out a little bit. He asked if I thought the guy was going to make his move soon or just take off. I told him about our little plot to light a fuse under Hester, and he asked if he should come out tonight. I demurred, saying only that this might take a few days to work. Or not.

I checked in with the sheriff; he informed me that Cubby had been released to recuperate at home. I was surprised he'd gone directly from ICU to outpatient release, but apparently the hospital was more afraid of its own community bacterial problems than of what might be lurking at Cubby's house. I told him about our move to shake up the Lee women, and he agreed that Hester might react. He said he was on the way over to the Johnsons' house with one of his detectives to have a little chat and would call me if he learned anything of tactical significance.

"Like where he's been holing up?"

"Just like that," he said. "Although that old carriage house across the river is the likely spot. Our forensics people found plenty of signs that it had been occupied."

"He's got another hole over on this side," I said. "If it isn't on Hester's property, then it's over here at Glory's End somewhere."

"Remember—make him come to you," he said. "You go out on patrol, he'll have you."

"We'll keep that in mind," I said.

"We?"

I told him about Carol. He was quiet for a moment.

"You know why she left the Job?"

"She told me it was because of a shootout of some kind that went bad, something she did, or didn't, do. I didn't press for details."

"She lost her nerve," he said. "There was a three-way gun-pointing situation, and the bad guy stared her down, shot her partner dead, and then, and only then, did she open fire. She put the mope down, but he put her in the hospital and gave her a gimp leg."

"I see."

"Do you?" he asked. "She's good people, Cam. Honest, kind, and intelligent. She sincerely regrets what happened and makes no excuses about it being someone else's fault. Still, don't get yourself into a tactical situation that requires her to be your only backup. I don't think she has it in her."

"No killer instinct."

"Right."

"Admirable in a woman, I think."

"If she's there as a woman," he said, "that's one thing. If she's there to help you fight this guy, that's another."

"I hear you," I said.

"You call us the moment you think you need real backup. Shots fired will do it for us. I'll have people ready."

"You call me if Cubby reveals anything useful, please." Then I thanked him and told him I'd keep my cell on.

Carol called and said she'd be out in half an hour, after picking up something for us to eat. I'd thought about what Sheriff Walker had said and almost told her to stay home. On the other hand, she sincerely wanted to help, and I think she may have wanted to take another shot at proving herself. It was entirely unnecessary, of course—she didn't have to prove anything to me or anyone else. Still, that was my sense of it, and besides, I liked her company.

The evening came on with a wash of warm, humid air and the threat of another thunderstorm at some point. We ate out on the front porch because the house was too hot except on that semiunderground floor. The builders knew what they were about, but I wanted to be able to see around the lawns and that broad sweep of grass leading down to the river.

I talked to Carol about what might happen, which ranged from absolutely nothing to a pitched gun battle inside the house. "The idea is to make him come to us," I said. "Assuming he's coming at all."

"Then I should move my vehicle," she said. "Park it over at the cottage or back in one of those barns. It might be useful if he thinks it's just you and him."

I looked out at the lovely vista of fields, lawns, and acres of trees, changing shape and color as the sun went down and that hot, humid breeze stirred all the greenery. Then I had a thought.

"Let's move inside now," I said, getting up and picking up the remains of supper.

"Why? It's so nice—oh," she said.

"I'm guessing he's been watching us for a while," I said, "and possibly right now. If he's doing it through a rifle scope, he has a problem, because there are two targets. One will not survive the first shot."

"The other might live to tell the tale," she said.

"Yeah. Something like that."

She shivered at the thought that someone might have crosshairs on us. We tried to keep it casual but almost collided at the front door trying to get through it. She laughed nervously as I pushed her gently through and into the house. The mutts came with us, still hoping for table scraps. They say dogs can't count, but mine sure can.

"Hester was appalled at the thought of our tearing this house down," she said, sitting on one of the beds, which I'd set up in the same drawing room in which the old lady had lived. "Spitting mad. Seriously high dudgeon. The appropriate authorities will be notified. Lawyers will be unleashed in angry battalions."

"How about Valeria?"

"Happily spaced out on some kind of prescription joy juice," she said. "Very much on her side these days. I could see one of the wounds, and it looked painful."

"What in the world could be hidden here that would inspire Hester to have somebody murdered?"

"You think she ordered Callendar to shoot the dog trainer?"

"No, I think that's just how this crew goes through life: Do what I say, and do it now. If you do it poorly, I'll have your ass for it. It's also very convenient if you live a hundred fifty years back in time; what crimes against the 'slaves' you do don't count against you."

The light in the western sky died as a dark curtain of thunderclouds rose up over the foothills. "So what brought him back?"

"I think she told him to make me go away, and then left it up to him as to how and when. I think he'll up the ante now, because the will's probably useless."

"If that's true, why would he come at all?"

"Because Hester's pissed, and also scared of something. So far, Callendar has failed. We know what happens to Lees who fail."

"Oh," she said. "Should we make sure the house is secure?"

I'd already done that, but it wouldn't hurt to do it again. "Let's start with the basement," I said. I took Kitty with us and left Frick in the kitchen and Frack on the main floor. That put a dog on every level with access to the outside.

I'd secured the basement door with the same rig Callendar had used against me, after first pulling that iron bar into the basement. He couldn't get in, but we could get out. We checked the rest of the basement to make sure we hadn't missed anything, and I made Carol step into the tunnel so I could test the restraints. She seemed glad to get back in. I knew the feeling.

The lowest, partially underground floor had windows, and there wasn't much we could do about them. They were smaller than the big ones on the main floor but still large enough to admit a determined human. I'd wired up the camera we had used over in the cottage to survey the stairway coming up from the kitchen to the main floor, which was the best I could do. I'd have loved to have a few hundred feet of black fishing line and some tin cans to lay out a web on the floor, but we were fresh out.

In the kitchen we checked the access to the springhouse and secured that door from our side. We set up some pots and pans under the two windows so that anyone sliding through should drop one on the floor. I showed her the word CALLENDAR chiseled into the mantel rock. She ran her fingers over it and wondered what it meant.

"Cubby said it was important, but I can't figure out why. It is old, if that plaster's any indication."

"You'd think it would have been centered," she said.

I looked at it. She was right. The name had been carved left of center on the long stone.

I found the hammer Cubby had used and began to whack gently on the blackened plaster to the right of the name while Carol held a flashlight on it. Sure enough, as the plaster bits fell into the hearth, more letters appeared. When we were done, though, we still had a mystery.

CALLENDAR KILLED THEM ALL, it read.

"Killed who?" Carol asked.

"Beats me," I said as I became aware of the rising wind outside. "Storm's coming in. We should probably get upstairs."

"You going to leave a dog down here?" she asked, pointing to Frick.

"That would be a smart move," I said, "but they're scared of thunder and lightning. No way will she stay down here if I'm upstairs."

As if to make my point, the first drumroll of thunder echoed across the river bottoms, and Frick immediately plastered herself to my leg.

"You are a useless mutt," I told her.

Her expression said, *Take me upstairs. Don't make me bite you.*

The storm lasted an hour this time, ending with the skies drained and one tremendous, crack-of-doom thunder boom that announced its departure from the county. I'd watched the monitor throughout the storm, but I'd forgotten what a lightning flash could do to an IR camera. If Callendar had approached the house, I'd have never seen him in all the blank white screens. The good news was that the spring storm had also washed out all of the heat, and now a cool, clear breeze came through the windows. I hated the thought of closing them, but there were no screens, and there would be bugs galore if we didn't.

Carol went into the bathroom and reappeared ten minutes later in a sweatshirt tracksuit. Practical, decidedly unenticing, and warm enough for the night temps in this old house. She'd planned ahead. I hadn't, so I would have to sleep in my clothes.

"Shall we keep watch together, take shifts, or what?" she asked, sitting down on the bed she'd appropriated.

"I'm going to sit up for a while," I said. "Have a Scotch and try to figure out what his possibilities are."

"I'll join you in a Scotch," she said, "but then I'm used to early bedtime."

We sat out on the front porch again, but back against the front wall of the house behind one of the columns so as to be less conspicuous. We talked about not much, and finally she brought the conversation around to the night in the alley that had ended her police career.

"Such as it was," she said. "Four years street, then a shield. Then the shooting, and I was out."

"You did better than most," I said. "Lotta guys never leave the street."

"A fair number don't want to," she said. "You know, the politics, dealing directly with bosses. Most of my friends on the force preferred to chase bad guys."

"The sheriff warned me not to let you stay here tonight," I said. Then I told her what he'd said. I figured it might come easier if I said it instead of her. She smiled in the dark.

"He's right," she said simply. "I do not have the killer instinct. I hesitated, and killed my partner."

"The bad guy killed your partner, Carol. Maybe you could have prevented it, maybe not. Usually the way something like that gets prevented is for the cop to shoot first, and these days, there's a lawyer waiting behind every bad guy happy to make some money from any mistakes."

"Bet you could have prevented it," she said.

"At the end of my career? Sure, probably. As new as you were? When I was that age I would have gone for the hero medal and shot first—and probably missed and killed a passing nun. The key thing is this: If the incident destroyed your self-confidence as a cop, and the rest of the cops believed you owned it, then you did precisely the right thing—you got out."

"Would you have left the force?"

"Absolutely," I said. "The whole cops-and-robbers thing is usually a bluff, when you get right down to it. The bad guys see a confident crowd of blues surrounding them, they give it up. When one gets cornered and decides to actually fight, we usually lose some people. They're feral. They can smell a hesitation. It's atavistic."

"You make it sound so simple," she said, "but I still feel bad about it."

"You're human," I said. "That's almost a disadvantage when dealing with the wild ones. You have a conscience and some empathy. Most of the really bad guys we go up against have neither."

"And Callendar? Is he one of the feral ones?"

"He shot that woman practically in the face. He made her turn around first, because she was looking at the house. Yeah, he's one."

I felt her shiver in the darkness. "I think I want to go home," she said suddenly.

"Want me to escort you home in my car?"

"You're not mad?"

"Dear heart, I'm relieved. You don't need another trial by fire. I loved the company, but I don't need the distraction, either."

"Ow."

I laughed. "Take off, pretty lady. You're simply using your head. Call me when you arrive at the house and you're locked in."

"I'm so sorry, Cam," she said.

I hugged her and told her it was all right. "Beat it, Pilgrim," I said in my best John Wayne accent.

"That's terrible," she said. "Really bad."

She gathered her stuff from inside, and I walked her

down across the wet grass to her car. I reminded her to call me when she was safe in the house, and off she went.

Fifteen minutes later my cell phone rang. It was Carol.

"Home safe," she said.

"Thanks for dinner," I said.

"You're welcome. It was just some leftovers I threw together."

"Okay, then. I'll call you in the morning."

"Yes, please do."

I hung up the phone and went inside. I couldn't lock the door from the inside, so I wedged a chair under the dual handles. I checked on the dogs and then stopped.

Some leftovers I threw together?

She hadn't cooked anything. She'd gone to the grocery store and hit the deli line.

*Fuck me,* I thought. That was a duress signal.

I called Sheriff Walker's office, got the duty officer, told him who I was, and asked them to rush a unit over to Carol Pollard's house because she might have an intruder holding her. The sheriff must have left some stringent instructions regarding any calls from me because there was no chatter, and two cars were dispatched at once.

Ten minutes later I got the call I'd been dreading. It was the sheriff himself.

"She's not there. Her ride's not there. I have a unit backtracking to your place, but there's no sign of her on the roads. What's going on?"

The sheriff showed up with two additional units a half hour later. I watched as he hurried across the grass through the light rain and then took down the barricade at the front door. I saw one of the cruisers turn around and go down the driveway, while the other crept around the hill to explore the barn area. We went into the back of the house to get away from all those tall windows.

"How'd you know?" he asked, and I told him.

"So he went to her house?"

"I think he was here, out front somewhere, and he either ambushed her on the driveway with some obstacle or got her at the gates. She would have shut the gates behind her, coming in."

"Contact?"

"Nothing yet."

Another thunderstorm was rolling across the distant countryside over on the Virginia side of the river, its thunder occasionally rattling the windows. It was going to be one of those nights.

"You know what the deal's gonna be," he said.

"Oh, yes."

He looked over at the Scotch bottle, and I went and fixed us up with two fingers each.

"You've got three options," he said. "He calls, you give it to us. That's the smart option. Or he calls and you tell him to fuck off."

"Or he calls and I go."

"That's the dumb option."

"Is it? This one's a killer. Remember the Craney woman? One round in the face? He made her turn around before he shot her. So she'd know."

"Of course I do," he said, "but one of my D's had the brilliant idea of going to his Web site, the one advertising the hunting expeditions. Talked to a couple of past clients. Guy's known in guide circles as a guarantee."

"What's that mean?"

"If he sets the client up on a trophy buck, and the client gets buck fever and blows it? He nails the buck, and then it becomes the client's trophy. His MOS in the army was sniper. Just like you. You wouldn't stand a chance."

"Nor does Carol," I reminded him.

He finished his Scotch, eyed the bottle, but then put the glass down on the table.

"I can try to cover you with a SWAT crew," he said.

"They're urban, not field guys, right?"

He nodded. We both knew they'd be mostly useless out there in the weeds at night. The Bureau's hostage rescue team could do it, but Callendar probably wasn't going to wait.

"Lemme show you something," I said, and we went down into the kitchen. He looked at the inscription on the mantel stone.

"Any ideas?" I asked.

"One," he said. "That looks pretty old. This might be what Hester Lee is afraid of."

"How so?"

"The train robbery. Maybe the original Callendar had something to do with that."

"Like what?"

"Beats me. Maybe he was the inside man."

My cell phone began to vibrate audibly. The sheriff looked at me.

"Showtime?" he asked.

The listing in the window said CAROL POLLARD. He was letting me know he did in fact have her. Then the screen shifted to a text message.

YOU FOR HER, it read.

"Showtime," I said. I texted back: WHERE & WHEN?

LOSE COPS, he answered.

I showed his answer to the sheriff, who wondered aloud how he could see us and then remembered the cruisers. There was another rumble of thunder across the river, although it didn't seem to be getting any closer. The rain outside had settled into a drizzle.

WHERE AND WHEN, I texted.

No answer.

"I've gotta do this," I said.

He nodded. "We'll leave here, go upriver to the highway bridge, cross the Dan, and come down on the q.t. to that burned-out house. I've got a boat out there. We'll muster some assets up at that carriage house and wait for your call."

That sounded like as good a plan as any. I thanked him for letting me take a shot.

"You like that lady?"

"I do, actually," I said. "We got comfortable with each other."

He finished his Scotch and then fished in his pocket for some spearmint gum. "You get this business done tonight, you better watch yourself," he said. "She'll git ya."

"I can think of worse things," I said.

"Me, too," he said.


I waited an hour while the storm across the river passed on to the east. It was still drizzling, and the occasional grumble of thunder could be heard across the entire countryside. I had everything I needed except some raingear. Wouldn't you know. Finally I turned off all the lights, called the dogs together, told Frack to assume the watch in the house, and took the other two out to the front porch with me. I was dressed in field gear and carried the shotgun and my SIG. I put my cell phone in a sock and stuffed it into my shirt pocket.

I thought I knew where he might he holed up, because I'd finally remembered what Valeria had said after getting her hide ventilated. *Him? He's in the bridge.* It had made no sense at the time, but then I also remembered the crumbling fortifications around my side of the bridge. I thought it was possible he could see the big house from that vantage, hence the order to lose the cops. It was as good an objective as any, so out we went.

The sky was black as ink, and there was tangible energy in that warm, muggy air. I thought about taking the utility vehicle, but there was no direct route up there to the abandoned rail line suitable for wheels. Conscious of long guns,

I took the indirect route, however, going down the drive to the two-lane, west along the road until I was up on the major's favorite ridge, and then north through the pines toward the burial ground and the ruins of the bridge. The dogs ranged ahead for the most part, but Frick seemed to want to hang back. I suspected the stormy night was affecting her, and I was glad that other thunderstorm had passed on by.

The grass was wet and I was wetter by the time we made it into the deep piney woods. I kept pulling the cell phone out of its protective sock to see if there'd been any calls, but the screen remained blank. All the woods creatures were probably bedded down, so we moved unchallenged, but probably not unseen, over the carpet of soggy pine needles. At last we came out onto the hillside overlooking the cemetery and the darkened bridge abutments. I stepped behind a tree, went into text mode, and then placed a call to the sheriff's cell phone.

APPROACHING THE BRIDGE, I texted.

COPY, he answered. NO HEAT.

I sent him an R for roger and replaced the phone in its now slightly damp sock, making sure it was still on vibrate.

"No heat" meant that they had IR gear on the river and had detected no signs of life on or around the bridge. It was comforting to know they were out there, but I knew better than to assume that there was no one around.

I started down the hill, my muscles tensed for a gunshot. If he was on or in the bridge emplacements, it would be child's play for a sniper-trained shooter to hit me in the open like that. I was betting that he wanted to crow a little before we got it on. If I was wrong about that, I'd be dead.

A warm and then suddenly cool breeze lifted off the ridge as I started down the hill toward all those leaning gravestones in the tall grass. My night vision was just about perfect by then, so when I glanced left and up the hill, I could almost make out the approaching thunderstorm. All the brand-new tree leaves were making that weird something's-coming noise, and I hurried to get down off that exposed hillside, mindful of the lightning patch up above me.

I tripped over one of the stones and almost went sprawling as the wind strengthened, definitely cooler now as the thunderhead seven miles above my head began to collapse. Both dogs closed in on me, and Frick went into her leg wrap mode. I moved as quickly as I could through the gravestones, aiming for the railroad embankment while trying hard to avoid cracking a shin. Then the world turned bright white, followed by a terrific clap of thunder that sent me to my knees. I could barely hear the residual rumble as the sound spread out over the county, and for the moment I was blinded. In that flash of light, though, I had seen two figures standing astride the empty track bed, halfway between me and the bridge. One was Carol, and the other was a large black figure with a bright white face and what looked like some kind of weapon that he was holding at port arms.

Callendar Lee, at long last.

I held position for another minute while trying desperately to get some night vision back, but my eyes were staring into an orange glow no matter how much I blinked, and my ears were still ringing. That had been close enough for me to smell the ozone. I could feel the dogs nearby, but they were certainly as blind as I was by then, too.

Of course, Callendar was probably also blind. Had he seen me? The first drops of rain patted onto the gravel. I called Carol's name, my voice sounding tinny after that thunderclap.

I thought I heard her yell and reflexively rolled to one side of the track bed, just as something cut the air by my cheek. I never did hear the gun, but by then I was rolling down the embankment on the downhill side, trying not to lose the shotgun. I ended up about twenty feet into the weeds and quickly pointed the gun up at the track bed in their general direction.

I still couldn't see.

*Neither can he,* I told myself, but I was wrong about that. The ground exploded next to my left cheek, and I frantically rolled again. I thought I heard the dogs scattering into the weeds nearby. Smart dogs.

The next round blew dirt against my right cheek, which is when I realized he had me spotted and bracketed, and he'd keep shooting until I got the message.

I stopped rolling. I put down the shotgun and raised my hands, then stood up, slowly, still blind as a bat. The rain was getting a little bit heavier, and there was some grumbling from the direction of that big black cloud.

I blinked frantically and finally could make out a few objects inside that orange corona. Two of them were moving toward me. I kept my hands out in front of me, wondering if I'd snapped the SIG into its holster. I usually did.

A second flare of lightning, but this one was cloud to cloud. It lit everything up like a welding arc. He had Carol in front of him, and he had that damned white mask on his face. No wonder he could see and I couldn't.

Carol, probably as blind as I was, stumbled as she came across the gravel embankment and then went sprawling. I heard her grunt painfully, and then she was still. Callendar ignored her and kept coming until he was standing ten feet from me. I could only guess that it was him, since I could see his silhouette and the white blur where his face should have been. I couldn't see the rifle, and then understood that that was because it was pointed right at me. The dogs. Where the hell were the dogs? *C'mon, mutts, now's the time to take his ass out. Don't be shy.*

Another lightning flash, not close but bright enough for

me to see that the shepherds were occupied. Two large
Dobies were confronting them, and the shepherds were
very slowly backing up.

"It's been fun," he said, raising his voice to reach over
the sound of the rain and a new breeze sweeping down
from the cemetery hill.

"Wait," I said. "I've got to know: who's the woman I'm
supposed to have killed?"

"She doesn't exist," he called. "That was all bullshit. A
distraction, to make you think I was serious."

"After Summerfield, I always thought you were serious," I called back.

"You kept coming anyway," he said.

"So this is all about the will?"

More thunder from that cloud, but no lightning. The
breeze had turned into a steady wind, though, and it was
definitely cold air now. In a minute we would be drowning.
The sounds of a big dogfight erupted to my right, but that
white face never flinched.

A new flash of lightning, behind me this time, lit the
area up before he could answer, followed by a bang of
close-by thunder. When I realized I could still see, I half
hoped that it would blind him for a second and tensed to
take a dive. Except what I'd seen in the lightning flash instead made me freeze in total amazement.

In the air, rising over the railroad embankment in a fluid
black arc, came the major on his horse, which crashed down
behind Callendar in an explosion of gravel and dirt just as
another lightning flash erupted. I caught one terrifying
glimpse of that huge cavalry saber flashing down, and then
the horse and rider were thundering away to my right, coming so close to me that I sat down without even realizing it.

Then the real rain came down like a waterfall, together
with more lightning and thunder and wind, to the point
where I could do absolutely nothing until it slackened off
for a moment.

I crawled forward, keeping low because of all the lightning. I couldn't see much. The blinding rain was sheeting down so hard now that it stung my hands and face. I was looking for Carol, but instead I put a hand into a warm, sticky mess. I recoiled, even as the rain quickly rinsed my hand. The major, abroad in the night and enveloped in his madness, had decapitated his own son.

"Cam?"

"Keep calling," I shouted over all the racket. "I can't see you."

"Here," she said, and I finally found her in the maelstrom, lying flat on the ground as I had been, trying to become one with the earth. We clung to each other for a moment, and then she asked what had happened. I told her, and she shuddered.

I realized I could no longer hear the sounds of dogs fighting, although the rain was getting heavier again. They could be ten feet away and I might not hear them. I started to call for them but then thought better of it. If the Dobes had driven them off, my calls would bring the worst kind of trouble right to us.

I asked Carol if she was hurt. I had to shout into her ear over the storm's incredible racket. I thought I heard her say the word "okay," so I gathered her up and we started to climb back up. I headed on a diagonal across the embankment, aiming for the ruins of the bridge fortifications. It was the only shelter around, and we needed to get off this damned lightning patch. Carol probably had no idea of what I was trying to do, but she wasn't going to leave me just then.

We were only about thirty feet away from the bridge abutment when all of a sudden I felt rather than heard a deep humming in the ground and sensed all the hair on my body start to stand up. That's when I realized we were crawling over steel. They'd apparently left the last thirty feet of track buried in the ground, and we were straddling it on our hands and knees.

" 'Bye," I said to Carol, or tried to, anyway, and then the world turned bright white again and all the noise finally stopped.

I awoke with my face in water. Not my whole face, just one side. I smelled wet dog, opened the one nonsubmerged eye, and stared into Kitty's teeth. Then I realized she was tugging me along the ground while another dog, who I assumed was Frick and not one of the killer Dobes, was pulling on my sleeve in the same general direction. It felt like I was being dragged through a big puddle until I realized, mostly from the smell, that I was on the edge of the Dan River. My vision was back to its orange glow phase again, but the storm had gone silent. In fact, the whole world had gone silent.

I tried to stop the dogs and get loose, but none of my muscles would do anything other than quiver. And hurt. I felt like I'd been slammed onto the ground by the entire front line of the Green Bay Packers. My mouth hurt. My teeth hurt. The fillings in my teeth hurt. My joints felt like they had been detached and then reattached with barbed wire. There was a terrible taste in my mouth, and my tongue was swollen into the size of a balled-up sock. The sock hurt.

Then there were lots of lights, which I finally realized were flashlights. A man's face appeared in my cone of orange vision. He was talking. I couldn't hear a thing, and I still couldn't move. The dogs backed off, and then people took over the dragging.

I closed my eyes and thought of Carol, of how nice it had been during our time together, and how nice it would be if we could just climb into a big warm bed and sleep off this terrible, brain-ringing hangover.

Which is pretty much where I woke up. It was a nice warm bed, unfortunately sans Carol Pollard, but it would do. The first thing I noticed was that my vision was no longer tinted orange. I thought I could hear a low, murmuring noise, but it was overwhelmed with a ringing sound. My left wrist hurt where there had been something stuck in my arm, probably an IV. Or maybe that's where the lightning had gone in. I focused this time and saw that it was, in fact, a handy-dandy IV. I felt wonderful, actually. Warm. Lucid. Content.

"Goo-o-o-d morning," an unreasonably happy voice warbled next to the bed. "And how are we feeling this morning?"

I turned my head to focus on what turned out to be a nurse. Turning the head may have been a mistake, based on the audible crackle of my neck vertebrae. Nurse Tweety Bird saw me frown, made an adjustment on the pretty plastic bag above my head, smiled at me like the angel she was, and then I was away again to Never-Never Land. Wonderful.

The next time I woke up, Nurse Tweety had been replaced by Sheriff Walker. Lousy trade. I thought he might have a twin, but then they solidified into my good buddy, the High Shareef of Rockwell County in all his uniformed glory.

"You warble and I'll scream," I said.

"Okay," he said. "We hereby declare this a warble-free zone."

The "we" part bothered me for a moment, but then my head cleared.

I remembered. Where was Never-Never Land when I needed it? He saw me break through.

"Ah," he said, "there you are."

"Where's Carol?" I asked.

"Resting comfortably, not far away. You remember what happened?"

I looked over his shoulder at the bright blue day outside.

"Rain. Thunder. Lightning. I remember the lightning."

"I'll bet you do," he said with a grin.

"Am I in trouble?" I asked.

"Physically? No. At least the guys in the white coats don't think so. You laid hands and glands on God's halo and were treated accordingly."

"I remember that," I said. "Jesus H. Christ."

"Yes, the believers think he's a full partner."

"God'll git you for that," I said. "How's Carol, really?"

"Sedated. Burns on her hands and knees, just like you."

I looked at my hands. I hadn't noticed them before. That's because the palms were swathed in white bandages. Now that I was finally paying them attention, they jointly rewarded me with a lance of serious pain in full stereo. I think I whimpered.

"There were rails there," I said. "They were supposed to have picked up all that shit after the war."

"Apparently it was a union job," he said with a straight face.

I closed my eyes for just a minute. An hour later he was back, with two paper cups of coffee. I praised him for being a gentleman and a scholar and gratefully sipped some truly obnoxious yet wonderful black coffee. It was hard, with the bandages.

"We're trying to figure out the headless m-f up there on the tracks."

It took me a moment, but then I remembered that huge horse and the rider with that equally huge cavalry saber. "The major arrived," I said. "Saw the overseer being menaced by a masked Yankee agent. Jumped his horse over that embankment and took said m-f's head right off."

"You're kidding."

"I'm not, and it's worse than you think." I reminded him about Callendar's true relationship to the family at Laurel Grove. That rocked him back a little.

"He killed his own son?"

"No," I said. "Technically, yes, of course, but actually?

He saw the overseer being menaced by a stranger with a gun, doubtless an enemy agent, and he acted to defend the Honor of the Glorious Cause."

"Holy shit."

"Exactly," I said. "You need to go sweat those Auntie Bellums. Find out what the fuck this was really all about. It couldn't have anything to do with some bogus will from the dusty past."

He sat back in his chair. My head was clearing fast, and I realized he was well and truly shocked by what I'd told him.

"I want to see Carol," I said.

"You sure?"

"I'm sure. I got her into this mess."

"Okay," he said. "This IV thing seems to have wheels."

A different nurse appeared. The room became an angel-free zone that resounded with the words "absolutely not," but the sheriff was a big guy and I was more than just a little determined. Once I swung my legs out from under the covers, however, I realized that Nurse Ratched might have a point. The room moved around for a minute, and I found out that there is a limit to what painkillers can do for you. Then she gave me one of those I-told-you-so looks, and I stood up. Fortunately the sheriff caught me before I fell right on my keester.

"Get a chair," he told the nurse.

"I don't work for you," she retorted.

"Get a fucking chair and do it now!" he thundered, and she just about flew out of the room. A moment later, magically, there was a wheelchair. I tried to sit down with as much dignity as I could muster and damned near missed the chair entirely. That had been some really spiffy lightning. God's halo indeed.

The sheriff pushed me down the hallway while rolling the IV stand alongside. "You're good at this," I said.

"Had lots of practice," he mumbled, and then I remembered what had happened to his wife. *Good going, dipshit,* I told myself.

He rolled me and my IV stand into another room, and there was Carol Pollard, or at least her face. Her very white face. The rest of her looked much diminished under the covers. My heart jumped a little when I saw her. Then she opened her eyes.

"Hey," I said, taking refuge in the universal southern greeting.

"Well, hello, handsome," she said. "Who might you be?"

The next day they discharged me into the custody of my loyal buddies from Hide and Seek Investigations. Once outside in the sunlight they proposed that I let them check me into a really nice hotel down in Triboro, where they would ensure that I had the best of care. I told them I wanted to go back out to Glory's End.

"You're shitting me, right?" Tony said. "You're not still going through with that, are you?"

"I am."

"Take him back inside," Horace said. "He's still out of it."

"What happened to the mutts?" I asked.

There was some hemming and hawing, and then Pardee said that they had a little surprise for me.

"Where is it?"

"Glory's End," they said in unison. I was glad to see that they knew defeat when it looked them in the eye.

"What is this surprise—they're not hurt, are they?" I couldn't remember why I thought they might be hurt.

"They're okay," Horace said, "and you like German dogs, right?"

"They're German shepherds, last time I checked."

"Great," he said. "Let's roll."

The surprise was real when we got to the house. The

sheriff was there, along with the county animal control lady. Sitting on the front lawn were five dogs instead of three. Two shepherds flanking two Dobes, and then Kitty sitting out in front of the pack in the place of boss dog. Frick and Kitty were sporting the stains of veterinary anti-septic spray, as were the two Dobes. It was obvious, how-ever, that they were now all the best of friends. Peace in the valley.

"I give up," I said from the passenger seat in Tony's ride. "How the hell did this happen?"

"The cops down at the river that night were focused on getting you and Carol out of the storm. These guys showed up here the next morning when Horace came to get all the video gear."

"Last I heard it was a war to the death out there," I said.

"Well, they've all got holes in 'em, but there they are. They've been to the vet."

I knew what had happened. It had been war to the death until that lightning bolt, and then instinct had taken over and all four of them had decided to depart the county. My guys came back to get me, and the Dobes had probably discovered their human's remains out there on the track bed. No more orders, no more fight. If you can't beat 'em, join 'em.

"The question is," the sheriff said, walking up with his animal control deputy, "whether you want them or you want us to take them."

"They seem to have joined forces," I said. The animal control deputy looked disappointed.

"I assume that little formation indicates the pecking order?" he asked.

I nodded. "I'll try it," I said, getting out of the car. "As long as they're not still mad."

My guys were all over me, even Frick, who got knocked down a couple of times in the commotion. The Dobes never moved. I finally put my shepherds on a down and then walked over to the Dobermans. They were both impressively muscled females, and thankfully, they were immediately submissive. We made our introductions, and then the sheriff said we needed to talk.

I yelled, "Find it!" at the shepherds, who took off in all directions, followed by the Dobermans. It would take them a while to realize that they didn't know what they were looking for.

We settled into the porch chairs while all the mutts spiraled around the yard looking for God knows what and the squirrels worried. There were some cardboard boxes with the electronics gear piled to one side, but otherwise the house looked just about the same.

"So," I said. "Does anyone know what this was all about?"

The sheriff put up a hand. "I conducted an extensive interview with Hester and Valeria Lee," he said. "Had the ADA with me, and they had a lawyer from Chapel Hill with them."

"Mexican standoff?"

"No, actually. Once I laid out the details of what had happened that night, Valeria broke down, and Hester just seemed to melt into the floor like that wicked witch in the *Wizard of Oz*. It seems that this was really all about two important secrets."

"I'm all ears," I said, even though I was still having trouble hearing anyone over the ringing.

"The first was that the original Callendar Lee's son was in fact the inside man of the train robbery that night. He'd been a clerk in the Richmond treasury, and he'd learned something important about that train. Which brings us to the second secret."

"Gold," I said.

"No," the Sheriff said. "Something actually more useful. Bearer bonds."

"What's a bearer bond?" Tony asked. Horace put a hand up; he was the financial guru at H&S.

"A piece of paper," he said, "usually in certificate form, that tells any bank to pay the bearer, hence the name, the sum of money or, commonly, stock, denominated on the face of the bond."

"Correct," said the sheriff. "It seems that in the final year or so of the Confederacy, Jeff Davis's secretary of the treasury was concerned about the safety of their gold hoard. He made an arrangement with the companies who bought whatever cotton could be smuggled out across the blockade to pay for it in bearer bonds on the Bank of England. That way, if they ever had to move the capital, which became increasingly likely once U. S. Grant started down through Virginia, a trunk full of bonds was a whole lot simpler than several tons of gold bars."

"The bonds were on that train?"

"Apparently so," he said. "Buried among all the government documents were one or two trunks of bearer bonds."

"And Callendar Jr., the clerk, knew which ones they were," I said.

"That's what she told us. There was also some gold, but not very much. The original Callendar Lee hired the roughnecks to come in and hold up the train. They got the gold. They were never told about the bonds."

"So the Lees got the bonds."

"What good were they?" Tony asked. "The government was defeated."

"That's the beauty and, of course, the vulnerability of bearer bonds. They might have been issued to the Confederate government, but a bearer bond doesn't say anything about who owns it. The bearer, the guy who has the piece of paper in his hot little hands, he owns it. If he or she shows up at the Bank of England's teller window and requests payment, he or she gets the money. Which is what the Lees did for the next several decades."

"Wow."

"That's why they became illegal in most states here," Horace said. "Especially once the states started imposing income taxes. A bearer bond was a great way to make money with no paper trail whatsoever."

"As long as whoever issued the bond was still solvent, yes," the sheriff said.

"Naturally," I said, "the Lees' precious family honor couldn't stand a hit like this. Both for Callendar's involvement in the massacre as well as the fact that they stole a part of the Confederate treasury."

"Okay," Tony said. "I hear all that, but what's it got to do with this place?"

The sheriff looked at me. "For one thing, this explains what that inscription says down there on the mantel: Callendar killed them all."

"Well, hell, she must have known that was there. Why not take the damned stone down and pitch it in the river?"

"Have you seen that mantel?" I asked. "It must weigh two, maybe three tons. No, what they did was cover it up with plaster."

"Still," Pardee said, "I'd have burned the house down years ago and just not worried about it."

"I can understand that," I said. "This house, this property, part of their so-called glorious heritage. None of them could bring themselves to do that. It was easier to control who lived here, you know, the so-called right kinds of people. That probably wasn't so hard, what with all the Lees in the courthouse, the local law offices, and so on."

"Maybe there's another explanation," Horace said. "The bonds are still here."

That comment produced a moment of profound silence, but then Tony shook his head. "Too long, man," he said. "Too many generations of Lees living off those things.

What they've managed to do over time is convert the bonds into two point five mil worth of property, which is another reason not to burn the house down, when you think of it."

I agreed. Except now they'd never get it. Besides, in this day and age, I wasn't sure that anyone presenting a nineteenth-century bearer bond in London would get the time of day, except maybe to discuss it as a collector's item.

"Did Hester admit she sicced her baby boy on me?"

"Nope," the sheriff said. "Hester admitted nothing regarding the events here or in Summerfield. Knew nothing about any of that. Valeria just kept crying, which is as good a way to avoid answering questions as any."

"So what's going to happen to them, then?" I asked him.

"The Lees? Well, that's an interesting question, and you will play some part in the outcome." He stopped there, waiting to see if I would work it out.

"Lemme see," I said. "Callendar, the guy who shot the dog trainer, and probably my original ghost, and who tried to air-condition my house—he's dead. He, in turn, was killed by an insane old man, who happened to be his father. I can attest to that fact. So can Carol."

"No, she can't," the sheriff said, and, of course, he was right. Carol had lost her memory. They had had to tell her what her own name was.

He sat back in his chair with an expectant expression on his face. "Of course, they were all in on it," he said. "Even Cubby Johnson, to a certain extent. You know that and I know that—but proof?"

I just stared at him. He waited. Then I got it.

"Guys," I said. "You know the meaning of the word 'deniability'?"

"As in what we don't hear, we never heard?" Horace said.

"Yup."

"We'll see you in town, boss," he said, and they all three got up and left.

"Okay," I said once they'd gone. "This is the South. What's the deal on the table?"

"Isn't it obvious?" he said. "You do still want this place, right? You want to live out here in this county and be treated respectfully?"

"Oh, my," I said.

"Well?"

"So: I decline to bring charges against the nutters next door. They remain in their haunted house, the major keeps riding, Valeria becomes a spinster, the Johnsons keep their jobs, and any legal issues with that long-lost will evaporate."

"In short, everything stays the same," he says. "Except you own Glory's End, and you have the lock of the century on your neighbors, who will continue, of course, never to speak to the proprietor of Glory's End."

"Wow."

"Well, hell," he said. "We can't try the major, and Hester has to live with what he did and the fact that she lit that fuse in the first place. She and her daughter now know they'll never have Glory's End; on the other hand, the daughter will inherit Laurel Grove because her nasty brother is holding his head in the cold, cold ground."

"And because they'll know that I know the true history, they'll leave me the hell alone."

"They'll also know that I know, which is even better insurance that they will leave you alone."

"Nothing changes, then."

"Not much ever does out here, Lieutenant. Especially across the road. Hester has aged ten years this past week; she is destroyed, I think."

I got up and stretched my legs. He was right, of course. This was the solution. "Who thought all this up?"

"Hester's attorney," he said. "He and I got together for a toddy, and he indulged in some idle speculation.'

"Don't tell me," I said. "His name is Lee."

"Wayne Anthony Marion Lee, Esquire, to be precise. He'd be a good guy for you to know, actually."

I started to laugh. It hurt my head, but it was almost worth it. Then I remembered Carol. I asked him if she had family who could take care of her.

He shook his head. "Her parents were killed in a car accident. She has one sister, but they don't speak, and she wasn't interested in helping out. Something about Carol's time on the force in Raleigh."

"She has nobody?"

He shrugged. "As I recall, she has you," he said.

I thought about that. Of course I would help. I'd do whatever it took to nurse her back to health and hopefully memory, but the practicalities of that were daunting. The sheriff read my thoughts.

"Carol volunteered at the hospital and the library, among other places and causes in town," he said. "There are ladies all over town who will help her get back on her feet, but you're the best candidate to help her understand what happened to her and why. All in the due course of time, naturally."

"Goddamn, sheriff," I said. "That might lead to a committed relationship of some kind."

"Fancy that," he said. "I told you she'd git you."

"I'll need some time to think about all this," I said.

"Absolutely," he said. "I'll give you about a minute."

We grinned at each other.

"Deal," I said. "Deal all around."

He drove me back into town, where I joined up with the rest of my gang, who were indulging in one last fry-fest at the local café. My hands were still bandaged, and my joints would have been perfect for some extreme yoga, but I managed to join in. Pardee and Horace went back to the city with all our gear, and Tony drove me over to the hospital to see Carol. It was awkward, of course. She remembered nothing but had been told some things about who she was and assured that she would mend physically. The nurses at the hospital all knew her and liked her, and I knew that they'd be watching me like a hawk for the next several months. We talked for a little while, and I felt better about my commitment to the sheriff, and to Carol. We were both going to learn some things, and there wasn't the first inkling of regret on my part about the situation.

I asked Tony to take me back out to Glory's End, where I could retrieve my vehicle and settle in my new herd of dogs. He took me there, promised to come out and check on me for the next week or so, but then left me to it.

I wandered around that big empty house again, wondering if I shouldn't just go back to the city and give this strange but fascinating place a pass. The more I thought about it, though, the more I wanted to do it—the house and Carol Pollard. Maybe I would run for sheriff one day when Hodge Walker packed it in; maybe not. Maybe I'd just walk the fields with my dogs, watching out for quicksand, abandoned wells, ticks, and sex-crazed teenagers, all the while restoring the house as best I could. I wanted to find the lost slave graveyard and restore that, too, and to do something about all those boys up the hillside. Heck, I might go buy a metal detector and go exploring for buried treasures.

I heard a noise above my head and looked up. A tiny bird had gotten into the house and was batting around the ceiling, that godawful ceiling with the patchwork of all the gaudy wallpaper, with its fantastic embossed beasts, the gilt edging on the individual panels, scrolls and swirls of antique writing, and the swooping numbers.

Large numbers. Lots of zeros.

I looked again at the individual panels and stared hard at those numbers. Then I began to laugh. I'd need a ladder to make absolutely sure, but now I thought I knew why the

Lees had never just burned the house down with its incriminating inscription in the kitchen. They'd hidden the bonds here instead of at Laurel Grove, in plain sight all these decades, pasted to the ceiling. These were probably the last of them.

The approaching sundown was streaming golden light into all the rooms and positively illuminating the bonds, if that was what they were. I'd have to get one down and then find someone who could authenticate it. I'd been to England. I knew that people there held documents going back a thousand years and used them to prove titles and all sorts of things. If in fact they were still worth anything like their face values, I'd have to find some suitable charities.

Another item for the restoration project. Projects, plural, actually: my new life, restoring Carol Pollard, and, finally, restoring Glory's End. *You said you wanted something to do*, I reminded myself.

There was a sudden commotion in the main hall. The dogs had chased a squirrel into the house and were going hell for leather to capture it. Shepherds and Dobies were skidding over those wood floors like Wile E. Coyote and the Road Runner. I yelled at them, and they all, including the squirrel, blasted out the front doors and down the steps.

I went out onto the porch and dropped into one of the rockers. I sensed that I was on the cusp of a sea change in my life. My escape to the countryside had been turned on its head, with the countryside now firmly in control. I was going to stay here, but I had to play by the unwritten rules. I couldn't know how things would work out with Carol, but I was very fond of her and more than willing to re-engage, even help bring her back.

All of this, Carol, restoring the plantation, settling into the warp and woof of the rural south, would take a long time. I might have to give up the pursuit of bad guys indefinitely. Instead I would have to settle for the occasional tin cup of bitter coffee up at the high rocks with the major while we discussed the increasingly grave situation up in Richmond.

The dogs clattered back up onto the porch and dropped on the floor, panting happily. The squirrel laughed at them from a tree. Everything was going to be okay.